Praise for The Fren

'A warm and captivating myst[...]

'A delightful, original and cleverly plotted murder mystery'
A.A. Chaudhuri

'Greg's writing is as transporting as it is cosy, and his characters
are gloriously intriguing'
Ellie Keel

'Charm, character, croissants and crime – the perfect French
mystery'
Annabel Kantaria

'Colourful characters, a beautifully drawn location and a mystery
within a mystery make this an eminently satisfying cosy'
Neil Daws

'A devious murder wrapped in an even bigger mystery – a delightful read for bibliophiles and Francophiles alike'
Robert Holtom

'Intricately plotted with captivating detail, this cosy murder
mystery will keep you guessing'
Eve Smith

'A marvellous mysterious well-paced tale in an evocative rural
French setting that stole my heart'
Nina Millns

GREG MOSSE is a 'writer and encourager of writers', husband of internationally bestselling author Kate Mosse. He has lived and worked in Paris, New York, Los Angeles and Madrid, mostly as an interpreter and translator, but grew up in rural south-west Sussex.

In 2014, he founded the Criterion New Writing playwriting programme in the heart of the West End and, since then, has produced more than 25 of his own plays and musicals. His creative writing workshops are highly sought after at festivals at home and abroad.

His first novel, *The Coming Darkness*, was published by Moonflower in 2022, followed in 2024 and 2025 by *The Coming Storm* and *The Coming Fire*.

Following his successful 1970s cosy crime series, the Maisie Cooper Mysteries, his new collection of Provençal village whodunnits begins with *The French Bookshop Murder* and *The Château Murder*.

Also by Greg Mosse

The French Village Mystery Series
The French Bookshop Murder

The Maisie Cooper Mystery Series
Murder at Church Lodge
Murder at Bunting Manor
Murder at the Theatre
Murder at the Fair
Murder at Sunny View
Murder at the Wedding

The Alex Lamarque Trilogy (Moonflower)
The Coming Darkness
The Coming Storm
The Coming Fire

Secrets of the Labyrinth

The CHATEAU *Murder*

GREG MOSSE

HODDER &
STOUGHTON

First published in Great Britain in 2026 by Hodder & Stoughton Limited
An Hachette UK company

The authorised representative in the EEA is Hachette Ireland,
8 Castlecourt Centre, Dublin 15, D15 XTP3, Ireland (email: info@hbgi.ie)

1

A CIP catalogue record for this title is available from the British Library

Paperback ISBN 9781399746915
ebook ISBN 9781399746922

Typeset in Monotype Plantin by Manipal Technologies Limited

Printed and bound in Great Britain by Clays Ltd, Elcograf S.p.A.

Hodder & Stoughton policy is to use papers that are natural, renewable
and recyclable products and made from wood grown in sustainable forests.
The logging and manufacturing processes are expected to conform
to the environmental regulations of the country of origin.

Hodder & Stoughton Limited
Carmelite House
50 Victoria Embankment
London EC4Y 0DZ

www.hodder.co.uk

For Lily

ZOE'S SKETCH OF
RUSSELL ON THE ICE

PATRICK'S QUICK FAMILY TREE

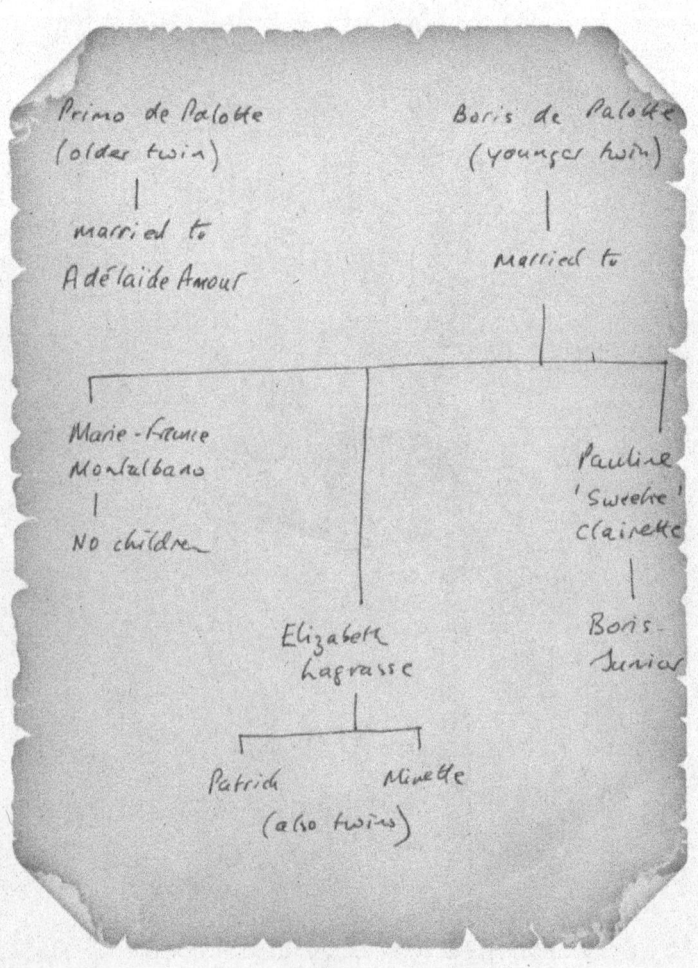

Primo de Palotte
(older twin)
|
married to
Adélaide Amour

Boris de Palotte
(younger twin)
|
Married to

Marie-France
Montalbano
|
No children

Pauline
'Sweetie'
Clairette
|
Boris-
Junior

Elizabeth
Lagrasse

Patrick   Minette
(also twins)

Cast of Characters

Zoe Pascal

Adélaïde Amour, celebrated actress and mistress of Château Palotte

Junior, Adélaïde's unhappy ten-year-old nephew

Russell, a Jack Russell terrier

Primo de Palotte, Adélaïde's husband, master of Château Palotte

Boris de Palotte, Primo's twin brother, Junior's father

Sweetie, née Pauline Clairette, third wife of Boris, Junior's mother

Elizabeth de Palotte, née Lagrasse, second wife of Boris

Marie-France de Palotte, née Montalbano, first wife of Boris

Patrick Lagrasse, co-owner and waiter at the Auberge Sainte-Catherine, son of Boris's second wife Elizabeth

Minette Lagrasse, Patrick's twin sister, co-owner and short-order cook at the Auberge Sainte-Catherine, daughter of Boris's second wife Elizabeth

Caroline Robin, solicitor and notary public

Monsieur Alain, *majordome* or butler

Maisie Cooper, Zoe's elderly half-sister

Gaspard Astor, *boulanger* or baker

Didier 'Didi' Astor, also *boulanger*, his son

Isabelle Valgarde, actress whose phone no longer rings

Emilie Constant, the oldest resident of Saint-Paul-de-Palotte

Bernard Dupin, minibus driver and tour leader

CAST OF CHARACTERS

PROLOGUE

It was a bitter January morning, the first Monday of the cold new year. At Château Palotte, half an hour north of the beautiful Provençal hill town of Sainte-Catherine, the decorative artificial lake was frozen over, three inches thick. Boris Junior – an unhappy and neglected ten-year-old, born to parents of wildly dissimilar ages – was clumsily skittering stones across the ice.

I don't know what to do.

He left the lake, pulling his tartan scarf – a present from his kind Uncle Primo, not his distant father, Boris Senior – tighter around his throat.

I'll go and see the stags.

To reach the woods in which the deer were penned, he had to cross the impressive lawn and take the path round the side of the château, through a five-bar gate that he took care to close.

Or I'll be in trouble again.

Boris Junior didn't like being in trouble, but it did at least mean people were paying attention to him.

The woods were deep and shadowy, even though the oak and the beech had lost their leaves. The dark-green needles of the conifers still provided a partial canopy. Protected from the chill wind, he spent twenty minutes exploring, without coming in sight of either the old stag or his harem of does. He did, however, catch a glimpse of the younger stag, prowling unaccompanied, his noble antlers erect – but looking friendless and lonely.

What did Papa say? He said: 'One day, Junior, you will have to replace me. Perhaps sooner than you think.'

Boris Junior knew that his father – after whom he had been named, though everyone called him simply 'Junior' – was unwell. Sometimes Boris Senior had to stop halfway up the awkward stairs of Château Palotte to catch his breath. Now and then, his father's chin sank to his chest and he could barely speak.

And Uncle Primo is the same. Why won't anyone tell me what's wrong with them?

Junior pushed his small white hands into the pockets of his quilted anorak, a garment too thin for the frigid weather, but he had grown out of what his mother called his 'good coat' and no one had found time to go into Aix, the nearest city, to buy him a new one.

He kicked at the blackened leaf litter around the base of an oak where the dull winter light was brighter. To his surprise he uncovered a shiny, ash-grey slow worm, about the length of his forearm, writhing in surprise at having been brought out into the open. From his lessons at school, he knew that slow worms were common in Italy and south-eastern France, and that they were, in reality, neither worms nor snakes.

They are lizards with no legs.

He followed the creature, pushing more leaves aside to prevent it from going back into hiding. At the same time, he glanced round for a weapon, a stone, perhaps, or a fallen branch to use as a club.

There was a length of oak just two paces away. He hurried to pick it up, the slimy surface of the bark unpleasant under his fingers. A woodlouse scampered over the back of his pale hand like a tiny tank. He brushed it off with a shudder, then turned quickly back to where he had last seen the sinuous, writhing slow worm.

It's gone.

Junior sighed with frustration, feeling he had just missed an important opportunity.

I need to know what it feels like to kill.

I

THE VERY DEAD OF WINTER

One

'I CAN'T TALK ABOUT IT'

Zoe Pascal, an attractive and intelligent woman in her fifties, was the owner of *La Librairie de Mes Rêves* – 'The Bookshop of My Dreams'. It was located in a stone building that had once been the village school in Sainte-Catherine, a beautiful hill town in a gorgeous location in the Verdon nature park, itself a ravishing corner of magnificent Provence, in the warm and fragrant south of France.

But it was neither warm nor fragrant today.

Zoe was on the first floor. She lived above the shop, overlooking the town square. It was a picture-postcard scene made up of biscuit-coloured buildings, curved clay tiles and cobblestones. But her neighbours' geraniums had all been scorched by frost. The bare lime trees were groping the damp chill air with twiggy, skeletal fingers.

She saw Patrick Lagrasse, joint owner of the friendly café, Auberge Sainte-Catherine. One of Zoe's many new friends in the town, he was delivering coffees to the early market traders, including charming Elise Guillaume, who looked after Zoe's courtyard rockery and front-door oleanders, and Robert Petit, the overattentive rotisserie chicken man.

After all the drama and excitement and, yes, fear, I still have no regrets about turning my whole life upside down.

In the involved and intriguing drama known in the popular press as 'the French bookshop murder', Zoe had had to use

5

all her courage, intelligence and intuition. Her field of action had ranged from the narrow streets of Sainte-Catherine and its octagonal Templar church, out into the fields of lavender and sunflowers and grapes, across the gorgeous countryside where clues were hidden far apart from one another in space and – trickier still – in time.

But that was back when the autumn sun still shone and my life seemed easier.

Zoe had been successful in solving the village mystery. Its conclusion had been, on balance, a happy one.

Except for the poor victim, of course.

She went downstairs, made herself coffee from the shop-floor filter machine, lit her wood-burning stove and sat down, watching the flames, musing on the coincidence of having 'assisted the police' back in Sussex in her youth.

Was it an accident that I was, finally, able to solve 'the French bookshop murder'? In other circumstances, might I be able to do the same again?

Although she did not yet know it, Zoe was about to embark on a new adventure in which things would play out very differently. The cast of characters would be smaller, the terrain much tighter and, in theory, more manageable, trapped in a snowbound château in the very dead of winter.

And, for Zoe, being close to murder would also bring her close to danger.

*

That, however, was all in the future. In Sainte-Catherine, the Christmas holiday season was still in full swing and the Feast of the Kings was imminent, an important festival that took place on the sixth of January, the date on which the Magi – the Three Wise Men – were supposed to have arrived at the nativity, having followed the magical star.

Until this year, newly resident in Provence, Zoe hadn't known that, for some people, Twelfth Night was bigger than Christmas Day itself. Every shop in Sainte-Catherine made an enormous effort with displays and decorations, adding carefully kept figurines of the Magi to their nativity scenes, alongside donkeys, sheep, pigs, shepherds, Marys and Josephs and innocent babes.

Although the Feast of the Kings fell mid-week, the celebrations continued right through to the weekend, with many of the townspeople receiving visits – relatives and friends from across Provence and from further afield. To Zoe's delight, it gave a boost to everyone's commerce.

In the cold late autumn and early winter, the open-air market on Place Sainte-Catherine had been reduced to intermittent and dismal sessions on just Wednesday, Saturday and Sunday mornings, packing up early as the light began to fail. But, for the period spanning Christmas, New Year and Twelfth Night, the stallholders were present every day of the week. Among the most popular was the one belonging to Zoe's friend, the vineyard owner and winemaker Marcel Maurice. Marcel had surprised and delighted Zoe by selling *glühwein* – hot mulled wine – made from his own red grape vintages, embellished with his own secret recipe of Provençal herbs and spices.

In addition to its swollen local population of family members, many winter tourists visited Sainte-Catherine, obliged to park in the large car park in front of the *mairie* because the narrow, cobbled streets didn't allow vehicle access. The guest house run by Denis Allard and Davide Quillan had apparently been booked up since the previous year. Zoe's friend Bernard Dupin was kept busy, too, bringing his minibus visitors on private tours of the region, always including a stopover at 'The Bookshop of My Dreams' – where, he knew, coffee and tea and pastries were always available, between the shelves.

So, it was a busy week and, by the time Sunday evening rolled around once more, Zoe felt in need of a proper break.

Surely I can afford to take a few days of holiday?

She opened her laptop to find that the internet was awash with last-minute options. She considered grabbing her passport, packing a bag and driving, on the spur of the moment, to Marseille airport in order to make the short hop by plane across the Mediterranean in search of North African warmth. She opened a weather app and found that Marrakesh was a pleasant eighteen degrees.

Distracted, she served her last customers. They drifted out the door, allowing in a gust of bitter wind, carrying with it a few flakes of snow; then the phone rang.

It was a raucous noise, one that Zoe didn't enjoy, but she hadn't got around to changing the tone. Tearing herself regretfully from the vision of bargain-basement holiday deals in southern Morocco, she picked up.

'*Oui, âllo?*'

'*C'est moi,*' came the gnomic reply, meaning 'it's me'.

Zoe recognised the voice of her old friend Adélaïde Amour, a successful actress ten years Zoe's senior who had, in a way, been her mentor. They had met in 1972 when Adélaïde – a youthful, sometimes semi-clothed 'starlet' – was witness to a murder on-stage at Chichester Theatre.

'How lovely to hear from you. Are you coming to visit Sainte-Catherine again?'

'No, I can't. Not just now. How are you? Not too busy, I hope?'

Adélaïde's warm contralto voice contained an unaccustomed element of tension. And there was a buzzing on the line, not loud enough to obscure what she was saying, but intrusive all the same.

'Pretty manic, actually,' said Zoe.

'I've been in California,' Adélaïde blurted.

8

Zoe knew that her friend's career had recently been on an upward trajectory.

'How exciting. Something good?'

'Time will tell,' said Adélaïde with a hint of frustration.

'Is it a new part in a film?'

'I can't talk about it.'

'Because you don't want to jinx it?'

'Because I had to sign an NDA. You know what one of those is?'

Zoe laughed and told her friend: 'Sometimes I get the impression you think I'm still sixteen years old. Yes, I know about non-disclosure agreements. I imagine they want you to play a famous person, or the story is based on facts from the real world and there are lawyers involved.'

'Something like that. Anyway, you must come.'

'To California?'

'No, to my home, to Château Palotte. Last time I came to see you, you let slip that you were intending to take time off at the end of the holiday season.'

'I did, yes,' said Zoe, warily.

'That's now, isn't it?'

'I suppose so,' said Zoe with a yearning glance at the cafés and minarets of Marrakesh on her laptop.

This is not what I was planning.

'So, you can come?'

'Do you mean now?' she asked weakly.

'It's my husband Primo's seventieth birthday midweek – and his brother's, too, obviously, as they're twins. It's about time you met them. Plus, there will be guests and parties all week.'

'I see.'

That sounds exhausting and, really, I think I'd prefer a nice holiday.

Zoe racked her brain for a reason to refuse. She had never met Primo or his twin and, though she didn't know why, something in Adélaïde's tone made her wary of doing so.

'Please say you will?' Adélaïde insisted.

Mentally asking forgiveness of her friendly Jack Russell rescue dog, she said: 'You wouldn't want me to bring Russell to a week of celebrations. He'll be in the way.'

'Don't be silly. I loved meeting Russell at your lovely bookshop. Then maybe we can talk about the secret thingy . . .' Adélaïde's voice faded, the background buzz taking over. Zoe asked her to speak up. 'I'm trying to be discreet,' Adélaïde told her. 'I'm on the phone in the kitchen and I don't want anyone to hear. I was just saying that it's a story from my life.'

'You mean the project with the NDA?'

'Actually, forget I said that,' Adélaïde retorted, sounding annoyed with herself. 'Please tell me you're coming and that you will arrive imminently?'

Zoe pondered.

Is this really what I want to do with my few days off?

She clicked the weather app on her laptop to reveal the forecast for the Verdon nature park where Château Palotte was located: snow and bitter winds, temperatures at or below zero.

'And your whole family will be there?'

'Every last peculiar one. I need you, Zoe. They outnumber me.'

She sounds odd. I think she's serious.

'What's really happening, Adélaïde?'

Her friend's voice changed. 'Oh, hello there. I didn't see you come in.' It changed again. 'Zoe, I have to go. There will be a place laid at dinner. Please, please, please?'

If I go, I'll have to take all my warmest clothes and a hot water bottle.

'All right.'

'You will? I knew you would.'

'You're asking for my help and, apart from Maisie, you're the only person left alive who knows me from those days, when I was just a child. And you did give me my first big break at the Avignon Festival and . . .'

Zoe stopped speaking, realising that Adélaïde was no longer there, that the annoying buzz had become a dial tone.

She hung up and frowned.

I'd like to know who it was who came in and interrupted. I hope Adélaïde's all right. Her ideas seemed all of a jumble. Is it just professional stress that made her thoughts bounce around like that? Or is there something else going on that I will only find out about when I get there?

TWO

'I WISH I COULD SEE
FURTHER AHEAD'

Zoe got her things together, packing enough for three nights in her small wheelie suitcase, including her hot water bottle. Because she was going to a kind of stately home, Zoe decided she ought to take her posh camel-hair coat – the one that draped down to mid-calf – and a long wool dress in pale blue that was suitable as evening wear. Then she removed half of the contents in order to accommodate her compact blower heater.

I won't stay a full week. I'll stay for Adélaïde's husband's birthday, then make my excuses and leave.

Her quilted gilet and ski jacket from Decathlon were utilitarian at best. That meant, however, that she could stuff them into the crevices round the heater.

I'm going to need my rucksack, too. That will make it look like I've come for a long stay, but I really don't think I can cope without all these extra bits and pieces.

She contemplated her lovely wood-burning stove, installed by the local handyman, Gato Merino, in the heart of the shop. It was quite safe to leave it to burn out. The apartment above was equipped with electric convector heaters, which she set to a trickle in order that the place should not become damp and icy while she was away.

Because she was in the habit of buying fresh food each day, there wasn't much in the fridge and most of what there was would keep because it was preserved in either vinegar or oil. There was, however, a loaf of rye bread wrapped in a tea towel that she decided to take with her, along with a small block of Emmenthal cheese, half a *saucisson* and her Swiss Army knife. She put them all in the side pockets of her rucksack then lugged everything downstairs.

As it happened, her eye was caught by something on her shop counter. It was a little pile of advertising leaflets, shoddily printed and inadequately proofread, that Adélaïde had brought over: 'For display so that your multitude of customers, who come to revel in the glory of the woman who solved "the French bookshop murder", get it in their heads to come and visit us here at Château Palotte. God knows, the money would come in handy.'

She picked the top one up. It told visitors – who were allowed to visit on Tuesdays and Thursdays between ten and twelve o'clock – that, in the early Christian era, the village of Saint-Paul-de-Palotte had been a modest settlement on the plain, clustered along the banks of the River Rigolet. Successive incursions by marauding Goths persuaded the locals to take the important defensive step of moving their homes – lock, stock and barrel – to higher ground. The inconvenience of being further from the ready water supply was, Zoe presumed, compensated by the security of a strong, circular wall of stone houses creating a bastion against attack, with narrow streets and a tiny church.

Zoe put the leaflet in her pocket and dragged her wheelie suitcase outside, perching her rucksack on one of the square granite bollards that lined Place Sainte-Catherine. Rain and snow were falling together from the lifeless sky. She locked up with Russell skittering around her ankles, displaying his usual limitless doggy enthusiasm for whatever life had to offer.

'I'm sorry to tell you, we're going out in the car,' she told him.

He caught the tone of her voice and calmed down. Zoe pondered the fact that she was in the habit of speaking aloud to Russell in both English and French.

He's so clever, though, it doesn't matter which.

'You make up your own mind as to what you choose to understand, don't you?'

Encumbered by her long coat, tightly packed rucksack and the little wheels of her suitcase bouncing on the cobbles, Zoe made awkward progress across the square. Though it was late, she could see people inside Ambroise Caille's estate agency – a middle-aged couple with two teenage daughters. Zoe assumed they were tourists, looking for a second home in the exquisite Verdon nature park.

She continued down through the narrow streets and saw, with a tinge of regret, that a Sunday evensong service was underway in the octagonal Templar church. Many of her neighbours and friends would be there. She wasn't a believer herself, but the routine of the liturgy had recently become a gratifying habit.

On Place Saint-Bertrand, the Auberge Sainte-Catherine was serving its final two customers, bundled up against the cold under its orange umbrellas. Patrick Lagrasse, in his tight white shirt and traditional black apron, was gliding balletic-ally towards them with the card machine.

Down at the car park in front of the *mairie*, the town hall, she saw a sad-looking French *tricolore* flag, flapping listlessly in the cold breeze. Her narrow lock-up garage was one of several, cut into the hillside. She unlocked her combination padlock using 0511, the fifth of November, her birthday – or rather the day on which she had been abandoned as a foundling at St Richard's Hospital in Chichester in south-west Sussex.

She slithered in, with only just enough room to part-open the driver's door of her elderly van, known both to her and to the mechanics at the Total garage as 'Renée the Renault', named after 'Good King René' who first brought Muscat grapes to Provence. Russell jumped onto her lap and tried to take possession of the driver's seat.

'Get on your own side, hound.'

He did so without complaint and stood up on his hind legs with his front paws on the dashboard while she eased Renée forward, stopped, got back out and went through the rigmarole of locking up again, her mind on other things. She had been trying to remember a distinctive – perhaps unique – Provençal word that would be perfect for describing the dismal weather.

Simultaneous rain and snow.

Zoe pulled away and Renée the Renault's wheels briefly spun in the freezing slush, but the road ran gently downhill so she was soon on her way. Russell did his best to maintain his precarious position until they left the circuit of street lamps on the ring road and found themselves in the darkly featureless countryside, only illuminated by the short throw of the headlamps. Then he gave up.

Oh, I know: aiganèu.

Through the spattered windscreen, she saw that the clever word was becoming redundant. Snow was definitively taking over, beginning to lie on the tarmac, collecting in the furrows of the ploughed-over sunflower field. With Russell now curled up on the passenger seat, unaware of their destination, Zoe had her first premonition of what was to come.

Adélaïde sounded very jittery. Why was the invitation so last minute? Is the noble Palotte family – with its ancient, grandiose château and landscaped gardens – perhaps short of money? The prospect of a big new Hollywood project with a self-important NDA doesn't seem to be making Adélaïde happy, either. I'm beginning to feel uneasy. I wish I could see further ahead.

The steering twitched on a patch of ice.

And I don't just mean my headlamps on the road.

Three

'YOU'RE A BRAVE LITTLE DOG, RUSSELL'

Zoe didn't enjoy driving at night and, the closer she came to her destination, the deeper the snow lay at each verge. In twenty minutes, she passed only half a dozen cars going in the opposite direction. Then, for the first time, someone came up behind her, far too close, as was the French habit.

She decelerated in order to allow them to zoom by. Unfortunately, there were too many twists and turns, so she spent several uncomfortable kilometres dazzled by their headlamps in her wing mirrors.

At last, on a brief straight, the car – a silver Audi – overtook. As it came alongside, she was surprised to recognise the passenger, illuminated by the phone screen he was consulting. It was Patrick Lagrasse, waiter and joint owner of the Auberge Sainte-Catherine. An unseen companion was beyond him in the driver's seat.

Is that his twin sister? I wonder where they're going?

Zoe had met Patrick back in September, on arrival in Sainte-Catherine, and had taken to him immediately. He was perhaps thirty years old as was his sister, Minette – who Zoe hadn't met – who worked long days in the Auberge Sainte-Catherine kitchen. After the summer season, they shut up shop to holiday for eight weeks in a secluded village in a hard-to-find cove on the Italian

Riviera. They then returned for the period of Christmas, New Year and Twelfth Night, before closing up again, awaiting the spring.

The other car disappeared up the road, travelling at impetuous speed. Zoe wondered if perhaps they were on their way north towards one or other of the nearby ski resorts.

That's one of the wonderful things about living in Provence. Going to the mountains or to the seaside or across the border into Italy can be a spur-of-the-moment decision. I imagine they're in a hurry to get there before the mountain roads are closed by snowfall. That trip would be beyond you, Renée.

She was following the river, the Rigolet, glimpsed now and then by Renée's headlamps reflecting off the water. There was thick ice at the banks.

She entered an area of oppressively thick woods, so dark that they made Zoe feel those headlamps must be failing. Then she emerged from the tunnel of trees to see a huge pile of felled timber at the side of the road and, a few kilometres ahead, a conical configuration of electric lights, reminiscent of a giant Christmas tree. She knew it to be made up of the windows of the village of Saint-Paul. The brightest lights, at the summit of the cone, belonged to the château that was her destination.

The last few thousand metres went by faster, despite the thickening blanket of white, because the road was almost straight.

If the temperature falls far below zero tonight, will Adélaïde suggest skating? The pamphlet says there's a lake. That's the sort of impetuous gamble I'd expect from her. But how will we know if the ice is thick enough?

Saint-Paul was built on an escarpment, with the houses rising steeply from the plain to the summit. The lake, lawn and formal gardens of Château Palotte followed a gentler slope to the east. This was the direction that Zoe took, aiming for the gates at the bottom of the drive.

Then, abruptly, Zoe trod on her brakes, seeing two stags fifty metres ahead, caught in her headlamp beams, colliding and twisting their antlers together, gouts of steam puffing from their nostrils. It was, she thought, a rut – a ritual combat for superiority in a herd.

She stopped the car and got out, shutting the door quickly so that Russell couldn't follow, then stood very still, unnoticed by the combatants. The antlers clashed again and there seemed to be a marked difference in strength. One animal was clearly older, bearing the scars of previous conflicts on its heavily muscled shoulders. The fur around its face was discoloured with age. The other was slimmer but more agile, quicker to change direction, to retreat then advance, making rapid thrusts and then, self-protectively, dodging away.

The pauses between clashes became longer. The older animal stood its ground but no longer made any thrusts of its own, reduced to stoically enduring its opponent's sallies. Then, abruptly, it was over. The older stag turned and walked away, through the gate and away across the ink-black fields.

Where on earth does it think it's going?

The younger one disappeared up the drive and away under some trees.

Where did they both come from, in fact?

Zoe got back in and, with another spin of her narrow tyres, sidled through a pair of heavy metal gates between tall stone pillars. One of them was sagging with a broken hinge. The drive was bumpy and ill-kept. Several times, she bounced through potholes on her way to a dilapidated carport with a corrugated asbestos roof. She parked alongside an elderly BMW estate car with a personalised number plate: 1972 AA.

That has to be 'AA' for 'Adélaïde Amour'. Heaven only knows what it must have cost. Or has she owned the number for many years from back when life was more affordable?

From the carport to the château, she had to climb a slippery external staircase. The borders alongside the path were

18

planted with lavender, visible by the light of a halogen lamp above the impressive front door, set in a stone-built tower. The lavender trunks were woody, the fronds long and straggly because no one had thought to prune them back after summer flowering. The *aiganèu* – snow mixed with rain – had given way entirely to decorative flakes, like in a movie, silently filling up the crevices in the soil and applying a gentle dusting on the shoulders and sleeves of her camel-hair coat.

Dazzled by the harsh glare of the halogen lamp, Zoe struggled with her wheelie case and her rucksack. She was met near the top by an elderly servant. He was slow and bent, stepping sideways from one tread to the next.

'I must introduce myself,' she told him. 'My name is Zoe Pascal and I'm a very old friend of your mistress, Madame Adélaïde. I expect you've worked here for a very long time. Are you the . . .' Zoe hesitated, searching her memory for the correct French equivalent of 'butler'. '*Le majordome?*'

'*Oui, madame. Je m'appelle Alain,*' he replied.

'Is that a family name or your first name? I don't want to say anything foolish or be inadvertently rude.'

'Alain is my family name. Everyone calls me by it, which is normal for a *domestique*.'

Zoe was taken aback by the word *domestique*, meaning 'servant', because she was under the impression that it was no longer used, that it was seen as . . .

Well, not insulting but not particularly respectful either.

'Allow me to take one of *madame*'s bags,' he said.

'There's no need, really—'

'There is every need,' he told her firmly, his head at an odd angle because his back was so bent.

Zoe wanted to argue but, in the end, Monsieur Alain didn't wait. He grasped the suitcase handle and she could see no way to refuse his demand to be allowed to fulfil his professional role. He carried it more easily than she had anticipated, despite his awkward gait.

The front door at the top of the steps was closed so Zoe ran ahead to open it. The hinges screeched and she was greeted by an enormous waft of hot, dry air.

Monsieur Alain told her: 'The mistress prefers a warm house.'

Zoe thought she caught a twinkle in the elderly butler's eye.

Is that criticism or indulgence?

They went inside. Monsieur Alain walked on with his burden, presumably heading for her accommodation. She let him go, thinking she ought to make herself known to her hosts, but the corridor was empty. No one was there to greet her.

I wonder if they'll put me in some distant lonely eyrie?

Zoe took off her rucksack and her long camel-hair coat, settling both on a large oak carver chair that almost had the dimensions of a throne. She heard a yap from outside and realised that Russell had lagged behind. She opened the door a crack and he slithered in, looking as though he was wearing little white slippers. She bent down and discovered that it was snow clinging around his paws, caught in the short white bristles and then accumulating, like a snowball rolling downhill.

She made him stand patiently on the doormat while she removed it with her fingers. He endured the indignity without complaint then, as soon as it was over, ran off and disappeared down a stone staircase on the left of the corridor.

'Where are you going?'

She followed him down a set of worn, stone steps. At the foot, she found a brightly lit space with an old-fashioned kitchen table made from planks of sturdy beech, an impressive stainless-steel stove, a wine rack, an enormous fridge and so on. Russell had already found himself somewhere to curl up – a smelly old dog bed. He looked completely content.

You're a brave little hound, Russell. You take everything in your tiny stride. I actually think you're looking forward to this more than I am.

Her mind went back to her and Adélaïde's first meeting, so many years before.

That led to murder. But there's no reason it should do so again.

Four

'RUSSELL!'

This was a mistake.

Monsieur Alain, the *majordome*, had returned, announcing that she, Zoe, was alone at Château Palotte.

Which surely is a very peculiar way to receive a guest.

'Everyone is out? Are they in the village, in Saint-Paul? Should I go to join them?'

'They are in another village, Saint-Julien, *madame*, for dinner with friends,' he informed her, gravely. 'They will return quite late, I imagine.'

I was promised dinner, wasn't I?

'But I saw Adélaïde's car?'

'Monsieur Primo likes to call upon a hire vehicle, a minibus, so that the whole family can be accommodated together. In that way, no one needs to abstain.'

He meant from alcohol. Again, this was said with an amused twinkle.

'Fair enough. Will they soon be back?'

'After midnight, *madame*, I expect.'

Zoe felt a surge of frustration.

This is already a waste of my precious free time.

Zoe declined Monsieur Alain's offer to prepare her 'a light supper', allowing him to lead her to a distant and damp-smelling room, along a mildewed and creaking corridor, decorated – if that was the appropriate word – with faded watercolours that barely distinguished themselves from the bubbled and discoloured wallpaper.

In that lonely room, Zoe nibbled a little of her rye bread, *saucisson* and Emmenthal cheese, then slept in sheets that smelt as though they had been correctly laundered but not properly dried, with a penetrating draught scything from a window too misshapen with age to close entirely.

*

The next morning, in a spirit of self-preservation, Zoe woke early.

I could leave right now, perhaps penning a note to explain my haste. A business emergency perhaps? But Adélaïde knows I don't open the shop on Mondays.

She dressed and went downstairs to the ground-floor corridor, bringing her wheelie suitcase with her. Not a sound could she hear; not a soul could she see.

She approached the mighty front door and turned the large iron lever that served as an outsized handle. It released a catch but the ancient oak boards, strapped together with metal bands and studded with heavy black nails, refused to budge.

I'm locked in, like a prisoner.

Zoe scanned the hallway for a place where the key – undoubtedly also outsized – might be kept. Then she realised that she was not completely alone. There was noise from halfway down the corridor, a wheezing and a scraping as someone, weary of their labours – perhaps even of life itself – wrestled with poker and ash shovel, lighting a fire.

Zoe left her suitcase and followed the sounds. She was delighted to discover that the flames of a jolly blaze were already chasing one another up the chimney of an impressive dining room with French windows that opened onto a terrace, above

23

the snowy lawn. The fire was being nurtured by the same dusty butler in grey livery she had met yesterday. When he stood up from the hearthrug, he still remained bent and stooped.

'Bonjour, Monsieur Alain.'

'Bonjour, Madame Pascal.'

'No one else up?'

'Not yet.' With a vague gesture, he indicated a set of inadequate breakfast provisions on the vast table, including a battered cereal box and a blue-and-white milk jug, a smeared glass cafetière, a sticky marmalade jar and two awkward lengths of yesterday's *baguette*, all of it contrasting wildly with the luxurious white tablecloth and the ancient polished floorboards. He told her: 'If *madame* needs anything, I will be downstairs in the kitchen.'

'Thank you.'

He left her and Zoe sat down to drink a cup of disappointing, watery coffee.

At least the room is warm and there's no draught.

She amused herself by scorching a slice of yesterday's stale French bread at the fireplace, sliced in half longways and offered to the flames on a telescopic brass toasting fork. Once the bread was on the verge of being burnt – just how she liked it – she carried it back to the table and applied a lavish quantity of butter and marmalade and had almost finished it when she was joined by a pale and unprepossessing boy, his hair uncombed, his teeth almost certainly unbrushed.

'Bonjour. Comment vas-tu?' she asked.

The boy seemed to feel no compulsion to break the silence that closed around Zoe's cheerful request to know how he was.

'What's your name?' she asked.

'They call me "Junior",' he told her grudgingly.

Zoe had a good memory and, on her visit to Sainte-Catherine, Adélaïde had explained a little about the set-up at Château Palotte.

'So, your father is Boris Senior, Monsieur Primo's twin bother?'

He glanced suspiciously at her from beneath his blond monobrow, awkwardly half smiled, then poured himself an enormous bowl of sugared cereal, *Trésors Chocolat-Noisettes*, parcels of ultra-processed wheat containing blobs of sickly Nutella.

Zoe poured herself a second watery coffee. Despite his lack of conversation, Junior still managed to disturb the quiet of the dining room with his noisy, rhythmic slurping. Simultaneously, he turned the pages of what looked like – for a boy surely not yet in secondary school – an inappropriate Hollywood glamour magazine.

Zoe finished her toast and once more considered abandoning Château Palotte.

But I can't bring myself to slip away before Adélaïde's even got up. I'll have to find something to do until the grown-up members of the household finally appear.

She left the dining room and descended to the well-equipped basement kitchen, down a stone staircase whose treads were worn and chipped with – she knew from the pamphlet – more than two hundred years' use. There, by the light of slot windows high up in the walls, she saw Monsieur Alain busy at the stove and, still asleep in the pungent soft bed left behind by a previous canine tenant, she found Russell. He opened an eye and she smiled, thinking how lucky she was to have been able to adopt such an optimistic, perky character.

Russell was a barrel-shaped terrier with short legs, smooth white fur and an appealing tan-coloured face. A few months earlier, he had been a stray without collar or name tag, just a weather-beaten bandana round his neck. Zoe had taken him in because he looked so shivery and sad and because, one day, she had driven away from the car park at the foot of the hill town of Sainte-Catherine, refusing his entreaties to accompany her. When she had returned, two hours later, she had found him sitting in the same place, waiting for her, the expression on his patient, handsome face so poignant and trusting that she had been unable to do anything else.

'Does *madame* need something?' Monsieur Alain asked.

Unused to being addressed in the third person, Zoe hesitated before replying: 'I thought I might pop out for a walk.'

The sound of the 'W-word' roused Russell completely from slumber. The butler indicated the stovetop on which a variety of breakfast foods were sizzling.

'Once I have taken the family's trays upstairs, will *madame* require hot food?'

'No, thank you.'

I won't be staying long.

Together, Zoe and Russell climbed the perilous stone stair. Remembering that the front door – at the foot of the western tower – was locked, she went to the other end of the corridor, to a stone vestibule at the foot of the eastern tower. It was untidy with boots, shoes, coats, hats and scarves. The less-impressive rear door was only bolted, allowing her to open it onto a walled vegetable garden. On the far side of the snow-filled planters was a pedestrian gate beneath an arch of clay tiles that she thought must allow access to the frosty lawn.

Once through the gate, Russell darted back and forth while Zoe kept a steady path, momentarily wondering what hoofed creatures had left so many criss-cross tracks in the frost and snow.

Oh, it must have been the stags.

Beyond the lawn was a frozen lake, about thirty paces across. To her surprise, Zoe discovered that Junior had got there first, inadequately dressed in a quilted anorak and tartan scarf. The boy was amusing himself by throwing pebbles across the surface of the ice, tossing them clumsily as if no one had ever shown him how to skim stones – as seemed more than likely.

I wonder if the grown-ups pay any attention to the boy? Adélaïde said it's Primo and Boris Senior's seventieth birthday. That's quite old for Boris Senior to have a . . . a ten-year-old?

Russell explored the perimeter of the lake, not yet emboldened to venture onto the ice.

If Russell was interested in sticks, I might get Junior to throw one for him, but Russell thinks such childish tricks beneath him.

The terrier conducted his interactions with the human world on his own terms. And he had a knack of looking Zoe in the eye and seeming to ask her unspoken questions to which she had no answer. Several times, in her investigation into 'the French bookshop murder', Russell had prompted her on a new train of thought. Once, in danger on a lonely road, he had saved her from serious injury – if not worse.

He is my tiny, brave chevalier.

The sun had only recently risen and was still very low in the sky, dazzling out of the east, the direction from which a cold wind also blew. Junior had walked out four or five paces onto the ice. She considered calling him back, but the surface seemed firm beneath his feet, with no ominous sounds of shifting or cracking.

He's not my responsibility, but I hope he doesn't fall through. If he does, I'll have to try and drag him out.

Zoe had no children. She was, as the women's magazines and podcasts would insist on calling it, 'happily childless'. This was neither by accident, nor by tragedy nor by conjugal betrayal, but by choice.

Russell seemed to become intrigued by Boris Junior's behaviour. Zoe watched – with a degree of apprehension – as dog followed boy, snuffling at the inert and odourless surface, his pointed face creased into something like a frown. Then his odd gait made Zoe smile.

He's trying to stand on tiptoe to keep the pads of his paws from the cold.

From Adélaïde's pamphlets, Zoe knew that the lake was fed by a river, the Rigolet, that ran down out of the mountains to the north. Further in its wanderings, the Rigolet wound past Zoe's home town of Sainte-Catherine before tumbling and twisting onwards, ultimately becoming a part of the mighty River Rhône. At Château Palotte, however, it was momentarily stalled in its desire for oblivion by a low dam.

She also knew that the artificial lake was designed to feed, beneath the lawn, a subterranean reservoir – 'an amazing construction, capable of providing fresh water all year round, even at the height of the scorching Provençal summer'.

Zoe followed the edge of the lake, not wanting to test the ice with her own sixty-five kilos. Junior was a wiry, unathletic boy and probably weighed only thirty-five or so, and Russell just five or six. The direction took her to the southern neck of the frigid body of water, frozen solid to a concrete lip, over which, come spring, the waters of the Rigolet would run free once more. In fact, a slender cascade still flowed through a narrow outfall, before tumbling icily on.

Zoe mounted an arched wooden bridge that gave access to the far side of the stream, beyond which serried lines of bicentennial trees, formally laid out in the eighteenth century, comprised a monument to Château Palotte's 'glory days' before the French Revolution turned all the old feudal certainties upside down.

She shielded her eyes from the low glare. Junior was marching out close to the middle of the lake, at least fifteen paces from the edge. She couldn't quite see what he was doing, but Russell was close at hand, confusedly investigating the inexplicable cold surface without smells.

Zoe saw Junior raise his hands above his head and understood, with a chill of trepidation, precisely what it was the boy was about to do. Junior had been back to the bank to collect a rock, one of the egg-shaped stones eroded smooth by the tumbling Rigolet, but much bigger and heavier than the pebbles he had sent clumsily – innocently – skittering across the ice.

'*Junior, arrête,*' she called.

She was too late. He didn't stop. Despite his thin, weedy arms, Junior managed to throw the rock several paces away from where he stood. It fractured the ice and sank instantly into the icy depths. The section of the frozen surface on which the boy stood remained intact, but Russell was directly caught up in the catastrophe, a large panel of ice tipping and shearing like an arctic floe, his little paws scrabbling without purchase, his claws unable to find any grip.

'Russell!' cried Zoe.

He slipped out of sight.

Five

'I Wish I'd Never Come'

Because the wind from the east was constantly scouring the surface of the lake, Zoe was both appalled and relieved to see the terrier beneath the surface, as if through frosty glass, desperately doggy-paddling, surely drowning, yet moving towards her with the current.

'Russell!' she cried out for a second time.

Zoe ran to the far side of the hump-backed bridge and knelt down in the frozen grass and mud at the edge of the lip, close to where a narrow channel of frigid water still flowed, trying to drag another egg-shaped stone – like the one Junior had used to fracture the ice – out of the frozen ground.

At first, Zoe could get no more purchase than Russell's claws had found on the tipping ice floe. Finally, at a cost of several damaged nails, the stone came free and she bashed it on the ice by the rim, smashing it into slush. The flow brought Russell close and she reached her arms into the punishingly chill water, her fingers losing sensation but able to grasp the writhing, sodden barrel of her dog's muscular little body, heaving him out, clutching the shuddering, gasping animal to her chest.

'You're alive,' she gasped.

He coughed and spluttered, foolishly wriggling to be free. She ran her numbed hands along his coat to squeeze out most of the chill water. Then, clumsily, with trembling fingers, she undid the poppers on her cheap Decathlon ski jacket to tuck him inside.

It was a horrible sensation, the icy water soaking through her quilted gilet into her turtleneck jumper. But Russell's shuddering began to diminish and she felt his tentative tongue lick her chin.

'You gave me a terrible fright,' she told him, her voice unsteady. 'But it wasn't your fault.'

From where she knelt, on the cold bank of the lake, she could see Junior, running away across the lawn towards the walled vegetable garden. She levered herself awkwardly to her feet.

'We must go and get warm and dry indoors,' she told Russell. 'There's a fire in the dining room.'

Junior's silhouette against the frosty grass disappeared through the pedestrian gate. Zoe wondered if – sad and poorly brought up, perhaps not knowing any better – Junior had deliberately tried to hurt Russell.

Surely not?

Her teeth began to chatter.

But I can't be sure . . .

In the artificial lake, the panels of ice broken by Junior's heavy stone seemed already to be knitting themselves back together. Zoe had a brief and frightening flashback to her moment of panic when she had seen poor Russell, carried by the current, sealed beneath the frozen surface.

'You're all right. We're both all right,' she told him.

She recrossed the arched bridge. He gave her another half-hearted lick and she hurried up the lawn, the exercise compensating a little for the icy water soaking through her clothes, running down insidiously into the waistband of her trousers.

This is horrible.

The lawn levelled out and she headed for the same entrance to the walled vegetable garden that Junior had used.

I wish I'd never come.

★

As things turned out, the crisis at the frozen lake would soon be relegated from headline to sidebar. And the question of whether or not Junior had meant to do what he did would become important for quite different reasons.

Zoe couldn't yet know it, but she was about to become implicated in much deeper, more grown-up questions, leading – with implacable inevitability – to murder.

Six

'THAT TERRIBLE BUSINESS
AT THE THEATRE'

Zoe saw no sign of Junior in the vegetable garden, nor in the house itself as she made her way along the corridor to the dining room and peeked in, without fully opening the heavy door. Primo de Palotte, Adélaïde's husband, was standing at the window, an unmistakable upright figure, despite his seventy years. She knew him from his photograph in the pamphlet.

Who does he remind me of? I think it's Patrick Stewart, in character as Captain Picard in Star Trek, *but an older version.*

Primo was wearing corduroy trousers in an aggressive shade of scarlet, a mustard-yellow jumper and a stylish tweed jacket, more redolent of Paris than the Hebridean island of Harris. She was on the point of making her presence known, when she realised that there was something odd in his pose.

Primo's forehead was pressed to the glass and she had a moment of surreal concern that he might be dead. Then she saw that his hands, clasped together in the small of his back, were restless and uneasy, the fingers moving through and past and round one another, like a bunch of unhappy worms.

With her coat done up to conceal her damp garments, she put Russell down and he ran off in search of the warmth of the kitchen and his soft bed. At the sound, Primo turned, an expression almost of distress on his well-proportioned features, the cheekbones high, the nose prominent, the chin reasonably firm considering his advanced years. Then he smiled and Zoe recognised the quality of his expensive orthodontic work.

It's almost eerie to have such perfect white teeth in so old and lined a face.

'Good morning, Madame Pascal. I'm so pleased to meet you.' He said all that in careful English, before continuing in French. 'Adélaïde told me you're an early riser. I hope you slept at least an hour or two. I imagine you felt the draught. It is, however, one of the few bedrooms adequately served by the ancient plumbing. Did you touch the radiator?'

'Should I have?'

'Absolutely not. My only hope is that your bed provided a comfortable middle ground between the scalding cast iron and the ill-fitting window. You were first downstairs?'

'With Monsieur Alain and then Boris Junior. Did you happen to see him?'

Primo looked worried.

'Why? Has he been difficult, the poor boy? You know he knows no better?'

'It's really nothing.'

'I hope you will forgive him?'

Primo spoke without much emphasis, as if apologising for his nephew's misdeeds was no more than a weary habit.

'Of course,' Zoe told him.

He tuned back to the glass. There was an awkward pause, then he added: 'It's an unsmiling landscape, isn't it?'

'The lake is lovely.'

'No, the formal French garden beyond, with its regimented layout of trees and shrubs. I'm more English in my tastes. Had I been around two hundred years ago, I would have overseen a more haphazard arrangement, a subtle improvement on wild nature.'

'There's probably a place for both philosophies,' said Zoe.

'You had breakfast, did you?' asked Primo, after another pause, his breath condensing on the windowpane.

'It was great fun toasting the bread at the open fire with that telescopic fork. Is it very old?'

'I used to love doing that when I was a boy.' Primo turned and smiled his vulpine smile once more. 'I never use it now. Perhaps I should teach Junior?' His eyes meaningfully met hers. 'I'm glad you came. I've been looking forward to meeting you – as have my brother and his wives. As a clan, we're a little self-absorbed but quite good company when you get to know us – at least, some people say we are.'

'Adélaïde didn't go into detail, but I'm sure it's true,' said Zoe, generously. 'Big families are always fun.'

'Would you sit down for a moment? I'd like to be able to offer you some decent coffee, but I'm afraid we don't run to that. Boris and I have both been warned off by our physician. Although he and I are probably getting to the point where we're butting up against the question of whether life is worth extending, if it's all privation and no jubilation.'

As he said this, he raised a comic eyebrow, making Zoe laugh.

'That would be splendid,' she told him. 'Would you excuse me for a moment? I'll be back directly for some of your medically moderated coffee.'

She slipped out into the corridor, found her small suitcase by the front door, located a clean winter base-layer and a T-shirt to put on over the top and got changed in the downstairs loo, a frigid room with ancient plumbing at the foot of the eastern tower.

She stuffed her wet things in the outer pocket of her suitcase, then she took a moment. There was still a jangle of adrenaline in her bloodstream.

My poor Russell.

She returned and found Primo ready to resume the conversation where they had left off.

'Is it wise to sacrifice everyday pleasures for increments of longevity?' he wondered aloud.

'I suppose it depends on the lengths of the increments?'

'Short-term sacrifice is sometimes the only way to achieve long-term gain. Don't you agree?'

'I know exactly what you mean,' she told him. 'I had a lovely life in London but I knew I wanted something else, and to get that something else needed sacrifice. I had to go far away from everything I knew – albeit to one of the most beautiful places on the face of the Earth – and start again.'

'You seem to be making a success of your new life in the south of France? My brother, Boris, became almost obsessed with your exploits in "the French bookshop murder". Quite the headline. Good for business?'

'Actually, yes, but that's not what I meant to say. It was this. I like the word you used, "jubilation". You may have come across those terrible people on the internet who try to persuade everyone to live in monastic discomfort, throwing away ninety per cent of their possessions and folding their colour-coordinated socks in pristine drawers?'

'I'm not sure who you mean. I'm not really abreast of popular culture.'

'What I mean is, I like the Spanish word for retirement, which is also—'

'*Jubilación*,' he interrupted, finishing her sentence with a smile. 'That's right – an invitation finally to take the time to enjoy life.' He gestured to the table. 'Please, will you sit, just for a moment? There is something I hoped to discuss.'

Zoe could see that he wouldn't take a seat until she had done so herself. She perched on one of the heavy dining chairs and ran a finger along the luxurious white tablecloth. Then, of course, he was obliged by his good manners to pour coffee for them both and bring it to the table with slightly trembling hands.

It's a good job I take mine plain black so he doesn't have to return for sugar or milk or cream.

'It's decaffeinated as well as weak,' he told her, sadly.

In order to be polite, she raised the cup to her lips, swallowing a tiny amount.

'What did you want to talk to me about?'

'That terrible business at the theatre when you and Adélaïde first met.'

'Good heavens,' said Zoe. 'That was so long ago.'

'I would very much appreciate it.'

'Isn't it Adélaïde's story to tell?'

'I would prefer not to pain her with dredging up unhappy memories.'

Then why speak of it at all?

'Do you want to tell me why it's on your mind?' Zoe asked.

'Can it be sufficient that I have a pressing reason? Will you be very kind and trust me on this?'

The same glimpse of distress – the one that she had seen when he had first turned from the chilly windowpane – was in his eyes and Zoe didn't feel she could refuse. She took her time, however, relating an outline of the circumstances, as far as she knew them, having been very much a bystander, concluding: 'I was only sixteen. It was my half-sister, Maisie, who combined with the local police force to investigate the circumstances and bring the truth to light.'

'And Adélaïde?' prompted Primo, very focused.

'She, too, was a mere bystander, as far as I am aware. She was in the cast, of course, so she was present on stage when the murder took place.' Zoe racked her brains and dredged up some of the names of the other actors, plus the director and stage manager and the theatre's chief executive, all of whom had been suspected, one way or another. 'Is this getting us anywhere? What were you hoping to find out?'

He surprised her by asking: 'How many of them are dead?'

'Quite a few, I imagine. As I said, I was only sixteen.'

'Would you be willing to make a list for me – with your memory of their respective ages?'

'Can you explain to me why?'

Again, his reply surprised her.

'I don't think I should burden you with my reasons, my dear.'

'Burden me in what way?'

'If I told you that,' he replied, quietly, 'it would be tantamount to telling you why I am asking you to be so generous and relive those unhappy moments.'

Zoe was unsure why she felt so wary.

After all, it's ancient history.

'Can I perhaps think it over?'

There was a tense silence, then the tone of Primo's voice changed, from polite insistence to apology.

'No, this was a mistake. You are right, of course. I shouldn't have broached the subject without Adélaïde being present. And I don't think, on so brief an acquaintance, I have the right to impose on your memories.'

He grasped the edge of the table, rucking the luxurious white cloth, pulling himself upright, again standing tall and straight, but it seemed to cost him a significant effort. Zoe rose with him, glad to abandon her feeble coffee.

'As you wish,' she told him, politely.

They went out into the corridor. Zoe began explaining that she ought to go downstairs to find Russell. Just then, however, she heard his claws on the stone stair, presumably because he had heard her voice. Her small suitcase was still by the front door with her wet clothes in the outer compartment, darkening the fabric. Primo took a heavy iron key out of the right-hand pocket of his scarlet corduroys and unlocked the door, pulling it wide, letting in a squall of powdery snow.

'Good heavens,' he exclaimed. 'It's settling in for another day. Still, I think I'll take a turn round the village, before it becomes impassable.'

Zoe gulped and asked: 'Are we in a frost pocket in Saint-Paul, about to be snowed in?'

'No, have no fear. That was just my little joke.'

Zoe felt disproportionately relieved.

'How far will you go?' she asked.

'A brief circuit, nothing more. I might drop in on Madame Valgarde, a dear old friend of ours.'

Zoe imagined an elderly spinster, someone who had never left the village and would, proudly, tell anyone who asked: 'They'll have to carry me out in a box.'

Primo descended the slippery, snowy steps and branched to the right through another tall gate in a mossy stone wall. Watching it close, Zoe felt compromised by his questions. It was thanks to Adélaïde that she had gained her first big breaks in theatre, leading to an intensely satisfying career in straight dramas and, more importantly – because the money was better and the contracts longer – musicals.

It was doubly unsettling because Primo seemed . . . What was the word I twice thought of? Oh, yes, 'distressed'.

She frowned.

How old was Adélaïde when she married Primo de Palotte? Was it twenty years ago? Fifteen? Perhaps in that difficult phase of an actress's career when they find they can no longer be cast as young and seductive, but they aren't yet old enough to play elderly matriarchs.

Zoe had a brief daydream in which she unlocked Renée the Renault and climbed in, with Russell jumping up onto her lap, then scrambling across to the passenger seat to stand on his hind legs with his front paws on the dashboard, anxious to make sure she was taking the correct route home.

He gave a brief yap as if to encourage her to turn the daydream into reality.

'Russell, we can't go home – not quite yet. Adélaïde told me she needs my help.'

Given his traumatic near-drowning, Zoe felt truly apologetic.

Once this is all over, I'll take a good deal of persuading if I'm to visit Château Palotte again.

Seven

'THIS AWFUL MAUSOLEUM'

Just then, Monsieur Alain, the stooped and elderly butler, was engaged in a circuit of the first and second floors with a heavy tray and a stainless-steel food warmer. Despite his bent spine, muscle memory and force of habit meant he managed it without mishap.

His 'round' of bedrooms was reassuringly familiar. Eight members of the household were currently in residence. Madame Adélaïde was an 'intermittent' because she was often away filming. Primo, Boris Senior and Boris's first wife, Marie-France, were the 'permanents', along with Boris's third wife, known as Sweetie, and their ten-year-old son, Boris Junior.

For a moment, Monsieur Alain let himself contemplate the oddity of the arrangement.

Happily, though, we have rooms to spare.

Monsieur Alain had known the twins, Primo and Boris, for more than forty years; Marie-France, too. Elizabeth, Boris's second wife, he had known almost as long – another 'intermittent', an occasional visitor from her publishing work in Paris.

Apart from Madame Adélaïde, the only member of the older generation in gainful employment.

There were two other guests present that he had known from birth: Elizabeth's thirty-year-old children, Patrick and Minette.

They are either already out of doors for a jog or we won't see them until lunchtime.

He had reached the landing.

Here we go.

★

First to receive her scrambled eggs and toast was Elizabeth de Palotte, *née* Lagrasse. She – like her children, Patrick and Minette – used her maiden name, both socially and at work.

Elizabeth was up and busy, having made her own coffee with the pod machine in her bedroom. She was in the habit of eating at her smoked-glass desk, wearing two dressing gowns against the cold because hers was one of the rooms where the radiators never got properly hot.

As Monsieur Alain came in, she was leafing through the typescript of a contemporary romance novel entitled *Amour à Mort*, meaning 'Love until Death'. The hard-nosed publisher she worked for as a freelance editor had judged it 'disappointing', though that wasn't an opinion they were willing to share directly with the author. That tricky and thankless task, requiring exquisite diplomacy, they had delegated to Elizabeth.

Munching her tepid eggs, she mentally enumerated the novel's many and varied flaws.

A lack of detail in the characterisation; uninspiring everyday locations without interest or charm; insufficient drama to delay the inevitable romantic resolution.

She wasn't yet sure how she would go about helping the author address these obvious deficiencies.

Authors can be so touchy and easily hurt ...

★

Monsieur Alain went to call upon Boris's third wife, Pauline Clairette, known as Sweetie. He was not surprised to discover that she had slept on a comfortable *canapé-lit* – a sofa bed – in the dressing room alongside the marital bedroom.

I expect Monsieur Boris has had another bad night.

★

A minute or two later, Sweetie was still toying with her rapidly congealing scrambled eggs when her son, Boris Junior, came in without knocking. She pulled her negligée hurriedly closed across her surgically enhanced chest.

'What are we doing today?' Junior asked.

'Nothing worth mentioning,' said Sweetie. 'The same as every day in this awful mausoleum.'

★

Monsieur Alain had already moved on, otherwise he might have taken silent offence at this insult to his home for so many years. But he was already lifting the warmer's lid to reveal well-done sausages and unctuous *boudin* – a kind of black pudding – that were Boris de Palotte's favourite morning meal.

As the butler transferred the meats to a surprisingly large breakfast plate, Boris sat up in bed and licked his lips, thanking God in an improvised 'grace' for the blessing of his blood-rich breakfast.

★

Back in her chilly bedroom-cum-office, Elizabeth tidied the stack of A4 paper comprising *Amour à Mort* and turned her attention to another typescript – much more dynamic but with its own, very different problems. *Treize à la Douzaine*, meaning 'Baker's Dozen', was 'true crime' – at least, that was the author's claim.

42

It's almost always an issue. Authors can't help themselves embellishing the 'facts', massaging them into a more compelling shape in the desire to entertain and to sell. The trouble is, though, it can't be both true and made up, at one and the same time.

*

Monsieur Alain left Monsieur Boris happily chewing and made his way to the bedroom of Marie-France de Palotte, *née* Montalbano.

Marie-France's bedroom was in the western tower, overlooking the front door and the bifurcated pathway leading to the village and the carport. As usual, Monsieur Alain discovered Boris's patrician first wife already up and dressed, wearing a beige trouser suit beneath which he knew – from his responsibilities in the basement boiler-and-laundry room – that she always wore thermal tights and vests.

'Nothing for me, Alain. We have a lunch. I won't eat until one.'

'*Oui, madame.*'

The butler made his way back downstairs to the kitchen. He set the stainless-steel warmer on the large beechwood table, lifted the lid with a weary sigh, grabbed a fork and began eating the leftovers directly from it. Meanwhile, he surprised himself with an unexpected train of thought.

We are creatures of tradition and habit – every day the same. But, among the family, something has changed.

He forked another mouthful.

Something that bodes ill, though I'm not sure for whom. For Monsieur Primo, above all? Perhaps for Château Palotte, itself?

Eight

'To Kill Poor Russell?'

Zoe was keen to leave, still, but needed to speak to Adélaïde first. She left Russell in his comfortable doggy bed downstairs and returned to the dining room where Monsieur Alain had lit the fire. No sooner had she sat down than Junior came back in, his Hollywood glamour magazine rolled up in his right fist, as if he had turned it into a weapon.

'Good morning, again,' she said, carefully.

'Am I in the way?' he asked, his eyes darting around the room. 'I'll go.'

'No, don't do that,' Zoe told him. 'I was hoping to talk to you. Have a seat. Perhaps Monsieur Alain will bring some hot food.'

'I just want some more of my cereal.'

He refilled his used bowl with *Trésors Chocolat-Noisettes*, looking small and puny on the large dining chair. Then he hesitated, looking sideways at her.

'Can I show you something?' he asked.

'Yes, go ahead.'

'You knew my Aunt Adélaïde,' he asked, tentatively, 'when she was young, didn't you?'

'I did. Why do you ask?'

Junior turned the pages of his magazine, finding a review of Adélaïde's recent success in an action movie about uncovering a traitor in the heart of Interpol, the global police agency. In it, Adélaïde was dressed in a sober black suit with a white collared blouse, her hair severely brushed back and her face not obviously retouched. In a corner of the page, however, was an older photograph from much earlier in her career, from just before the triumph – and the murder – at Chichester Theatre when she and Zoe had first met. The movie was called *Sirène* – 'mermaid' in English. Adélaïde was depicted almost nude, her 'modesty' maintained by artfully positioned seaweed.

'Yes,' Zoe told Junior. 'I knew her back then.'

'What about this one?'

Next to the 'mermaid' image was a striking studio portrait of Adélaïde with another actress with similar bone structure but much darker skin. The image was from later in Adélaïde's career. Both were dressed in very revealing evening gowns.

Junior asked: 'Why do women take their clothes off but men don't?'

'Good question,' said Zoe, surprised.

'I think it makes them look silly.'

'You won't have to worry about that sort of thing for ages. You're only ten, isn't that right?'

'Yes,' he said grudgingly. 'But that doesn't mean I don't hear what people are saying.'

'Saying about what?' asked Zoe.

'Money, mostly. That's all the grown-ups want to talk about.'

There was a pause as he served himself some milk.

'Are you quite often bored, Junior? Tell me, what do you like doing?'

'I wish Papa would give me my PlayStation back.'

He began eating, using his spoon once more like a shovel, slurping with each mouthful.

'What do you like to play?' asked Zoe, fearing it would be a fighting game with blood splatters on the screen.

'I like *Zelda*,' he told her. 'You have to find a sacred relic to restore the balance of Power, Courage and Wisdom.'

'That sounds splendid,' said Zoe, wondering why Boris had confiscated it.

Monsieur Alain re-entered.

'Madame Pascal is perhaps aware that the others have eaten in their respective rooms, except for Madame Adélaïde and Madame Marie-France, neither of whom take breakfast. Should *madame* prefer, I could prepare an omelette?'

'Actually, that would be delightful. I hope my dog isn't in the way?'

'He's very quiet and good,' said Monsieur Alain. 'Herbs or cheese?'

'May I have both?'

'Of course. *Herbes de Provence* and Emmenthal.'

'*Merci, beaucoup.*'

The *majordome* left and Zoe listened for more movement in the quiet house. Hearing none, she took the plunge and asked Junior: 'Did you think about the fact that Russell, my dog, might have drowned under the ice of the lake?'

Junior didn't reply at first. He kept his eyes down. Then he mumbled: 'I don't know.'

'I wasn't sure if it was an accident, Junior, or if you were doing something that you didn't realise could turn out to be serious?' He said nothing. She went on: 'Or was it deliberate and you just didn't think properly about the consequences?'

Junior scraped sweetened milk from the bottom of his bowl. He reached for the cardboard box for yet another help-ing. Zoe put a hand on it to prevent him. He looked up at her, an inscrutable expression on his childish features – but with eyes that seemed impenetrably dark.

'Which was it?' Zoe insisted.

There was a pause with just the hiss of a damp log on the fire to break the silence.

'I wanted to know what it would be like,' he told her, finally, in a whisper.

'What, exactly?'

'To kill it.'

'To kill poor Russell?' asked Zoe, shocked.

'No, not your dog.'

He gave up on the cereal and folded his hands in his lap.

'I don't understand,' Zoe told him. 'What then?'

'Just a thing,' he told her desperately. 'It could have been anything. I didn't think of it being yours.'

'But why?'

'I wanted to know how it would make me feel.'

Nine
'Is He Dead?'

The doorbell rang. Zoe hoped Monsieur Alain would answer it. She couldn't drag herself away from the extraordinary conversation with Junior.

He wanted to know what it would feel like to kill.

Zoe told him: 'That was the wrong thing to do, breaking the ice. You realise that now, don't you, Junior?'

'Yes, I do,' he said.

That sounds like he's simply giving the answer I expect, rather than showing any real understanding.

'Do you promise to never do anything like that ever again?'

'Yes,' he told her, and she thought at last she had broken through.

'Truly?'

'I promise.'

The doorbell rang twice more. Regretfully, Zoe went and opened up onto whirling snow. Standing in its midst, wearing a chic ski jacket and overtrousers, plus a stylish fur-lined hat, was Zoe's friend and solicitor, the effortlessly sophisticated Caroline Robin.

'What are you doing here?' Zoe asked, unable to hide her surprise.

'I could ask you the same, but Adélaïde warned me you'd be here. Anyway, I'd rather come in first.'

'Of course.' Zoe stepped aside and Caroline entered and stamped her ski boots on the mat. Zoe asked: 'Are you a friend of the family?'

'I hope I have that honour, after all these years,' said Caroline, unpoppering and unzipping her ski jacket, revealing a burgundy twin-set in fine merino wool. 'But I also work for them.' Zoe held her jacket while Caroline sat on the enormous oak carver chair to remove her boots and over-trousers, beneath which she was dressed in white skinny jeans and thick-soled socks. 'Let's go down to the kitchen. It's usually the only warm room in the whole château.'

With regret that she had to abandon her unfinished conversation with Junior, Zoe fell in with this idea, following her friend to the basement floor where Monsieur Alain looked up at them in guilty surprise, his face illuminated by a rare shaft of sunlight from one of the high slot windows.

'Forgive me, Madame Pascal, if I've been foolish, but he seemed so hungry and desperate and the hard dog biscuits didn't seem to his taste.'

Worrying that he's done the wrong thing is making him address me more normally.

Zoe saw that Russell had manipulated the elderly servant and was enjoying his own omelette, served in his dog bowl on top of some dry kibble.

She smiled and told the *majordome*: 'That was very kind of you. Is that for me?' she asked, indicating the hot skillet on the stove.

'*Oui, madame.*'

'Perhaps Madame Robin should have it as she's only recently come in out of the snow?'

'As *madame* wishes,' said Monsieur Alain, reverting to type.

Zoe and Caroline sat at the large rectangular kitchen table.

'Do you have no other shoes?' she asked her friend.

'My bag's still in the car,' said Caroline, already eating.

'I will shortly bring Madame Robin's bag and place it in her usual room,' said the butler.

'Thank you, Alain,' said Caroline.

'You're staying?' asked Zoe.

'Yes,' said Caroline. 'I'm on birthday duty.'

Zoe didn't press for more information because she knew Caroline didn't like talking while eating and, potentially, it was inappropriate to discuss her 'duty' in front of the *major-dome*. Zoe's own omelette arrived and Monsieur Alain left them. She found she was very hungry, finishing hers almost at the same time as her friend. Russell, unusually, jumped up onto Zoe's lap.

'Is he missing you because he's not allowed upstairs to sleep on a corner of your human bed?' asked Caroline.

Zoe laughed, replying: 'I should never have admitted I let him do that.' She became more serious. 'He is a little needy, though. He had a shocking experience earlier on. I think it's made him nervous.'

Zoe told Caroline about the incident at the frozen lake.

'That poor boy,' said her friend.

'You mean Junior? Yes, he is. But, just before you arrived, when I asked him why he had done it, his answer was extremely peculiar.' Zoe gave Caroline the gist of the conversation. 'What do you think of that?'

'It sounds very natural and normal to me. Little boys are interested in fighting and death and pulling the legs off flies and poking the corpses of rotting moles. You can't say they aren't.'

'He is ten, though,' protested Zoe.

'Anyway, we mustn't dilly-dally. There's the announcement to be made.'

'What announcement?'

'Primo leads the family down to the market hall to tell all his tenants about their bonuses. Each gets a kind of rebate on their rent at the end of the calendar year and it's made public around the birthday. It's charming, actually. Primo takes the money and invests it, the profit accruing to the tenants.'

'They all get the same?'

'Far from it. Primo discusses with each of them where they think their rent money should go. Some opt for very safe things like interest-bearing cash accounts, others for wildly inappropriate gambles like crypto-currencies or oil-fields in Kazakhstan.'

'Some will be happy, others not?'

'Yes. This year, because of world events, the people who took the safer options will be happiest. You and your book-shop are bucking the trend.'

'Yes, it's been extremely satisfying. Of course, what the papers called "the French bookshop murder" was a big boost. In a gruesome way, it made the shop a destination, otherwise I wouldn't have allowed myself to take this week off.'

'Good heavens, Zoe, you're not staying for seven days in this mausoleum?'

'No er, I mean, I'm not sure. Perhaps. Adélaïde wants me to, so I suppose I might. The thing is, I intended to . . .' She sighed. 'To tell you the truth, I would rather be in sunny North Africa at an all-inclusive hotel.'

'I don't blame you, but spring in Provence is always just around the corner.'

'You can't mean that?'

'This weather will break soon. You see if I'm not right.'

They put their plates and cutlery in the dishwasher and Car-oline went upstairs, crossing over with Zoe's friend Patrick from the Auberge Sainte-Catherine. His presence, like Caroline's, was a complete surprise. He and Zoe exchanged a few words of greeting, then Patrick told her: 'We're running late. We have to go into the village for one of the birthday events.'

'Yes, I know, but could you possibly explain more about what it's for?' Zoe pleaded. 'I feel lost among all Adélaïde's relations. And – I'm sorry to be rude – I have no idea why you're here.'

Patrick grinned and told her: 'Had Adélaïde not explained already, we would be asking you the same question. Minette and I have been coming to the château for "the birthday" for most of our lives. I'm surprised nobody told you. Everybody knows one another's business in Sainte-Catherine.'

'That's true,' Zoe acknowledged. 'But I'm still a new-comer. Can you tell me now?'

'It's quite a long story—'

'Or just fill me in on the event we're all going to in the village?'

'Oh, that's easy. Primo inherited the Château Palotte estate by virtue of being born ten minutes sooner than his brother – which may or may not have rankled with Boris for nearly three-score years and ten.'

'But I was under the impression that inheritance in France is guaranteed to all the children, that they have to receive at least quarter shares? Isn't that right?'

'Normally, yes,' said Patrick, 'but not when everything is tied up in trusts before the parents' demise. It all passed absolutely to Primo.

Someone called from upstairs: 'Hurry up, everyone.'

'And Caroline is the Palotte family solicitor as well as mine?' Zoe asked.

'That's right.'

Led by multiple voices, Zoe and Patrick headed for the dining room where they found the entire family assembled. Primo had changed out of his scarlet cords and mustard-yellow jumper and was dressed in a sumptuous three-piece tweed suit. Adélaïde was a pace away, in a fur coat and fur boots. Zoe thought there was something uncomfortable in their slight separation.

Patrick took Zoe round the room and briefly introduced her to the assembled family members. He began with Boris de Palotte, Primo's twin brother, who Zoe thought seemed unhappy.

Possibly under the weather?

He was swamped in what the ex-British Prime Minister John Major once memorably called the 'single European overcoat', a sludge-green tent-shaped thing, reminiscent of a Tyrolean cape. He was arm in arm with his young wife, known as Sweetie, who was well wrapped up in an enormous white puffer coat.

'It's a pleasure to meet you,' Zoe told them.

Patrick then presented her to Boris's previous wives, the elderly Marie-France and the middle-aged Elizabeth, who wore – respectively – a long charcoal-grey down overcoat and a similar one in bright yellow.

Not knowing they had met, Patrick led her to Junior who was standing very close to the fire in his quilted anorak and tartan scarf, looking uneasy. Then Patrick introduced his sister, Minette. Zoe mentioned a few mutual Sainte-Catherine acquaintances, taking in the fact that brother and sister were almost matching in jeans and close-fitting, hi-tech blousons, plus woolly hats and warm gloves.

'Ah, Caroline,' said Primo, advancing on the solicitor and shaking her hand. 'Thank you for coming in this atrocious weather. I hope the roads were not too difficult?'

'It is my honour to be here, Monsieur de Palotte,' said Caroline, revealing to Zoe a previously unseen strand of deference in her character. 'I hope I haven't kept you waiting.'

'And Madame Pascal,' said Primo, moving politely on. 'Our special guest.'

Zoe found herself resisting the urge to curtsey, simply replying: 'Good morning, Monsieur de Palotte.' Without quite knowing why, she felt the need to conceal the fact that they had already spoken, adding: 'I hope you slept well?'

'Call me Primo, please. And one doesn't, in my condition.' He looked left and right. 'Shall we?'

Zoe and Caroline led the family out of the dining room into the wide corridor. Zoe helped her friend back into her expensive ski jacket and boots, then they shuffled aside for Primo to lead them out. He opened the wide front door with a screech and it swung quickly inwards on a stiff, snowy gust. Zoe held on to it as Primo carefully stepped over the sill, into the accumulating snow. She noticed, with a sharp shadow of worry, that it came up over the lace-holes of his brown brogues.

Poor man. Whatever he meant by 'in my condition', he doesn't also want to catch a chill.

Adélaïde gave Zoe a grateful smile and slipped out to follow him down the steps between the unpruned lavenders, their blooms dry and withered. Zoe and Caroline came next, descending half a dozen slippery treads to the fork which led left to the carport and right to the gate into the village.

Then, shockingly, Zoe heard Primo gasp and saw him shudder. His knees buckled. Adélaïde leaned in, struggling to support his weight. Zoe stepped in to assist but found they had no choice but to lower him gently to the ground.

'Is it a heart attack, a stroke?' she asked.

Adélaïde didn't reply. Her eyes were fixed on a point a few metres away.

With a feeling of trepidation, Zoe tracked her gaze to a mound of grey livery, already part-concealed by snowfall. But the blanched white face of the elderly butler, Monsieur Alain, was visible, turned towards them, his dentures protruding beyond his lips, his awful staring eyes as lifeless as the sharp stone step that had deeply gashed his seamed forehead.

'Is he dead?' Adélaïde asked, her breath a waft of steam in the freezing air.

Zoe considered the fact that there was no such vapour emerging from poor Monsieur Alain's nose or mouth.

Not even the faintest wisp.

'I think, Adélaïde,' said Zoe, 'that he must be.'

Ten

'BUSINESS AS USUAL'

The word on everybody's lips was, not unreasonably, 'accident'. Monsieur Alain was an old man. His mobility was reduced by his severe stoop. The narrow stone staircase was slippery and any imperfections – cracks or loose stones liable to make someone trip – could easily have been hidden by the snow.

In the aftermath, as a stranger to the family, Zoe felt like a spare part. On discovery of the corpse, she had taken a large stride away across the lavender border, allowing those with a closer relationship to the elderly servant to attend to him. Primo had still said nothing but Adélaïde had got him up off the ground.

Sweetie asked, with a kind of childish insistence: 'How did it happen? Why won't anyone tell me how it happened?'

Boris Senior, her husband, took a deep breath, giving Zoe the impression that he was winding himself up into making a speech. 'This is a dark day—' he began.

He didn't get any further because Elizabeth, his second wife, interrupted, saying sharply: 'Be quiet, Boris.' Then she and Patrick and Minette stepped away to converse very quietly with Marie-France. Zoe wondered if they were reconstructing the possible sequence of events. In her imagination, she was doing the same.

To start with, where is the suitcase? That's why Monsieur Alain left us alone in the kitchen, to go and fetch Caroline's bag from her car. But it's nowhere to be seen, meaning he fell on the way down. And why would he have done that, given that he must have gone up and down these steps, including in bad weather and in winter, many thousands of times over his time at Château Palotte?

Primo and Boris moved closer to one another and to the corpse, their necks bent, almost as if they were imitating the butler's habitual pose as a kind of tribute. In a touching display of shared grief, Zoe saw them put their arms around one another.

The pattern of conversation reconfigured. Adélaïde, Marie-France and Elizabeth came together near the front door. They, too, began conversing in hushed undertones. Then Sweetie joined them, repeating her answerable question.

'How did it happen?'

There was an awkward moment when no one seemed to know what to say.

The wind continued to blow, whipping squalls of snow-flakes across all their faces so that every one of them – the bereaved elderly twins, the wives, the younger twins, Zoe herself – kept turning their heads to brush away the ice that was trying to form on their lashes. Zoe realised that Junior was missing. She supposed that he had run back inside, frightened by the awful sight. She felt sorry for him, aware that nobody else seemed to have noticed his absence.

They really do seem very uncaring with regard to the poor boy.

Primo and Boris broke apart and Primo, with his authority as the older twin by just ten minutes, said: 'Adélaïde, my dear, would you please call the doctor? His professional expertise is not required because it is too late, but I suppose he should attend in his capacity as registrar of deaths.'

Adélaïde went inside without a word and Zoe realised that Caroline was nowhere to be seen.

She's probably already gone to put the official wheels in motion.

Marie-France and Elizabeth followed, leaving Sweetie abandoned.

'What shall I do?' she asked her elderly husband, plain-tively.

'Go with them, Pauline.'

'What have I done wrong?' she demanded. 'You only call me Pauline when I've done something wrong.'

'Nothing, Sweetie, my dear. Please leave us alone together, my brother and me.'

With a desolate glance, Sweetie turned away and followed the others indoors. Primo and Boris said nothing, their eyes returning to the dead butler.

Zoe spoke to Patrick and Minette: 'What a terrible thing to have happened.'

'I liked him,' said Patrick. 'Many times, with his scoliosis, there was talk that he should be forcibly retired and given somewhere to live.'

'But where would he have gone and what would he have done?' asked Minette, rhetorically. 'That was always the question. He had no other life.'

'Nothing outside his work,' said her brother.

'Thirty years ago,' said Minette, 'he probably had five or six servants working under him.'

'What's the position now?' asked Zoe.

'Only he lives in,' said Patrick. 'Lived in, I mean, with all the heavy work done by outsiders, as and when.'

'Don't you think,' said Zoe, 'that we should encourage the two gentlemen to go inside?'

Primo and Boris were once more holding on to one another, either for physical or for emotional support.

'You can't stay out here like this,' said Patrick.

'Uncle Primo, you both need to come indoors,' said Minette. 'This won't do.'

The two men turned their heads, as if synchronised. Reluctantly, they climbed the treacherous steps, one after the other, and Patrick and Minette went to walk in front and behind them to make sure another disaster couldn't ensue.

Once the door had closed, Zoe found herself alone in the whirling snowflakes. She looked carefully at the place where Monsieur Alain had fallen. Because of the smudges in the snow, she thought she could see the exact spot where he must have toppled over, falling forwards in his descent, striking his head on the leading edge of one of the steps, and then his momentum rolling him over onto his side so that his face was angled back up towards the house.

I hope it was quick and he didn't lie here in the cold, wishing that help would come.

Shivering, Zoe followed the others indoors. To her surprise, they were gathered in a disorganised confab in the corridor. From their muddled conversation, she grasped that – in addition to calling the doctor – Caroline and Adélaïde were in touch with the village mayor, calling from Primo's office on the first floor. Apparently, just as soon as the body had been taken away by an ambulance or mortuary van, they were going to head down to the market hall in order that Primo should make his eagerly awaited announcement of his tenants' annual bonuses.

'It will be business as usual,' he insisted.

Adélaïde appeared at the foot of the stairs with the news that two members of the emergency services – often known in French as the *pompiers*, usually translated as the fire brigade – would be along shortly.

'Accompanied by the doctor, too?' said Primo, earnestly.

'Caroline has done all that needs to be done,' Adélaïde confirmed.

Zoe thought her friend looked extremely shocked, very white, her lips pinched.

Is there something she wants to say but doesn't dare? What a horrible situation for everybody.

'I suggest,' said Primo, 'that we all go downstairs to the kitchen for a shot of brandy to warm ourselves up and give ourselves courage for the ceremony.'

'It's what Alain would have wanted,' declared Boris, pompously. 'Later on, we must organise a proper burial service, brother. Perhaps the bishop could be prevailed upon to preside.'

'We might do that,' said Primo, giving Zoe the impression that he would like nothing less. 'Let's leave those questions for later on, Boris. Would you mind?'

Adélaïde led Primo down the basement stairs. The others followed and Zoe abruptly became worried that Russell would make a disgrace of himself as everybody trooped in. She, of course, was last – apart from Caroline who was upstairs on the phone again – and Junior, who was still nowhere to be seen.

Happily, Russell took the sudden influx in his stride, moving from person to person in order to discover which of them were 'dog people' and which weren't. Meanwhile, Elizabeth emerged as the person most *au fait* with where everything was and swiftly had a tray of glasses ready. The brandy came from a locked cabinet, opened by Primo, inside of which Zoe saw, in the brief period that the door was ajar, an impressive array of spirits, in particular single-malt whiskies from celebrated Scottish manufacturers.

The process of pouring out created a silent hiatus. Nobody was going to drink until everybody was served, then they were all delayed further because of Boris's desire to break the silence with a speech that, Zoe thought, everyone found excruciating, though they all listened respectfully.

'Alain served this family for forty years. Is it more than that? I'm too shocked to know. Going on fifty? I am indescribably hurt. No, that's the wrong word. Not hurt. Confused by his passing.' He shook his head, gravely. 'It seems to me that, as one ages, far from speeding up, time feels more laborious as the seconds grind by, change upon change, eroding our hopes and our spirits. But, with the example of our Lord and Saviour, Jesus Christ, we endure. We know

– and happy, we are, because of it – that we can trust in salvation thanks to His sacrifice.' Boris left a pause, then intoned a sepulchral: 'Amen.'

Zoe wasn't sure who it was who repeated the word. Two or three voices murmured it, she thought, as a kind of Pavlovian response. Nobody made the response with any real gusto, however.

'To Alain,' said Primo, quietly.

This was greeted more enthusiastically.

'To Alain,' everyone chorused.

Finally, they drank and Zoe found she was very glad of her brandy. She had stayed outside longer than anyone else and felt quite chilled. As Caroline had said, though, the kitchen was probably the warmest room in the house. Zoe supposed there was a boiler lurking somewhere close by.

Some desultory conversation ensued about the timeline of Monsieur Alain's employment, leading to a consensus that he had been with the family for forty-eight years. A few meagre stories were exhumed about events at which the butler had been present but in which he had, if truth were told, played little part. Zoe discovered that he had joined the household as a teenager on being orphaned, his father dying in the French army while serving in Indochina and his mother from an unnamed illness.

He wasn't as old as his stoop made him look.

The lurching conversation was finally interrupted by the distant ringing of the front doorbell. Patrick said he would go and find out who it was, adding: 'There's no need for everyone to troop back out.'

'I feel I ought,' said Boris, looking from face to face, as if seeking approval.

'Do you have to?' asked Sweetie.

'It's a question of family responsibility—' Boris began.

Primo told him: 'I would be grateful if you stayed at my side, brother.'

'Of course, my dear fellow, of course.'

Watching this exchange, Zoe wondered if Primo had made the request in order to prevent his twin going upstairs and taking over, undermining the quiet dignity of the butler's final voyage in the care of the *pompiers*. Suddenly weary of the complicated relationships between all the Palotte relatives, Zoe asked: 'Would you all excuse me? I'm sure you don't need me to accompany you to the ceremony in the village.'

'Oh no,' said Adélaïde. 'But you must, Zoe, please.'

'Really?'

'Would you?' Adélaïde's tone of voice was so earnest that all other conversation ceased and everyone turned to look at her. 'I mean, if you don't mind. It really is a lovely event. I'd like you to share it with us and see the good that Primo does, the generosity of his treatment of his tenants and . . .'

Adélaïde's voice trailed away, like an actress unable to remember the strong climax of a speech written especially for her, for this very moment. She looked like she knew she had spoiled the effect.

Why is it so important to her that I should see her husband in a good light? She seems to need my support but still hasn't really told me why.

Eleven

'SURPRISINGLY ALONE'

'In that case, if you would really like me to be there, Adélaïde, of course I will come with you,' said Zoe. 'Would you just excuse me for five minutes? I'll be back down shortly.'

Zoe ran upstairs, the first flight taking her to the ground-floor corridor. She found it empty and the heavy front door slightly ajar. She was tempted to go and see what was happening, but resisted.

There's a difference between taking a legitimate interest and nosiness.

She bounced up the second flight to the dingy corridor with the main first-floor rooms. She ran along, past the insipid watercolours, to her own damp-smelling bedroom in the eastern tower. Going inside, something gave her pause.

My things have been moved.

She stayed where she was, just inside the door, her eyes scanning the bed – which she had made before coming downstairs – the bits and pieces on the nightstand, the open suitcase and the rucksack alongside, the change of clothes draped on a useful chair.

I wish I could see what it is that's been shifted.

She corrected herself.

Or taken.

She heard footsteps once more, through the ceiling, pacing back and forth.

Junior? He's been suspiciously absent for some time.

Her eyes slid pointlessly from object to object.

There's nothing I actually need up here. I just wanted to get away from them all for a few minutes.

She sat down on the edge of the bed, closed her eyes and took a few moments to focus on her breathing, trying to ground herself. She had known grief and how it could corrode the present, but there was something else, too.

I don't react well to being surrounded by unhappy families – bitterness and recrimination, passive aggression, jealousy and disappointment.

It was all a result of having been left, as a tiny baby, at the door of St Richard's Hospital in Chichester, as a foundling, like in an old-fashioned story by Charles Dickens. As a child, she had been starved of love, raised in inadequate 'care', latterly by harsh foster parents who, on her sixteenth birthday, when the state was no longer obliged to pay for her upkeep, had abandoned her at a rural bus stop with no money and just a small suitcase for her meagre possessions.

Things might have turned out very badly for Zoe had she not had the great good fortune to be taken in by Phyllis Pascal, the owner of the local Jacobean manor house. A severe but charitable countrywoman, Phyl had, eventually, adopted Zoe, bringing her in contact with the remarkable amateur detective Maisie Cooper, her half-sister by adoption, and, by extension, with Adélaïde Amour.

Because these thoughts were running rapidly – almost indiscriminately – through her mind, Zoe felt a sudden need to touch base with her old friend. She found it hard, however, to act on the impulse. She felt herself enveloped by a disagreeable fog of loss, casting a pall over her unhappy emotions.

Phyl is already dead. And there are eighteen years between Maisie and me. Like Monsieur Alain, I can't expect her to go on forever. How will I feel if I end up surprisingly alone?

She unplugged her mobile phone from a fragile double socket on the wall beneath the nightstand and woke the screen. Annoyingly, the device hadn't charged. It was still on seven per cent, even less than when she had gone to sleep the previous evening.

That should be enough, however.

Maisie's number was the most recent she had called. She tapped and, soon, heard it ringing, feeling deeply aware of the physical distance between them.

Eight hundred miles. Thirteen hundred kilometres.

Maisie picked up on the fifth ring. Zoe greeted her warmly and asked her how she was, what she had been doing.

'Are you still troubled by your tumble?'

'You've interrupted the physiotherapy for my wrist. I have to squeeze a tennis ball,' Maisie told her. 'Then I pick up a tin of baked beans and put it down again. I think I've given them the impression that I'm weak and feeble.'

'You're not weak and feeble,' said Zoe. 'I expect the fracture is knitting together nicely. You're still in the prime of life.'

'I've reached the age where I don't fall over, I "have a fall". It's awful,' Maisie added, good-humouredly.

'That's other people's words, not yours.'

They went on to discuss the respite home for which Maisie had become responsible after Phyllis Pascal's death. Then Maisie asked: 'You sound tentative, Zoe. I know what that means. Something's happened and you're beating about the bush.'

Zoe smiled at the old-fashioned expression and began to tell her story, starting with Adélaïde's unexpected invitation for Primo and Boris's birthday. Unfortunately, she took too long and was nowhere near getting to the unexpected tragedy of Monsieur Alain's death when she was interrupted by Patrick's strong voice from the stairs.

'We're about to leave,' he called.

Zoe spoke into her mobile phone. 'I have to go with them. Adélaïde has asked me especially. Just before I do, is there anything you can tell me about the murder at Chichester Theatre all those years ago that Adélaïde might be ashamed about?'

'Zoe,' said the distant, patient voice, with an edge of surprise, 'that's neither my story to tell, nor do we have the time, if you're being summoned.'

Patrick repeated his appeal: 'Zoe, are you there?'

'*J'arrive, vas-y*,' she shouted back, meaning 'I'm coming, go on'. Then she asked: 'Maisie, can I call you later? Dredge up those memories and put them in order for me, will you?'

'They're as fresh as paint,' Maisie told her. 'Some of us never forget.'

Zoe hung up, put the phone in a pocket and left her room. Patrick had already left, taking her at her word. She followed the corridor and plodded heavily downstairs, pondering the fact that Maisie hadn't denied that Adélaïde might have something of which to be ashamed.

Primo was definitely worried. Otherwise, he wouldn't have tried to get me to … to talk about Adélaïde behind her back.

She considered her friend's appeal for her help.

Is there more to the Chichester Theatre story than a vague accusation? Might there be someone trying to cause trouble by raking up the past? People are so ready to think: 'There's no smoke without fire.'

The Palotte family was once again confusedly assembled in the hallway. Junior brushed past Zoe at the foot of the stairs, still in his inadequate anorak and posh tartan scarf. Beyond the gaggle of heads and hats, someone she couldn't see opened the door and, even at the back of the line, Zoe felt the bitter breeze forcing itself indoors.

She followed them out. From her higher vantage point on the rubber outdoor mat, she saw them picking their way carefully down the stone steps. She wondered if she ought to call out to them to lock the front door. The only key she had seen had been in the pocket of Primo's scarlet trousers.

Or maybe they've already forgotten that Monsieur Alain is gone and there's no one to guard the place.

She shut the door and had another thought.

Monsieur Alain opened up this morning so he must also have a key. I wonder if it's still in his pocket on its way to the mortuary?

She heard Russell yap from within, on the far side of the heavy timbers.

'*Reste-là, on revient*,' she told him, meaning: 'Stay there, we'll be back.' He snapped another sharp complaint before falling silent.

Because of her hesitation, the Palotte family had moved out of sight, past the place where the butler's body had been discovered, along the right fork and out into the village through the wooden pedestrian gate, set in a tall stone wall beneath an arch of clay tiles, like the one that led from the vegetable garden onto the lawn. Zoe descended six steps and inspected the spot where Monsieur Alain had first been seen by Primo, causing him to gasp and collapse.

For a second or two, I thought he'd had a heart attack. I must ask Adélaïde about the seriousness of his condition.

The snow continued to fall. The area where Monsieur Alain had lain was compacted by many feet. On the edge of the step on which she thought he must have struck his head, though, a smear of blood was visible, already brown and crusty.

Did the emergency services photograph that as evidence? It won't last if the weather turns to rain.

Zoe reimagined the butler's body, his feet on a higher step than his hips which were, in turn, higher than his shoulders, with his face awkwardly turned back towards the house.

I suppose that doesn't matter if everyone considers it an accident.

She focused on the stone tread where he must have slipped or tripped, brushing away the snow with her gloved hand, finding no irregularities or loose stones.

Too many people have come tramping through.

She took off her right glove and rubbed her fingers through the dried-up blooms of the lavender bush closest to her, on the right-hand side, dislodging the snow, bringing the delicate, calming fragrance to her nostrils. Then she frowned, seeing that the bush was broken near its base where the main trunk, about the thickness of her thumb, entered the snow-covered soil. With a feeling of trepidation at what she might discover, she checked the other side of the stair, but found the bushes intact.

She stood up, glancing around, an idea forming in her mind of what she ought to be looking for.

A stick or a fallen branch, not too thick or heavy, but a metre or so long, enough to wedge between two low lavender bushes and trip up an old man on a slippery stair.

Her heart began to race. She took a deep breath to still it.

Which begs two questions. Was it done deliberately? And, if so, who was the intended victim?

II

ACCIDENT OR MURDER?

Twelve

'I Didn't Do Anything'

Patrick appeared, framed in the pedestrian gateway beneath the clay-tile arch.

'Adélaïde asked me to come and look for you. She thought perhaps you might have got lost in the village.'

'No, I'm sorry,' Zoe told him. 'I had to take a phone call.'

'Not bad news, I hope?'

Zoe realised her face must look very serious and worried. She made an effort to brighten up.

'Not at all, but I couldn't get them to let me go,' she lied, mentally asking Maisie's forgiveness. 'I'm sorry to have made you come back. What happened with the *pompiers*?'

'They were very efficient. The local policeman turned up.'

'He didn't want to ask anyone questions?'

'No. He just shook his head sadly and said: "It comes to us all." Why do you ask? What do you imagine he might want to know?'

'I expect I've read too many detective stories,' said Zoe, 'where nothing can be taken at face value.'

Patrick laughed, saying: 'And you solved your own "book-shop" mystery.'

He led her into the narrow streets of the village of Saint-Paul-de-Palotte, past a useful general store, outside which was a yellow post box, then a *boulangerie* – a bakery – and several stone-built houses. Then the lane opened out into a square in whose centre was a market hall with open sides, a historic post-and-beam structure with fifty or sixty chairs lined up beneath its cobwebby roof. Every seat was taken and there was a hum of many simultaneous conversations, although conducted at a discreet volume, reminding Zoe of how people behave in church or at funerals.

Patrick led Zoe to the front of the 'audience' and showed her a chair that had been kept free next to Adélaïde. She sat down and was surprised when her old friend removed her glove and took her hand. Zoe was transfixed for a moment by the distinctive evidence of age – the prominent veins and tendons, the liver spots.

I still have an image in my mind of Adélaïde as a lovely young woman. And the excellence of her make-up and coiffure means that image hasn't been entirely overwritten by the passing of time.

On Adélaïde's far side was Junior, then Sweetie, Boris, Patrick, Minette, Marie-France and Elizabeth. Zoe was pleased to see that Junior was snuggled under his mother's arm, then she wondered if it was merely a ploy to make him sit still. Caroline was in the row behind with an empty chair alongside her.

In front of the audience was a small daïs made up of some heavy planking across a knee-height, brick-built enclosure, stained with soot, clearly used as a hearth. Zoe supposed it often served as a barbecue for village parties and festivals.

Primo was seated alone on the makeshift daïs, in a wooden-armed chair, not unlike the oak carver in the hallway at the château, sedately removing his leather gloves. Standing beside him was a youthful woman in a dashing Desigual coat with a loud and colourful design, who introduced herself as the mayor of Saint-Paul-de-Palotte and, with a dazzling smile, recited a passage of archaic French from the medieval foundation of the village that Zoe – and others, she was sure – found hard to follow.

At the conclusion of her speech, the mayor climbed down off the rustic daïs and took the empty seat at the far end of the second row, next to Caroline. Primo reached into the side pocket of his tweed jacket and removed a high-quality cream envelope. It was thick with papers. His wiry fingers – even more obviously marked by age than Adélaïde's – folded back the flap, then he looked up at the audience and began, in a strong, composed voice.

'Friends, neighbours, we come together on an unexpectedly sad day. Some of you will have seen the *pompiers* arriving at Château Palotte. Others may already know that our *major-dome*, Monsieur Alain, has died. I will not copy the example of the annoying obituaries in the newspapers and conceal the reason. He tripped and fell in the snow and wind, engaged in the honest labour that, for so long, he had jealously guarded for his own.'

Primo left a pause. The audience under the heavy roof was still and quiet. Glancing round, Zoe saw a mixture of smiling faces and sad eyes, creased with fond memories but also a sense of loss. Then, to her surprise, Primo put his fat envelope down on his knees and began to clap. Zoe felt Adélaïde remove her hand from hers to follow suit. Then the entire assembled community of villagers was applauding the memory of the life of the dead butler.

After what felt like a minute, Primo stopped clapping and the audience soon did the same.

'*Bon voyage*,' he said, loud enough to be heard but, Zoe felt, the words were really for the private attention of his butler's departed spirit. Then he became more businesslike. 'Life goes on.' He took a sheaf of slips of paper from the envelope. His eyes narrowed as he read the details of the first. '*La famille Astor*.'

A burly man, sitting just behind Zoe, got up and approached the daïs, stopping before it without climbing up. Because he was seated, Primo's eyes were more or less level with those of Monsieur Astor as he handed over a slip of paper. Zoe saw writing upon it, but couldn't make out what it said. The burly man responded, in a ritual tone: '*Bon anniversaire, Monsieur de Palotte.*'

Primo replied to this wish for a 'happy birthday' with 'happy new year': '*Bonne année, Monsieur Astor.*'

The burly villager went to sit down and there followed twenty-two virtually identical interactions – Zoe counted them – all following the same pattern. As each head of family received their rebate notice, the same words were exchanged, then they returned to their seat, some unable to resist glancing at the details, others quickly folding their slip of paper in half and putting it away out of sight.

The entire event took not much more than ten minutes. The final tenant – the order was alphabetical – was a very handsome, middle-aged woman with a darkish skin tone whose smooth deep-brown hair was styled with a severe centre parting. She wore a long, black overcoat and took her time making her way to the front of the market hall, then received her paper with what looked like a conspiratorial smile.

'*Bon anniversaire, Monsieur de Palotte.*'

'*Bonne année, Madame Valgarde.*'

The woman returned to her seat and Zoe experienced *déjà vu.*

Don't I know her?

The mayor climbed back up onto the daïs to announce: 'In light of today's sad news, the Palotte family will return to the château and not take part in the traditional toast.'

Primo stood and Adélaïde hurried to help him down, his stiff limbs making it awkward. As he walked away, followed by his relatives, the villagers applauding once more, Zoe thought Primo looked extremely wearied and, perhaps, embarrassed by the attention.

But it happens every year. Surely, he must be used to it? Or is the estate doing badly so he's had to be less generous than usual?

The family left the market hall and made their way along the narrow street, heading past the bakery and the general

74

store. Monsieur Astor and a younger man who looked very much like a slimmer version of him – Zoe assumed his son – removed the heavy planks from the brick-built hearth, revealing half a dozen ice buckets standing in cold ashes, each one containing a bottle of some kind of sparkling wine, perhaps champagne, perhaps a different local vintage. Zoe slipped away as the corks were popped and the villagers' conversation became noisy and insistent.

The snow still fell. Sheltered from the breeze, she hesitated outside the window of the general store, taking a feigned interest in a display of elderly postcards and useful plastic household equipment. Once she was certain that she'd waited long enough, she followed, pausing at the château gate to make sure the coast was clear, then searched with her eyes for a branch or stick that might have been placed across the stone stair in order to trip Monsieur Alain and send him tumbling.

How many times had he navigated those steps without any problems, including in bad weather? Hundreds? Thousands?

In the back of her mind, of course, was the idea that it might well have been another sinister prank from Junior, Boris and Sweetie's – possibly – maladjusted son. But she couldn't see anything that looked suitable.

Discouraged, she climbed to the front door and went inside, wincing as its hinges screeched. She carefully wiped her feet and followed the hallway to the dining room where she found Junior playing with the fire, poking at the larger logs with a damp length of branch.

'Hello there, what are you up to?'

Junior jumped, startled, and threw the damp stick onto the conflagration in the wide hearth.

'I didn't do anything,' he said, then ran out of the room, an expression of utter terror on his pale, dark-eyed face.

75

Thirteen

'An Unexplained Death'

For a few moments, Zoe simply stood where she was, turning her head from the fireplace to the door and back again. Then, mentally rebuking herself for her hesitation, she snatched up a long pair of fire tongs and grappled with the cumbersome stick that Junior had tossed onto the flames. Because the fire was burning so vigorously, the timber was already smouldering, despite its damp bark and smattering of lichen. There was a bare knuckle about two-thirds of the way along that made it distinctive.

It must have fallen months ago, lying on the damp ground all winter, but then Junior found it and . . .

She eventually managed to close the tongs on the branch, crossed the room and, with her left hand, turned the handle of the French doors onto the terrace and kicked them wide open, almost dropping the branch on the floor.

She just managed to get it out of doors, letting it fall onto the carpet of snow. It hissed and she rolled it over twice with the toe of her boot to make sure that it was completely cool, then picked it up in her gloved hands and walked quickly round the outside of the house to the slippery stone steps. When she reached the place where she thought Monsieur Alain had fallen, she positioned the branch across the stair, discovering that it fitted snugly between two lavender bushes, the one on the left intact and the one on the right broken at the base.

What do I do now? This is complete supposition. And this branch could have ended up across the path in many different ways, given the strong winds that have been battering the region.

Feeling self-conscious, she glanced over her shoulder towards the western tower that rose, steadfast and ancient, above the front door of the château.

I wonder whose window that is on the first floor.

She examined the stick, looking to see if there might be a mark where it could have been dragged against the broken lavender trunk. She raised it to her nose, feeling foolish, but unwilling to discount the possibility that a faint fragrance might remain. Unfortunately, thanks to its brief passage through the flames, all she could discern was smoke and charred bark.

But, surely, Junior looked and sounded guilty?

Zoe descended the stair and took the right fork towards the gate where she was able to hide the stick in a pile of snowy leaves that had been blown in a heap against the stone wall. She still couldn't convince herself.

Junior is in the habit of being told off. He might have seen the expression on my face and reacted as he did from that, not because he actually did anything wrong.

Zoe ambled slowly back round the house to the dining-room window, her eyes down, lost in thought.

And, at breakfast, I as good as accused him of trying to drown Russell and he more or less admitted it.

Once she had closed the French doors, she took out her phone and discovered that the combination of the passing of time and the cold day had reduced her battery to only two per cent. She ran her fingertips rapidly back and forth across her scalp, sending a sprinkling of snow onto the white tablecloth.

According to poor Monsieur Alain, apart from Patrick and Minette and Junior and me, the others all had their breakfasts in their rooms.

She imagined the stooped butler tottering up and down, from the basement to the upper floors, carrying his stainless-steel food warmer and, presumably, cutlery and crockery and condiments. She sat down on one of the firm dining chairs and idly traced a shape on the heavy cotton cloth with the nail of her right forefinger. Her mind returned to the obvious supposition – but also to an unanswered question.

If Junior placed that branch across the treacherous steps as a prank, did he mean to trip somebody in particular, or did he not care who his victim was?

Zoe tried to put herself into the mind of the unhappy ten-year-old.

Is it conceivable that Junior formed the idea of tripping up Primo because of his father Boris's money problems?

Had it not been for Caroline's arrival and the butler going out to fetch her suitcase, Zoe knew that everyone would have expected Primo to be first down the steps, because of his role in leading the whole family into the village for the ceremony.

Now that I think about it, that seems horribly plausible.

Zoe went upstairs, past the wan watercolours, to her bedroom. She opened the door and hesitated, looking around. This time, she didn't get the impression that anybody had been inside during her absence. She plugged in her mobile at the loose socket, alongside the bedside lamp, made sure that it was charging then went back out into the first-floor corridor.

For a few moments, she stood still and listened. In the solidly built château, all sound was muffled, but she could faintly discern more than one conversation, the nearest one quite close at hand.

She followed the first-floor corridor to a room on the left, probably above the dining room, and hesitated with her ears pricked. A heavy, close-fitting door prevented her from working out what was being said, but she thought she could hear two voices, one male and one female. Then the cadence of the conversation changed, the handle began to turn and she walked quickly on. At the head of the stairs, she looked back to see Caroline emerging and waited for her.

'This is quite the to-do,' she said, weakly. 'Will it create more work for you? I suppose it must.'

'Why do you ask?'

'As the family solicitor? An unexplained death must have a way of generating confusion and paperwork?'

Caroline looked, as always, extremely chic but also extremely serious.

'In what way is Alain's death unexplained?'

Zoe suggested, in a quiet voice: 'Perhaps we could go somewhere more private where we can speak without being overheard. I need your advice.'

'Perhaps we should,' said Caroline in a tone that suggested disapproval. 'You're not letting your imagination run away with you, are you, because of the events back in Sainte-Catherine with "the French bookshop murder"?'

'Perhaps,' admitted Zoe. 'That's possible. But, all the same, might you have fifteen minutes . . . ?'

She left the thought hanging. Caroline sighed.

'All right. Where do you suggest we go?'

'We could walk down to the lake and then find shelter under the trees if the snow gets heavier. Who were you talking to?'

'That's Primo's office.'

'Oh, I didn't know. I haven't really got the hang of where everything is.'

'I have to make a phone call, then Primo and I have other matters to discuss. Shall we say in half an hour?'

'Yes, let's. I'll be downstairs.'

'I'll find you. Don't worry.'

Caroline bustled away and Zoe was left alone. To her surprise, she heard music.

Someone's playing a piano and people are singing.

The sound was not particularly melodic and the instrument was badly in need of tuning, but it was joyful and it drew her downstairs, to the main corridor, carpeted with a threadbare runner, either side of which were dark oak floorboards that ran into tall skirting boards, then ancient wainscoting in the same timber.

Zoe knew by now that there were two state rooms on the south side of the corridor. She had spent quite a lot of time in the second one along, the dining room. The reception room nearer to the front door was less well known to her.

The door was closed – a heavy six-panel affair, painted cream by some distant ancestor and not retouched since. Every detail of the complicated wooden carving was choked with soot or cigarette smoke or dust.

Perhaps all three.

Now that she was close by, she could count three voices coming from within, one male and two female, singing a traditional Provençal folk song. She opened the door, taking in an incongruous meeting-room table surrounded by chic office chairs that wouldn't have looked out of place in Silicon Valley. At the opposite end was a blazing fire faced by a few armchairs. In between was a baby-grand piano on which was a tray of glasses and bottles. By the window, on the floor, were four large clay pots containing herbs brought in from the garden to protect them from frost.

A floorboard creaked beneath her tread. It just happened to fall in a pause between two verses. Silence abruptly fell and three faces turned towards her.

The first was Adélaïde's, seated at the piano, an expression mixed of sadness and pleasure on her still-beautiful features – wide-set eyes, equally broad mouth, strong cheekbones and carefully curated hair.

The second was Minette, tall and dark with an athletic build but a pale complexion.

Someone who doesn't often see the sun.

The third face belonged to Patrick Lagrasse, looking immensely handsome in a well-cut dark-grey suit over a pale-blue turtleneck jumper.

Adélaïde jumped up from her piano stool, crossing the room in three dynamic strides, enfolding Zoe in her arms.

'Isn't this just too awful? Poor Alain. Are you feeling sorry you came? We've been trying to cheer ourselves up. Where's Russell?'

'He's quite happy downstairs. I'll take him out in a bit.' She turned to the others, smiling to soften her confusion. 'Now, would it be possible for you to explain . . .'

Zoe lost her thread, not sure how to put it.

Adélaïde suggested: 'The complicated tribe I married into?'

'Yes,' said Zoe with relief. 'All I really know is that your husband was a confirmed bachelor until you met him, plus the brief introductions earlier this morning.'

'Yes,' said Adélaïde. 'Primo lived an austere life devoted entirely to the pursuit of wealth.'

'Successfully,' added Patrick, with an approving smile.

'Obviously,' said Adélaïde. 'That was his nature. One mustn't fight what one is. But the complications I'm talking about are not on his side.'

Minette interrupted: 'Patrick and I form a complication all of our own.'

'Let me tell it,' Adélaïde insisted. 'I am the oldest person present. It falls to me.'

Patrick and Minette smiled indulgently, simultaneously replying: 'Go ahead.'

'Primo's twin brother Boris married three times. Patrick and Minette are the delightful offspring of Boris's second marriage.'

'They are your husband's twin brother's second wife's children. You are their step-aunt?'

'I suppose,' replied Adélaïde. 'It's what modern people call a blended family. Or not blended, just thrown together, like oddly assorted ingredients in a not very palatable dish.'

'Strawberries with meat,' said Minette unexpectedly.

'Anchovies and maple syrup,' suggested Adélaïde.

'Scrambled eggs and custard,' said Patrick, then contradicted himself. 'No, actually, that might work. Fried eggs and custard.'

'You still look baffled, Zoe,' said Adélaïde. She gestured to the tray on the piano. 'Perhaps a drink, before we go on?'

'It feels early still, but I don't suppose it is. What do you have in that lovely cocktail shaker?'

'Gin and white vermouth – Noilly Prat, as it happens – and zest of orange,' said Minette. 'We brought the bottles from the Auberge. Primo's spirits are kept under lock and key.'

This apparently innocent remark caused a momentary feeling of discomfort, though Zoe couldn't see why.

'That will do nicely,' she said.

Adélaïde invited Zoe to take a seat by the open fire on which half a dozen logs of Mediterranean oak were burning, with long tongues of flame licking the cavernous chimney. Catching her expression, Adélaïde asked: 'Is it very hot in here?'

'It is rather,' said Zoe.

'When I got back from Los Angeles, the whole place was icy. I could see my breath indoors.'

A good-natured argument took over, from which Zoe learned that the heating at Château Palotte was a long-term issue. Both Primo and his twin brother Boris considered the fall in temperature occasioned by the winter season to be a reason to put on more layers of clothing, rather than stoke up the central-heating boiler or light extravagant fires.

Using words Zoe was sure she had uttered many times before, Adélaïde declaimed: 'There's no reason for us all to live like medieval peasants who have invaded the home of their feudal overlords but don't know where the matches are kept and have no idea how to run the place in a civilised fashion.'

'Speaking of feudal overlords,' said Zoe, 'you'll never guess what I saw down by the gate last night.'

'Was it Junior lighting a bonfire or something?' asked Adélaïde.

'Or sacrificing a rabbit on a slab of stone?' asked Minette, harshly.

'How gruesome,' said Zoe, wondering if she was serious. For a moment, she considered telling them what had happened to Russell on the ice. Then she realised she felt sorry for Junior and didn't want to add to his troubles. 'You are joking, I hope?'

'More or less, I expect,' said Adélaïde. 'But the boy's a monster. Go on. What did you see?'

'It was all perfectly visible because of the beams of my headlamps. It made me get out of the car.' She left a tiny pause, then told them: 'Two stags, rutting.'

'What a drama,' said Patrick, grinning. 'Did you hear that, Minette?'

'No, I didn't,' called his sister. 'I was rattling the ice in the shaker.'

'The stags are rutting.'

'*Mon Dieu,*' she exclaimed, meaning 'my God'.

None of them seems to think this is serious news. That's a relief.

'And the older animal,' continued Zoe, 'defeated by youth, just wandered away across the fields, while the younger one stalked back inside, haughty and proud of himself.'

'The combat ended,' said Adélaïde, thoughtfully. 'Succession was complete.'

Oh, is that a hint about Primo and Boris? Apparently, both are in poor health. I suppose either one would inherit from the other – not just the wealth of the Château Palotte estate, but also the social status.

Minette added: 'Youth must always triumph over age, in the end.'

For some reason, the comment made Zoe shudder.

Can she possibly mean Junior?

Fourteen

'THAT MAY BE THE MARTINIS TALKING'

Minette replenished their drinks in traditional martini glasses, upturned cones on narrow stems. Adélaïde raised hers in preparation for a toast.

'We've already drunk to poor Alain's memory. Let's drink to everyone else's good health and, above all, happiness, at least for the duration of poor Zoe's visit.'

'Unlikely outcome,' said Minette. 'But yes, agreed.'

Zoe wondered how to break it to Adélaïde that she intended to leave as soon as – politely – she was able.

'And we're all in for the duration,' said Patrick.

Minette added: 'Saints preserve us.'

Patrick shuffled an extra chair into the semicircle at the fire and they all sat down.

'The duration of what?' Zoe asked.

'The birthday events.'

'What do they consist of?'

'Give it time,' said Patrick. 'All will become clear.'

'Or not,' said Minette. 'Either way, you're better soused than sober.'

Zoe wasn't sure she concurred.

'Where is everybody else?' she asked. 'In fact, who is "everybody"? Can you give me a detailed rundown on who's in residence?'

'I'll explain because I have the most logical brain,' said Minette.

'Agreed,' said Patrick and Adélaïde, in unison.

'You already know,' Minette went on, 'that Primo and Boris are twins, both seventy years old in a couple of days?'

'Yes,' said Zoe. 'And Primo inherited the Château Palotte estate because he was born ten minutes earlier.'

'Precisely,' said Minette. 'Despite his wealth and position, until his fifties, Primo lived a solitary life of expensive pleasures, at which point he met the mature but still-entrancing Mademoiselle Amour. His head was turned. He renounced his vows of celibacy—'

'He never made any vows of celibacy,' argued Adélaïde.

'I exaggerate for effect,' conceded Minette. 'He and Adélaïde were joined in holy – and also, I expect, carnal – matrimony.'

'Really, Minette,' scolded Adélaïde.

The younger woman ignored her: 'By which time his insatiable sibling and twin Boris was on the verge of marrying for a third time.'

'And all three wives are with us?' Zoe asked, enjoying her cocktail.

'Alive and kicking,' said Minette.

'No, I mean in residence in the house?'

'Oh, yes.' Minette assumed a serious expression. 'Now, no one interrupt. Zoe, there are no survivors from the generation above. Boris's and Primo's parents and aunts and uncles and so on are all dead so they, alone, are the doyens of the Palotte dynasty. Primo, as discussed, married fairly late in life with the delicious Adélaïde. For obvious reasons of female physiology – despite Adélaïde appearing ever young—'

'An eternal forty-nine for her publicist,' chipped in Patrick.

'Really, Patrick,' protested Adélaïde, laughing.

'Don't interrupt. For obvious reasons of female physiology,' Minette repeated, 'they have no children. To turn to Boris, he first married Marie-France Montalbano. I can't tell you when, precisely, but I do know that Marie-France is sixty-eight, two years younger than he. They had no children but the marriage was apparently a success, joyful and insouciant, albeit undermined by infidelity on both sides. They parted as friends in what must have been, for Boris – and therefore for the Palotte estate – a costly divorce.'

'How interesting,' murmured Zoe, realising that her glass was inexplicably empty.

'No butting in,' repeated Minette. 'Next came Elizabeth Lagrasse, fifty-five years old today, mother to Patrick and to me. She's an editor, you know, of books, fiction and non-fiction. I expect you're itching to ask why we carry our mother's name? Because, although he brought us up, we are not Boris's children. His and our mother's marriage was marked once more by infidelity.'

Zoe glanced at the others. Adélaïde and Patrick seemed rapt.

I suppose they know all this so well that it's not much mentioned and it's a surprise to hear it said out loud. But is no one going to tell me who the father of Minette and Patrick actually is?

'In this dynamic train of events, we're coming into the station,' said Minette. 'Boris and our mother, Elizabeth, divorced when he was fifty-nine, eleven years ago, in order to "clear the decks", allowing him to marry his – possibly final, certainly most foolish – wife, known as Sweetie, christened Pauline, family name Clairette. After a sumptuous wedding and honeymoon, Boris soon provided the seed and Sweetie the fertile terrain for the propagation of a new generation of the Palotte family, the appalling Boris Junior.'

'And they will all be present throughout the birthday week?' Zoe asked.

'Absolutely. The first and third wives live here full-time.'

86

'Marie-France and Sweetie?'

'That's right. You're a fast learner.'

'It would probably be a good idea for me to write it all down in a family tree.'

'Oh, yes,' said Adélaïde, excitedly. 'Then we can add dates of birthdays and precise ages and things.'

The three of them began arguing about when each family member's birthday fell. Zoe contemplated them, apparently light-hearted and carefree. She felt the party in the piano room was serving as a kind of wake, a way to dispel the sadness of Monsieur Alain's death. But there was something else, too, an undercurrent of deeper feeling.

Does this mean that Boris Junior – for whom they all seem to have nothing but pity – is the heir apparent to the elderly twins, Boris and Primo, both of whom, according to Primo, suffer from an unnamed medical condition that limits their indulgence in coffee and perhaps other stimulants?

'You look very serious,' said Adélaïde, suddenly. 'What are you thinking about?'

'How happy you look,' said Zoe, which was in part true. 'I'm delighted to be here.'

'That may be the martinis talking. I hope your delight lasts. Somehow, though, I doubt it.'

Zoe heard Caroline's voice from the corridor, calling her, so she excused herself. She fetched Russell from the downstairs kitchen and put on her outdoor clothes while Caroline pushed her feet into her après-ski boots. They exited the château through the French doors of the dining room, onto the snowy terrace. While Russell scampered back and forth, Zoe told the story of the rutting stags. Caroline looked pensive.

'The deer are controversial,' she said. 'Up above the château is an area of fenced woodland.'

'I've not yet been that way.'

'They're supposed to be trapped inside. Now and then they get out. I don't know how. And the main gates, down

87

on the road that leads towards the Verdon Gorge, don't work properly.'

'How do you mean?'

'You must have seen. They used to be motorised, but one of the hinges in the old ironwork has given way, so they've just been left standing open. How did the rut conclude?'

'The older one, defeated, simply wandered away along the road. Where will it end up?'

'I don't know, but that's just the sort of thing that's bound to cause trouble,' complained Caroline, shaking her head. 'Imagine if it caused a road accident or fell in someone's swimming pool. The responsibility would come back to Primo.'

'To Primo specifically?'

'As head of the family, yes. I'll call the man who deals with the forestry on the estate. He'll check on the fences.'

Zoe listened with interest to her friend's phone conversation, understanding that the man on the other end was a Château Palotte tenant with a loud voice who helped with issues of arboriculture, who thought the stags had probably got out due to 'careless ramblers not closing the gates'.

Once Caroline had finished, Zoe asked: 'Why hasn't the main gate been fixed?'

'Because Primo hasn't been able to find an artisan who will guarantee to make it work without replacing the original stone and the original hinges. That's him all over. He can't bring himself to change something that has stood for two hundred years.'

Because of the cold, they had been moving quickly and had arrived at the far end of the lake. They climbed onto the little arched bridge. Zoe put her gloved hands on the balustrade to look down at the narrow channel where the water ran unimpeded from beneath the ice. She could make out the rock she had desperately prised from the frozen mud and used to smash an opening in order to pluck Russell from the frigid water.

I must tell Adélaïde about that at some point, though I don't really want to add to her worries.

Then, of its own accord, her mind wandered through a kind of exhibition of memories, each one evidence of Château Palotte's dilapidation or neglect, including the unreliable central-heating system, the ugly asbestos roof on the carport and the broken iron gates.

Possibly, despite the brave face everyone puts on things, Primo can't afford the repairs.

Fifteen

'AN EVIL WILL'

'Well?' Caroline asked.

Zoe dragged herself back to the present, standing on the little bridge above the outfall from the artificial lake.

'Has Primo always been like that, you know, someone who wants to preserve at all costs?'

'That's a very perceptive question,' said Caroline. 'I've worked for the family for nearly twenty years and he's always been a perfectionist. Is that what you wanted to talk to me about?'

Zoe looked back across the lawn towards the château, through the swirling snowflakes. The medieval, stone-built turrets at each end looked drab and cold. The more modern – though still antique – accommodation in between them seemed gloomy and unwelcoming, with lights in only two windows, the dining room on the ground floor and Primo's office above. Russell was quite far away, sniffing among the roots of the trees along the drive.

'I'll tell it in the order it came to me,' Zoe told her friend.

She went on to describe the sequence of events from her arrival, including seeing Monsieur Alain managing surprisingly well with her bags on the steep stone staircase, profiled against the glare of the halogen.

'And?' Caroline asked.

'Admittedly, it wasn't anywhere near as snowy or slippery at that point.' She described her brief inspection of the place where Monsieur Alain had fallen that morning, just before

Patrick came back and summoned her to Adélaïde's side at the ceremony in the market hall. 'He's very attentive to her,' she concluded.

'Patrick and Adélaïde get on very well. They have the same sense of humour and love of life. Should we keep going, Zoe? Anyone looking out of the south windows will think we look peculiar, locked in earnest consultation on this funny little bridge.'

'Good idea.'

They walked on, under the serried lines of trees, laid out with careful precision. In the privacy of the formal landscape, Zoe reprised the story of all her encounters with Junior, right through to finding the branch in his hands in front of the dining-room hearth – and the look of terrified guilt in his eyes.

'I'm torn between the idea that the branch might have fallen in the strong winds or that Junior could've put it there as a prank. Then, of course, there's the more serious interpretation, that he might have had a . . . *Ah, flûte,*' she added, using a French expression indicating minor frustration. 'There's a legal expression I can't remember.'

Caroline nodded and supplied the Latin phrase: '*Mens rea,* literally an evil will, a guilty mind, a malign intent.'

They had arrived quite close to the iron gates onto the road to the Verdon Gorge. Zoe thought about the responsibility that Primo had borne for the majority of his adult life – maintaining the château and the estate, providing for his family and, in a way, for his tenants, all with a sort of feudal generosity. She could see how, over time, that would evolve into a deep-rooted desire to preserve and maintain, not to change or allow to be destroyed.

'The right-hand gate,' she said. 'It looks like it could fall at any moment.'

'Don't tell me that,' said Caroline. 'There's already enough going on and there's the concert to consider with quite a large audience.'

'A concert? Good heavens. Will it go ahead?'

'Primo is a man of his word. He wouldn't cancel a commitment if he was at death's door.'

Zoe shuddered. 'What a sinister thought.' After a pause, she decided to take the plunge. 'Is there plenty of money, you know, in the family, in the estate, sufficient to meet all his pressing demands?'

'There are always choices to be made,' said Caroline, 'but I'm not privy to every detail and I'm sure you'll understand when I remind you that you didn't hear it from me.'

'You know why I want to know? You asked me about letting my imagination run away with me. I'm trying to work out if I'm caught up in another murder mystery. It feels like one of those stories where everyone is gathered in one place and plenty of them have a motive. One way or another, every one of them is set to inherit something, surely?'

'That's not a motive to kill an innocent and ancient butler.'

'Unless the wrong person died.'

Caroline looked shocked. 'You mean Primo.'

'I do – or Boris?' The snow was growing more insistent. For the time being, they were sheltered beneath semi-deciduous trees that hadn't lost all of their leaves. Zoe pressed her point. 'Will you entertain the idea that someone else could have been the intended victim? It was the accident of your arrival that sent Monsieur Alain out into the cold.'

'I take your point, but that only applies if it wasn't an accident, and everything points to it being one.'

'Even Junior's look of guilty terror?'

Caroline reproduced precisely the idea that Zoe had turned over in her own mind earlier on. 'He's got a guilty conscience about poor Russell. No wonder he's wary of what you'll say or do next.'

'You think I'm foolish, fearing something else is about to occur?'

'Something else?'

'Something else bad.'

Caroline sighed. After a pause, she admitted: 'There is an atmosphere at Château Palotte that I've not experienced before.'

'What sort of atmosphere?'

'A sort of watchful tension.'

'Then you share my concern, my suspicions?'

'Now you've told me all that, I'm afraid perhaps I must.'

'Were you discussing any of this with Primo before I met you in the corridor?'

'No,' said Caroline, carefully. 'Again, I can't divulge the substance of a professional consultation. It could be linked, however. Overall, I'm not saying you're right, but I didn't know then what I know now.'

Zoe felt the first few snowflakes pierce the partial canopy and find their way onto the back of her neck, inside the collar of her ski jacket. Twenty or thirty paces away, she saw Russell poking about at a frozen molehill and called his name. He looked up, bounced into action and came barrelling towards them, like a damp, furry meteor. She crouched and picked him up.

'What have you been doing?' she asked him.

His paws were muddy and there was wet dirt round his snout. He wriggled and whined so she put him down.

'I must get back,' said Caroline. 'There's a family meeting. It always follows the ceremony.'

'Do you think I might have a chance to speak to Adélaïde first?' asked Zoe.

Caroline checked her watch and told her: 'Maybe, if we're quick.'

Russell went ahead, running on and then twisting and scampering back to them, through the trees then over the bridge and up the lawn beside the lake. Zoe didn't speak because she was lost in thought.

I need to ask Adélaïde for the real reason why she asked me here so insistently.

When they arrived on the terrace, Zoe found the snow had formed a brand-new pristine carpet that she felt reluctant to mar. Through the glazed French doors, she could see Adélaïde and Patrick in close conversation, standing in front of the hearth.

I may be imagining this – and everything else – but that looks like a very earnest discussion. Do they have shared suspicions, too?

Caroline brushed past, leaving a set of heavy footprints across the snowy terrace. She opened the French doors, invited Zoe to precede her, then Russell beat them both into the room, hurrying under the table and out the other side in order to compete for space with the two humans in front of the fire.

Adélaïde and Patrick turned towards Zoe. In their eyes was a characteristic expression that Zoe recognised from the gossipy backstage world of London theatre.

They were talking about me.

Sixteen

'HOW SOULLESS AND SAD'

There was no time for Zoe to find out precisely what Adélaïde and Patrick had been saying about her – either by asking outright or coaxing it out of them with subtlety – because Boris entered the dining room to tell everyone, in his usual pompous tone: 'We are all expected.'

And that was that. Without a word or a gesture of acknowledgement, Caroline and the others left Zoe with a sense that she had been excluded from a party that she didn't, in any case, want to attend.

Good luck to them.

Russell disappeared back to the kitchen. While the others were all next door in the drawing room, presumably seated in the chic office chairs at the modern conference table, she stoked the fire so it wouldn't go out.

After all, there's no butler to keep it going.

Wondering what her inattentive hosts had planned for lunch, she went upstairs to her room and found her mobile charged to sixty-two per cent.

So, the socket does work after all.

With a tinge of excitement at the potential transgression, she decided that now was her chance for further exploration of Château Palotte, perhaps even the other residents' rooms.

It would be quite justified. Adélaïde has asked me here because she wants my support, but I don't know enough about who everyone is. And now there's the question of how and why Monsieur

95

Alain died – including whether he was actually the intended victim. Having a good look round can only help.

Emerging from her room, she found the next one along was being used as a store, chock-full of boxes of paperwork, some dating back at least thirty years, as she could see from the labels on a teetering pile near the window. There were also sundry items of superannuated office equipment, including an elderly Amstrad computer and a dot-matrix printer, plus a lumpy mattress in green-and-white ticking on a narrow single frame and a straw-seated chair whose joints had been disassembled by time and misuse.

The next room was Primo's office. Zoe was – oddly – relieved to find it locked.

Otherwise, I would have been tempted to go in and snoop and that, surely, would have been an intrusion too far.

Thinking about the question of security, she frowned.

Downstairs there's a locked liquor cabinet. Primo's office is locked, too, and there seems to have been a bit of a rigmarole with the front-door key. Is there a problem with pilfering and snooping?

She nodded, slowly.

And I'm sure someone was in my room in my absence.

After that, she discovered the room that Caroline was staying in, recognisable from her very smart clothes, laid out with careful precision across the bed and the other furniture as if for inspection.

In order to mix and match and create different outfits.

On the bedside table was a tablet computer whose screen Zoe touched in order to waken it. She was unable to get any further because it required a passcode. Then she snatched her hand away.

What are you doing, Zoe?

She continued along the corridor. Next came the staircases, a straight one down to the ground-floor hallway and a spiral one up to the second floor. After them, she found a very feminine dressing room that she deduced must belong to Adélaïde, with lots of make-up and hair-care products and complicated lingerie and a single divan bed. It led, through a communicating door, to a bathroom and then two older rooms knocked together, as revealed by the mouldings in the ceiling, separated by a joist where a wall had once been.

Primo's room.

It was a remarkable space, with a massive four-poster bed, several pieces of good-quality antique furniture and a separate area for a sofa and two matching Louis Quinze armchairs. Between them was an inlaid coffee table with a delightful marquetry top. Stylish Art Deco ornaments covered the mantelpiece and the top of a chest of drawers. Two paintings adorned the walls.

Good heavens, I think they're by Bonnard.

Peirre Bonnard was an artist associated with the Provence region whose treatment of light in the impressionist style Zoe found utterly dazzling.

She had to exit through Adélaïde's room because the door to the corridor from the larger bed-sitting room was locked. Beyond Primo's accommodation, in the western tower, was another bedroom whose contents resembled Adélaïde's, but each item spoke of an older era and more sedate fashions. On a desk by the window Zoe found a few envelopes, both social and official, addressed to 'Madame Marie-France de Palotte', revealing that Boris's first wife continued to use her married name.

And her window overlooks the place where Monsieur Alain died – although that's not so important if you consider that she was there at the time, in the family procession.

Zoe retraced the corridor to the spiral staircase and climbed to the top floor, thinking about how impractical the château would become, in time, for each of its ageing occupants.

She went straight to the western end and discovered that the room above Marie-France's bedroom, also in the tower above the front door, was set up for television watching with an old-fashioned cathode-ray set, housed in a dedicated mahogany cabinet, plus a modern flat-screen perched on top. Zoe tried the remote and the device came to life at excessive volume, so she turned it off again without finding out what the programme was.

Some daytime rubbish, I expect.

Leaving the TV room, she felt a flush of guilt and stood listening for the sound of any approach. There was none. She decided to go on, hoping she wasn't pushing her luck.

I ought to have dashed about more quickly.

After another bathroom, she found a dressing room with a pull-out *canapé-lit* – a sofa bed – that was occupied by someone whose taste in cosmetics and fragrances was much less sophisticated than Adélaïde's, and whose loud clothes, including some chic items by Chanel, had been left in appalling disorder, some trampled underfoot on the deep red carpet.

These are Sweetie's things.

Next door to Sweetie's untidy accommodation was another locked door.

Boris's room, I suppose, next to Sweetie's, with Junior as far away as possible at the far end of the corridor.

Next came a door that hung invitingly open, revealing a comfortable bed-sitting room, large enough to accommodate a queen-size double, a small wardrobe and a compact chest of drawers, plus a weary-looking computer, very conspicuous and out of context on a smoked-glass desk. A typescript of a contemporary novel entitled *Amour à Mort* – 'Love until Death' – lay tidily beside the keyboard.

This is Elizabeth's room, Patrick and Minette's mother. Minette told me she worked in publishing. It's the only one that has a sense of the world outside the walls of this extraordinary mansion.

Zoe noticed the coffee machine and a large plastic container of pills. The label on the latter told her that it contained 'five hundred powerful doses of caffeine, soluble, fully vegan and without undesirable additives'.

That seems rather a lot. Is Elizabeth behind in her work and needs to pull all-nighters because she's a freelancer without job security?

Next came a bathroom, then the penultimate room on the upper floor was also open so she was able to discover from its contents that it was shared by Patrick and Minette, equipped with two single beds, laid out like a hotel room, with everything slightly too close together.

Almost as if they were children, still.

The final room, in the eastern tower, above her own, had a barren air, despite being crowded with a selection of toys and books, many of them suitable for a child younger than Junior. On the white IKEA chest of drawers were two small boxes of Lego for building models of *Star Wars* spacecraft. Beside them was a *Star Wars*–themed board game – what the French called a *jeu de société*, a 'social game'. Unfortunately, it was entirely untouched, still tightly wrapped in its cellophane.

I suppose these were gifts, from a time when the adults found him more congenial.

The duvet cover on the narrow single bed was decorated with scenes from the *Star Wars* universe.

They found something he seemed to like and stuck with it.

On the mantelpiece above an empty hearth, she discovered a handful of Christmas cards, inscribed with peremptory good wishes, each one containing a twenty-euro note, as if the grown-ups had got together and decided what would be an appropriate – if antiseptic – gift for the boy, then they had all done the same.

How soulless and sad. And I don't suppose there's even anywhere for him to spend his money in Saint-Paul-de-Palotte.

She thought about how, with the elderly butler dead on the cold, snowy steps, not one of the grown-ups had thought to look out for the ten-year-old child for whom it must have been an appalling shock.

Perhaps the shock of discovering that his prank had ended in tragedy.

Seventeen

'OLD GUILT IS STILL GUILT'

The family conference in the drawing room with its modern conference table and baby-grand piano broke up. Zoe heard the voices and skipped hurriedly downstairs to see what was next on the birthday agenda. As the family went their separate ways, she learned that Patrick and Minette had an appointment forty minutes away by car, in the Verdon Gorge where, they told her, they were looking forward to '*un coup de varappe*'.

Zoe was astonished. 'You're going rock climbing?'

'It's a wonderful location,' Minette told her. 'And it's quite safe. There are permanent safety lines if you keep to the designated routes.'

'Then we have a dinner invitation,' said Patrick. 'But, tomorrow morning, we'll see you bright and early.' He reminded Zoe that they were in the habit of rising early in order to prep for the day's service at the Auberge Sainte-Catherine. 'It's a hard habit to break, even during the holidays. We'll be up at six-thirty and you probably will, too?'

Patrick knew this because Zoe sometimes dropped in on the Auberge at that time.

'Yes, all right. I'll see you then.'

Their departure left Adélaïde and Zoe alone in front of the fire. The logs had burnt down and it was no longer so stiflingly hot. All the same, Zoe felt her cheeks were red from the huge heap of glowing embers. Adélaïde's chair was a little further away and she seemed composed and unflustered – at least, on the surface. There was, Zoe recognised, a wariness in her eyes.

I wonder what that's about? Is it something we've already discussed or a new topic that she hesitates to broach?

'Where is everyone else?' Zoe asked for a second time. 'Out at some pre-birthday function?'

'Precisely. And there's another one this evening. The village always organises their own "thank you" celebration at some point in the birthday week or, if the birthday actually falls on a Sunday, the previous one.'

'Will Junior go with them?'

'He might, unless he's in bad odour. I'm not sure.'

'If not, where would he be?'

'In his room, I suppose,' said Adélaïde vaguely.

'That sounds miserable for him. Won't he be lonely?'

'Perhaps.'

'What sort of celebration?'

'A remorselessly jolly one with burnt meat from the barbecue and songs sung by local children.'

'That sounds charming.'

'I've asked to be excused so that you and I can have some time together.'

'That's good,' said Zoe, preparing to bite the bullet. 'I wanted to tell you something—'

Before Zoe could finally break it to Adélaïde about what had happened between Junior and Russell down at the lake, her friend was on her feet.

'Let's go with them.'

'This evening?'

'No. Let's go with Patrick and Minette.'

'Don't you want to tell me about why you were so keen for me to come to Château Palotte? You sounded so worried on the phone.'

'I can't, Zoe,' said Adélaïde. 'Will you please be patient? I just need a few hours off from all my worries. You do understand, don't you?'

'Fair enough.'

'You see, I've just realised, when I do tell you, it will make it all so much more real.'

Because Zoe had been so busy since arriving in Sainte-Catherine at the end of the previous summer, she had not yet had time to visit the extraordinarily picturesque Verdon Gorge, or to see the famous vultures, soaring insouciantly between the walls of rock. Despite the cocktails she had drunk, Adélaïde was a good and precise driver. Her elderly BMW was comfortable, even with all four of them on board, with old-fashioned leather seats and an excellent heater.

On the way there, they found a restaurant in one of the many delightful Provençal villages. Over a light lunch, Adélaïde and her step-niece and step-nephew demanded 'the full story of the French bookshop murder', in all its confusing and then frightening detail. Zoe obliged, then Patrick sketched the Palotte family tree on the paper tablecloth and gave it to Zoe, remarking with a grin: 'For you to study and learn.'

After lunch, Zoe found herself vicariously exhilarated by watching Patrick and Minette rock climbing, especially when Patrick lost his grip and allowed himself to suddenly fall back, snatched out of the air by his safety line.

Once the '*varappe*' was over, Minette reminded them that she and her brother were expected in Aix-en-Provence, the nearest large town, for dinner that evening, so that was where Adélaïde took them, arriving late in the afternoon. Zoe suggested visiting the Musée Granet to see the exhibition of paintings – many of them of local scenes – by Paul Cézanne. Then they split up.

'We'll take a taxi back later,' said Minette.

Zoe felt proud to be able to introduce Adélaïde to a wonderful restaurant that she knew from lunching with her solicitor, Caroline Robin. La Table Provençale was a jewel, with a magnificent local menu from which they chose, sitting out of doors in their coats under the branches of an olive tree.

By the time they had finished their early supper, though, the weather had turned again, becoming much colder. They were glad to shelter in the warm capsule of the BMW for the journey home. Adélaïde parked under the carport, next to Patrick and Minette's silver Audi, and they climbed the outdoor steps to the front door. Zoe could feel her shoes slipping on a film of ice.

Once indoors, they revived the fire in the drawing room and each went back to the same armchairs, facing the hearth. Adélaïde resumed their earlier conversation.

'It must have made a difference to your reputation and status in Sainte-Catherine when you solved a murder?'

'That's overstating things. I didn't so much solve it as find myself accidentally at the centre of things. It was nothing like when Maisie got to the bottom of the murder at the theatre, for example.'

There was a pause as Adélaïde seemed to accommodate herself to this thought.

She looks a bit like a boxer who's just ridden a solid punch.

'That's a coincidence,' Adélaïde murmured. 'Maisie Cooper, the amateur detective from so long ago, your half-sister and my friend.'

'I hope I haven't done the wrong thing, bringing it up. In what way is it a "coincidence"?' Zoe asked.

'You're not the first person to reference that ancient history,' said Adélaïde. 'I suppose I'd better show you something. You'll have to hang on a minute.'

Adélaïde left the drawing room, very agile on her still-slender pins, leaving Zoe to stand and pace. She tried a few triads on the piano, finding its discords made her want to grind her teeth. She walked round the ugly modern table, more suited to a contemporary boardroom than a château, and looked closely at several impressive artworks on the walls. One, she was sure, was an early Picasso drawing, in ballpoint and pencil on a paper tablecloth, presumably from some early twentieth-century Parisian café, framed under expensive anti-glare gallery glass. A second looked very much like another Bonnard, a similar study to the ones in Primo's bedroom. A third was more cartoonish, with blocks of colour and robust-looking figures, possibly by Fernand Léger.

I can't quite make out the signature. If it is genuine, though, what are these three objects worth? At least half a million euros each, surely? Perhaps more if they have some art-history significance that I'm not aware of.

Adélaïde returned with an envelope in one hand – it looked very much like the one Primo had handled on the makeshift stage, containing the tenants' bonuses – and a bunch of keys in the other.

'We'll have to be quick. I need to put this back before Primo gets home.'

'Is that his private correspondence?'

'In a sense but, at the same time, it concerns me more than it does him.'

'And it's connected to the Chichester murder?'

'Before I show it to you, let me just make something plain. Your friend and mine, the brilliant Maisie Cooper, was there at the *dénouement* of the mystery, when the perpetrator was unveiled and all the complicated misunderstandings and red herrings elucidated. More importantly, though, the right person was killed, if that makes sense. It was someone who had done many bad things and who would otherwise have gone to prison for a long time.'

'Why are you telling me this?'

'In a complicated mystery, there are sometimes trivial points, individual actions, that have no real importance but, because of their proximity to murder, they take on a darker aspect.'

Zoe began to feel that she knew what Adélaïde was getting at.

'Someone has accused you,' she suggested, 'of wrong-doing, back in the mists of time, when I was only sixteen years old?'

'Yes,' said Adélaïde, grimly. 'How clever you are to guess. But let's not discuss the passing of the unforgiving years. It's professionally damaging.' Adélaïde was still standing on the threshold of the drawing room. 'Let's sit down again and you can read it yourself and tell me what you think.'

They did precisely that, Zoe taking the page with a certain amount of reluctance because it was very clearly addressed as a 'private and confidential' communication to 'Primo de Palotte, Château Palotte, Saint-Paul-de-Palotte'. The envelope was expensive, made of thick vellum in a pale beige shade, with a textured surface. The flap was still gummed down securely, but the top seam had been cut with a sharp paper knife. Inside was a single sheet of paper of much lesser quality, taken from the feed tray of an everyday printer, perhaps. There was no return address or date, just three paragraphs of text.

> I am writing to tell you about a secret your wife has kept from you. I can do this because I know someone who was there. It all happened a long time ago but that doesn't make any difference. Old guilt is still guilt.
>
> I'm talking about when your wife first became an international star, the first time she had to do acting in English. I bet she's never told you what really happened. I don't think you want anyone else to know. I

bet you think it would be a shame if anyone did. It's probably a good idea to ask her the real reason why she went to Los Angeles.

When I say 'a good idea', I don't mean that you will like her answer.

Zoe turned the piece of paper over, looking for a continuation, but there was none. Handing it back to Adélaïde, she remarked: 'It seems incomplete. Could there have been a second sheet?'

'I don't believe so. I saw it in Primo's hand one day in his study. I crept back in later to read what it said.'

'When was that?'

'Just after I got back from California. Tell me, since you've been here, has my husband . . . ?'

Adélaïde looked pained and left the question hanging. Zoe felt she had no alternative but to make Adélaïde aware of her odd conversation with Primo, when she had come across him with his forehead pressed to the cold glass of the dining-room window. She concluded with: 'When you saw him with the letter in his study, how did you know it was important?'

'Because of his expression,' Adélaïde told her. 'He slipped it out of sight, in amongst some financial documents, so I knew I would have to sneak in and read it.' Adélaïde said this as though she had been entirely within her rights. 'I am his wife, after all. I wasn't going to leave him to fret on his own.'

'It wasn't in a safe or anything?'

'It was on his desk, but back in the envelope.'

'Do you think he's aware that you've read it?'

Adélaïde frowned and asked: 'How would I know?'

'From his behaviour, how he looks at you?'

'That's a good question. I'm not sure. Well, what does it mean?'

Zoe gave it back and told her: 'It looks very much like a prelude to blackmail.'

Eighteen

'A KIND OF PSYCHOPATH'

Zoe watched her friend take in the idea that the mysterious letter might be a prelude to blackmail. Once again, she thought, Adélaïde resembled a boxer who was trying to recover from a heavy blow.

'Don't you think?' Zoe prompted.

'Not a friendly warning, then?' asked Adélaïde, sounding hopeful.

'About what? From whom?'

'Someone who thinks that Primo has married beneath his status and is advising him to cut short our relationship?'

'Someone who believes in class and thinks you are not worthy?' asked Zoe, surprised.

'That sort of thing, yes.'

'They've left it pretty late. You've been together fifteen years, haven't you? Do you have any suspicions?'

'I was hoping you might, as an outsider, take a stab in the dark.'

'Would you show it to me again please?' Adélaïde handed it over. Zoe scanned it and said: 'The tone and the style of expression are not particularly sophisticated. I suppose that's something that might be easily disguised.'

'You mean a grown-up could write in slightly childish language,' said Adélaïde, perceptively. 'Or it's genuinely from you-know-who.'

'What are you thinking?'

'The same as you, I expect. It would be just the sort of damaging, evil prank that I would expect of Boris and Sweetie's appalling son.'

'Where would he have got the envelope? How would he have posted it. Is there a printer in the house?'

'The envelope is from a rack on Primo's desk, where there are also stamps. Junior is a child of the modern age and, despite his tender years, is quite *au fait* with word processing and all the rest of it. Any post can quickly be dispatched from the letter box next door to the village shop. That's less than a hundred metres from our front door.'

'But how would a child of ten years old have discovered something to your discredit – sorry, to your alleged, potential discredit, not assuming at all for a moment that it's the truth – from so long ago?'

'Yes, that's another question. Eavesdropping, I expect.'

'But on whom? Everyone involved must be ancient.'

'I'm not ancient. You're not ancient.'

'No,' admitted Zoe.

Adélaïde sighed then tried to explain without explaining: 'I told you I'd signed an NDA. Can you not put two and two together?'

Zoe paused, her mind busy, then she said: 'The Hollywood project is some kind of re-enactment or reassessment of the murder at the theatre?'

'Exactly,' said Adélaïde, very quietly. 'And there have been discussions by phone and via email. Perhaps Junior has winkled out or eavesdropped my password. I expect you can guess what it is? The same as my—'

'Don't tell me,' Zoe insisted. 'How will the story be treated, documentary or fiction?'

'Documentary. There's a vogue for it on streaming services. Perhaps you know all about that?'

'Not especially. And what would be your role?'

'Executive producer, narrator, talking head, presenter. They want to delve into every aspect and they're prepared to pay handsomely.'

'Do you need the money?'

'Everyone always needs money,' said Adélaïde.

There was a brief pause, then Zoe at last said: 'I need to tell you something about Junior.'

She explained to Adélaïde the drama that had happened down at the lake in which Russell had almost drowned. She tried to make sure that no obvious blame attached to Adélaïde's ten-year-old nephew, portraying it all as an unfortunate accident. Adélaïde, however – even though she hadn't been there – jumped to the opposite conclusion.

'I sometimes feel that child is a kind of psychopath. He's almost inhuman.'

'You can't mean that.'

'Seriously, I'm not sure how to explain. Junior seems to have no connection or sympathy with anyone or anything.'

'Not even his parents?'

'Especially not his parents. Boris Senior is far too busy losing money with his wild business follies and as for his mother, Sweetie . . .' Adélaïde sighed with exasperation. 'Sweetie is twenty-nine years old, married to a seventy-year-old, and she has the mind of a twelve-year-old schoolgirl.'

'That's very harsh,' said Zoe.

'It's no wonder she and Boris Senior produced such a little alien. What was that terrifying novel where the village was haunted by impostor children who could all communicate by telepathy and the poor mothers were unaware that they had been impregnated without their knowledge?'

'That was *The Midwich Cuckoos* by John Wyndham.' Zoe smiled, trying to lighten the tone. 'But you know it's just a story, not real life.'

Through a gap in the heavy drapes on the tall French windows of the drawing room, they saw the harsh halogen light had come on outside, indicating that they would soon no longer be alone.

Adélaïde was quickly on her feet. Grasping Zoe's shoulder, she whispered: 'Go and stall them. Make a fuss. Repeat how delighted you are to be here and ask them about the family coat of arms or some other rubbish like that. Hurry.'

Adélaïde ushered Zoe out into the corridor and even gave her a little push in the right direction. Meanwhile, she bounced athletically up the stairs, presumably *en route* for Primo's study to replace the 'private and confidential' letter.

Zoe stayed still for a few moments. Then, hearing the creak of footsteps on the landing above her, she went to greet the new arrivals, just as the large iron handle tilted down and the door swung inwards, almost catching her on the toe because it was so wide and took up so much space.

Sweetie entered, accompanied by confetti-like snowflakes, wearing a smart Chanel suit, navy blue with shiny bronze buttons. Her eyes were very heavily made up, with 'smoky' eyeshadow and thick lines of kohl pencil ending in what the fashion magazines called a 'flick'. Her hair was cut in an unbecoming blonde bob. Without the make-up and the severe coiffure, Zoe thought she would be very pretty indeed.

'Good evening. How was the party in the village?'

Sweetie blinked, nonplussed, then she said, vaguely: 'Oh, yes. You're the bookshop woman.'

Her eyes are red.

'Yes, that's right.'

'Adélaïde says you're very clever.' Sweetie pulled a tiny handkerchief from the cuff of her navy-blue jacket. 'She thinks the world of you. It must be nice when people take you seriously.'

'Shall we shut the door?' said Zoe.

'The others are coming – slowly of course, they're all so old. Tell Boris I've gone up to bed, would you?'

Sweetie sniffed, took a deep breath, appeared to compose herself, then almost ran along the corridor and up the stairs to the first floor.

I hope she doesn't meet Adélaïde sneaking about in Primo's office.

Outside, feet were crunching on snow, proceeding slowly up the external staircase. A man's voice called out: 'Sweetie? Where have you got to?'

Zoe stayed where she was. Eventually, they arrived in single file, headed by a man who looked strikingly like Primo de Palotte but who, she knew, was his twin brother, Boris.

'Good evening. Your wife asked me to tell you that she's already gone up.'

'Did she?' asked Boris, rhetorically. 'Oh dear.'

He stepped carefully over the threshold and walked on, leaving Zoe with a strong whiff of his pungent aftershave – sandalwood, musk and fruit. Once his billowing coat was gone, Zoe could see Primo and the other two ladies climbing the slippery outdoor steps with great care.

They are cautious because of what happened to Monsieur Alain. And because Primo is seventy, Marie-France sixty-eight and Elizabeth fifty-five. I'm 'a mature woman', though I still feel like a teenager sometimes – now for example, as I stand here with a foolish grin on my face, wondering what I'm going to say to them.

On the snow-covered outdoor mat, Primo waited politely while Boris's two former wives came inside, both in their long down overcoats, Elizabeth, the younger one, in bright yellow, Marie-France, the older, in charcoal grey. Zoe repeated her greeting and asked if they had had an amusing time at the party.

Elizabeth said: 'It was so kind of the village.'

Marie-France told her: 'The same childish folk songs, year after year – it's close to unbearable. They had some choice things to day about you, Madame Pascal.'

'They did?'

'Lots of them are very interested in your sleuthing, especially young Didier, the son of our village *boulanger*.'

'I've been so busy, I feel that's all quite a long way in the past,' said Zoe.

'The past has ways of intruding on the present,' insisted Marie-France. 'Isn't that right, Primo?'

'Let the poor man come inside, Marie-France,' said Elizabeth, mildly.

Zoe realised that Adélaïde's elderly husband was waiting patiently for the ladies to remove their coats. Snow was settling on his thin hair as they, in their turn, were procrastinating on the mat with slush from their après-ski boots melting on the mat. Primo looked shrivelled and old, but his good manners precluded him from asking them to hurry.

To expedite things, Zoe offered to help and, soon, they were all four indoors, Primo unwinding a cashmere scarf from around his scrawny neck. His fingers were very thin and white.

'You all look absolutely frozen,' said Zoe. 'How about something warm to drink in the kitchen? Or, if you prefer, a fire is lit in the drawing room.'

Adélaïde came dancing downstairs, saying to everyone: 'You're back. Was it great fun?'

'It was but now I'm for my bed,' said Primo. 'Goodnight, Marie-France, Elizabeth. To you, too, Madame Pascal,' he added, punctiliously. 'I will look forward to renewing our acquaintance in the morning.' Adélaïde proffered her arm and, with an awkward smile that only just exposed the tips of his startlingly white false teeth, he told her: 'Thank you, my dear. How good of you to wait up.'

Zoe watched them go, thinking that – despite his words – there was a stiffness between them. She became aware of Marie-France and Elizabeth exchanging the tail end of a look that, had she caught it sooner, she might have thought malicious.

'Patrick and Minette will be back from Aix soon,' she informed them. 'And they tell me they will be down for breakfast at six-thirty.'

'Yes,' said Elizabeth. 'I expect they'll go for a run. I, on the other hand, will read until two and not be down before ten.'

'Are you a big reader?'

'Elizabeth works in publishing,' said Marie-France. 'Reading is by way of being her job.'

'Mine, too – but it's also one of my greatest pleasures,' said Zoe, then regretted the defensive tone she could hear in her own voice. 'What are you reading at the moment?'

'A romantic novel called *Amour à Mort* and a collection of true-crime stories called *Treize à la Douzaine*,' said Elizabeth. 'Your French is very good but do you know what that means?'

'We have a similar expression in English, though we call it "a baker's dozen" rather than "thirteen to the dozen". Is it any good?'

'The question,' said Elizabeth, 'is whether or not it's true.'

In her head, Zoe made the obvious connection with what Adélaïde had told her – the disturbing letter.

Or is that mere coincidence?

She told Elizabeth: 'In Sainte-Catherine, in my bookshop, non-fiction makes up an important part of my sales.' She turned to the older woman. 'Do you enjoy reading, too, Madame de Palotte – or should I call you Madame Montalbano?'

'Can we make a pact to call one another by our first names?' suggested Marie-France. 'It will make things much easier.'

'Yes, of course,' said Zoe. She yawned. 'Excuse me. Is it very late? I've lost track.'

'It was coming up on eleven when we left the market hall,' said Elizabeth. Then she yawned, too. 'Oh, dear, it's catching.'

Zoe bid them both goodnight, explaining that she had neglected her dog and needed to give him a walk before she retired. She went downstairs to the basement kitchen and found Russell curled up in the dog bed. He had one eye open, beadily observing her approach.

'*On y va*,' she told him. 'Let's go.'

Russell ran past her and she hurried to catch up, finding him scratching at the back door, the one that opened from the eastern tower into a walled vegetable garden. It was bolted top and bottom and she worried that someone might lock them out by mistake. She decided to leave it ajar and just let Russell poke about the barren winter borders, picking up his feet daintily through snow that came up to his little knees. Zoe began to feel guilty about letting the heat out.

I wonder if Marie-France, with her patrician air, disapproves of Adélaïde. Could she have written the letter? But why would she have waited so long?

The answer was obvious.

Because she's only just discovered the malicious – possibly discreditable – story about the murder at the theatre.

A loud animal call came from beyond the wall, similar to that of a bull but with a sort of hoarse cough underneath the resonant bellow. Zoe crossed the snowy ground and opened the gate onto the lawn, keeping one ungloved hand on the frame and the other on the latch, not wanting Russell to slip out.

I seem to remember there's a special word for the call of a stag.

The night was dark and still. The ground was luminous white, with a single trail of dark hoofprints crossing the freshly fallen snow, but the stag was nowhere to be seen. An ancient Irish poem came into her mind, a text she had once had to recite in a play in which she had played the narrator. It was a modern English translation but still atmospheric, seeming to capture, very precisely, both her mood and the strange environment she had unexpectedly found herself trapped in.

My tidings for you. A stag bells.
Rivers freeze and ice sighs.
A wild goose raucous in grey skies—
Its cold-caught wing foretells
A season of snow. My tidings for you.

She was pleased to have remembered the technical term.

That's right, it's archaic but the stag 'bells'.

Russell came snuffling round her feet and she hurried to close the gate.

Why do I feel 'trapped', though?

They went back inside the tower.

I'm trapped by obligation. Adélaïde needs me, though she hasn't fully explained quite what she expects from me. But I owe it to her to help. She was the reason I got my first breaks in theatre. My small successes all came about because she supported me and put me on the right path. Without Adélaïde, I would never have been able to buy 'The Bookshop of My Dreams'.

She shot both bolts, top and bottom.

I do wish, though, that I understood exactly what's going on among these extraordinary people.

Nineteen

'Is That Sobbing?'

Back indoors, Zoe took Russell downstairs to the kitchen and looked in the cupboard under the big stainless-steel sink where she found some more of the dry kibble Monsieur Alain had mixed with the omelette.

Ah, good. That's a bit of luck.

In the fridge – which was almost bare – she discovered an elderly piece of Cantal cheese, like a strong, hard cheddar, with mould growing unimpeded on its surface. She pared away the green and cut some unblemished shavings to improve Russell's dinner, then refilled his stainless-steel water bowl.

'You'll be fine here. There's no need to come searching for me upstairs.'

Busy eating, Russell appeared to pay no attention. She poked him with her toe and he looked up with an expression of long-suffering patience.

'I don't want to see you before six.' She checked her watch. It was just gone half past eleven. 'Or maybe later.'

Russell stopped eating, having wormed his tongue into every cheesy nook, leaving only dry biscuit behind. He turned round three times in the smelly dog bed and curled up. Zoe crouched down and stroked his smooth white fur, his tan forehead.

'If you were capable of purring, I believe you would be doing so right now.'

She stood up, wished him 'goodnight' and made her way up two flights of stairs, then followed the corridor to her distant room. The radiator felt very cold.

I suppose the heating's already gone off.

She put on the bedside light and plugged in her blower heater at a socket close to the door. The room was soon warm without being stuffy or uncomfortable, because there was still a cooling draught from the ill-fitting window. She put the rye bread and cheese and *saucisson* from her fridge next to the cold glass, to help it keep.

She flossed and brushed her teeth at an ugly, oversized basin in a corner of the room, then changed into her treasured White Company pyjamas – of which she had three sets. She got into bed, turned off the bedside light and rolled onto her side, then sat up again in order to set an alarm on her phone.

I'd like to catch Patrick and Minette before everyone else is up. I'd be glad to know more about the circumstances at Château Palotte. I bet they're the most likely to share the unvarnished truth.

★

A little later, in the deep of the night – she wasn't sure exactly when – Zoe was woken by footsteps overhead, making the floorboards creak. Blearily, she thought about the shape of the château, illustrated in the amateurish promotional leaflet, with an ancient tower at either end and partially modernised eighteenth-century habitation in between.

I'm on the same floor as most of the others, but there is another storey above me. Whose room was it . . . ?

Lying very still, not quite awake, she was able to track the sound of the footsteps through her ceiling, towards the window then back to the centre of the room. Then, the creaking stopped and she heard another sound, faint and disturbing.

Is that sobbing? It sounds like a child. Oh, yes, Junior . . .

After a minute or so, that stopped, too, and Zoe drifted back into her unremembered dreams.

★

When Zoe woke again, the panes of glass in her ill-fitting bedroom window were as dark as black mirrors. She checked her phone.

Six-twenty.

She felt well rested and got out of bed without resentment. The blower heater had done a good job, although her skin felt tight from the very dry atmosphere. She turned it off and went to the ugly sink in the corner to run the tap over her hands and push her wet fingers through her short grey hair, restoring some volume. She dressed in the same clothes as the day before, but with fresh underwear, added her coat so she might take Russell out for an early trot, then opened the door on the long, dingy corridor.

It was intimidatingly dark but she didn't want to turn on any lights and disturb the household. Fortunately, her mobile phone's home screen was bright enough to allow her to navigate. She descended the wooden staircase, wincing with each squeak.

In the dining room, she found herself alone and set about preparing a fire in the large grate. The basket of kindling was two-thirds empty but the few sticks that remained were very dry and quick to catch with spills of newspaper poked between them. The room, however, began to fill with smoke because of the plug of cold air trapped overnight in the chimney, preventing it from drawing.

She crossed to the windows, drew back the heavy drapes and opened a pair of full-height French windows onto the snow-covered terrace. The wind that struck her cheeks was bitter.

Patrick and Minette came bustling in from the corridor, both dressed for exercise.

119

'Good morning. How did you sleep?' she asked them.

'Fantastic,' said Patrick.

'Uncomfortably in a narrow child's bed,' said Minette.

'How far will you run?'

'The perimeter of the gardens,' said Patrick, 'not counting the woods, is just over three kilometres, down through the village and back up again.'

'The climb really gets the blood pumping,' said Minette.

'I envy your energy,' said Zoe. 'How long will it take you? I was hoping we might have a chat.'

'Not long,' said Patrick. 'By the way, the *boulanger* will be here soon, bringing pastries.'

'How will I let him in?'

Patrick looked sad and explained: 'No one will have locked up without Alain to remember.'

There was a brief pause as the memory of the butler's unexpected death washed over them.

'And is no one else up?' Zoe asked, making an effort to smile.

'Good heavens, no,' said Minette. 'I'll be surprised if we see anyone before nine at the earliest.'

'In that case,' said Zoe, 'we'll have plenty of time. Enjoy your run.'

They left and she returned to her fire, feeding it with eight or nine more spills of newspaper, eventually raising enough heat for the smoke to rise up through the two floors and out into the pre-dawn sky. She added a few more sticks of kindling and some mighty logs of Mediterranean oak in a triangle, like the struts of a teepee. These, too, were very dry and soon caught. She heard Russell's claws on the floorboards and remained crouched as he came to join her.

'How are we this morning?' she asked.

He licked her knuckles then wandered out through the French windows into the garden, apparently impervious to the cold. She watched him exploring, then shivered and fastened the doors behind him.

Leaving the fire to burn up on its own, Zoe went downstairs to the kitchen and found the electric kettle stone cold on the counter. She filled it to the maximum and flicked the switch to set it to boil. In the ancient white fridge that stood taller than she, Zoe located a mason jar half full of what smelt like Colombian coffee. She couldn't find a cafetière but she did discover a Pyrex jug in one of the cupboards below the counter.

I suppose I could give it a stir and maybe locate a tea strainer through which to pour it out.

This Heath Robinson method turned out not to be needed because she discovered a packet of Melitta filter papers between the bread bin and a bowl of eggs, plus a filter funnel under an upturned saucepan on the draining board. As the coffee dripped through, Zoe felt herself drifting back towards sleep. She roused herself to open the fridge again to see what there might be to eat.

There was very little. In fact, it resembled her own fridge, with five or six things in jars, preserved in oil or vinegar, including some high-quality anchovies, some honey and a vacuum-packed bag of fresh penne pasta. That reminded her of her conversation with Adélaïde and Patrick and Minette in which they had each come up with bizarre combinations of food.

I should have brought down my rye bread and saucisson *and cheese.*

She shut the fridge and watched the last few drips soak through into the Pyrex jug. She found a mug on the draining board and took her coffee upstairs to the dining room, which still smelt strongly of smoke. She reopened the French doors. Russell slipped in and she left them ajar in order to clear the fug. She drank her coffee with the warmth of the fire behind her and the bitter wind once more on her cheeks.

Alone in a strange house, she felt restless, impatient for Minette and Patrick's return.

I need to take every opportunity I can to understand the complex web of characters in this extraordinary place. I have to help Adélaïde with her awful blackmail situation and I feel a duty to look deeper into Monsieur Alain's death. No one else seems to want to.

With a meagre dose of caffeine beginning to circulate in her bloodstream – she had a suspicion that it might actually be decaf – Zoe decided to explore the château once more.

I wish I'd looked at my phone to find out precisely what time it was when I heard Junior sobbing. It could have been anything from half past midnight to just before dawn.

She corrected herself.

No, I got up before dawn. It must have been around the tipping point of the night, no longer yesterday but not quite today – maybe three or four o'clock?

Russell gave her a look that seemed to mean: 'What? No proper walk?' Then he returned to the warm kitchen.

Zoe walked the length of the ground-floor corridor, from the front door at the base of the western tower, past the drawing room and the dining room that made up almost the entire south-facing façade. On the opposite side, there weren't any rooms, just built-in cupboards, one of them filled with all kinds of household junk, the others empty and damp-smelling. Beyond all that was a ground-floor bathroom and then the vestibule at the foot of the eastern tower with its bolted door onto the walled vegetable garden.

Zoe went upstairs, walking on the balls of her feet in order not to make too much noise on the ancient treads, then took the narrower staircase that climbed in a spiral to the very top, with shallow wooden steps without carpet. Using her mobile phone screen for illumination so as not to have to turn on any lights, she ascended to a hallway with clean lino-leum flooring.

To her surprise, at the far end, she saw a tray on the floor outside the room from which she believed she had heard weeping.

So, Junior didn't go to the party in the village. He just sat on his own and ate dinner in his lonely room.

By the light of her phone torch, she inspected the tray.

Lasagne from a tin-foil dish.

She headed back downstairs and was just in time to hear and see the front door closing and a brown-paper bag on the seat of the oak carver chair. A delicious fragrance of butter and sugar already hung in the chill morning air.

The pastries dropped off by the baker.

She realised that she was glad.

I'm absolutely ravenous.

Twenty
'YOU'RE STUCK WITH US'

Back in the dining room, Zoe put the paper bag of pastries on the white cloth of the dining table. As she took off her coat – because the room was now warm – the historical leaflet about the château fell out of her pocket. For the first time she noticed the Palotte family crest, pictured at the top of the page, a stone turret with a rampant stag on either side.

Hence the stags in the grounds. That seems very much in character for Adélaïde's husband, Primo, the Anglophile 'lord of the manor'.

She opened the leaflet out and found the diagram of the building, with a turreted tower at each end. She didn't have time to study it for very long because Patrick and Minette appeared in the French doors, making her jump, their breath visible on the chill air that accompanied them. Patrick closed up and told Zoe: 'My fingers are like ice.'

'Mine, too,' said Minette and they both went to stand by the fire, rubbing their hands together.

'I think I heard Junior crying last night,' Zoe told their backs. 'I don't know what time it was.'

'Poor kid,' said Patrick, without turning round.

'Do you know what he was doing while the others were at the party in the village?'

'I don't. Do you, Minette?'

'No, and I don't suppose they care so why should we?'

'Someone gave him supper in his bedroom,' said Zoe, then felt a chill as a horrible idea came into her mind. 'He wouldn't have been locked in, would he?'

Minette turned and said: 'Maybe.'

'Is it likely? Who would take such a drastic step?'

'Boris, Sweetie, Marie-France – but they would say it was for his own good.'

'Not your mother?'

'She tries very hard with Junior. She feels his neglect very deeply,' said Patrick. 'But there's a limit to what she can do if his parents won't pay attention to him and speak shortly and belittle his ideas.'

'Neglect is a strong word,' replied Zoe. 'And Primo?'

'He does his best, too. He tries to look after all of us, but I think he's finally deciding that nothing good comes of getting involved in "Boris's shenanigans".'

Patrick sounds very serious when he says that.

'But he pays for those "shenanigans"?'

The two of them had their backs to her once more.

'He does – always has done.'

Zoe asked: 'Does Marie-France live in the château full-time?'

'Yes. Goes on holidays with them, too,' said Minette.

'What does Sweetie think of that?'

'Hates it, I imagine.' Patrick turned from the flames with a sympathetic smile. 'Boris has much more in common with Marie-France than with Sweetie, obviously. At the same time, he disparages our mother, his second wife, as "manly" because she earns her own modest living.'

'How did he and Sweetie come to meet? How did they come to marry?'

Minette asked: 'How do you think?'

'I don't like to guess.'

'Sweetie was taken on as a personal assistant and,' Minette added slyly, 'I imagine she has excellent skills.'

Patrick laughed and remarked: 'He took a fancy to her.'

'You must have heard,' said Minette, 'about the "dangerous age" for older men.'

'I have,' admitted Zoe.

'Every age has been dangerous for our Boris Senior,' said Patrick.

I wonder if that was what Sweetie was crying about when they came in from the evening reception in the village last night? Boris can't have got bored of her, can he? She's his third wife. Is it possible, at seventy years old, that he can have his eyes on a fourth?

Minette got busy. She opened the dresser at the far end of the room, revealing a variety of accoutrements for making coffee – a plastic jug kettle, two large cafetières, three two-litre bottles of Evian spring water, a glass jar of individually wrapped biscuits, a bowl of sugar lumps. It all resembled the 'facilities' in a high-class hotel. There were also two shelves of crystal wine glasses.

Just then, through the generously glazed French doors, Zoe saw the sun nudging up beyond the lawn, rising in the east with a fan-shaped array of orange-yellow shafts, pointing up into a small quadrant of pale-blue sky.

'Was it slippery going down into the village?' she asked.

'Not too bad,' said Patrick.

'It was icy on the way back up,' said Minette.

'Where is the *boulangerie*?'

'At the top of the village, level with the gate from the château. You would have seen it on the way to the event in the market hall.'

'I didn't notice. I suppose it was shut at that point.'

By this time, Minette had prepared two cafetières of coffee. She brought them to the table with cups and saucers in very fine china, decorated with a blue willow pattern. Zoe assumed this was another aspect of Primo's Anglophilia – his love of all things English.

But that doesn't matter right now. This is my opportunity.

'I don't quite understand the set-up here,' she said as innocently as she was able. 'Can you tell me more about what's going on?'

'In what way, "going on"?' asked Patrick, his mouth full of buttery croissant.

'The relationships and, I suppose, the day-to-day living arrangements.'

'Are you getting a sinister vibe?' asked Minette, pulling a *pain au chocolat* in half to separate the two sticks of confectionery. She dipped one piece in her coffee. 'I wouldn't blame you.'

'I'd just like to understand,' said Zoe, neutrally.

'It's not like before,' said Patrick. 'A few years ago, it was joyous.'

'That's the word,' said his sister.

'Everyone got on well?'

'When Junior was little and they sort of shared his care and found him charming. Though not Boris, who never paid him any heed and was besotted with his pneumatic young wife. Then it started to go bad.'

'Why, though?'

'Boris Senior felt pushed out by the child and, I suppose, a baby is more malleable than a small person who wants to achieve their own independence,' said Patrick.

'And is bored out of his mind,' said Minette.

'Does he not go to school?' Zoe asked.

'He does, but the weekends drag and the holidays are long,' explained Patrick.

Minette added: 'Like we said, our mother, Elizabeth, did her best to be a "kindly aunt", but she's only in residence for special occasions. Primo taught him games, ludo and snakes-and-ladders and draughts. Then he went too fast with backgammon and chess and there were sulks and tantrums. Then Primo tried to initiate family board games but, again, they were too sophisticated for the child.'

'And made the elders argue,' said Patrick, 'so that was no better.'

'What about excursions and things?' asked Zoe.

'Sweetie used to take him into Aix-en-Provence,' said Minette. 'But not for Junior's benefit. She would go to her hairdresser or her nail artist or her spa treatment, leaving him with a childminder, someone she and Boris had used when Junior was an infant, but totally inappropriate by that time. I mean, the childminder liked the extra money for watching Junior, but her apartment wasn't set up to amuse a growing boy. Sweetie bought him a PlayStation and that worked well for a while because he was on it day and night, but Boris decided that it was "corrupting" and took it away and locked it up somewhere.'

'Oh dear,' said Zoe. 'How sad it all sounds. Did you say your mother has given up trying?'

'No, she would never do that. It makes her furious,' said Patrick. 'She always does her best when she's here.'

'Where does she live otherwise?'

'Paris,' he told her. 'Where else? A not-great apartment on Rue Jacob in the Latin Quarter, close to the publishing house from whom she gets most of her work.'

'She's a freelance?'

'Yes.'

'Doing well?'

'She has to work,' said Minette, sounding cross, 'because she's spent all her divorce settlement, apart from the little apartment, and Boris can't help, even if he wanted to, because he's always been a mug in business and it's only Primo's generosity that's kept him afloat all these years.' Then she surprised Zoe by saying: 'That's a problem for Sweetie, too, I reckon.'

'In what way?'

'I expect,' said Minette, 'that she bought into the idea of Boris as an elderly rich husband that she could profitably outlive. The truth is very different. I think even Sweetie's slow synapses have at last worked it out. With the benefit of hindsight, she's finally calculated that she ought to have directed her gold-digger energy at Primo rather than Boris.'

That's pretty brutal.

'But that would have clashed with Adélaïde meeting Primo and—' said Zoe.

Patrick interrupted: 'No, Primo and Adélaïde came together earlier.'

Zoe said nothing as the twins continued to eat and drink, listening to the sounds of the house, expanding with the hard-working central heating and the hot chimney. She heard no footsteps or other evidence that they might be overheard.

'Did you say all that about gold-digging in jest,' she finally wondered aloud, 'or because you know that Sweetie—'

'You think I sound cruel,' said Minette. 'You have to understand that it's our inheritance, too. Without Sweetie and her undelicious offspring, we were next in line for Boris's portion. Or Patrick was, but I think he would share.' She smiled at her brother and asked: 'Wouldn't you?'

'I suppose,' deadpanned Patrick, then he laughed.

'And, remember,' resumed Minette, 'Boris Senior was and is next in line to Primo.'

'Not Adélaïde?' queried Zoe.

'No,' said Patrick. 'Like your British royal family, inheritance of the Palotte estate is in the male line. I quizzed our solicitor about it.'

'Caroline?'

'Yes. She told me the trusts are watertight.'

'Fair enough,' said Zoe. 'To sum up, Junior is unhappy because no one pays him any attention and he's become more and more difficult. Your mother, Elizabeth, has to work because her circumstances demand it, but she's still on good terms with her ex-husband Boris and with his first wife, Marie-France.'

'And *Maman* – Elizabeth, I mean – tolerates Sweetie,' said Minette, 'is kind and polite to her, but understands her for what she is.'

Not wanting to get drawn into any more character assassination of Boris's third wife, Zoe pressed on with her summary.

'Primo supports his twin brother whenever he has a financial crisis, which is regularly. And both of them are unwell?'

'That's true,' confirmed Patrick.

'They don't like it being discussed,' chipped in his sister. 'I imagine Adélaïde would give you the details if you asked.'

'Who have I missed? Tell me more about Marie-France. How does she live?'

'Entirely at her ex-husband's expense,' said Patrick.

'Which means, at the end of the day,' snapped Minette, 'Primo's expense which is, by extension, our expense.'

There was a pause while they all, as if synchronised, finished their coffees. Patrick poured more from the second cafetière and Zoe asked, with a hint of trepidation: 'And Adélaïde?'

'We love Adélaïde,' said Patrick, his delicate willow-pattern teacup halfway to his lips.

'How exactly did she and Primo get together?' asked Zoe. Then she added: 'Am I being very nosy?'

'Yes,' said Minette, brutally, 'but you're stuck with us, so why not? About fifteen years ago, Primo put money into a film Adélaïde starred in, probably her first really good "mature" role. There are some very advantageous options in France where investors can set their tax burden aside and—'

'I understand how the finances work,' said Zoe. 'It was more the emotional connection that I wanted to understand.'

'You know what I think?' demanded Minette and Zoe feared it was going to be another harsh assessment. She was surprised, therefore, when Minette told her: 'Adélaïde had already ploughed through a goodish career, twenty years at that point, in a man's world, being ogled and belittled and all the rest of it. Primo showed her respect and took an interest in her professional opinions. When the film did well and she was offered better parts, he invested in her next one on the proviso that she was also made an executive producer.'

'And this was before they became a couple?'

'Yes, at least eighteen months. Then they surprised everyone at the Cannes Film Festival by arriving together on the red carpet, arm in arm, with Adélaïde showing her ring to the cameras. They'd got married on their own at a swish resort in Mauritius or Réunion or somewhere. I can't remember, now.'

'What a lovely story,' said Zoe. 'Respect blossoming into love.'

'The marriage service was entirely private,' said Patrick. 'I've always wondered why I wasn't invited, but I never wanted to ask for fear of spoiling our relationship. Adélaïde was very good to me when I was younger. It's really thanks to her that—'

Above their heads, the floorboards began to creak.

'They're on the move. That's probably it for our private conclave,' said Patrick. 'Do you feel better informed?'

'I do,' said Zoe.

There are motives everywhere for resentment and jealousy. And Adélaïde is worried about potential blackmail. Plus, there's a coldness between her and Primo that she's pretending not to notice. He, if I'm not mistaken, has money worries. The documentary project might help with that, but it also seems to risk uncovering things that Adélaïde would rather were kept hidden.

'Are you sure?' Patrick wondered. 'You look uncertain.'

'Much better informed,' she insisted.

But I can't say I feel reassured.

III

A DEEPER MYSTERY

Twenty-One

'IT'S OVER'

Zoe felt that she had learned quite a lot about her hosts from the unguarded tongues of Patrick and Minette.

But I need to know more.

She returned to the basement kitchen. A corridor led off the warm space in both directions. Because the only illumination came from high slot windows near the ceiling, it was gloomy. She turned on the electric lights and explored the passage to the west. It led into a bare, stone room with an empty drying rack that descended via strings and pulleys from the ceiling. It also housed a vast central-heating boiler, a washing machine and a diminishing stack of logs.

Probably crawling with spiders.

On the floor alongside was a pile of dusty, faded newspapers.

A fire hazard, surely, all this?

Zoe recrossed the kitchen and tried the other direction, along another basement corridor, discovering a modern bathroom, then an unused servants' hall with a six-person dining table, then a round bedroom, also with high slot windows, presumably in the base of the eastern tower. It had a masculine air and felt bereft and sad, already missing its occupant.

This belonged to Monsieur Alain. There's a spare livery hanging in that wardrobe.

Russell came to see what she was doing. He clearly had the 'W-word' on his mind.

'Yes, all right, hound.'

Glad not to run into any other residents of the house – who she supposed were having tea or coffee in their rooms – she slipped out through the dining room, replenishing the logs on the fire.

I hope we don't run out.

Russell followed her outside through the French windows, across the terrace and onto the lawn. The air felt a little warmer, though still wintry.

Perhaps we're in for a thaw. I hope so.

With Russell weaving awkwardly round her ankles, she headed past the walled vegetable garden, away from the château on slightly rising terrain. She soon found herself at a five-bar gate that led into crowded, mixed woods – bare oak and beech trees, dark-green conifers.

Someone's left this open.

She went through and carefully latched the gate behind her, then was startled by movement in the undergrowth. Her heart beating faster, she scanned the shadows beneath the trees, then recognised the sounds as hoofbeats.

This must be where the stags are supposed to live.

She followed the edge of the woods, finding that the whole area was fenced, as was a large area of open grassland beyond. About a hundred metres away, just as she came out of cover, she saw six or seven female deer, quietly grazing, and smiled to herself.

How utterly lovely.

The moment didn't last. It was immediately spoiled by guilt at the realisation that she hadn't warned Primo that one of his stags had escaped.

I would have done so, but he ambushed me with his questions. I told Caroline, though, and she dealt with it.

She walked on. The woods were extensive and there was much to enjoy, out of the wind with the weather a little less withering.

Is it possible that Primo is jealous of one of Adélaïde's romantic entanglements from so long ago? I seem to remember her telling me that performing for the first time in English was so important to her that she took the decision to remain utterly chaste in order to focus one hundred per cent on her big-stage debut.

Zoe had an uneasy sensation that she had been underhand, talking about Adélaïde behind her back. She felt guilty about reading the disturbing note sent to Primo. She tried to suppress both emotions.

I'll have to get Adélaïde to open up, however much she hates the idea. Then, perhaps, I can get her and Primo to have things out, leaving me out of it.

She remembered the moment when Primo had shut their conversation down, clearly regretting broaching the topic.

He made himself feel ashamed, spying on his wife by questioning an old acquaintance.

Zoe didn't know what birthday commitments she might have later on, so she took advantage of the solitude to walk for another hour, only turning for home when Russell began looking up at her with appeal in his dark eyes.

'All right. We'll go back. Your little paws must be frozen.' He cocked his head and she felt obliged to add: 'No, I do not intend to carry you.'

They returned to the house by the same route, crossing the terrace, leaving slippery footprints in the slushy snow. Then Russell caught the scent of a rat or a rabbit, forgot that he wanted to be indoors and dashed off out of sight.

The fresh air had made Zoe feel hungry. Unlike Patrick and Minette, she hadn't wanted a pastry. She headed straight for the kitchen and opened the large fridge. To her amazement, she found it stuffed to the gills with all kinds of foodstuffs – unopened packets of speciality goods, raw cuts of meat wrapped in butcher's paper, jars and pots, fresh vegetables, salad leaves, cucumbers and onions.

There must have been a delivery while I was exploring. I wonder who brought it all in?

To the right of the fridge was a generous wine rack that now contained two dozen bottles. One after another, she gently pulled three out, interested to see what vintages were present, but not wanting to disturb their lees – their sediment. Two were classic clarets from Bordeaux, the third a very fine white Burgundy.

She heard the screechy front door distantly opening and closing, then waited as slow footsteps approached along the corridor and then down the stairs. A woman appeared, laden with a carboard box containing some more sophisticated, speciality goods. Zoe recognised her handsome face and dark complexion.

'Madame Valgarde, isn't it? My name is Zoe Pascal. I saw you at the ceremony. I'm a guest at Château Palotte.'

'I'm glad to meet you.' Madame Valgarde relinquished her burden on the kitchen table and smiled. 'I wonder, might you be able to give me a hand?'

'Of course,' said Zoe, automatically, then enquired: 'With what?'

'This evening's catering. Elizabeth said you might. Primo invites the village.'

'I suppose, under other circumstances, Monsieur Alain would have taken charge?'

'That's right. It's very sad.'

Madame Valgarde was wearing the same long black coat as at the market hall. Zoe remembered Primo mentioning that he might drop in on her that first morning and she had imagined an elderly spinster who never left the village.

She's not that at all.

Madame Valgarde unbuttoned her coat, taking her time. In fact, Zoe was beginning to think that everything Madame Valgarde ever did would be accomplished with a sort of leisurely sensuality. Next, she felt it was entirely in keeping when she discovered that, beneath her overcoat, the visitor wore a very becoming black dress, reminiscent of the uniform of an Edwardian governess, but in a flattering and flexible fabric. She hung her coat on a peg at the foot of the stairs, next to two or three aprons.

'What needs to be done?' Zoe asked. 'Is it a sit-down meal?'

'No, just endless canapés. By the time we've finished, you will hate the sight of a caper.' Madame Valgarde laughed and Zoe found herself entranced by the symmetry of the newcomer's features, her clear, darkish skin, her striking hazel eyes, her friendly good humour. 'As long, Madame Pascal, as I'm not dragging you away from more important tasks.'

'I'm actually at a bit of a loose end. But, if we are to work together, you must call me Zoe.'

'And you must call me Isabelle.'

'Pleased to meet you, Isabelle.' They shook hands and Zoe heard a distant yapping from the direction of the first floor. 'Would you excuse me? I'll only be a minute.'

She ran upstairs to the front door, opened it and found Russell looking very bedraggled and cold, too wet and muddy to be picked up.

'Come on,' she told him. 'Let's get you dry and warm.'

His paws left little wet marks on the floorboards and on the heavy stone steps of the basement stairs. As they reached the kitchen, Zoe saw Isabelle Valgarde looking at herself in the reflective steel door of the fridge, turning left and right, smoothing her black dress over her hips.

She really is a very attractive woman – and she knows it. I wonder who else has noticed?

Zoe bent down to rub Russell dry with one of the smelly blankets from the dog bed. Just then, a noisy rumble of unhappy conversation and rapid footsteps became audible as, somewhere above, a difference of opinion was being aired. Zoe thought it was Boris and his second wife, Elizabeth.

Oh dear. That's all we need.

Concealed by the table laden with ingredients, she was out of sight when she heard a single set of footsteps on the kitchen stairs and a man's voice, demanding in an urgent whisper: 'What are you doing here? I've already told you. It's over.'

There was an eerie silence because Isabelle Valgarde made no reply. Zoe began to think she couldn't remain out of sight, crouched behind the table, any longer.

'Well?' the man insisted.

If I emerge, it will look like I've been deliberately eavesdropping.

To her relief, with a sound of footsteps retreating up the stairs, the man's voice repeated: 'Over, I tell you.'

Zoe stood up and, apologetically, told her new acquaintance: 'I'm so sorry, Isabelle. I didn't mean to—'

'Never mind. You heard Boris. He says it's over.'

'Please, forget I was even here,' said Zoe.

'I imagine you wish you'd never set foot in Château Palotte. I almost do myself.'

That's an odd jump.

'I came to support my friend.'

'Adélaïde?'

'That's right.'

'I'm sure you're a tower of strength.'

Zoe didn't know what to say to this comment. It sounded, at one and the same time, both complimentary and dismissive.

There was another eerie pause. During it, Zoe asked herself two things.

What, precisely, does Boris think is over? And is it possible that the reason Sweetie was crying when they got back from the village reception was because of Isabelle Valgarde?

Twenty-Two

'OLD AGE IS A SHIPWRECK'

The awkward silence between Zoe and Isabelle, standing either side of the kitchen table, was broken by Adélaïde's voice, calling from the upper hallway.

'Zoe, are you there?'

She called back: 'Yes, I am.' Embarking up the stairs, she and Adélaïde met halfway, perched awkwardly, one above the other. 'What's going on?'

'The aftermath of the family meeting. Everyone's unhappy,' said her friend. 'The only person who will remain unaffected is Caroline, of course. In the end, it doesn't matter to her. We're just another handful of feuding clients.'

'I'm sure she doesn't think like that.'

Adélaïde ignored this attempt at a more positive view of proceedings and declared: 'I'm beginning to regret asking you, Zoe. I thought your presence would be a comfort, but you're just one more thing to worry about.'

'We could go somewhere private and you could tell me what's happened?' suggested Zoe, quietly, aware that Isabelle was not far away in the basement kitchen. She could hear her moving pots and pans, in preparation for their marathon of canapé making. 'It might do you good to unpack it all. I'm sure things are nowhere near as bad as they seem.'

'I can't,' said Adélaïde, unhappily. 'Primo and I have another social obligation – lunch with some appalling people in Valon, the village where they have the lavender festival.'

'What sort of appalling people?' speculated Zoe, still try-ing to lighten the tone. 'Philistines who have never seen a single one of your films?'

'Completely the opposite and worse. They think of themselves as aficionados of cinema and, because I'm a commercial success these days, they look down on me as a sort of fallen angel because I no longer star in movies with meandering, incomprehensible plots that nobody wants to pay to go and see.'

'Someone should tell them there's room for all sorts,' said Zoe. 'Why must you go?'

'Primo has a very strong sense of his obligations. Surely that's become clear by now?'

'Do you not have a say in the matter?'

'It's probably better that I accede to what he thinks is best.'

There was a tiny pause during which Adélaïde looked inscrutable and Zoe wondered: *How exactly should I take that comment?*

'Fair enough,' she said.

'What I'm wearing won't do, either,' said Adélaïde. 'I'll have to go and change. I'm sorry to abandon you. What will you do for lunch? We really are the most terrible hosts.'

'I'll admit that this would have been a singular experi-ence, even without poor Monsieur Alain's fall. As for lunch, I hadn't given it any thought,' she lied, her stomach rumbling.

Adélaïde put a hand to her mouth, her eyes wide.

'Tonight's reception – the catering – what will we do?'

'Madame Valgarde is downstairs. She's going to prepare canapés and I told her I would lend a hand.'

'Isabelle is here?'

Adélaïde brushed past Zoe, who wondered what would happen next.

Is she pleased or cross?

When she caught up with her friend, she was standing with her hands on Isabelle's shoulders and Zoe was struck by the similarities in their bone structure, their wide-set eyes, their generous mouths, albeit with very different skin tones.

Of course, Isabelle is the second actress in the studio portrait in Junior's Hollywood glamour magazine – the one with the revealing evening gowns.

It was still unclear whether this was a happy reunion until Adélaïde said, with a return of her usual positive energy: 'Thank you, darling. I couldn't be more grateful. How did you know to come and save us?'

'Elizabeth phoned me. I'm happy to help.'

'Ah, Elizabeth, always trying to fix us.' Adélaïde embraced Isabelle more tightly. 'Please make sure that Zoe eats something. I've failed to make her welcome and we have to go out again.'

'Primo looked very weary this morning,' said Isabelle. Zoe could see her face in a sort of close-up over Adélaïde's shoulder. Her voice sounded serious, but she looked impassive, like a still from a movie. 'I suppose he won't cancel?'

Adélaïde released her and took a step back. 'You know he never would.'

Isabelle smiled and her face brightened with the abruptness of someone turning on a light.

'Yes,' she said. 'Poor Primo – a prisoner of his expectations of himself.'

Zoe felt there was a strong complicity between the two women, equally glamorous in appearance but unalike in character. Isabelle seemed steady and composed while Adélaïde veered swiftly between moods. Although Zoe had always admired Adélaïde's energy, she wondered, treacherously, if it might be difficult to live with full-time. She asked: 'How did you two meet?'

'There's no time for that now,' said Adélaïde. 'I'm already making us late.'

'Go,' said Isabelle. 'Impress people. All will be well when you return.'

Zoe accompanied Adélaïde to the front door where Primo was waiting patiently, dressed in his three-piece tweed suit and tan brogues with a mustard-yellow scarf knotted around his neck.

Adélaïde told him that she had to change. 'But I'll be back down in three minutes. You'll see.'

She hurried away, leaving Zoe and Primo alone in the hall-way, with no sound of any other resident of Château Palotte nearby.

'Can I reiterate my sympathy at your loss?' said Zoe. 'Monsieur Alain, after all these years, must have been a friend as well as an employee.'

'In a sense, that's absolutely true,' said Primo. 'I relied on him like a friend, but he would never have accepted that description of our relations.' His tone changed. 'I wonder, might I take this opportunity of asking you if you've had a chance to talk to Adélaïde?'

'About the murder at the theatre?'

'Yes.'

'Barely,' said Zoe. 'And, this evening, there's another social event, I understand. Will it go on late?'

'Yes, it will, and everyone will be tired at its conclusion.' He yawned then excused himself. 'I'm sorry. That's very indecorous of me. This is all very wearing. Would you mind . . .'

His voice faded and he sort of stumbled towards the oak carver chair. Zoe sprang into action to give him an arm and help him into it, with the impression that she had prevented him from falling.

'Do I need to call a doctor?' she asked.

'No,' he told her, with a little gasp. 'This is quite normal.'

'Surely it can't be—' she began.

'Believe me.' He exhaled, noisily. Her left hand was still on his right arm. He covered it with his own. She felt a slight tremor. 'Old age is a shipwreck,' he told her, quietly.

'Is that from a poem?'

'Charles de Gaulle said it about Marshall Pétain, the French collaborationist leader who threw in our lot with the Nazis. *La vieillesse est un naufrage,*' Primo repeated, relishing the phrase. 'I feel it, too, in my own case.'

'You seem far from old,' said Zoe.

'A slow shipwreck,' he told her. 'My mind is captain of a doomed vessel. It remains alert, but can do nothing to prevent the ship of my body from running onto the rocks.'

Despite his gloomy conversation, Primo was beginning to have a better colour. To break the mood, Zoe asked: 'What is everyone doing for lunch?'

'They have all made their own arrangements.'

'Everyone has gone out?'

'Yes,' said Primo. 'Boris and Sweetie and their unhappy offspring are breaking bread with our lady mayor and her mother, Emilie Constant, accompanied by Marie-France and Elizabeth. Patrick and Minette have gone into Aix for what Minette told me would be – not entirely good-humouredly – "a break from this madhouse". Caroline has accompanied them because she has a meeting of her own at her office. They will return together.'

'Isabelle and I are alone?'

Primo looked startled.

'Isabelle Valgarde is here?'

'Madame Elizabeth asked for her assistance with this evening's reception. I thought I might lend a hand, too.'

'Does Boris know?' asked Primo, sharply.

'He does, yes.'

'Has there already been a confrontation?' he asked, perceptively.

Somehow, Zoe couldn't bring herself to lie, even though she could see that this was news that her friend's elderly husband didn't want to hear.

'I'm afraid there was.'

'What was its character?'

145

'One-sided,' said Zoe.

'Please go on.'

'Boris twice insisted: "It's over." Isabelle said nothing in return.'

True to her promise of speed, that was the moment when Adélaïde came back to join them, wearing a fabulous green dress in a fabric that seemed to change colour with the light. Over it, she had chosen a long cardigan in soft yellow wool that came down beyond her knees.

'You look an absolute picture of 1920s fashion,' Zoe told her.

Adélaïde was about to reply when she frowned and asked her husband: 'What's wrong? What's happened?'

'Nothing, my dear,' said Primo, helping himself to his feet by leaning on the arms of the oak chair. 'I was merely taking advantage of one of life's pauses.'

'I'll drive,' Adélaïde told him. 'It will be over before you know it.'

Zoe stood in the doorway and watched them leave, through lightly swirling snowflakes, all the way down the slippery outdoor staircase to the carport, where Adélaïde got in on the driver's side of her sagging BMW and Primo took the passenger seat. The car pulled away.

I hope the roads are not just clear for the outward journey, but also for the return.

She thought about Patrick and Minette and Caroline, also away across country.

Am I going to end up snowed in with just Isabelle and Boris's family, attempting to keep the peace between his mismatched, feuding wives, his unhappy son and his reluctant mistress?

Twenty-Three
'DOES ADÉLAÏDE HAVE FRIENDS?'

Zoe shut the front door and returned to the warmth of the kitchen where the stainless-steel worktops beside the stove and the beechwood table were now scattered with packets and jars. Isabelle gave her a quick rundown of what she intended to prepare 'for the village'.

'Monsieur Astor the baker will be up shortly with the *baguettes*. We will cut them into thin rondels, flavour them in several ways, then bake them crisp to serve as bases for each canapé. Then we will dress them in batches of two dozen with the various combinations of the ingredients you see in front of you.'

'That all sounds delicious. Before we begin, however,' Zoe suggested, 'do you think we might eat something ourselves? I'm famished and everyone else has gone out.'

'Good idea. What shall we have?'

'I don't want to take any ingredients that will upset your plans.'

'A Provençal stand-by, then, pasta with a tomato-and-olive sauce.'

'Sounds marvellous.'

'And a good handful of fresh basil leaves.'

'Wonderful.'

Zoe tried to get Isabelle to allow her to make her own lunch, but her new acquaintance wouldn't have it. She asked Zoe to heat water in the kettle and pour it into a saucepan to bring to a rapid boil, then add the fresh *penne* from the fridge – ridged tubes of pasta. Isabelle herself opened a good-quality tin of tomatoes into a separate saucepan and lit the gas burner beneath, bringing the pulp to a slow simmer with a substantial pinch of salt from a large clay cruet alongside. Meanwhile, she delegated to Zoe the task of thinly slicing a dozen green olives and fetching basil leaves from the plants growing in tubs in the drawing room.

'At least a dozen large ones or twenty smaller ones, for the garnish.'

Zoe ran upstairs. She had seen the plants at the martini party in their green-stained clay pots, brought indoors from the terrace to protect them from the worst of the weather. Seen up close – there was parsley, basil, thyme and oregano – the plants looked like they were on their last legs, but she managed to find a dozen decent, unblemished leaves.

Back in the kitchen she showed Isabelle her harvest and asked: 'You know the house well? You're a regular visitor?'

'Why do you say that?'

'Because you knew I would find basil leaves in the drawing room.'

'Yes, I understand the logic. I meant, why did you mention it?'

'I was just making conversation. I'm not trying to pry.'

'Heaven knows,' said Isabelle, 'there's enough going on without an outsider getting involved.'

'I'm not an outsider,' Zoe told her. 'I'm one of Adélaïde's oldest friends.'

'Does Adélaïde have friends?' quibbled Isabelle. 'Isn't she rather a sort of beautiful lonely clipper, sailing the ocean of life alone?'

'She and Primo seem very close, don't you think?'

'Perhaps he's the solitary clipper, then, not her,' said Isabelle, stirring the sauce. 'And Adélaïde is a lonely albatross that has done him the honour of alighting on his rigging for a day and a night, before continuing her lonely pilgrimage.'

'I wouldn't presume to judge,' said Zoe, carefully. 'We've not seen one another so frequently these last few years.'

'I'm not judging either. We all have to live with the choices we make,' said Isabelle.

She's talking like somebody who has experienced loneliness. Is she also being critical of Adélaïde? I think she is, but she and Adélaïde seemed very pleased to see one another. Was that not genuine?

'How did you and Adélaïde meet?'

'I was number one on the call sheet for Adélaïde's break-through film,' said Isabelle, 'the movie where she met Primo because he had invested in it. Do you know the story?'

'A little of it, but what does that mean, "number one on the call sheet"?'

'It's the billing and it defines the daily paperwork for shooting times and locations, who's required where and when, so everyone is always listed in the same order of importance. It's an enormous deal in cinema, whether an actor is number one or number two or number six. Whole projects can stand or fall on whether the agents and the producers can agree.'

'Like the order of precedence in a royal wedding – who sits where, alongside whom.'

'I wouldn't know. Anway, I thought that movie was going to change my life but, instead, it changed Adélaïde's.' She left a pause and, as if to indicate the topic was closed, tossed the slices of green olives into the sauce. She gestured to the pasta. 'That's overcooked, isn't it?'

'Oh, sorry.'

Zoe fished out a little tube of *penne* with a wooden spoon, tested it with her thumbnail, then drained the whole pan into a battered colander, giving it a good shake. The pasta looked a little gloopy.

'Cut me a quarter of a lemon,' said Isabelle. 'They're in the fridge.'

Zoe fetched a gorgeous piece of fruit and found a knife block on the stainless-steel worktop. She used the smallest blade.

'Is this right?'

'Perfect.' Isabelle squeezed the wedge of lemon into the tomato sauce, gave it a final stir and turned off the heat, instructing Zoe to pour the pasta on top. 'And give it a good shake – not a stir because that *penne* looks too soft.'

Zoe did as she was told, remarking: 'You've made quite a lot just for me.'

'I'm looking forward to it, too. Let's sit and you can tear the basil leaves on top.'

Isabelle fetched a bag of grated Emmenthal from the fridge and sliced it open with Zoe's paring knife, leaving it lying on the clean boards of the kitchen table, then located two large bowl-plates in an eye-level cupboard. By this time, Zoe was getting the hang of the layout and found spoons and forks in a wide cutlery drawer, plus a large serving spoon in the one beneath. She invited Isabelle to dish up, but the other replied: 'Serve yourself.'

Zoe did so – copiously – then offered the spoon across, wondering if Isabelle would take just a token quantity to keep her company.

'No, I won't need that. You've taken about a third.' Isabelle poured another third directly from the saucepan into her bowl-plate and, abruptly, laughed, giving the impression of a light being illuminated on a sombre afternoon. She said: 'I'm no longer an actress, if that was what you were wondering. I don't have to starve myself as a matter of routine, and this terrible weather means we all need to fuel up as we hunker down, waiting for spring.'

They both added plenty of cheese and, for a little while, they ate in silence, with Zoe in a rush to satisfy her hunger pangs. But she was still, in the back of her mind, worrying about the deepening drifts of snow.

If we get cut off and trapped, 'waiting for spring' – as Isabelle called it – it will become a kind of nightmare.

Twenty-Four

'ONE IS NOT THE EQUAL
OF THE OTHER'

Facing Zoe across the kitchen table, Isabelle chewed sedately, with a small frown on her lovely brow. Eventually, Zoe thought that her lack of conversation might appear rude, so she asked: 'Do you miss acting?'

Isabelle finished her mouthful before placidly replying: 'I do. People such as Adélaïde and myself, we need constant validation.'

'What did you find to replace it in your life?'

'Nothing ever has, not fully.'

'That sounds rather desolate,' Zoe prompted, but Isabelle merely smiled and made no reply, adding another handful of cheese before taking another mouthful. 'I'm sorry,' Zoe continued, 'that I overheard what Boris said to you. It was not my intention to—'

'He was indiscreet. I indicated your presence with my eyes and he – to my surprise, because he is a slow-witted man – understood my unspoken meaning, that there was someone there. I don't believe he knows it was you. You will have noticed, however, that he couldn't resist repeating his portentous phrase: "It's over." I suppose you are curious about what he must have meant.'

Isabelle took another mouthful and Zoe told her: 'There's no need to share anything that isn't my business.'

There was a small pause before Isabelle wondered aloud: 'But you said you had come to Château Palotte in order to support Adélaïde?'

'I did.'

'Then the peccadillos of her husband's brother might be important?'

'True.'

There was another pause. Zoe wondered what would be the best way to express what was on her mind.

'You are a very intelligent and accomplished woman, Isabelle. Boris seems . . .' She stopped, not knowing how to complete the sentence without giving offence. 'He doesn't seem a natural fit – with you, I mean.'

'No,' said Isabelle.

Placidly, she carried on eating and Zoe felt obliged to do the same, not pressing the point, speculating whether she had gone too far.

We are, after all, about to spend a couple of hours in close proximity, collaborating in the manufacture of fiddly canapés.

Once their bowls were empty, Zoe washed up while Isabelle removed the remaining ingredients from the fridge, then leaned on the edge of the stainless-steel counter, her knuckles white from the pressure, and unexpectedly offered: 'It was a mistake too brief to merit the idea of being "over".'

'There's no need to tell me if—' Zoe began.

'It's a simple story. It goes like this. I spend too much time alone. At a party here in the château, I drank too much and I think, somehow, I forgot that, although they are twins, one brother is not . . .' She left a pause, sighed, then added in a tone of explanation: 'I was born and raised on the island of Martinique in the Caribbean. My first language was Creole. We have an expression: "*Yon pa vo lot.*" It's derived from French, of course: "*L'un ne vaut pas l'autre.*" Do you understand?'

'Yes, "one is not the equal of the other". I see,' said Zoe, with a feeling of being out of her depth in the extraordinarily intricate family dramas of Château Palotte. 'Can I ask if you and Primo have ever—?'

'The fact that you ask shows how little you know him.'

'I don't deny that. As you said, I want to understand for Adélaïde's sake.'

'We met Primo at the same time, Adélaïde and I. You might say we had equal chances. She won in all ways – reputation, future roles, critical validation, marriage.'

Thinking of her first conversation with Primo, Zoe asked, as lightly as she was able: 'People have mentioned his "austere" intelligence. What do you think he might do if he discovered something to her discredit?'

'You mean, would he utterly change his mind, that she would become sullied and undesirable?'

'I'm not sure what I meant.'

'Then how can I answer?'

You are right. That is what I meant, however.

Zoe watched Isabelle looking through the pockets of her coat, still on its hook at the foot of the stairs. Zoe found a Tupperware box for the leftover pasta and pushed it to the back of a shelf in the fridge. Isabelle located a folded sheet of handwritten paper from a pocket and smoothed it out on the table.

'Run your eye over this,' she told Zoe. 'I hope you can read my chicken-scratch handwriting.'

Zoe did as she was asked, now and then asking for clarification. Meanwhile, the glamorous Isabelle donned an apron, accentuating her delightful figure as she tied its string, then separated the many ingredients into different food-prep areas on the table and worktops. There were ten canapés on the list.

> Cucumber with whipped goat's cheese and herbs
> Saucisson *with finely chopped pickled onion and parsley*
> *Prosciutto cured ham with avocado*
> *Preserved tomatoes with bell peppers and toasted garlic*

Smoked duck with tangy mandarin orange
Artichokes and smoked salmon
Coulommiers cheese with grated carrot and lemon juice
Creamed green lentils with fresh thyme
Slivers of roast pork with crispy apple slices
Chopped beetroot with roquefort blue cheese and honey

Once Zoe had finished reading, she looked up and saw that Isabelle's organisation was impeccable.

'This all seems delicious and so varied that—'

The front doorbell rang insistently. While Isabelle opened jars and packets and pots, Zoe went upstairs to find burly Monsieur Astor, the first villager to receive notification of his rebate from Primo, standing on the rubber outside mat in the snow. He was carrying a sheaf of freshly baked *baguettes*, each one in its own narrow paper bag.

'They smell wonderful,' Zoe told him. 'I feel I know you because I saw you at the ceremony. My name is Zoe Pascal. I'm a friend of Madame Adélaïde.'

'To have such a friend is lucky, indeed,' said Monsieur Astor, gallantly. 'My son Didier and I will see you later.'

He put the *baguettes* in her arms and bustled away, almost taking a tumble on the steps, laughing good-humouredly as he regained his balance and forked right towards the pedestrian gate. Zoe noticed that the snowfall was accumulating more and more. The suspicious damage to the trunk of the lavender bush to the right of the steps was now almost completely out of sight.

Perhaps that's no bad thing.

She shut the door and went back downstairs, shivering a little from the blast of outside air.

Isabelle told her: 'Get the *baguettes* out of their bags so they don't become soft. The rondels should be not too thick. You ought to be able to cut twenty-four from each stick.'

'I'll do my best to make them even.'

While Zoe was sawing away with an elderly bread knife, Isabelle peeled and minced an entire enormous bulb of purple garlic, opened two small jars of black-olive tapenade and squeezed out a tube of high-quality tomato purée onto a chopping board. Then she ground up fresh rosemary with salt and olive oil using a pestle and mortar.

'These,' she told Zoe, 'are the four flavourings with which the rondels must be baked, with just a smear on each one.'

'Are the flavourings meant to co-ordinate with particular toppings?'

'No, it's mix and match. Some people would disapprove, but I think it makes them more interesting.'

'So, for each batch of twenty-four canapés, destined for one of the ten toppings, there will be four sets of six crispy bread bases, each one flavoured differently.'

'Exactly, Zoe.'

Isabelle's face was bright, her hands working quickly and efficiently.

She's enjoying herself. I hope I don't make a mess of things and let her down. I wonder what her life can be like, such that this menial – although creative – task should give her such a lift.

They worked on, mostly in silence, with an economy of movement, without rushing. The rondels of *baguette* entered and then emerged from the oven in batches, laced with either garlic, rosemary, tapenade or tomato purée. As they added the toppings, Zoe was impressed to discover that the crispy bread didn't become soggy because the smears of flavouring seemed to seal the surface.

This is going well. I wish I could just accept all this innocently purposeful activity at face value.

It was a slow and pernickety process but, eventually, enough rondels were ready to begin plating them up using a set of large cardboard serving platters, decorated with a Christmas pattern of dark holly leaves and red berries, just the right size to accommodate twenty-four canapés each.

After nearly two hours, these platters covered almost every kitchen surface, even including the cast-iron frames over the burners on the stovetop.

They both stood back and Isabelle said, with a smile of satisfaction: 'I think we deserve a sit-down, don't you?'

'Yes, I agree.'

Isabelle took a seat at the table, folding herself gently onto a hard chair. Her graceful movement reminded Zoe of one or two leading ladies she had worked with in the West End who would make a thing of sitting down without looking behind them, creating an enticing performance out of that simple act.

Zoe made them both a cup of rooibos tea to which Isabelle added a thin slice of lemon. Zoe sipped hers, watching a vague and distant look coming into Isabelle's eyes, as if she was suddenly there but elsewhere.

That looks like regret. Has Isabelle just realised that she's sort of cos-playing at being Madame Primo de Palotte and that soon the real châtelaine, Adélaïde, will return to squeeze her out once more?

The moment stretched out.

If Isabelle resents Adélaïde for 'stealing' her breakthrough in that movie – and also carries a torch for Primo – might her connections to the world of show business mean that she's a good candidate for being the author of the threatening letter? Several times I've noticed a certain distance or coldness between Adélaïde and Primo. If that's correct, could Isabelle's rumour-mongering be the cause?

Zoe couldn't help a frown from creasing her brow.

And might that have been Isabelle's precise intention?

Twenty-Five
'It Smells of Luxury'

After all the fiddly and sophisticated food preparation, Zoe felt in need of a shower. Leaving Isabelle in the kitchen, she quickly ascended the two flights of stairs, aware of a range of odours clinging to her hair, her clothes and her skin, principally the toasted garlic. They had been careful, however, not to burn any of the cooked ingredients, which would have left a stronger taint.

She collected her toiletries and a change of clothes from her bedroom and went to the closest shared bathroom on the dingy corridor. The shower didn't have very much pressure and was quite awkward to get underneath because it was too close to the taps of the bath. But, with a little gymnastic stretching and bending, she managed it, emerging from the hot water feeling pleasantly clean, but aware of a chilly draught from yet another ill-fitting window.

She was soon dressed again, choosing to put on her pale-blue woollen evening dress – the one she had packed 'just in case'. Before going downstairs, she decided to sit on the bed and try Maisie again. Her old friend picked up just as she was about to give up, on the tenth or twelfth ring.

'Oh, I am glad I caught you,' Zoe told her. 'Do you have ten minutes?'

Maisie told her that she did and asked: 'By the way, what sort of weather have you got in the south of France? I saw on the news that there's a fierce cold snap all the way from southern Spain, across to the Alps.'

'It's utterly Baltic,' said Zoe. 'Lots of the château's residents are out and about and I've begun to wonder if they might get snowed in at their respective destinations. Adélaïde has so many social responsibilities that we've barely been able to speak. Please can you tell me about what happened at Chichester Theatre. I only have vague memories of the drama.'

'That's reasonable. You were very much on the edge of those events.'

'Before we go back over it, can I tell you some more details of what's been happening here?' Zoe summed up – as concisely as she was able – all of her conversations and all of the dramatic events: the butler's tragic tumble; Primo's brother's unlikely one-night stand with Isabelle Valgarde; Boris's third wife's eyes, reddened with weeping; some smaller details and the sense that everyone was keeping up appearances but no one was truly happy.

'I suppose,' said Zoe, 'the thing I want to know is whether there is any truth in the idea that Adélaïde has something to be ashamed or guilty about. I know you don't feel you have the right, but could you unbend just a little? I promise it will go no further.'

'You can't promise that, Zoe,' said Maisie, gently. 'Should there be an official investigation, you will be bound to tell the truth, the whole truth—'

'And nothing but the truth,' said Zoe, completing the ritual phrase. 'Please, though? I know, if you were here, you would want me to help Adélaïde, but how can I if I'm uncertain what is true and what is . . . What do I mean?'

'Rumour-mongering,' said Maisie. 'All right. To begin at the beginning, I'm not sure how much you will remember, but the heart of the matter was the fact that the climax of the play, on stage at Chichester Festival Theatre, involved a set of gallows and a safety line.'

'Something was tampered with?'

'Exactly, and only the cast and crew had access at the crucial time. The murder played out in front of an appreciative but unsuspecting audience of more than twelve hundred.'

'How awful,' said Zoe.

'I was helping to coach Adélaïde with the archaic English text, but the important thing is this. The person who was sent to prison for the murder was, undoubtedly, the perpetrator. The only area of doubt was whether they might have had an accomplice – not someone who, metaphorically, loaded the gun, if you see what I mean, but who might have done something to prevent the crime . . . but chose not to.'

Maisie left a pause. As on her previous phone call, Zoe sort of 'heard' the distance between them, the eight hundred miles of snowbound continental Europe and damp British Isles.

'And Adélaïde might have been that person?' she tentatively asked. 'Did you confront Adélaïde with the question?'

'Of course.'

'What did she say?'

'She tapped her very white teeth with a well-kept fingernail and told me: "Maisie, you think of everything." In other words, she refused to be drawn.'

'And now, looking back, what do you think?'

'Given all you have told me, I wonder if there might be someone out there, with knowledge of those events, who is asking themselves that same question, aware that celebrity guilt is a popular interest in the worst of the media, and is hoping to profit from it.'

'And the victim?'

'He was an awful man. I did have sympathy for him. His life was cut short. He might have learned the error of his ways and changed for the better. No one knows the future. Avaricious, selfish and bullying though he was, change was not beyond him. Change is not beyond any of us.'

An argument began in the background. For a full minute, Zoe listened to Maisie speaking calmly to two residents of the Bunting Manor respite home, then Maisie returned, saying: 'I'll have to go. Call me back tomorrow or the day after, so I know that all is well.'

'You think there's something I should be worried about?'

'*Mieux vaut prévenir que guérir,*' Maisie told her. 'Off you go. All my love.'

'And to you, too.'

Zoe ended the call, a thoughtful expression on her face.

That's an interesting phrase Maisie used: 'Mieux vaut prévenir que guérir.' *But is it always 'best to prevent rather than cure'? I sometimes feel that trying to do so can make the bad outcome more likely.*

Throughout the telephone conversation, Zoe had been sitting on the side of her bed. She noted with frustration that her phone hadn't continued to charge and gently moved the plug in the fragile socket to reconnect it. She was also feeling very cold in just the blue wool dress and bare feet. She remedied that by pulling on some warm winter tights. She compromised her usual preference for flat footwear with a pair of sensible 'character' shoes that she had kept from her theatre days, black with a blocky heel.

She looked through the remainder of the clothes she had brought, discovering there was nothing she could reasonably add to her top half, unless she was to wear her camel-hair coat indoors. She decided to check Adélaïde's wardrobe, sure that her friend would have something suitable for her to borrow.

The corridor was empty and the door to Adélaïde's dressing room unlocked, as before. She went inside, finding it very tidy, with everything put away and all the drawers and cupboards closed.

Because she needed something longish to go with her evening gown, she tried the full-height wardrobe and found a glorious velvet dress coat in deep purple that would work perfectly with the pale-blue wool. She tried it on, turning left and right in front of an antique *cheval* mirror on a mahogany stand. On the left breast, a delightful silver brooch, in the form of the Palotte family crest, glinted luxuriously. Annoyingly, the lace fringe at the cuff caught on the winder of her watch.

She was about to take her watch off when she heard the screechy front door opening and closing and, immediately after, Adélaïde's voice, telling Primo to go and sit by the fire in the dining room while she ran upstairs: 'For your medication.'

Zoe went and stood in the doorway, waiting for Adélaïde to appear from the stairwell. She soon did, looking serious and pressed for time.

'I'm sorry to be in the way,' Zoe told her, apologetically. 'Do you mind if I borrow this?'

'Absolutely not. It looks better with your colouring than it does on me,' said Adélaïde, probably untruthfully. She bustled inside the dressing room and disappeared through the communicating door into the bedroom, emerging fifteen seconds later with a large plastic pill sorter, with sections dividing it into the days of the week. 'Come downstairs and join us in five minutes,' she ordered. 'Not straight away. Give him some time.'

'I will.'

Zoe felt a wave of anxiety on Primo's behalf, but also at a loose end. Of course, she was going to do as Adélaïde had asked, but was unsure how to occupy herself.

Five minutes of doing nothing in someone else's dressing room is a long time.

She smiled to herself.

I should have brought a book.

Her smile became a frown.

Actually, I must find something to read in bed this evening. Primo said everyone would be tired and go to bed early.

There was no bookshelf in Adélaïde's dressing room, so she had another riffle through the wardrobe, mildly interested to see what else might be in there. Not being a 'dedicated follower of fashion', it didn't detain her long.

She moved on to the dressing table. It was crowded with toiletries and hairbrushes, an eyelash curler, a pair of tweezers, a smoothly polished olive-wood jewellery tree with multiple branches, on which were perched or draped a dozen rings and seven or eight necklaces and bracelets.

To her delight, among the cosmetics, Zoe found a huge flagon of Chanel Number 5, a perfume that she knew had become horribly unfashionable but which she adored. She used the glass stopper to dab some on her neck and wrists and smiled with delight.

It smells of luxury to me. I don't care what other people say.

She returned the huge perfume bottle – it still had a cardboard ticket tied around the neck indicating that it was a Christmas gift from Primo – to its gap in front of the mirror. Tucked into the frame, between the silvered glass and the polished teak, was a sheet of A4 printer paper, folded over four times into a narrow strip. Zoe wouldn't have given it any thought, except for the fact that she could, by chance, see the first few lines at the top of the page, beginning with: *Dramatis Personae.*

It was a Latin phrase that she knew well, meaning 'cast of characters'. Also visible were two names on separate lines beneath, Adélaïde's own and that of the murder victim from the tragedy at Chichester Festival Theatre.

Zoe felt a sudden, unnatural stillness. She didn't want to move the piece of paper, for fear of Adélaïde noticing, but had an almost irresistible temptation to do so. Then, on reflection, she realised that she didn't have to. She knew what the rest of the list must comprise.

Adélaïde has been thinking over those events and has written out a list of everyone present, starting with herself because she must have been 'number one on the call sheet', as Isabelle would say. Then, I bet, she's gone down through the company, including the director and general manager and the lighting technician and everyone else she could remember.

Zoe heard a ticking sound that she thought was coming from the heating pipes under the floorboards, expanding as the boiler down in the basement accelerated its work for the increasingly bitter cold of the evening.

I wonder what conclusions she came to.

Twenty-Six

'To Kill Me and Resurrect Me'

Eventually, Zoe decided that Adélaïde's requested pause for five minutes without interruption for Primo were up. She left Adélaïde's dressing room, removed her watch – because its winder was still catching on the lace cuff of the dress coat – and left it on the bedside table in her room. Then she descended the stairs to find Primo and Adélaïde huddled close to the fire in the dining room, having pulled two heavy chairs away from the long table, close to the flames. Zoe saw that they had banked the fire up with almost all the remaining logs. She picked up the enormous woven-willow basket and told them: 'I'll go and refill this.'

They both turned their heads to look at her, rather blankly, Adélaïde with a vague smile that didn't quite reach her eyes and Primo with a bad colour, pasty and damp.

'Where will you go?' asked Adélaïde. 'Not out into the wilds of this terrible weather?'

'There's a stack of logs in the boiler room. Didn't you know?'

'Oh, yes. I suppose I might have done.'

'I assume they're kept there so they become good and dry?'

'Possibly,' said Primo. Then he sighed and said: 'We will miss Alain in more ways than we yet know.'

Zoe left them and lugged the basket carefully downstairs, calling out to Isabelle who replied from the modern bathroom next to Monsieur Alain's lonely room.

'Like you, I've taken a shower. I'll be up shortly.'

Zoe noticed that Isabelle had used the intervening time well, folding a stack of paper serviettes into the shapes of fifty or sixty graceful swans. They made a surreal sight because the only place Isabelle had found to put them, once made, was on the floor.

The logs in the boiler room were very dry and, therefore, surprisingly light. Zoe picked them up in pairs, knocking them together to dislodge any spiders. She was still able to lift the large basket, even when it was laden above the brim.

But there aren't many left behind.

She lugged the basket upstairs, navigating the staircase cautiously. Adélaïde and Primo were still on their hard chairs, but they looked more comfortable, sitting back from the flames. Zoe noticed the pill dispenser in Primo's hand, sort of drooping from his slack fingers, and feared it might fall to the floor.

Perhaps coming open and mixing up all the different medications.

She put the basket down in the corner of the hearth, within the brass fender.

Someone ought to find some metal polish for that. It's already not gleaming like it did yesterday, when Monsieur Alain was still alive to look after it.

'How was your party?' she asked.

'Lunch was late,' said Adélaïde. 'We stood about and talked until we had nothing left to say to one another, then we had to sit down and make more conversation at the table.'

'What did they serve?'

'Cassoulet, would you believe?' Adélaïde scoffed. 'The idea?'

'At least it was lunchtime, not evening,' said Primo, quietly.

'What's wrong with cassoulet?' asked Zoe, innocently.

'The heavy meat, the fat, the indigestible beans, the thick congealing paste at the side of one's plate . . .'

'Wholesome and sustaining,' said Primo with a weak smile.

'But it didn't agree with you, did it?' insisted his wife.

'And the people?' prompted Zoe.

'We should have been eight but it was just us and our hosts, the so-called cinema aficionados. Two sets of other guests were unable to come due to the snow and ice – a likely excuse.'

'I've not been out. Is it very bad?'

'The snow is persistent and it's cold enough to be accumulating in every dip. And these country roads are not the ones the authorities think of gritting. Perhaps we shouldn't go out again until this cold snap is over.'

'Was it dangerous?'

'Adélaïde is a very good driver,' said Primo, formally. 'I felt quite safe.'

There was a pause. Zoe contemplated her old friend and mentor.

Adélaïde always seemed to me the sort of person who would live slightly apart from the world, managing her relationships at arm's length, like in Isabelle's image of her as an albatross alighting on the rigging of Primo's clipper.

Adélaïde tenderly took the pills from Primo's hand.

If it's true that he's seriously ill, I think Adélaïde will miss him very much when he's gone. I had no idea she was so devoted to him.

'Is there anything else I can do for you?' Zoe asked. 'Should I contact a doctor?'

'No, thank you,' said Primo. 'I will soon go into hospital for what they call an "intervention". It may moderate or cure my condition, or it may not be successful at all, in which case we will progress to a more drastic option, if they consider me strong enough.'

Zoe waited to know more, not wanting to ask. It was Adélaïde who explained.

'Primo suffers from atrial fibrillation. That means his heart beats fast and slow, mostly fast, and sometimes dances the fandango.'

She said this with a smile, though her eyes were creased with worry.

'That must be exhausting,' said Zoe.

'It is,' said Primo. 'The stairs . . .' he told her, waving a vague hand. 'Up and down and up and down . . .'

'The château probably isn't very practical.'

'No,' said Primo, 'but some things in life must not be . . . You see, I am a link in a chain, not the chain itself.'

'You wouldn't consider living somewhere more practical, perhaps with professional medical attention?'

'You make a good point, Zoe,' said Adélaïde. 'What a good idea.'

She spoke with an edge of gentle irony, as if taking advantage of Zoe suggesting it to reinforce a suggestion that she had made many times herself.

'Some things cannot be mended,' said Primo. 'If the medical profession is incapable of improving my condition, does that mean I should give up on the things most dear to me – this house, the grounds, my deer, my sense of my own past and the legacy of those who came before me?'

He spoke very quietly and looked calmer and less pasty than when Zoe had first reappeared with her basket of logs. Zoe thought about mentioning the broken gates and the escaped stag, but decided to stick to the current topic. 'I don't know anything about atrial fibrillation. Is it something people live with for a long time?'

'It can be,' he told her. 'The irregular and accelerated pulse brings a risk of clots. Should a clot arrive in the lungs or the brain, it can be fatal or, perhaps worse, create a life-changing disability that might render survival a burden rather than a blessing. My brother Boris is also a sufferer. Did I say that?'

'How awful for you both. And the drugs you take? I suppose they slow your heart down?'

'Beta blockers and thinners, among other things,' he told her. 'They do their best.'

'Primo goes into hospital next week,' said Adélaïde. 'Can you imagine what they are going to do?'

'I have no clue,' said Zoe.

'They will stop his heart and start it again.'

'Good heavens.'

'I suppose it can be said,' mused Primo, 'that they intend to kill me and resurrect me.'

'How will they do that?' asked Zoe, glad to see that he was smiling at the extraordinary idea.

'With a giant needle, apparently,' said Primo. 'The consultant told me it was like "rebooting a computer". I had to break it to him that I had no clue what that meant. He explained – like me, he is an Anglophile – something to do with "boot straps"?'

He said the last two words in English and Zoe had to admit in reply that she didn't understand the image, either.

'The procedure is called cardioversion,' said Adélaïde, her voice brittle and worried. 'If it doesn't work or if it only works for a little while, they will proceed to another one called ablation with cryo-therapy and hot wires burning away malfunctioning tissue.'

'Is that what it is?' asked Primo, mildly. 'I was refraining from looking too far ahead. Boris is always trying to make me talk about a future I may never see.'

'You seem much more yourself than when I first came down,' said Zoe.

He touched the tips of his fingers against the pulse in his opposite wrist. After half a minute, he announced: 'About ninety, almost normal.'

Isabelle arrived with two of the ten platters of canapés. She laid them on the white tablecloth and said, with a flourish:

'Zoe and I have worked wonders. She has a gift for following orders.'

'How marvellous,' murmured Primo, a wary look on his face.

Adélaïde, however, was immediately on her feet, congratulating Isabelle: 'You are the best. I can't tell you how much I was dreading having to try and cobble together some inferior snacks. I am the worst hostess.'

'But you make up for your practical incompetence,' said Isabelle, evenly, 'with your exceptional charm.'

The expression of wariness on Primo's face deepened into worry. Zoe felt she ought to say something.

'Shall I help you bring up the other trays?'

'Please do.'

Isabelle left the dining room and Zoe followed, aware of a murmured conversation between Adélaïde and Primo behind her.

Each time I see them meet, Adélaïde makes a big effort with Isabelle. What I thought was friendship is, in fact, condescension – perhaps even guilt?

Downstairs, she and Isabelle picked up another two trays each and brought them up without stopping for further conversation. Primo was toying with the telescopic brass toasting fork and Adélaïde was straightening the curtains, drawn across the cold glass, shutting out the darkening, snowy landscape.

Still without another word, Isabelle returned to the basement kitchen. Zoe accompanied her and, together, they brought up the remaining four trays of twenty-four canapés each.

That makes two hundred and forty in total, in all their varied splendour of colours and contrasting flavours. How many people are coming? If it's the same crew we saw in the market hall, I'd say about fifty. Add in the residents of the château and that makes only four canapés each. It doesn't seem enough, even for a stand-up drinks party.

The answer to this conundrum came straight away. The doorbell rang and Isabelle told Zoe: 'That will be Gaspard Astor.'

Zoe went to answer and discovered the *boulanger* standing on the rubber outdoor mat, his shoulders hunched against a squall of snow, carrying two enormous rectangular baking dishes, each one fifty centimetres across and seventy centimetres long, hot and steaming from the oven.

'*Tarte aux poireaux,*' he announced, '*et quiche aux lardons.*'

Zoe adored a rich and savoury leek tart so she was delighted. She could take or leave the bacon quiche. Because she had hesitated, Gaspard Astor smiled and used the French equivalent of the English waiter's warning 'mind your backs'.

'*Chaud devant.*'

She stepped aside and he took them directly to the dining room, indicating to Zoe that he knew the house well and was a welcome – perhaps frequent – guest.

Or, rather, a welcome help. He's an employee, in the end, isn't he? He doesn't have a closer connection?

'Thank you, Monsieur Astor,' said Primo, politely, rising from his hard chair by the fire and shaking the man's hand. 'They look marvellous.'

'They're still wobbly but let them sit for twenty minutes and they'll finish setting.'

'Will Didier be joining us?'

'My son wouldn't miss it,' said the *boulanger*. 'Speaking of which, I must go and change.'

He left and no one troubled to show him out, reinforcing the idea that he was used to coming and going without ceremony. Isabelle enlisted Zoe's help in bringing all the swan serviettes up from the basement, which took several trips because they had to be balanced on trays in precarious piles and seemed determined to fall to the floor. In the end, they managed it.

'I should have made the swans up here,' said Isabelle, smiling.

Surprised by an unexpected lightness in her mood, Zoe realised that it was because she and Isabelle were alone once more.

I suppose Adélaïde and Primo have gone to change.

Isabelle spent some time rearranging the table and asked Zoe to fetch 'some implements for cutting the tart and the quiche'.

Zoe concealed her weariness. The dining room was very warm from the huge fire Adélaïde had built up, especially since she had shut the curtains on the cold glass of the tall windows. Zoe removed her borrowed velvet dress coat and hung it over the back of one of the chairs. The pin of the silver brooch came loose so she reattached it more securely, but it remained precarious, the metal old and tired.

Yet again, she descended to the basement kitchen, at first searching in the wide utensil drawers. Finding nothing suitable, she chose instead the two largest knives from the block on the stainless-steel counter. They were long and well kept, with bone handles, each keen blade sharpened by hand to a wicked edge.

She brought them back upstairs, recognising that Isabelle had made the table look lovely, the trays of canapés offering their enticing variety of colours and promised flavours, between the flocks of pristine paper swans, and the two enormous rectangular tarts, one at either end.

'You would make a wonderful *châtelaine*,' said Zoe, then regretted it as she remembered the complicated circumstances – the fact that Isabelle had been beaten to Primo's affections by Adélaïde and had more recently, to her great regret, become entangled with the inferior twin, Boris. 'I'm sorry – that was a silly thing to say.'

'No, I agree with the sentiment, if not the tense. Shall we say, rather, that I "would have made" a wonderful *châtelaine*?'

Zoe could think of nothing to say in reply. She felt foolish, staring at Isabelle's remarkably symmetrical face, so like Adélaïde's but with a sadness in her eyes that spoke of loneliness and disappointment.

*

Later on, when the worst had finally happened, Zoe would look back on this moment.

That was when I first felt sure of it – that events were moving inexorably towards more tragedy.

Twenty-Seven

'THEY ARE VERY
DIFFERENT PEOPLE'

The next group to return home to the château was – and this still felt very bizarre to Zoe – Boris de Palotte and all three of his wives, resembling a strange, multigenerational family. As she helped the patrician Marie-France out of her coat, she thought again about the fact that Boris's first two marriages had been ended by infidelity.

On both sides, that's the interesting thing. After all, it's not unusual to hear about a man with wealth or power or celebrity – or all three – trading in an older wife for a younger one every now and then.

'Next year, Boris,' said Marie-France, 'however much it makes you feel like the "big man", I will decline to play *Snakes and Ladders* with the village children.'

She stalked off down the corridor. Sweetie told her husband that she was going upstairs, too.

'Come up. I want to talk to you,' she added in a small voice.

'Yes, dear.'

'Will you play this with me?' Junior asked his mother in a plaintive voice. He was holding a chess set that, from the partial wrapping paper still clinging to it, looked as though it had been gifted by the village in parallel to the actual birthdays of the elderly twins. 'Just for one game?'

'I don't know how,' said Sweetie, sadly.

'I'll show you,' insisted Junior. 'Uncle Primo taught me.'

Zoe remembered being told about Junior being difficult and fractious, a year or two earlier, over board games that were probably too advanced for him.

'We can all play,' said Sweetie. 'But not right now.'

The three of them moved off, leaving Zoe with Elizabeth who told Zoe, once the others were out of earshot: 'It drives me wild how inattentive they are, almost as if they are deliberately being unkind to that boy as a sort of cruel experiment.'

'You can't mean that.'

'It's almost criminal. And I wouldn't be surprised if, the older and frailer Boris becomes, the more Sweetie will like it. She will increasingly be in charge.'

'I hadn't looked at it like that. I suppose that's natural in a May-to-December relationship. The younger partner takes over more and more of the practical responsibilities. But is that Sweetie's natural domain?'

'She was a professional PA, remember, when she entered our orbit.'

Elizabeth sat down on the oak carver chair to take off her outside boots. 'I'm going to have a word with the boy.'

Zoe wasn't listening. She was lost in thought.

If Elizabeth is right about Boris and Sweetie, that makes Boris's one-night stand with Isabelle Valgarde all the more surprising. Sweetie is perhaps prepared to care for him in his inevitable 'slow shipwreck' of age, as Primo called it, but I don't think that role would suit the ex-actress Isabelle.

Zoe asked what they had all been up to in the village and Elizabeth told her the story of their luncheon and afternoon. Apparently, the event had taken place in a community hall and had comprised a delightful pot-luck meal to which a dozen villagers had brought concoctions based on old family recipes, all of them inspired by the ingredients of southern France.

'That sounds charming. You were there quite a long time, though. What happened next?'

'There were board games.' Elizabeth laughed. 'I know it sounds childish, but it's a bit of a tradition in the village in winter. I think it comes from the fact that, historically, this area has often been cut off by snow and ice.'

'Really?'

'Yes, quite regularly.' In response to Zoe's pained expression, Elizabeth added: 'But never for very long. There's no need to worry.'

'You didn't have any mishaps on the way back to the château on foot? When I let you in, I could see the snow was still falling and lying deeper and deeper.'

'We did not. All is well,' said Elizabeth, reassuringly.

'Have you looked up an accurate forecast?'

'Whether the forecasting is accurate or not is a moot point. Time will tell. The geography around Saint-Paul-de-Palotte means that we live in a microclimate.'

'Everybody always says that,' replied Zoe, with a smile. 'People always think that their particular locale has special weather.'

'In our case, it's true. Anyway, how have you got on?'

'I've been helping in the kitchen. You were right to ask Isabelle for help. She was marvellous. Oh, by the way, I did wonder if you might have a book that you could lend me? It's silly, isn't it, given I own a bookshop? I forgot to pack one and I do like to read in bed before going to sleep.'

'What sort of thing do you like?'

Zoe told Elizabeth that, during the adventure that turned into 'the French bookshop murder', she had been reading a novel by Fred Vargas about a murderer who used the presence of wolves in the southern French landscape to cover up their crimes. 'I think she's a brilliant author and, oddly, that story ended up being a helpful touchstone in solving the mystery.'

'Then I have just the thing. And you won't need to worry about breaking the spine or turning down the pages. It's in paperback and I've already read it. Come up to my room and I'll find it for you.'

Zoe followed her up the two flights of stairs, her legs aching.

It's pretty full on – this whole birthday thing. Perhaps I'm making something out of nothing, thinking there's tension and unhappiness at every turn. It might just be a reaction to the constant pressure on everybody to be upbeat and bright and conversational at every moment. And poor Monsieur Alain's death has made that much harder.

Zoe followed Elizabeth into her room, noticing again the particular atmosphere of a place where purposeful work was done, rather than just another social space.

Where time is merely passed.

The paperback book that Elizabeth had promised was another Fred Vargas novel entitled *Quand sort la recluse*, meaning 'when the recluse emerges'. It reminded Zoe of her worry about biting spiders in the woodpile because the 'brown recluse', though tiny, was common in the south of France, equipped with an evil necrotic venom.

'In the novel, does the murderer use spider venom as a weapon?' she asked.

'You'll have to read it and find out,' said Elizabeth with a smile.

Faint with distance, the front doorbell rang again. Zoe thanked Elizabeth for the book and ran downstairs with it in her hand. When she got there, she saw that the handle was moving but not completely disengaging the latch, as if the person outside was struggling. She opened up and found Patrick on the rubber mat with snow in his hair and two half-cases of wine bottles in his arms, trying to get in with his elbow. Behind him were Minette and Caroline, carrying a half-case each.

'Bravo,' said Zoe, with a smile, stepping aside. 'Essential supplies.'

They came gratefully indoors, out of the cold, stamping their showy shoes on the mat, before taking their burdens through to the dining room where they put them down on the dresser at the far end.

'Twelve white and twelve red,' explained Patrick. 'We picked them up direct from the vineyard, from your friend and ours, Marcel Maurice. We barely got up the track to his yard. What time is it?'

'It feels like five-thirty, maybe a bit later,' Zoe told him. 'Did you have a difficult journey? You all look quite frazzled.'

'We had a spin on one of the roundabouts,' said Patrick.

'It was very foolish,' said Minette.

'It was dangerous,' insisted Caroline, crossly. 'Patrick was driving too fast.'

There was genuine bad feeling between them, Caroline unhappy to have been put in danger and Patrick resentful of the criticism.

'The roads are becoming icy, then?' Zoe asked, mildly.

'Yes, they are,' said Caroline. 'Obviously.' She left the room, calling back over her shoulder: 'I'm going to change.'

Zoe, Patrick and Minette had the room to themselves.

'Did you enjoy your lunch?' she asked.

'Not bad, then we went to the cinema,' said Patrick.

'What did you see?'

'An old movie of Adélaïde's from when she wasn't so famous – no longer the gorgeous ingénue but not yet one of her serious mature roles. It was very pretentious. She was only in four or five scenes.'

Zoe told them: 'I'm just thinking back to when I first knew her and she was always sort of "searching" for her performance. Do you know what I mean? It gave her a kind of yearning quality on screen and on stage. I think her audiences responded to the earnestness of her desire to give the best of herself, beyond how wonderfully she was dressed, how gorgeous her appearance.'

'You really are a devoted friend, aren't you,' said Minette, and it sounded like a criticism.

'She was extremely good to me,' said Zoe. 'I owe her my career in theatre.'

'How come?' asked Patrick.

'I attended the Avignon Festival as her assistant, one summer in the early Seventies, and it just went from there. Perhaps you don't know, but theatre is a tight world and opportunities tend to come from people you've met, people you've already formed relationships with. It's a microcosm of life, I suppose. It's easier, isn't it, for your next project to include the people with whom you worked successfully on your last project?'

'Except with family,' said Minette, grumpily. 'You don't choose your family.'

'You're lumbered with them,' said Patrick, with good humour.

Zoe looked from one to the other.

Despite their closeness – working together at the Auberge Sainte-Catherine and the fact that they are twins – they are very different people. And I wonder if they had bad news about their inheritance from the family meeting? Will there be complicated trusts like when Primo inherited, when Boris was pushed completely aside?

Patrick and Minette left the dining room in order, as Patrick said: 'To change into something that meets Primo's expectations.' The doorbell rang yet again. Zoe went to answer, wondering how the family would have coped without her to take on some of Monsieur Alain's duties.

It was once more Gaspard Astor, the *boulanger*, this time with his son Didier. They were both dressed in lounge suits, Astor Senior's burly physique straining against the buttons of his navy-blue jacket, while Didier appeared almost swamped, as if his suit had been chosen with the expectation that he might grow into it.

'Not a delivery, this time,' said Monsieur Astor, with a smile. 'Are we early?'

Without her watch, Zoe told them: 'Bang on time, I think.'

She took them through to the dining room and the two bakers, father and son, set about cutting the enormous quiches into portions with the very sharp knives Zoe had brought up from the kitchen. Monsieur Astor told her about the recipes they had used and Didier chipped in with details of the provenance of the ingredients – 'all local suppliers'. The conversation felt like a tennis match, with Zoe standing near the fireplace, turning her head left and right like an umpire, to each end of the long table.

'They both smell delicious, Monsieur Astor.'

'You must call me Gaspard, and Didier is Didi to his friends.'

'Pleased to meet you, Didi,' said Zoe. 'How wonderful to work together with your father. Was it always your ambition to go into the family business?'

'It just sort of happened,' said Didi, vaguely.

'What's your favourite part?' Zoe asked.

'At this time of year, the warmth of the kitchen. It's going down to minus four overnight. Did you know?'

'I didn't,' said Zoe, with an involuntary shiver.

'I suppose some of the guests might not come,' said Gaspard. 'The village cobbles are pretty treacherous. But we know that already, don't we? Poor Alain.'

'Yes,' said Zoe. 'I know Monsieur de Palotte wants it to be "business as usual", but it does seem sad that poor Monsieur Alain's death has been left behind in rather an abrupt way.'

'Those that have, they don't need to give much thought to those that don't,' said Didier.

It took Zoe a moment to grasp his meaning. She said: 'In the end, we have to accept that it's the way of the world, don't

we? In an important company, for example, when a successful chief executive takes a new job elsewhere, the machinery
of the organisation takes over and life goes on. Isn't that the
case with an employee like Monsieur Alain, however long
he's been here?'

'We don't want bad feeling,' said Gaspard, not to Zoe but
to his son. His tone was severe. 'You hear me?'

'All right,' said Didi resentfully. 'Don't go on.'

Zoe's heart sank.

Oh dear. The upsets extend beyond the walls of the château.

Twenty-Eight

'I'M SURE IT WAS AN ACCIDENT'

Of the family members, Patrick was the first to reappear, greeting Gaspard and Didi affectionately, with a strong and manly hug for each. Then he set about opening the wine bottles with professional competence, using a corkscrew that he carried in the fob pocket of his waistcoat, worn with a red turtleneck jumper, smart trousers and shiny shoes.

Minette came in, wearing a smart red suit in an almost masculine cut with a cream crew-neck sweater underneath. She and Didi seemed on very good terms. They retreated together to a corner of the room to discuss the French football season and the extraordinary price recently paid for a new star player by the league leaders, Paris Saint-Germain.

'Have you always lived in Saint-Paul-de-Palotte?' Zoe asked Gaspard.

'Man and boy. Born above the bakery. I'll leave in a box, like Monsieur Alain, or rather, given the way of the world, a body bag.'

He said it with a smile, shaking his head, comically, and Zoe laughed.

'When you put it like that, the modern world does seem rather harsh,' she replied. 'A wooden coffin is a kind of celebration, or rather a memorial, a way of honouring—'

He broke in: 'And the body bag is waste disposal.' He laughed, a hearty, infectious sound. 'I wonder if they're compostable, like we are?'

Marie-France arrived in a startlingly formal old-fashioned gown in ivory silk, with beaded decorations that caught the light. With her usual patrician manner, she made a circuit of the room, speaking a formal greeting to each person in turn, including her family members. Then she sat on a hard chair near the fire, waiting for others to come to her.

Marie-France was followed by Elizabeth who kissed both of her children on the cheeks and spoke briefly about the film they had seen, a book adaptation from the 'art-house' period of Adélaïde's career.

'And Adélaïde's performance carried it?' Zoe asked.

'Yes,' said Patrick.

'She barely had anything to do,' said Minette, surprising Zoe with her dismissive tone.

My first impression was that Adélaïde and Patrick and Minette were all three good friends, but perhaps that's not right. Or it was right – but something has happened to change that?

Elizabeth moved on to chat with the baker and his son. She had chosen a warm-looking navy-blue dress, like Zoe's in soft wool, with long sleeves and pockets on the hips.

The front doorbell rang and Zoe went to answer, meeting a group of seven or eight villagers. As she was letting them in, another half dozen were on their way up the slippery steps and two more were coming through the pedestrian gate. Zoe felt odd, wanting to shut the door between the groups to keep the heat in, but couldn't bring herself to do so because it felt rude.

As Didi predicted, the evening is turning increasingly bitter. It's lucky the wind is in the north-east, otherwise it would be blowing the snow and the cold inside.

She welcomed the newcomers, several of whom she recognised from the ceremony in the market hall, and found herself behaving as if she actually was the new butler, offering to take their coats. She ended up with an enormous armful of outdoor wear and, not knowing what else to do with it, carried it downstairs to pile on Monsieur Alain's sad, tidy bed. She returned to the dining room and discovered another group already attacking the canapés, but still in their hats and coats and scarves. She collected their bits and pieces and took them downstairs.

Yet again the doorbell rang. This time, because she was in the basement, trying to explain to Russell why she couldn't take him out for a walk, Patrick got there first. As she reached the hallway, she met a troop of at least a dozen more guests from the village. They were all very jolly and had no hats or coats to remove. One of them told Zoe: 'We decided to run up as we are.'

From further conversation she grasped that these were the fans of board games who, presumably, had been playing and drinking since their lunch with Boris and his side of the Palotte family and were now in the mood to continue imbibing in different premises.

The fire in the enormous dining-room hearth had burnt down so Zoe squatted and added a few logs.

Not too many, though, because of all the human warmth from the many new arrivals.

Standing, Zoe saw that Primo and Adélaïde and Isabelle had finally joined the party. For reasons that – had she been asked – she didn't feel quite able to explain, she felt absolutely certain that they had arrived late, having snuck away somewhere private for their own important triangular conversation.

Do I think that because they've instantly scattered through the room, far from one another? I hope they've managed to unpack some of the awkwardness between them and turn a new page.

The party as a whole was going with a swing. Zoe felt proud that the canapés were all received with 'oohs' and 'ahs' of appreciation. She noticed that Gaspard and Didier remained at opposite ends of the dining table and were helping serve the leek tart and bacon quiche, shaking out the decorative serviette swans for the guests to use as plates. Meanwhile, Minette was offering drinks from the dresser, having opened the doors on the shelves of crystal wine glasses. They added to the gaiety by catching the light with their multiple facets.

Still more guests arrived, including an elderly woman using an aluminium walker with little wheels at the front of the frame. Zoe helped her to a chair near the hearth, beside Marie-France, finding that the woman's ungloved hands were like blocks of ice. Zoe talked to her about the weather and the frigid forecast, then the woman wanted to know how it was that Zoe spoke 'such excellent French with barely an accent'. She explained that she had been taught by her older half-sister, Maisie, who was 'properly bilingual'.

Because she was busy chatting, it was Patrick who went to answer the door for what turned out to be one last time, welcoming a family with a teenage daughter and a younger son, perhaps eight or nine years old. In this younger brother, she was pleased to see that Junior seemed to have found a friend. The boy had brought with him a small Nintendo console with a built-in screen. He and Junior immediately huddled in a corner, both perched on the same hard dining chair, observing with rapt attention the progress of their digital adventure.

Zoe excused herself from the elderly visitor in order to do her duty and circulate. She found herself explaining several times, in more or less the same words, how she came to have given up her London life in theatre to acquire the bookshop in Sainte-Catherine. That, of course, led on to a discussion of 'the French bookshop murder' and her role in bringing the facts to light. On the third occasion, telling the story as concisely as she was able, Didi Astor happened to be alongside. She soon realised that he knew almost as much about the events as she did herself, having followed them in the press and online.

'In one of the reports I read,' he told her, 'it said that you were involved in several murders when you were a girl.'

'When I was a young woman, not a girl,' Zoe told him.

'You were sixteen,' he argued. 'Is that not a girl?'

'I don't think so,' said Zoe, patiently. 'When you were sixteen years old, I imagine you thought of yourself as a young man, not as a child?'

'Maybe,' said Didi, grudgingly. 'Anyway, is it true?'

'I wasn't exactly involved. I knew people who were involved.'

'It must have been very exciting. Nothing ever happens in Saint-Paul-de-Palotte.' He lowered his voice. 'Don't tell my father I said so, but I can't wait to leave.'

'What does your mother think?'

'She left us, when I was tiny.'

'Oh, I'm very sorry. Please accept my sympathy.'

'I don't mean she died. She left us,' he repeated, in a tone that suggested Zoe had said something foolish. 'But I was too young to notice.'

I'm not sure that can be true. Babies and infants are aware of what's happening around them. Even if he doesn't acknowledge it, this young man must have a traumatic memory of abandonment – like I do.

'Do you ever see her?' asked Zoe.

She didn't receive an answer because, just then, they were joined by Elizabeth who, Zoe realised, had been hovering nearby, looking for an opportunity to join the conversation.

'Would you give me one of those last few pieces of bacon quiche?' she asked with a smile.

'That's a coincidence,' said Didi. 'We were almost just talking about you.'

Watching him lift a square on the flat of his long, sharp knife, Zoe wondered what that meant. He slid it onto the paper napkin that Elizabeth held in her left hand and, as he drew the blade away, it nicked the pad of her thumb, drawing a tiny drop of blood.

'Oh, dear,' said Zoe, reaching for a clean paper swan.

'No matter,' said Elizabeth in a strange voice. 'I'm sure it was an accident.'

She pressed her thumb against the side of her forefinger and moved away.

'She fidgeted,' said Didi. 'I didn't do it on purpose.'

Zoe was taken aback.

Good heavens. He sounds just like Junior, putting that stick on the fire, hoping it would be destroyed by the flames.

Twenty-Nine

'A PICTURE OF DESPAIR'

Didi's face had closed up like a clam, watching Elizabeth move quickly away, squeezing the nick to her thumb to stop it bleeding.

'Perhaps she did fidget,' said Zoe, calmly. 'What did you mean when you said: "We were almost just talking about you"? Which bit, exactly?'

Didi seemed to be weighing up whether he wanted to answer when Patrick suddenly addressed the noisy room, in a loud voice, clapping his hands to gather everyone's attention.

I'll have to find a moment to come back to this. Maybe I can get him on his own at the baker's shop. I have an idea there's a deeper connection to the Palotte family than I expected – perhaps even with Adélaïde's worries.

The general conversation ebbed and Patrick added, in the same carrying voice: 'As is traditional, the birthday drinks will be marked by a toast proposed by the oldest guest.' He was standing in front of the fire, which had burnt very low. He put a hand on the shoulder of the elderly woman who Zoe had helped into the party and announced her name: 'Madame Constant.'

She got to her feet with the aid of her walking frame and stood, a little stooped but bright-eyed, glancing up at Patrick in anticipation of performing her duty. There was a brief kerfuffle as anyone with an empty glass made sure that they had something with which to drink the elderly twins' health.

'Shall I?' she asked.

'The floor is yours,' Patrick told her, then addressed the room: 'Primo, Boris, I give you the doyenne of Saint-Paul-de-Palotte, Emilie Constant.'

'Thank you,' she said, then left a pause before beginning what sounded to Zoe like a speech learned by heart. 'If it is true that wrinkles show us, on the faces of the elderly, how much, in youth, they smiled, I must have spent my early years grinning like an idiot because my face resembles a dried prune.' Everyone laughed. 'If it is true that age should be counted not in years but in the number of friends accumulated over a lifetime of good deeds, it is no wonder that there are seventy of us and more in this room this evening.' People smiled and someone said 'bravo'. She resumed. 'Youth is a gift of nature and—'

She was interrupted by Junior and his friend fidgeting with the tiny screen. As Sweetie told them to stop playing, Boris strode over, snatched the device out of their hands and put it out of reach on the high mantelpiece above the hearth.

There was a horrible silence. Eventually, Madame Constant tried to restore the lighter mood.

'We are all friends here, I like to think. I was saying, while youth is a gift, freely given, age is a work of art, refined each day, which is why I'm such a masterpiece.' Fewer people laughed at this second witticism. 'Those of you who read your Bible or who remember your Sunday school lessons will recognise this text from *Proverbs*: "The rich person is not one who possesses much. The rich person is one who is content with what he has." I won't presume to judge Primo de Palotte's state of happiness, but I will add that he makes every effort to share his good fortune.' She left a tiny pause, then added: 'Supported, I don't doubt, by his brother, Boris.' There was a very muted reaction to this idea. 'Anyway, never mind youth. Age is cause for celebration. And three-score years and ten are plenty to justify this sumptuous week of merriment. Let us raise our glasses, with best wishes for life, health and continued happiness, to Primo and Boris.'

'Primo and Boris,' everyone chorused and drank.

Primo gave a brief speech in reply, including gracious thanks to the mayor – who, Zoe recalled, was Madame Emilie Constant's daughter – for her service to the village. Everyone drank again and, for a few seconds, that seemed to be it. Then Boris suggested a prayer.

'Perhaps I might lead with a few words of my own devising?' He didn't wait for an answer, solemnly intoning: 'Dear Lord, bless this house and all who live in it, as well as our dear friends and neighbours. Deliver us from the deadly sins of lust, gluttony, sloth, wrath, envy, pride and avarice.'

He left a pause, giving Zoe the distinct impression that he thought that certain people in the room needed to hear the 'capital vices' enumerated in order to recognise their trespasses. She couldn't help herself glancing around, but saw no obviously guilty faces.

Boris switched his attention to the seven holy virtues – chastity, temperance, charity, diligence, kindness, patience and humility – somehow giving the impression that he represented an avatar of each.

It's probably difficult to tell him not to go on like this. It's hard to insist that it's not an appropriate moment for a prayer.

Zoe saw that Adélaïde was helping Primo into a chair. He looked very drawn. Finally, after some further improvised pieties, Boris concluded.

'Peace be upon you,' he told them all. 'Amen.'

There was a chorus of 'amens' in reply, in a tone that suggested not piety but relief that the uncomfortable moment was finally over.

How is it that he feels empowered to bless this 'congregation'? Surely 'peace be upon you' is a phrase that belongs in the mouth of an ordained minister?

Chatter resumed as a queue of villagers approached Primo – who Adélaïde wouldn't allow to stand, though his punctilious manners demanded that he ought – offering their own personal good wishes. From the words exchanged, Zoe understood that each of them was, after all, happy with their new-year bonuses.

But those who aren't happy are perhaps not coming near?

Sweetie had returned the Nintendo and was taking a kind interest in the game. Boris, Zoe realised, was standing alone with no one to talk to. The party as a whole was shifting and flowing, while the younger Palotte twin – by just ten minutes – stood friendless and disregarded on the hearthrug.

She watched Boris turn to the log basket, fish out a lump of well-seasoned Mediterranean oak and toss it onto the dying embers.

Then he leaned a hand on the stone mantelpiece, bowing his head onto his braced forearm, looking for all the world like a picture of despair.

Thirty

'She's Not Quite Herself'

Time moved on and Zoe began to feel that she would give a lot of money for the chance to sit down and keep still and silent for half an hour. Then people began requesting the return of their outdoor apparel and, for the next fifteen minutes, Zoe was kept busy between the basement and the dining room, fetching coats and hats and scarves.

Eventually, all the visitors from the village had gone and the older residents of the château bid one another goodnight and disappeared to their respective bedrooms. Sweetie led Junior away by the hand. The time was a little after nine and everyone seemed drained and not particularly fulfilled.

In the dining room, Zoe frowned at the many crumbs and fragments of food scattered across the bare antique floorboards. Lots of paper serviettes had also been allowed to drop without being picked up, the rest scattered about. Patrick was busy shaving the edges of a cork to force it back into an unfinished bottle while Minette was damping down the fire, making sure the logs had settled in the embers and ash.

'What normally happens?' Zoe asked. 'Do you leave all this for the morning?'

'We are constitutionally unable to do that,' said Patrick.

'It won't take long with three pairs of hands,' said Minette, without resentment.

She seems much happier. Perhaps she just doesn't like crowds of people.

'How shall we go about it?'

'We'll burn the lot,' said Minette.

Zoe and Patrick collected the serviettes while Minette piled up the empty cardboard canapé platters. They put everything on the dying fire, including the scraps of waste food, and the whole lot burnt up in a blaze of flame.

The Astors had taken away their big rectangular baking trays but on every surface – mantelpiece, dresser, side table, main table, even the seats of some of the chairs – were discarded crystal wine glasses, most of them empty, but a few still containing the dregs of their final servings.

Patrick ran to fetch two large tea trays from the kitchen – the ones Isabelle and Zoe had used earlier to bring up the paper swans – and he and his sister took all the glasses downstairs in two journeys. Zoe followed to help stack them in the dishwasher while Russell weaved in and out between their ankles. Zoe served him some more hard kibble but he wasn't hungry. He needed to go out.

'I must take my dog into the vegetable garden for ten minutes. Then shall we push the hoover round the dining room?'

'We don't want to do it now, do we?' said Patrick.

'We'll be out for a run again early,' said Minette, 'but I'm happy to help after that.'

'We're not trying to avoid it,' said Patrick, smiling broadly. 'We're so used to it, working in the Auberge, that cleaning and tidying are as easy as breathing. By the way, has anybody told you you've been a wonderful help?'

'I was happy to make a contribution—' Zoe began.

'You've gone above and beyond. Have you and Adélaïde had a chance to talk?'

'Barely,' said Zoe, then she asked with feigned innocence: 'Does she have something special to say, do you think?'

'She's not herself,' he told her.

'I'm not sure what you mean by that.' Her mind went back to something that had made her feel uncomfortable and unwelcome. Now they were alone, it seemed a good moment to ask. 'Am I right, you were discussing me when Caroline and I came back from our walk? What were you saying?'

Zoe had made an effort to ask her question without resentment. Patrick took it in his stride.

'Just how much she appreciates you, and I told her a few ins and outs from the murder in Sainte-Catherine. Of, course, it strikes quite close to home for Adélaïde. I think this true-crime thing she's got involved with is worrying her.'

'Too close to home,' said Minette.

Russell yapped and Zoe realised that it wouldn't be fair to delay any longer, though she wished she could hear more.

'All right. Let's meet again after your morning run and complete the cleaning and tidying.'

'Agreed,' said the others in unison, then they all three laughed and the twins left her with a synchronised goodnight: '*Bonne nuit!*'

The Fred Vargas novel that Elizabeth had lent Zoe was on the kitchen table. She picked it up and took it with her outside, through the back door into the enclosed vegetable garden. Russell made a circuit of the stone walls while Zoe stayed beneath the feeble outside light, just enough for her to start reading. She quickly became absorbed in the story and was surprised when Russell snuck past her to make his own way back to the smelly dog's bed in the basement kitchen.

Zoe bolted the back door top and bottom and took herself upstairs, walking along the edge of the dingy corridor so as not to produce too many creaks and groans in the ancient floorboards. Her room seemed undisturbed and she wondered if the impression she'd had of her things not being where she had left them was the fault of Monsieur Alain coming and tidying, rather than a nosy or untrustworthy visitor.

I'm so tired I don't have the energy to work out if that would fit the sequence of events.

She washed and brushed her teeth at the ugly sink in the corner and changed into her pyjamas, before going to look out of the draughty window.

Zoe's room overlooked the terrace and the lawn. Snow was falling. Everything in the monochrome outside world was white or grey, including the frozen surface of the lake and the formal trees beyond. About a kilometre away, a car was going by, heading towards the Verdon Gorge, moving very slowly and carefully across the icy countryside. The draught from the ill-fitting window was like a knife.

But the radiator is scalding hot again. I don't think I'll need my blower heater.

She got into bed, reopened the book and continued reading, moving further and further into a complex, multi-stranded mystery in which several investigations were conducted simultaneously by the shabby, round-shouldered hero, Commissaire Jean-Baptiste Adamsberg. Around an hour later, the subplots began to fall away as the 'real story' emerged, a disturbing tale of poisonous spiders used as a weapon, as she had guessed.

I must remember to be careful when I refill the wood basket tomorrow.

Zoe smiled to herself.

There I go again, assuming it's my responsibility to maintain the fire.

She heard a scratching at the door and recognised it as Russell asking if he could come in. For some weeks, she had been promising herself that she would make a determined effort to wean him off sleeping in her bedroom.

Imagine if I had a gentleman caller. What would I do then? Tell him to make room?

She padded across the room and opened the door. Russell slid past her and jumped up onto the corner of her bed, as was his habit, as if he knew he ought to make an effort not to take up too much space. He turned twice round, then curled up, like a furry white croissant.

Maybe this disturbing novel wasn't a good idea. I'm beginning to feel a kind of dread.

Zoe got back into bed and curled up on her side, facing the window, just aware of the cold air on her face. Now very alert, she allowed herself to visualise some of the people she had recently met.

Gaspard Astor, the boulanger, seems very much a 'salt of the earth' sort of man, whereas his son Didi appears troubled. There was that odd incident with the knife and Elizabeth's thumb. If no one else will tell me why, I bet Isabelle knows, having lived in the village for many years.

Zoe frowned in the darkness.

Why does Isabelle live in Saint-Paul-de-Palotte?

She wondered if Isabelle might have been able to put aside enough money from her early career to cope with a long, unremunerated retirement. Her mind swiftly constructed an unhappy scenario in which Isabelle – despite what she had said – was Boris's long-term mistress, a kept woman, but unavowed.

Or known to the village? Would that generate new motives? There is also the issue of Adélaïde getting the breakthrough that Isabelle thought was hers – and getting the husband, too.

Zoe turned over onto her other side, away from the window.

Adélaïde is worried about Primo's health and about her own past. I will have to confront her and find out if there truly is something that might damage her career or even that she might be prosecuted for. Primo must be worried, too, because he tried to draw me into all that. And I'm not convinced that all is well for him, financially. The reason Caroline gave for not mending the gate – the lack of an artisan skilled in ancient techniques – seems convincing, but there's also the minimal staff and the fact that the château isn't well maintained. Plus, there's the constant drain of Boris and family as hangers-on.

Feeling annoyingly alert, Zoe sat up and rearranged her pillows, drawing the covers up under her chin.

I don't understand Boris because I don't understand pious hypocrisy and infidelity. It seems such an unhappy combination and such a dreadful mistake to make – repeatedly, too.

Zoe sighed in the darkness of the damp-smelling bedroom.

I suppose his excuse would be, on each occasion, that it was on both sides. I can't see either Marie-France or Elizabeth as natural-born philanderers but I suppose it was a long time ago in both cases. The trouble is, the one-night stand with Isabelle is more recent and is the obvious reason – though I can't be certain – for Sweetie's tears the other night. Poor Sweetie would have been confronted by Isabelle – looking slow and sensuous and glamorous – at the village celebration.

She checked the time on her mobile phone and discovered it wasn't excessively late, so she allowed her mind to continue searching for understanding.

Marie-France seems utterly dependent. I've heard no mention of income or private wealth. Elizabeth lives from pay cheque to pay cheque, a precarious freelance life. Boris has expensive business ventures that all end in failure. Junior attends the local state school, rather than being sent away to board.

Thinking about Junior gave Zoe a strange mix of emotions. There was the anger she still felt about him breaking the ice and almost drowning poor Russell beneath the surface of the frozen lake. But she also had sympathy for him, lonely and directionless in a house of feuding grown-ups.

And there is definitely a chance that he put the stick across the path, causing – whether he meant to or not – Monsieur Alain's death.

Zoe pondered something she had learned from Caroline about Patrick Lagrasse, early in her residence in Sainte-Catherine, well before the *dénouement* of 'the French bookshop murder'. Zoe wrinkled her brow, trying to remember the precise words.

Something like: 'He goes mad on his holidays, women by the string, like sausages.' But the only woman he seems close to here, apart from his sister, is Adélaïde.

Zoe found it impossible to see Patrick and Adélaïde's friendship as anything but platonic.

Minette has a severe, judgemental personality. I think I might be able to imagine her doing something drastic, without compunction, believing it the logical response to circumstances.

Zoe yawned and snuggled lower, feeling her mind becoming vague.

What do I mean by 'something drastic'? I'm not sure . . .

Her thoughts drifted, then the image of poor Monsieur Alain – his gashed forehead and gaping mouth, fallen on the snowy, slippery steps – sort of coalesced from the mist.

Has the worst already happened, or – as I found myself dreading when Isabelle told me that she 'would have made a wonderful châtelaine' – could I be about to witness another murder?

*

Snuggled cosily in her bed, Zoe had no way of knowing that wakefulness was common throughout Château Palotte. The reasons that the other residents found sleep hard to come by were all different: guilt for things done; guilt for things left undone; guilt for bad actions not prevented; guilt at sinister future designs; guilt over an abuse of power; above all, a desperate desire for self-preservation at any cost.

Zoe was right to be afraid – for others and for herself.

IV

SNOWBOUND

Thirty-One

'I WISH I WAS A GOOD BOY'

Zoe woke much later than she meant. She washed and dressed in her dismal room then went out into the corridor, pausing to listen to the sounds of the house and its occupants. Despite the distance, she thought she could hear loud conversation from downstairs.

To her great surprise, the entire family was already in the dining room.

Of course. There's no Monsieur Alain to take breakfast to their rooms.

The white tablecloth – stained from the previous evening's party – was strewn with the contents of the fridge, all the leftovers from the canapés that she and Isabelle had prepared. Three cafetières of coffee had been steeped and mostly drunk, weak brown liquid dribbling down from their spouts.

In another unexpected turn of events, Primo and his nephew Junior were by the fire, toasting bread with the extendable brass fork. Perched on the fender, they seemed – just at that moment – to exist in their own little bubble of contentment, while the emotions of the rest of the family, grouped around the table, were set to a steady simmer.

Marie-France and Elizabeth, seated with their backs to Zoe, were arguing about their relative rights as prior wives.

'There is such a thing as precedence,' said the older woman, referring to the fact that she had been Boris's first choice.

'But he had second thoughts, didn't he?' retorted Elizabeth.

At the other end of the table, Boris and Sweetie were arguing in an undertone, leaning into one another, their heads no more than a few centimetres apart. Behind them was the dresser in which all the coffee paraphernalia and wine glasses were stored. On top was a handful of half-empty bottles. From a distance, their pose might easily have been misinterpreted as intimate affection, but Zoe could discern the tension around their eyes, their downturned mouths.

Closer to the door and therefore closer to Zoe, Patrick and Minette were arguing about the long winter closures of the Auberge Sainte-Catherine, while eating cheese and crackers, for want of proper breakfast food.

'It doesn't make sense,' Minette complained. 'We need income all year round. We could do reduced hours.'

'That's not how it works for me. I need to get away completely.'

'So that you can spend the winter chasing one-night stands. How old are you?'

'Same age as you, my darling twin.'

'Can't you give me a thought, trapped in my kitchen-dungeon?'

Patrick shook his head, dismissing further conversation, and took another mouthful.

For reasons Zoe was unaware of, Isabelle was present once more, sleekly dressed as if for *après-ski* in some magnificent Alpine setting, her close-fitting down suit moulded to her perfect figure. She and Adélaïde had just finished opening the curtains onto the terrace, revealing that overnight snowfall had deepened the carpet of white, blurring every shape. They, too, seemed unhappy with one another.

'I wish you had confided in me,' Adélaïde was complaining.

'It wasn't your business,' Isabelle retorted, opening the French windows and stepping outside. Her moon boots sunk to the ankles into the perfect powdery snow.

'Is there any reason,' demanded Marie-France, grandly, 'why the door has to stand open?'

Adélaïde followed outside, despite the fact that she was underdressed, and closed it behind her.

Taking in all of these fragments of simultaneous conversation had lasted little more than a minute, with Zoe standing hesitant on the threshold. Then, to her surprise, it was Sweetie who walked almost the length of the room to bid her good morning.

'How are you?' Zoe asked. 'Did you sleep well?'

'No,' said Sweetie. 'How could I possibly?'

Zoe was stumped for a reply and grateful that Adélaïde came back inside, meaning she didn't have to find one. Sweetie returned to her chair and, through the French doors, Zoe saw Isabelle crossing the terrace, embarking on an apparently serene and graceful stroll across the lawn towards the lake.

'Zoe,' said Adélaïde. 'Please forgive me for repeatedly forgetting you are even here.' She pulled a sad face, reminding Zoe of when she was very much younger. 'And I just keep apologising, don't I? Did you bring warm-weather gear? Yes, of course you did. I remember you wearing it. Would you like to put it on and we'll wander out like the intrepid Isabelle and have a chat?'

Primo stood up, painfully levering himself off the brass fender.

'There won't be time, my dear. The church service . . .'

Junior got up, too, carrying a very fine-looking china plate with gilt all around the rim, on which lengths of toasted *baguette* were loaded.

'Put it on the table, dear boy,' said Primo.

Thinking he had a better colour, Zoe asked him: 'How are you, *monsieur*?'

'It's kind of you to ask,' he replied, with his habitual punctiliousness. 'I'm very much better than I was, but my brother and I appear to be unsynchronised, if you understand what I mean. I am improved but he is very poorly this birthday morning.'

'Oh, good heavens,' said Zoe. 'I completely forgot. It's today, isn't it?' She looked from one brother to the other, Primo standing very erect in his beautifully cut three-piece tweed suit, Boris slumped with rounded shoulders, seated beside his unlikely third wife. She told them: 'As Madame Constant said, congratulations on reaching three-score-years and ten. And, as we say in English, "many happy returns", which I'm sure you know is a wish for lots more contented birthdays to come.'

'A fond wish,' said Primo, distractedly.

Boris didn't reply. His elbows were on the table and there was a packet of indigestion tablets in his hand. He raised his head and Zoe saw that a blood vessel had burst in his right eye, giving him a sinister appearance. He finally addressed his brother.

'I suppose we must go ahead with today's events? You will not countenance postponement?'

'Anything we postpone,' said Primo, 'might mean never again. You can't have forgotten that next week I go into hospital in order to die and be brought back? There is a risk that they will fail, that I will remain on the table.'

'Oh, Primo,' said Adélaïde.

'Nonsense,' whispered Boris.

'If you are both on the same medical pathway,' enquired Zoe, addressing Boris, 'does that mean, *monsieur*, that you will soon be subjected to cardioversion as well?'

Boris took a deep breath but Sweetie replied for him.

'The doctors won't do it. He doesn't take his medicine or follow advice because he won't be told anything by anybody.'

'Not today, please,' said Boris, wearily.

Rather touchingly, Zoe thought, Junior had buttered a piece of warm toast to place in front of his father, opening the marmalade and offering him a knife. For a few seconds there was silence, then Boris spoke. 'I can't eat that.'

There was a chill in the room. The boy looked like he was about to cry.

'Boris,' snapped Elizabeth.

'It's all right, Junior,' said Sweetie.

Then his father put a lined and liver-spotted hand on the back of his son's neck and drew him in for an awkward embrace.

'It was a kind thought,' said Boris.

The expression on Junior's face revealed surprise and gratitude.

Poor boy, this is a rare event. Can it be that Boris is so unwell that the threat of death has concentrated his mind and made him want to mend his relationship with his son?

Soon everyone was on their feet getting themselves together for the birthday church blessing which would, apparently, be attended by members of the family alone. Zoe wondered if she would be co-opted as 'Adélaïde's friend' but no. She was left to pass the time as she wished.

She decided, first, to clear up, making everything clean and tidy, including hoovering and washing up and putting away. It took almost an hour, during which she also put on a quick load of laundry in the boiler room, hanging her things out on the drying rack when it was done.

She fetched the book Elizabeth had lent her and wondered where to sit. The dining room was warm but had nowhere comfortable. The drawing room had proper armchairs, but it was chilly, the radiators only tepid, and she didn't think there was enough wood left downstairs for her to light a second fire.

We're running quite low. Might it be possible to get a delivery, despite the ice and snow?

She chose the kitchen – so that Russell would know where she was – and read for half an hour. Then Patrick and Minette came back with savoury and sweet tarts from the *boulangerie* and with the news that the 'older generation', as they referred to them, were having lunch with the mayor and her mother, the doyenne of the village, Emilie Constant.

'Another tradition?' Zoe asked.

'Another element of the unchanging rigmarole,' said Minette.

'They seem to like it,' said Patrick.

'And Junior?' asked Zoe.

'He will have to endure it,' said Minette. 'But we thought you might like to come with us for some exercise?'

'I won't be able to keep up.'

'Not running,' said Patrick. 'A yomp through the woods.'

'Lovely.'

They all got togged up and strode out into the crisp day. Zoe and – even more so – Russell enjoyed themselves enormously. Several times they thought they had caught sight of the stag and his harem of deer, but could never be sure. After an hour, they were back at Château Palotte and Patrick sprung another surprise, showing Zoe a USB thumb drive.

'What do you think this is?'

'I can't guess.'

'Adélaïde's latest. I thought we might go up to the miserable television-room, eat our tarts and watch it under blankets.'

'That sounds like great fun, but won't everyone else come back when we're in the middle?'

'Their shared intention is to take a nap because of this evening's concert.'

'Tell me about that. How does it work?'

Minette argued: 'Must we? Let's begin or they might be back and some of them might be tempted to join us and you know they're all incapable of sitting quietly without asking who every character is the moment they appear and why they're doing what they're doing.'

'True,' said her brother.

They climbed the stairs to the second floor with Russell sniffing at what were, for him, newly discovered regions of the ancient house. Patrick found an almost invisible slot in the black carcass of the flat-screen television and Minette used the remote to access the movie and set it playing, adjusting the volume. They shared out the pastries and sat in lumpy armchairs, draped in blankets left ready on the arms, and – with a crescendo of dramatic music to accompany a rooftop chase – the film began.

★

At the same time – though Zoe, Patrick and Minette didn't know it – Junior had managed to persuade his parents to let him come home as the adult luncheon at the Constants' house ground on.

He returned to Château Palotte, climbed the stairs and lurked outside the television-room door, wondering if he would be allowed in or if what they were watching was forbidden to him, like the films his father liked to enjoy alone.

In the end, he moved away without interrupting the exciting sounds, returning to his room where the toys of his infancy outnumbered amusements appropriate for a ten-year-old.

He thought about his conversation with Madame Pascal and the reason he had honestly given for why he had tried to drown the dog.

I didn't need to do it, in the end. Now I know what it feels like.

He wiped away a tear.

I wish I was a good boy and people liked me.

Thirty-Two

'That's Rather Terrifying'

'Zoe,' said Adélaïde, 'please put on your unfortunate Decathlon ski jacket and come outside with me.'

The thriller film about Interpol had finished. Zoe had come downstairs to revive the dining-room fire, discovering Adélaïde alone, wondering aloud where Zoe had got to.

'All right. Give me two minutes.'

Zoe went via the boiler room for some clean clothes. She had no *après-ski* moon boots like most of the others wore but she had her oversized waterproof nylon hiking boots and a thick, second pair of socks. In addition to her base layer and sweatshirt, she added the unbecoming quilted gilet and then the economical sports-superstore ski jacket that Adélaïde had derided.

'Don't listen to her,' she told it, aloud. 'You don't have to be chic to keep me warm.'

Russell had come with her and was watching with an expression of gratified expectation on his handsome pointed face.

'Yes, we're going out,' she told him.

He jumped down and skittered round her ankles, giving two or three muffled yaps in what Zoe thought of as his 'indoor voice'.

'Let's go.'

She and Russell found Adélaïde in the ground-floor corridor.

'Don't you have a scarf?' her friend asked. 'Look in here.'

Previously unexplored, one of the corridor cupboards contained a profusion of outdoor clothes and equipment, including hard hats and boots for horse riding, waist-length waders for fishing, rods and reels, and a huge cardboard box of hurricane lamps. Zoe found a lovely cashmere scarf that she folded around her neck and tucked underneath her scratchy zip. Adélaïde found a red beret that she perched on Russell's head. He shrugged it off, picked it up in his teeth and shook it like a rat.

Zoe opened the back door to the vegetable garden with Russell desperate to be first outside, but he was brought up short by the fact that the wind had made the snow accumulate in a heap that came up to his chin. He looked up at Zoe with appeal in his lovely warm eyes so she picked him up and carried him to the pedestrian gate that led out onto the lawn. There, the snow lay thickly but he was no longer pushing through it like someone fighting a drift.

Adélaïde told her: 'It's over there.'

'What is?'

'The reservoir.'

The short winter day was almost done. Following her friend's gesture, Zoe noticed a new feature, maybe twenty paces away from the edge of the lake, which she hadn't seen before because it had been concealed by frost and snow. It was a door, set horizontally in the ground. Someone had opened it, pinning it back with a chain.

'What on earth is that?' Zoe asked.

'The venue for the concert. It's an underground cistern, built two hundred years ago in order to provide fresh water all through the hot Provençal summers. It's no longer needed with water on tap from the mains, so it's been repurposed and will serve for the big birthday event.' Adélaïde paused. 'I suppose you think us very foolish and indulgent.'

'Of course not—'

'It's put a terrible strain on Primo,' interrupted Adélaïde, then added, in an afterthought: 'And Boris too, I suppose, if we can believe him.'

'You mean he was pretending to be ill? Are you sure? He looked dreadful. Why would he pretend?'

'I don't know.' They had arrived at the surreal opening in the lawn. Zoe could see that another set of footsteps had recently approached the place and was not surprised when Adélaïde called out: 'Isabelle? Are you down there?'

Is Isabelle's presence the reason why Adélaïde couldn't give a full answer?

'Yes, I'm here,' came Isabelle's poised voice, distant and thin.

'She has very kindly been putting out the chairs. Follow me, Zoe,' said Adélaïde. 'But be careful. There is no handrail.'

Zoe thought dangerous stairs were something of a theme at Château Palotte. She followed Adélaïde down a set of damp stone treads that protruded from a wall that was furry with moss and lichen. One bright shaft of light was creating contrasts that Zoe's eyes found difficult. Her left hand against the brickwork, she carefully trailed her friend into the subterranean reservoir whose presence she had been made aware of by the promotional leaflet for tours of the château.

That's another good point. Why would Primo open to the public if the finances were sound?

Isabelle met them at the foot of the stairs, carrying a hurricane lamp. 'We'll need more of these,' she told Adélaïde.

'I know. Thank you again for stepping in. Do you know where they are kept?'

'The cupboard on the ground-floor corridor. I'll go now.'

'Thank you, Isabelle. Primo and I are very grateful for your assistance. I don't imagine Boris has told you so, but he is, too.'

Isabelle put the hurricane lamp in Zoe's hand, giving her the impression that she was being delegated the task of holding it because she was a person of less importance than the *châtelaine*, Adélaïde.

'Boris has not thanked me,' said Isabelle, her back to them both because she was already climbing the precarious stairs. 'Quite the opposite.'

Now that she and Adélaïde were alone, Zoe was able to have a good look round. The subterranean cistern was about the size of a tennis court and made up of a sequence of wide brick arches, about three metres tall at the apex, like the crypt of a church, the pillars breaking up the space. The floor was flagstones with damp patches here and there. In the centre was an array of rusty folding chairs with slatted wooden seats, set out in ten or twelve rows. They faced a stage made of scaffolding bars and planks.

'If this is an underground reservoir, is there a water inlet?' Zoe asked.

'Why?' asked Adélaïde, distractedly.

Zoe moved to the edge of the cistern, in a direction that she knew must approach the lake, a few metres above. Sure enough, high up in the damp wall, was an opening, fitted with a metal sluice that could be raised with a chain and pulley to allow the lake water to cascade down into the reservoir. The sluice didn't entirely fill the gap so a small slot of sky was also visible.

'That's rather terrifying,' she told Adélaïde. 'Imagine if it gave way and a great flood of freezing water came rushing in.'

'Oh, it's seized up and hasn't moved for years.'

'I hope that's true. By the way, I thought it would be Baltic down here, but it's quite mild.'

'Like a wine cellar,' said Adélaïde, 'making it ideal for the birthday concert. The minibus man brings in tenants from round about.'

'Do you mean Bernard Dupin?'

'I don't know. A little chap with a dark jacket and a peaked cap.'

'Yes, that's Bernard. He brings visitors to Sainte-Catherine and makes sure they all come to my bookshop to browse and have coffee.'

'That's nice of him,' said Adélaïde, her mind still elsewhere. She sat in the centre of the front row. 'Come and ask me your questions. I know you want to.'

Zoe joined her, leaving an empty seat between them because it seemed odd, in the big, empty space, to sit too close.

'Well, I suppose, the first thing is, why did you all get up so early?'

'Because there was no one to bring breakfast to the bedrooms, of course.'

'Yes, obviously, and you did all go to bed quite early.'

'Although not everybody went straight to sleep. Junior, apparently, went roaming through the corridors and ended up in Boris's dressing room where there's a pull-out *canapé-lit* that he shared with his mother.' Zoe was keen to probe further on the relationship between Boris, Sweetie and Junior, but Adélaïde continued: 'Patrick and Minette were first up, obviously, because that's their habit, and they laid out everything from the fridge, indiscriminately. The bread came from the freezer, which was why it had to be toasted. It would have been inedible otherwise.'

'I found it rather touching, seeing Primo and Junior perched on the brass fender together.'

'Yes, it's strange that the awful child is suddenly more in Primo's good books than I am.'

Thirty-Three

'AN ALMOST-IMPERCEPTIBLE FLAW'

In the damp reservoir beneath the lawn, Adélaïde's remark that Junior was more in Primo's 'good books' than she was didn't come as a complete surprise.

Zoe asked, lightly: 'What do you mean by that?'

'It's as if,' said Adélaïde with a faraway look, 'I was a fine piece of crystal that Primo has treasured for many years, only to find, all along, that there was an almost-imperceptible flaw.' She sighed. 'Ask me something else.'

'All right. What were Patrick and Minette arguing about?'

'The same as always. Patrick is satisfied with just getting by, whereas Minette feels that all her hard work, isolated in the kitchen, ought to mean more from life than she receives.'

'That fits their characters. Oh, where was Caroline?'

'She came down, got herself some coffee and went back upstairs.'

'Working?'

'I suppose so.'

'On what?'

'Yes, that's the question. I fear Primo has given her instructions.'

Zoe thought she might have an inkling what those instructions concerned, but could tell that Adélaïde didn't want it said out loud.

At least, not yet.

'What about Elizabeth and Marie-France? I thought I'd understood that there was a sort of connivance between them. Do you know what I mean?'

'For reasons that I can't fathom, they wanted to discuss, aloud, the possibility that both Primo, on the operating table, and Boris, through his general dissipation and his chronic dyspepsia, as well as his atrial fibrillation, might die.'

'They were discussing their inheritance and their rights?'

'They were.'

'No wonder there was such an extraordinary atmosphere. I barely felt I could enter the room, as if there was a force field on the threshold. You were much nearer to Boris and Sweetie. What were they saying?'

'I couldn't actually hear. From the way Sweetie's eyes kept flicking towards Isabelle, I think we can guess.'

'Am I right that Sweetie discovered Boris's infidelity with Isabelle on the night of the village party, when she came home with tears in her eyes?'

'She's not a child, however childishly she sometimes behaves. She must have suspected and then had her suspicions confirmed by how Boris and Isabelle behaved to one another.'

'Can you tell me why Isabelle is so keen to help with everything? It doesn't make sense to me.'

'You might be surprised to discover that she has, in common with Primo, a kind of heartfelt commitment to the village, adopting Château Palotte as a kind of mission. Being always available must bring her some kind of psychological or emotional reward.'

'You always greet her very warmly. You speak of her with appreciation and generosity. Is that to cover up what you really think?'

'And what is it that I really think?' Adélaïde asked, very quietly.

'I really can't tell,' said Zoe. 'You are an excellent actress.'

Russell, who had disappeared while they were crossing the lawn, came awkwardly down the stone steps, sniffing as he went. Once he had reached the damp floor, he made a circuit of the perimeter of the underground cistern, glancing every so often towards his mistress as if to ask: *What an earth is this place?*

'I'm not trying to keep you in the dark,' said Adélaïde. 'I asked you to come and stand by me throughout these interminable celebrations, after all.'

'So, what were you and Isabelle talking about?'

'When we were in the dining room, a professional matter; outside, what she refers to as the "mistake" of her "moment with Boris".'

'She actually told me out loud that it was a drunken fling with a kind of vicarious satisfaction.'

'For a moment, she was able to imagine that she was with Primo whom she has loved ever since they met all those years ago.' Adélaïde left a pause, then added: 'When he chose me.'

'I don't know how she can stand it. I think I would have moved away, begun a new life somewhere.'

'What if you still thought you might have hope?'

'You mean that Primo would, finally, choose her above you? I don't believe it.'

'That's very sweet of you, but perhaps you don't know me as well as you think. What else do you need to ask?'

'I'm not sure,' said Zoe. 'Maybe tell me more about the concert?'

'On the birthday, your minibus man brings the tenants from the estate who live outside the village, not because they can't all make their own way, but to create a sense of *bonhomie*. Actually, it's bigger than a minibus. I suppose it must hold two dozen people? Have you ever seen it?'

'I never have,' said Zoe. 'Bernard always has to park down at the bottom of Sainte-Catherine in the car park by the *mairie* while I'm trapped in the bookshop, looking forward to their arrival. Will Bernard definitely be able to get here?'

'What would prevent him?'

'The snow, of course, and the ice.'

'He's a professional driver. I imagine he has winter tyres or snow chains or something. Isn't that what people do?'

'I really have no experience,' said Zoe. She laughed. 'If I told my friends at home that I was in the south of France, in glorious Provence, where the sun always shines and the thyme and the lavender are always in bloom, that I was snowed in and ... Well, I don't think they would believe me.'

As Caroline had done, Adélaïde insisted: 'The weather will soon turn. You'll see.'

Zoe thought it was said with a kind of plaintive hopefulness, prompting her to ask: 'And the storm clouds over the château itself – I mean all the difficulties between the family members – will they disperse, too, do you think, once the pressure of the twin birthdays has gone by?'

'Maybe.'

'And what about your own ... I want to say "external issue", with the poison-pen letter. Have you spoken to Primo about it?'

'I have not.'

'In order not to make it real?'

'Because it reveals the flaw in what he believed to be unblemished crystal,' said Adélaïde.

Zoe wanted to press her further but was unable because she heard voices from outside.

'Shall I go and see who that is?' she asked.

Adélaïde didn't move. Finally, she said: 'That would be very kind.'

Zoe weaved round the chairs and the brick pillars of the subterranean reservoir and climbed the slippery staircase, running her hand along the damp wall as a precaution, emerging into the cold of a beautiful still day, illuminated by the last of the feeble, low sunshine in a frigid orange-blue sky. Russell came with her and scampered away across the snow to the lake's edge.

The voices she had heard were a handful of members of the local folk music orchestra, *Les Vautours*, meaning 'The Vultures'. Their van was parked over at the carport and they were trudging across the snowbound lawn with their instruments. Five in number – the band had a fluctuating composition, depending on who was available – they were all dressed in dinner jackets and bright white shirts, presumably with thermal underwear beneath. Zoe knew these particular members by sight but not by name.

'*Bonjour, messieurs!*'

'Madame Pascal,' replied the nearest musician. 'How nice to see you here.'

'Do you need any help?'

He told her confidently that they knew where and how to set up and embarked on the precarious steps.

While she was outside and there was still daylight, Zoe thought she might go and look at the sluice at the edge of the lake that controlled the ingress of water into the cistern. As Adélaïde had predicted, the mechanism looked completely seized with rust. Zoe peered in through the small gap. By the light of the single hurricane lamp down below, she was able to discern a couple of pillars and the forest of chairs beyond.

Someone called her name. It was Isabelle, crossing the lawn with more lamps dangling from her leather-gloved fingers.

'Can you help me with these?'

'Of course.'

Together, they redescended. In total, they positioned eight lamps, one at the foot of each of eight brick pillars. Isabelle had taken the precaution of bringing two boxes of matches, so she and Zoe were able to light four each, adjusting the wicks to provide a steady, smokeless flame inside each bell of glass. Once this was done, the cistern took on a completely new personality.

Like a Christmas grotto or a magical theatrical venue – which, I suppose, it is.

'Is there ever an issue,' Zoe asked, 'with smoke or with carbon dioxide making the air unfit to breathe?'

'There never has been,' said Isabelle. 'The door is always left open and that creates a kind of chimney, I suppose, because hot air rises. And there are two inlets for air.'

'Two?' queried Zoe. 'Isn't there just the sluice on the lake side?'

'There's an outlet channel, too,' said Isabelle, 'should the cistern reach overflowing. It's behind the stage, over there, at the same height as the sluice.'

Now there was more light, Zoe could see it clearly, a round opening close to the top of the wall behind the stage.

'Oh, I get it. It's a pipe that runs under the lawn.'

'That's right. It comes out below the little bridge.'

'And we're sure it's not blocked? Is it maintained, or has it been, by Monsieur Alain, for example? If the air became bad in here, it might be too late by the time anyone noticed, especially with a big crowd breathing all the oxygen. Some-one might find us all slumped in our seats.'

'What an idea,' said Isabelle, and the tone of her voice and the expression on her face led Zoe to think that Isabelle had had a sudden revelation, something that she had never real-ised until this moment. 'Let us hope not.'

By this time, The Vultures were in position on the stage. The performance was clearly going to be acoustic, without electronic amplification: two violinists; one guitarist; a drum-mer with a pair of tom-toms on a strap round his neck and soft beaters so as not to dominate; and an accordion, carried by the man who had spoken to Zoe.

Adélaïde roused herself to tell them: 'Come up to the house. I think you all know that poor Alain is no longer with us but we will do our best to find you something to eat and drink before everyone arrives.'

'Thank you, Madame de Palotte. We appreciate it. How are you, Madame Valgarde?'

'I get by,' said Isabelle.

'And how are the birthday boys?' asked the accordionist in a jocular tone.

'Primo is better than sometimes,' Adélaïde told him. 'Monsieur Boris is apparently very poorly.'

'None of us lives forever,' he commented with a rueful smile.

Neither Adélaïde nor Isabelle replied. The reason, Zoe saw, was that they were watching one another with a kind of predatory intensity.

Thirty-Four

'How Ill Actually Are They?'

Zoe felt it was one of those moments when, in the popular phrase, 'you could cut the atmosphere with a knife'. But it seemed that she was alone in noticing. Then the predatory intensity in the eyes of Adélaïde and Isabelle faded and Zoe wondered if she might have imagined it.

The five members of the band put down their instruments on the rudimentary stage of scaffolding planks. The two actresses – evenly matched in poise and beauty, if not in professional success and reputation – followed The Vultures up and out into the dusk, with Zoe walking pensively behind. Glad of the four layers that she was wearing on her top half, she continued in the rear all the way across the lawn, onto the terrace and in through the French doors.

The dining-room fire was burning down in the grate. The luxurious white tablecloth told a messy story of all that had been eaten there, over the past eighteen hours. Somebody – she supposed Patrick and Minette – had once more laid out all the eclectic remains from the fridge.

The band members – as habitués of the château – went directly to the dresser, opened the doors and found five crystal glasses that they charged with white wine from the unfinished bottles on top.

Isabelle said: 'I will go into the village to speak to Gaspard.'

Adélaïde replied: 'I will run up to see how Primo is getting on.'

They both left. To make herself useful, Zoe unloaded the last two logs out of the basket into the grate and went downstairs to the boiler room to replenish it. To her surprise, the machinery was silent and the room unusually cold.

She filled the basket to the brim, on the lookout for the insidious presence of tiny – but venomous – brown recluse spiders. She struggled back up the awkward stairs. In the ground-floor corridor, now overwarm in her coat and gilet and other layers, she realised that the indoor air was cool on her face.

Re-entering the dining room, she put down the log basket and was pleased to see that the band members were attacking some of the leftover delicacies – fine cheeses, preserved vegetables, anchovies, cured meats and so on – on the same varied mix of crackers and sweet biscuits she had seen at breakfast. She removed her ski jacket and draped it over the back of one of the dining chairs, then went back downstairs to check on the boiler.

Cold and still, almost like a dead thing.

She checked the power cable and the socket, its plug pushed firmly into the wall. She pulled it out and put it back in again, making no difference. On the control panel she found a button labelled '*Initialiser*', meaning 'reset'. She pressed it but nothing happened in response.

Without Monsieur Alain, will everything in the château progressively fall apart? What will be next to fail, beyond all the fractured relationships?

Zoe went in search of a fuse box, finding it high on the wall in the corridor that led to Monsieur Alain's untenanted bedroom.

Zoe flipped down the smoked-plastic cover and quickly saw that the RCD – the residual current device, an automated safety precaution in the event of earth leakage from an appliance somewhere in the house – had tripped. By the gloomy light of the high slot windows, she reset the RCD by raising the switch and immediately heard the distant whirring of the boiler pumps, enthusiastically restarting.

That's a relief.

Back in the kitchen, she discovered Elizabeth who told her she had come downstairs to find out what was going on because the lights had gone off and her computer had lost power and she had been obliged to abandon the editing job that she was embarked upon.

'You should be all right now. I've reset it. Were you working on the romantic novel or the true crime?' Zoe asked.

'Crime and romance often go together,' mused Elizabeth. 'Though romance is usually a subplot to the mystery.'

'Yes, that's true,' said Zoe.

'People talk about motive and opportunity, but the key is always the evil will.'

That's odd. I seem to have already had this conversation with Caroline.

'Are we talking,' Zoe asked, with a smile, 'about real life or fiction?'

Elizabeth didn't answer the question. Instead, she asked her own. 'Are you not dressing up? We usually do for the birthday.'

Caroline herself arrived, stumbling slightly from the bottom step, making Zoe lurch towards her to help.

'I began running out of battery on my laptop,' said the solicitor. 'Is there a problem?'

'There was but I've fixed it.' Zoe shared what she had done: 'Can I make you both some tea?'

'Yes, please,' said Caroline. 'It was probably time to get changed, in any case.'

Zoe turned away from them, filling the kettle and getting down mugs. Keen to continue her low-key investigation, she asked in an innocent tone: 'Is everybody a little calmer or happier since breakfast?'

At first, she received no answer. Fetching milk from the fridge, she saw a fleeting reflection of the two women in the stainless-steel door, hesitant, like video-game characters awaiting instructions.

She went on: 'It's such a shame poor Monsieur Alain didn't live to see the culmination of the seventieth-birthday celebrations. Primo and Boris must feel his loss very deeply. How ill actually are they?'

Elizabeth replied: 'Neither one will discuss it properly. Isn't that so?'

For a second, Zoe wondered how to answer, then she realised that the question was directed to Caroline.

'Their condition is debilitating and unpredictable,' the solicitor replied. 'The severest danger comes from the accelerated and erratic rhythms of each man's heart, with the risk of generating a clot that travels to either the lungs or the brain, either of which might be life-changing or even fatal.'

'And, if the cardioversion fails,' Elizabeth continued, 'I mean if Primo survives it but his atrial fibrillation persists, the next step is burning away heart muscle through ablation?'

'And the cryo-therapy, a very serious next step,' confirmed Caroline.

Zoe turned and put the two mugs of tea on the table.

'I've made it strong, after the English fashion, with milk. Do either of you take sugar?'

Neither of them did.

'I suppose you can't tell me what you've been working on?' Elizabeth asked Caroline, very directly.

'No, I can't,' said Caroline.

There was a pause during which Zoe almost expected the solicitor to add: 'I'm sorry.'

But an apology has no place where professional standards are in play.

'Well, thanks for that,' said Elizabeth.

She picked up her mug of tea and stalked away.

That's the first time I've seen her really cross.

Meanwhile, the kitchen was warming up, the boiler performing its function.

'Are the pumps and mechanisms making much more noise than before?' Zoe asked.

'About the same, I think,' said Caroline.

'That's a relief. Will you excuse me?'

Zoe ran upstairs to her room to put on her evening gown and the long dress coat in purple velvet, with its lovely silver brooch in the form of the Palotte family crest. When she came down, Caroline was still there, looking at messages on her phone. Zoe took her courage in both hands and asked: 'Has Primo instructed you to change the dispositions of his will?'

Her friend quietly put down her phone and picked up her mug to drink, giving an almost imperceptible nod.

Thirty-Five

'Like a Trap'

'I don't usually take milk,' said Caroline, inconsequently.

For a moment or two, Zoe was too shocked to speak.

So, Primo is disinheriting Adélaïde – or something like it. Can that be true?

'I'm assuming the repercussions for Adélaïde will be negative,' suggested Zoe, feeling that she was talking like a book and not knowing why.

Caroline nodded a second time, then they both turned their heads at the sound of the front door opening, audible from its screeching hinges. Then there were footsteps in the corridor above and Zoe was briefly worried that she and Caroline might have been overheard by whoever had opened up.

More specifically, that I myself might have been overheard, asking my indelicate questions. Caroline took care to say nothing of any consequence out loud.

'That will be the tenants,' said Caroline.

They both went upstairs and discovered Bernard Dupin – 'a little chap with a dark jacket and a peaked cap,' as Adélaïde had said – with two dozen assorted residents of the Château Palotte estate. Zoe greeted him with pleasure, his group's arrival coinciding with Gaspard Astor, the baker's arms full of a sheaf of fresh *baguettes*, held like a quiver-load of arrows.

Zoe felt destabilised by the sudden influx of happy voices, focused as she was on the uncovering of secrets and lies.

But the 'happy birthday' energy was infectious and she soon found herself chatting happily to strangers.

The party moved from the corridor to the dining room where it quickly became clear that the band members all knew the estate's tenants from previous years' celebrations and from concert venues elsewhere in the Verdon nature park. Gaspard helped everyone with the preparation of a still-eclectic mix of sandwiches and *tartines* – open sand-wiches. Outside, the sky was almost dark.

Zoe was passed from hand to hand, as it were, because of her role as the hero of 'the French bookshop murder' in which everybody was very interested. After twenty min-utes of increasingly loud chatter and merriment, Adélaïde returned with Primo on her arm. He looked as well as Zoe had seen him, though his expression was unhappy.

Closed off – almost, as if he resents Adélaïde's presence at his side. Can that be true as well?

He and Adélaïde began a circuit of the room, very much 'the lord and lady of the manor', greeting each tenant by name.

Boris was next to arrive, looking very down in the mouth and immediately sharing the news that, however bad he had felt earlier, he was now three times worse.

'My heart is beating almost too fast for me to breathe.'

Alongside him, Sweetie seemed actually worried. Junior, touchingly, trailed after them, holding her hand.

Caroline and Elizabeth entered, having put on smart but warm clothes, with an air of having 'had words' on their way down from their respective bedrooms. They too, however, clicked into social gear and embarked on their own separate circuits of the room. Zoe heard Caroline talking to some of the tenants in a manner that suggested that she represented them in their legal affairs.

I wonder if Caroline – or rather her predecessor in her legal office – was the person who created the complex trusts that made

Primo sole inheritor of his family's wealth, leaving Boris with nothing? And I wonder if the varied annual 'bonuses' create division and resentment?

Night fell and the windows became black. The party grew louder. Anyone who needed a snack seemed to have satisfied their appetite, except Didi Astor who stood alone near the fireplace, eating a long length of baguette smeared with butter and pâté, a picture of adolescent awkwardness.

He's not a teenager. He ought to be able to manage a semi-formal event like this one at his age.

The last dregs of wine were served and Zoe wondered if she ought to go to the basement kitchen in search of more. Marie-France came in and made a stately circuit. Then Patrick entered, carrying three wine bottles in each hand, their necks trapped between his strong fingers. He proceeded to uncork them with professional ease and enlisted Zoe's help in circulating and topping up with a bottle in each hand. She made a circuit, stopping several times to chat, then saw Patrick try to engage Adélaïde in conversation. But she remained entirely focused on her husband's social duties, nodding and smiling as Primo spread sober goodwill.

Minette arrived, added a couple of logs to the fire, gave her brother a filthy look and buttonholed Didi for what Zoe assumed was more football gossip.

This is all getting more and more complicated and unhappy.

One of The Vultures approached, entreating Zoe to come and replenish the band's drinks. They were standing over by the French doors onto the terrace. She splashed some of the noble white Burgundy she had seen in the kitchen wine rack into the five proffered crystal glasses.

Elizabeth was close by. Zoe went to fill her glass, too, but Elizabeth hastily put her hand over the top to refuse. At the same moment, Minette grasped her mother's arm and led her outside into the night, thrusting the French doors wide so that they clattered against the exterior stonework.

Oh dear.

With the chill breeze whistling in, a lull in conversation ensued and several people, in addition to Zoe and the musicians, turned their heads to witness the inaudible urgent conversation between mother and daughter, conducted against a patch of deep blue sky scattered with cold stars, illuminated by a bright moon.

Is this something new or just a restatement of old grievances? Or has Minette managed to find out what's eating Didi Astor?

'Perhaps this our cue?' said Primo, loudly, taking advantage of the relative quiet.

Using her strong theatrical voice, Adélaïde declaimed: 'If we are all ready, let's make our way down to the reservoir.'

Everyone began filing outside, crossing the terrace and gathering up Minette and Elizabeth as they went. The moonlight reflected off the snow, making it almost as bright as day. About half the attendees took their wine glasses with them, two or three of them stumbling on the slippery terrace and losing some of their contents. Zoe topped them up and saw another line of visitors, crossing the lawn from the village.

They didn't come in for nibbles. I suppose the local people had theirs last night, so today it was the tenants' turn.

The two lines of party guests converged at the entrance. One by one, she saw them begin their careful descent into the damp, subterranean reservoir.

Which looks, to me, more and more like a trap.

Thirty-Six

'I Don't Think I Can Cope'

The precarious staircase into the reservoir – transformed by the warm light of the hurricane lamps into a kind of grotto – meant it took a considerable time for everyone to descend and find a seat. Obeying some kind of unspoken rule, all the glasses were left in the snow by the entrance. Zoe did the same with her now-empty Burgundy bottles and was almost the last, with Patrick just behind her. She turned her head to ask him: 'If the chain gave way and the horizontal door was blown shut by the wind, would we all be trapped?'

He smiled broadly. 'What a gruesome thought! Why on earth would that cross your mind?'

'We're underground and I'm worried about the air.'

She explained the concerns she had shared with Isabelle. Patrick sniffed, theatrically. The smell of smoke from the lamps was, to Zoe's relief, much less strong than she had anticipated.

'All I can say is,' he told her, 'it's never been an issue in the past and, no, the door just sits in its opening. There's no catch or bolt or anything like that and it's definitely not difficult to lift from inside.'

'I'm glad.'

The staircase in front of them was now clear. Patrick went to find his place in the front row and Zoe decided to stay near the back, among people she didn't know well, where it was quite dark because the hurricane lamps had all been moved to surround the stage.

The accordionist struck up and the concert began, with all five members playing by ear, without need for scores or music stands. The high voices of the two violins, the muffled drums, the rhythm guitar and the lively accordion all filled the space, not in an echoey way, but rich and satisfying, concentrated by the acoustics of the vaulted ceiling. Impressed, Zoe realised that the previous versions of The Vultures that she had encountered had not all been of equivalent quality to this selection from their rolling cast.

These are their star performers, chosen for one of their most important events.

Polite applause greeted the end of the first number, then the tempo and volume increased. The two violins played in vivid counterpoint, never on the same note. Syncopated rhythms from the drums and guitar were exceptionally catchy, reminding Zoe variously – as the songs succeeded one another – of folk songs from the Balkans or from North Africa.

The accordionist switched from spiralling melodies to an oom-pah bass line. For the next three songs, he was the vocalist, his voice strongly flavoured by singing in several languages, French, Provençal and one she didn't recognise. Then they embarked on a song that Zoe had heard before, in Sainte-Catherine at the feast of Saint-Bertrand, a risqué one about the 'appetites' of the beasts of the field. It made Zoe think about the almost-surreal apparition of the stags, caught in the beam of her headlamps.

I didn't know at the time that those rutting stags were almost a commentary on the inhabitants of Château Palotte – everyone competing for dominance. That's the case most obviously with Boris and Primo, though Primo conducts himself always with impeccable dignity. But the idea could be extended to take in Boris's feuding wives or the obvious conflict between Isabelle and Sweetie.

230

She frowned.

And the subtler one between Isabelle and Adélaïde.

The musicians switched back to an instrumental number and Zoe disappeared further into imagination and memory, undisturbed by any lyrics.

I haven't had time to discover which electrical device blew out and tripped the RCD. I hope it isn't a dangerous short circuit.

She had a momentary vision of the château ablaze.

And there's no one left outside to see the flames and raise the alarm.

She undid the top two buttons of the long velvet dress coat she had borrowed from Adélaïde because the subterranean reservoir was now quite warm from all the human bodies.

There is clearly a serious rift between Primo and Adélaïde. What she was saying about him discovering that she has a 'flaw' must connect to Caroline's description of him as a perfectionist. Surely it's to do with the murder at the theatre in Chichester all those years ago – the one that the Los Angeles streamer wants to make a true-crime documentary about? Adélaïde's been in LA in person, but she has also been discussing it by email and she was on the brink of telling me her password. I wonder if it might be her personalised car registration number? If I can make a reasonable guess at it, others might and—

The bandleader introduced a 'call-and-response' number in which selected audience members stood up in turn to shout answers to questions in the lyrics, something that had clearly happened before.

Regardless of who's been prying into her business, the important thing is that Adélaïde thinks Primo has lost confidence in her and is worried that he has instructed Caroline to prepare a divorce and financial separation. Which, in a detective story, would give her a motive for wanting Primo out of the way before he had a chance to sign it.

The energy from band and audience became almost over-excited, but Zoe was only half present in the room.

Could Elizabeth be the author of the threatening letter, somehow to bring advantage to her children, Patrick and Minette? Or might it have been Boris or even Sweetie, for her own advantage and to favour Junior?

This train of thought was interrupted by a round of applause and Zoe noticed Bernand Dupin smiling at her from along the row. She smiled back.

A while ago it crossed my mind that the unnamed father of Patrick and Minette could turn up at any moment. That would put the cat among the pigeons. He could easily insinuate himself with either the village party or the group on Bernard's little bus, taking care not to be recognised. The organisation is pretty haphazard. I bet no one would question it if a tenant said: 'This is my friend. You don't mind if they join us?' Or might he have turned up even earlier, involved in Monsieur Alain's tragedy?

In a brief pause between numbers, she leaned over and asked Bernard: 'Are you worried about the snow and ice?'

'Not yet, Madame Pascal. I have winter tyres and there's always the hope that the weather is about to break.'

Everyone's very convinced that's true, but I'm glad I've got my emergency supplies on the windowsill in case we end up trapped – snowbound in Château Palotte, rather than down here in the cistern.

The band launched into a French sing-along number whose words Zoe didn't know, but everyone else did. She let it wash over her, pondering questions like the locking of the front door and where Monsieur Alain's key had ended up and her fanciful ideas about spider venom or even electrocution. Then, almost without her noticing, the song came to a rousing climax and the band struck up the schmalzy melody of the English 'Happy Birthday to You' tune that the audience sang in French with words that didn't quite fit the rhythm. During it, the elderly twins stood and turned to face the audience, Primo under his own steam and Boris assisted by Sweetie.

Zoe was glad when, a new round of applause having faded, neither man launched into a speech. The vocalist announced 'a final medley' and the band embarked on a circular tune embellished with virtuoso harmonies that reminded Zoe of klezmer music from the Jewish tradition.

People began leaving from the front, filing past the front row, offering good wishes to Primo and Boris, before crossing the reservoir and climbing the stairs, back out into the night.

After a few minutes of this, the music shifted as the melody evolved into a second, less excitable tune. The audience continued to file past and drift away. A couple more minutes passed, then Bernard Dupin finally stood up and told her: 'The family will be left alone. It is traditional.'

'Should I stay?' she asked.

'You are their guest? Isn't that so?'

'True, but perhaps . . .'

She didn't complete the thought because she had noticed that, in the transition to a third, still more sedate tune, the band were now on their feet themselves. Without stopping playing their acoustic, unplugged instruments, they too were climbing down off the stage, preparing to head for the stairs.

Zoe hung back, undecided. Bernard and the last guests filed forwards, greeted Primo and Boris, then doubled back on the far side of the chairs. The musicians followed, carefully ascending the slippery treads. Zoe decided to sidle down her row, heading directly for the exit without moving to the front. Up she went, one hand on the slimy wall, stopping halfway as the mellifluous sounds of the music faded, with the band playing as they crossed the snowy lawn, out of sight.

Zoe turned. Down in the subterranean reservoir, harshly lit by the eight hurricane lamps, the Palotte family plus Caroline Robin and Isabelle Valgarde were all on their feet, engaged in several simultaneous arguments whose words she could not make out but whose tone she could read in the livid expressions, the dabbed tearful eyes and the frustrated and angry gestures.

I don't think I can cope with any more of this.

She climbed the last few steps and found Bernard assembling his party in the bright moonlight. He bid her 'au revoir', admiring the silver brooch on the breast of her velvet dress coat: 'A lovely piece.'

'Thank you. It belongs to Madame de Palotte.'

'*Ah, la belle Adélaïde,*' he replied then turned to his passengers. 'Shall we . . . ?'

They trooped away, a line of shadows, across the glistening lawn to the carport, heading for their small bus. At the same time, the villagers were all disappearing like sombre ghosts through the pedestrian gate near the front door. That made Zoe think about the smouldering stick she had taken from Junior's hands and hidden close by, under a pile of leaves.

Maybe Junior did it – wedged the fallen branch between the woody stems of the two lavender plants – because someone told him to? Who would have the influence to make that happen?

She watched Bernard's bus pull away, its wheels spinning in the snow and ice, despite his 'winter tyres'. At the bottom of the drive, by the broken gate, the vehicle skated sideways and came within a hair's breadth of striking the left-hand pillar. Once on the road, Bernard crept along at little more than walking pace, only accelerating – still very carefully – on the straight.

Zoe picked up two big handfuls of wine glasses, sliding them upside down between the fingers of both hands, and took them back to the house, leaving them outside the French doors in the snow. She went back for the rest, plus the empty white Burgundy bottle, crossing over with the family as they emerged from the reservoir, in cold, uncommunicative silence, except for Junior who was crying like a much younger child.

Oh, how awful.

She hung back. Patrick emerged last, closing the horizontal door. He mooched away and Zoe began to shiver from her immobility. Eventually, the family disappeared in dribs and drabs through the French windows, out of sight.

I imagine everybody wants a bit of time off, each from everyone else. That famous quotation from Tolstoy's Anna Karenina *couldn't be truer: 'All happy families are alike; each unhappy family is unhappy in its own way.'*

Thirty-Seven

'THANK HEAVENS'

Once all the wine glasses were in the dishwasher, Zoe set it going, then put the white tablecloth in the washing machine on its own for a sixty-degree cycle. Her mind turned to the thorny question of the next day's breakfast and lunch.

Especially if we're snowed in. My emergency rations on the windowsill won't go far.

She opened the low door of the freezer compartment. Beneath some packets of frozen peas and sweetcorn and diced onions and so on she found two large metal trays labelled 'Lasagne'. She transferred them to the empty shelves of the fridge to begin defrosting, then stood for a moment, listening.

Even down here in the basement, I can hear creaks in the floorboards and on the stairs as people move about this creepy mausoleum.

Because she thought it was still making a lot of noise, whirring and stuttering, she went to look at the boiler.

Am I imagining it or does that not sound good?

Taped to the wall was a *fiche technique*, the boiler's specifications, including its brand and serial number and so on, plus the handwritten details of a plumbing engineer called Laurent Barge who, she supposed, was responsible for its maintenance.

I hope we don't find ourselves needing him.

She went upstairs, briefly meeting Minette on the landing.

'Goodnight,' Zoe told her.

'Unlikely,' said the athletic young woman, wearily, moving quickly away.

Back in her room, Zoe piled up her pillows and sat on the bed without undressing to continue reading the novel that Elizabeth had lent her.

★

Sometime later, Zoe found herself juddering awake, still sitting up, fully clothed, with her novel in her hand. She had a horrible feeling that she had forgotten something. Picturing herself in the kitchen, stacking the dishwasher with the wine glasses, it came to her.

Oh no, Russell. He wasn't there.

Slipping her mobile into her pocket, she ran down two flights of stairs to the basement, again aware of footsteps elsewhere in Château Palotte. She softly called his name, but heard no pitter-patter of claws or subdued 'indoor' bark in reply. She checked the drawing room and the dining room, then opened the French windows onto the terrace.

The air was icy on her cheeks, with a few lightly drifting snowflakes in the air, perhaps dislodged from the roof. She hastily did up the top buttons of her velvet coat.

This is odd. He's not been out this late on his own and I've assumed it was because he was frightened, still traumatised from his near-drowning.

The moon had moved a little way across the sky and was now directly above the château, in a wide gap in the clouds, easily bright enough to navigate across the snowy lawn to the opening into the underground reservoir. The horizontal door was closed but, as Patrick had promised, it was easy to lift and pin back on its chain, the more recent snowfall sliding off it.

Before embarking on the dangerous staircase, Zoe hesitated.

I feel I'm being watched.

She glanced around the glistening lawn, across the lake and towards the impenetrable and intimidating shadows of the formal woods.

Perhaps the stag has got out again and is observing me, an intruder in his territory?

She peered down the stairs, trying to make out the details of the very dark reservoir, but it was impossible. The hurricane lamps were all extinguished. She activated her mobile phone torch and shone it into the void.

If Russell is down there, perhaps he will see the light and come.

Zoe put her left hand on the mossy wall and began her descent, tentative at first, then forcing herself to be more decisive. When she reached the flagstoned floor, her torch beam didn't stretch very far across the forest of chairs and her eyes again found it hard to adjust to the sharp contrasts between areas of light and shade.

Oh, I wonder ...

Zoe crossed behind the rearmost row of slatted wooden chairs, heading for the place where she had been sitting, inspired by the touching memory of the day when she had left Russell in the car park in Sainte-Catherine, only to find him still there waiting for her two hours later, steadfast and shivering and hopeful.

Sure enough, there he was, curled once more like a furry white croissant on the seat of the very chair that she had used, fast asleep.

Thank heavens.

She picked him up and he roused himself to lick her cheek, as if to say: *I knew you'd come.*

It was hard to manage phone, torch and dog, all at the same time. On the stairs, Russell decided that enough was enough and he wanted to be put down, scrabbling at the front of her coat. Because the moon was shining directly in, she was able to put her phone away and still see clearly, placing him squarely on the step.

'Go on, then. Up you go.'

Russell did as he was told, climbing in a sequence of bunny hops, front feet then back feet. Zoe followed, noticing once more the surprising difference in temperature between the mild artificial cavern and the freezing outside world. She unhooked the chain and shut the door, following Russell back to the terrace.

Back indoors, she made sure the dining-room fire was damped down, to prevent sparks, then made her way upstairs. Russell scampered ahead, without even a pretence of at first going to sleep in the dog bed in the basement kitchen.

Up in her room, Zoe groped behind the curtain to fetch her emergency rations off the windowsill. The rye bread was a little firm but fine to eat. Happily, neither the Emmenthal nor the *saucisson* had frozen in the cold draught. She sliced some slivers from each with her Swiss Army knife and fed them to Russell with her fingers, telling him aloud: 'You must have been frightened down in that awful damp place. So this is a treat, the exception, not the rule, you understand?'

Saying this, Zoe wondered how Russell had become trapped.

Did someone go back to turn out the lamps, locking him in? They were still burning when I saw the family leaving.

She frowned, trying to visualise the family members, disappearing indoors while she had hung back.

Was Isabelle with them, or did she drift away with the rest of the villagers? And what about Caroline?

She undressed, folding her clothes on the top of her chest of drawers, feeling a strong sense of relief as she donned her pyjamas, turned off the ceiling light and slipped beneath the covers.

What a day. It's been endless.

Soon, her mind became pleasantly adrift in the darkness. Russell stirred on his corner of the bed.

'I'm glad you're here,' she told him quietly. 'Otherwise, I would feel horribly alone.'

Thirty-Eight

'DON'T BOTHER YOUR FATHER'

Zoe woke in more darkness, summoned from the middle of a sleep cycle by footsteps in Junior's room overhead. She checked her phone and discovered that the time was exactly eight o'clock, but the screen was still on 'night mode' because the sun was not quite up. Clumsily, she reached for the switch on the cable of her bedside lamp and toggled it three times with no response.

I expect I'll have to go and reset that RCD again, though the only real solution is to find out which device is tripping it.

She got out of bed, becoming quickly aware of the chill in the air. She crossed to the window and put her hands on the radiator beneath it.

Stone cold.

She opened the curtains. The sky was just lightening with a pre-dawn glow, but the view of the lake was obscured by dancing flakes. The draught from the bottom of the frame was nowhere near as bad, but only because the outside window-sill was banked up with snow.

It must have been falling for several hours and it doesn't look like stopping.

In the gloomy room, Zoe dressed in her everyday clothes, plus her ski jacket, two pairs of socks and her waterproof nylon boots, then had to grope her way downstairs to the kitchen because the ceiling lights were all out. Russell came with her and curled up for an additional nap in the dog bed.

By the light of her phone she located the consumer unit, high on the wall in the corridor outside Monsieur Alain's bedroom. As she had expected, the safety circuit breaker had tripped. On this occasion, though, when she pushed it up to re-establish power, it refused to stay in position.

This is not good news.

Pointlessly, Zoe tried the circuit breaker one more time. It instantly snapped back down, as if in rebuke. Hearing hesitant footsteps, she called out: 'There's a problem with the electrics.'

Adélaïde's voice replied: 'I guessed as much. It isn't the first time. There's an engineer who comes sometimes. The number is on the wall behind the boiler. You could ring him.'

They met in the kitchen, which was slightly less gloomy, with grey light entering from the slot windows high up in the walls, only just above ground level outside. Zoe said: 'Should I run down to the reservoir and retrieve the hurricane lamps? You could make the call while I do that?'

'Good idea.' Adélaïde took out her mobile phone and walked away, remarking over her shoulder: 'We should build up the fire in the dining room to give people a place to sit.'

'All right, I'll do that first. When I come back, do you want to tell me about what happened after the concert, what was said and so on?'

'Perhaps,' said Adélaïde.

Adélaïde turned on her phone torch in order to see the plumbing engineer's number clearly. As a precaution, worrying about short circuits, Zoe unplugged the boiler then gathered up an armful of logs from the diminishing pile of well-seasoned timber. She ran upstairs to dump them in the basket. The long mahogany table with rounded ends looked magnificent without its stained tablecloth.

She went back down for another armful of logs, wondering if there might be more somewhere. She included some smaller scraps of kindling and a few of the faded and

242

dusty newspapers. Adélaïde was sighing and listening to a robotic, pre-recorded voice giving a replacement number for Monsieur Barge, so Zoe toiled back up alone and began arranging her fire-lighting wigwam. Her eyes darted round for matches and found them on the high mantelpiece. She set one to the tinder-dry newspaper, which burnt up quickly but smokily.

Zoe opened the French doors onto the terrace to encourage the chimney to draw, revealing a pristine carpet of unblemished virgin white. The sky was a low ceiling of undifferentiated grey cloud from which snow continued to fall in dancing flakes, with a narrow slot of orangey-blue in the east.

Adélaïde entered, saying: 'He's calling me back.' She sighed. 'I don't blame you for fleeing our terrible manners last night.'

'Were you all very late to bed?'

'Would you believe it if I told you that I went from room to room, trying to keep the peace?'

'Yes. Why wouldn't I?'

'I'm afraid I have a reputation for being self-centred.'

'Not with me. Did you make any progress?'

'I spoke to everyone in private, plus lots of unhappy combinations. There were all kinds of comings and goings, including down to the liquor cabinet in the kitchen and back again. Plus, Junior ended up sleeping in Sweetie's dressing room, I think.'

'Did Isabelle come back to the house with you all?'

'She did. Primo asked her to do so in order to "clear the air".'

'Did they achieve that?'

'I don't know. I wasn't present with her and my husband and his brother.'

'And Caroline?'

'Both Boris and Primo sought words with her.'

'Together?'

243

'And separately,' said Adélaïde. 'Then Boris and Sweetie and Isabelle met in further conclave. Do you think we can shut the terrace doors now?' Zoe did so. Adélaïde asked: 'Did I hear you go out and come back in again?'

'Yes, I went looking for Russell and found him trapped in the reservoir.'

'Oh,' said Adélaïde, without – Zoe thought – any real depth of feeling for the misfortunes of small dogs. Adélaïde added: 'Then I had a call from Los Angeles at one-thirty in the morning because some foolish intern was incapable of working out the time difference.'

'Did you take it? Was it good news?'

'The finance is all in place. The trouble is, I don't want to rake over all that again.'

'The murder at Chichester Theatre?'

'Yes.'

'On the other hand, you need to do this true-crime show,' said Zoe, taking a chance, 'because Château Palotte needs the money.'

'Aren't you clever,' said Adélaïde, unhappily.

'You want to support Primo and thought it might fix the rift that has opened up between you.'

'So very, very clever,' said Adélaïde, only just audible. 'But it's the cause of the rift.'

Her phone rang and she answered on loudspeaker. Monsieur Barge, it turned out, was only forty kilometres away but on the far side of the Verdon Gorge, trapped at a job that would take him several more hours, in an old people's home.

'That must take priority,' came his tinny voice. 'After which, who knows if the roads will even be passable?'

'Of course, but any effort you feel prepared to make will earn our eternal gratitude,' Adélaïde told him. 'Whenever you arrive.'

'*Entendu*,' he told her, meaning 'understood'.

Adélaïde hung up.

'That doesn't sound very promising,' said Zoe.

'No,' said Adélaïde. 'It does not.'

Marie-France entered, dressed in a high-necked black day dress decorated with beads, like an Edwardian lady in mourning, over which she had chosen a velvet coat in bottle green, not unlike Adélaïde's purple one that Zoe had worn. In her usual haughty voice, she asked: 'Are we marooned? Will we freeze first, or starve?'

Sweetie and Junior arrived, the latter asking for his cereal. Sweetie told him to go and eat in the kitchen. Zoe recommended bringing his breakfast upstairs because the basement would be getting colder and colder. Junior looked at her askance then slithered away.

Caroline arrived, rubbing her hands together for warmth and telling everyone: 'According to the news on my phone, the road from Aix-en-Provence to Sainte-Catherine has been closed. And that one will have been gritted, unlike the ones around Saint-Paul-de-Palotte. We're definitely stuck.'

Patrick and Minette arrived, 'drawn by the warmth', as Patrick said. Zoe got the impression that brother and sister had made up – or, at least, were no longer in open warfare. *It would be hard to keep fighting while sharing that small bedroom.*

Elizabeth followed them in, yawning and telling everyone that she felt 'chilled to the bone'.

Marie-France asked: 'Do you see yourself as somehow special in that regard? We are all in the same boat, are we not?'

'A boat that is gradually disappearing beneath the waves,' said Patrick with a smile, reminding Zoe of Primo's idea that 'old age is a slow shipwreck'.

Minette asked about food, remarking: 'The locusts have eaten us out of house and home.'

Marie-France reprimanded her, saying: 'The tenants and the villagers came at the family's invitation. Should we begrudge them their annual treat?'

'I imagine most of them,' said Patrick, good-humouredly, 'think of it more as an obligation.'

'Hear hear,' said Minette.

'Please don't all start arguing again,' said Sweetie, surprisingly.

'Yes,' said Adélaïde. 'Please don't.'

Zoe saw Sweetie give Adélaïde a glance of such deep and heartfelt gratitude at this casual support that she had to look away.

'What are we going to do?' asked Caroline.

Zoe told them all about the circuit breakers and the boiler and the plumber and the lasagnes. Sweetie suggested asking 'that nice man from the village' to heat them up.

'Can you possibly not have learned the name of Monsieur Astor, the *boulanger*?' demanded Marie-France, who seemed determined to spoil the atmosphere every chance she got.

'I say . . . ?' came a weak voice from the corridor.

Adélaïde rushed out and Zoe heard her gently admonishing Primo for coming down alone. They entered the dining room and Primo insisted on formally shaking everyone's hand before finally being persuaded to take a seat.

'How did you sleep?' asked Adélaïde, from which Zoe deduced that they had not shared their enormous four-poster bed.

'Tolerably,' said Primo. 'But my heart is now racing. Has anyone seen Boris? Is he any better?'

'We left him to his rest,' said Sweetie. 'He was up very late with appalling indigestion. Junior and I slept in the dressing room.'

Just then, Junior himself returned with a rattling tea tray on which – rather touchingly, in a desire to be helpful – he had balanced mismatched cutlery, the butter dish, five or six pots of jam, plus odds and ends of the previous evening's *baguettes*. He put the tray on the table and asked: 'May I be excused? I ate downstairs.'

'Yes,' said Sweetie. 'Run along. Don't bother your father.'
'I won't.'

Zoe spread some sheets of newspaper on the polished mahogany of the dining table and moved the tray onto them.

Patrick remarked that, if Primo was in agreement, there was no need for them to 'contract hypothermia and expire unhappy'. He wondered if he ought to go downstairs and 'liberate a few bottles from the wine rack and the liquor cabinet'.

'Not for me,' Primo replied, offering the key from the fob pocket of his tweed waistcoat, 'but go ahead.'

Patrick added: 'For later on, not straight away. With the lasagnes, for example, once Gaspard has done the necessary.'

'I don't eat breakfast,' said Marie-France, 'as some of you may know. But neither do I enjoy balancing canapés and wine glasses of an evening. I ate almost nothing and am extremely hungry as, I imagine, you all are. I suggest we eat brunch, as soon as the food is hot, so we neither freeze nor starve.'

'The line may be a good one,' said Adélaïde, 'but there is no need to repeat yourself.'

'Well, I must say—' began Marie-France.

'I'm sorry,' interrupted Adélaïde. 'Please ignore me. It's a very good idea, Marie-France. I know Primo was too busy doing his social duty to have more than a bite or two. Zoe, would you be very kind and—'

'Of course,' said Zoe, jumping in. 'I'll do it now if you can unlock the front door?'

'I'm afraid,' said Primo, 'that I forgot that small duty, without Alain to remind me.'

'Never mind,' said Zoe. 'I'll be back shortly.'

Zoe hurried downstairs to fetch the two lasagnes, bringing them back up and putting them down momentarily on the big oak carver chair while she opened up. The steps were deep in pristine snow. She descended with care, finding a small drift piled up against the gate to the village. She pulled it open, revealing that the perfect cobbled lanes of Saint-Paul-de-Palotte resembled a Christmas postcard. In the windows of the shops and houses were points of friendly light.

The problem with the power is confined to the château.

She walked the short distance to the *boulangerie*, finding it delightfully warm and snug. She made her request to Gaspard who told her: 'We'll be only too pleased to help. They're properly defrosted. Didi will bring them up in forty minutes – a respectable time for a brunch.'

'Thank you so much.'

Zoe returned via the lane to the gate, squinting at the low sun that shone – albeit not for long – through a narrow slot beneath the ceiling of grey cloud.

Now I'm out, I should go and get those hurricane lamps.

She crossed the unblemished snow of the lawn with flakes collecting on her eyelashes, surprised to find that the horizontal door giving access to the reservoir was open.

I'm sure I shut it.

Warily, she descended just the first three steps, sniffing the air, still concerned at the idea that it might have become noxious. In the end, though, it seemed there was nothing to worry about.

She completed her descent and made for the stage. By coincidence, the low eastern sun was creating a bright shaft of light, angled down through the small gap – like a letter box – above the rusted sluice, creating a narrow, oblique beam onto the bare scaffolding boards.

Bare, that is, apart from the huddled shape of Boris de Palotte, curled in a foetal position, draped in his bell-like overcoat, as if trying to keep himself warm while the space all around had become cold and devoid of life.

As he was, very obviously, himself.

Thirty-Nine

'IS THIS ANOTHER MURDER?'

For Zoe, time briefly stopped. She had a flashback to Sainte-Catherine a few months before, with the discovery of another body, equally devoid of life, victim of 'the French bookshop murder'. She became aware, in the silence of the reservoir, of her own blood pulsing in her ears while Boris de Palotte's heart – despite the wild swings of his atrial fibrillation – would henceforth be forever still.

From far away came the strange call of the stag, an odd combination of a hoarse cough and a booming bellow. The text of the ancient Irish poem came back into her mind, a song of bleak midwinter foreboding at the arrival of 'a season of snow'.

Come along, Zoe. Pull yourself together.

She approached the stage. Boris was close enough to the edge for her to remain on the damp flagstones and reach out a hand to take hold of his wrist, intending to feel for a pulse. But the sparse flesh on his bony limb was already cold. She had to fight the urge to snatch her hand back. Illuminated by the shaft of cold sunlight, Boris's eyes were half open, the awful bloodshot one reminding her of zombie movies.

Is this another murder?

Zoe reversed to the foot of the stairs, trying to follow the exact same path across the flagstones that she had taken on the way in.

Because that might be important later on.

She did the same on the stairs, backing carefully out towards the grey light, moving painfully slowly, her mind juggling a host of conflicting ideas.

He might have come down to the underground reservoir to be on his own, for some privacy and peace and quiet, to think and make plans. Might he have been consumed with regret? But for what?

She thought about his cruelty to young Junior, his failed business ventures, his lack of friendship and respect in the village.

Did he know about Elizabeth's stash of super-strong caffeine tablets? Could he have stolen a handful in order to kill himself with an overdose, provoking a catastrophic crisis in his heart condition? That would only make sense if he had, for some reason, been forced to face up to the mess he had made of his life. Perhaps being confronted by Sweetie's misery or by the folly of his adventure with Isabelle?

She tried not to get carried away with supposition.

Or I suppose it's possible that he could have – innocently – succumbed to the cold or to the late night and the unaccustomed exercise, because he was allegedly 'very poorly' earlier in the evening. Or did he return to the reservoir to meet someone? But why? To plot in secret? Or to review the progress of his own murderous designs?

Zoe felt sure this was the right solution.

He would definitely have had the authority and influence to be able to persuade Junior to place the branch in order to trip Primo as he led the family to the ceremony in the village. Might he have asked his son to slip out in the dead of night so that he could give him more instructions, certain of not being overheard? I heard Junior's footsteps in the room above mine in the night.

Standing quite close to the top of the stairs, her head just emerging, she turned to face Château Palotte, grey and unfriendly in the cold light.

Or is he a victim? Did someone invite him to meet them here because they had their own mens rea, their own 'evil will'. Either way – those poor people. I'm about to turn their lives upside down.

The snow was still falling and the wind seemed to be picking up, out of the north-east. She had another – bleaker – thought.

Or am I actually bringing good news – to one or to some of them?

Because she hadn't fully emerged, her eyes were only just above the level of the grass. She was at a perfect angle to examine the snow-covered lawn, seeing her own footsteps, leading diagonally across the pristine white surface, towards the front door and the steps where Monsieur Alain had died. No other traces were visible in any direction, except for a few tiny indentations left by birds.

I wish I knew when the snow began properly to fall. Late enough that Boris left no footprints? Or, perhaps, they've been covered up? That would tie in with the fact that his flesh is already cold.

She returned her gaze to the darkness of the reservoir.

Although it's eleven or twelve degrees underground, remember, like a wine cellar. His wrist, like his other extremities, would become chilled quite quickly and feel cold compared to how warm my fingers are. I've been busy buzzing about and running errands and lighting the fire and traipsing up and down stairs.

Zoe began thinking about the order of events since the post-concert arguments in the reservoir had broken up. Then she made a noise of frustration.

You're being silly. You're not a doctor or a detective. You don't know how to calculate the time of death from the temperature of a corpse. Why are you thinking like you do?

The shaft of light from the sluice, high up in the wall, had moved with the progress of the sun through its slot in the clouds. It now cast its beam at the foot of the stairs, illuminating a puddle of damp in which something silver had fallen. Zoe redescended, keeping her eyes fixed upon it.

I don't want to look on Boris's corpse once more.

Then, to her surprise, she felt relief.

That's a stroke of luck.

She bent to retrieve the object, cold and wet from the flagstones.

It must have come off when Russell was scrabbling against my chest to be put down, after I found him. I didn't even know it had fallen.

The silver object was the brooch in the form of the Palotte family crest, two rampant stags either side of a stone turret, the one she had been wearing, pinned to the front of Adélaïde's velvet dress coat.

When the clasp gave way that first time, I should have just left it somewhere safe. I would have felt awful for losing it, as if I was a bad omen, a Jonah, bringing bad luck.

She put it deep and safe in her ski-jacket pocket.

Although the bad luck is already here.

She reascended, but only as far as the penultimate step.

What is my first priority? Primo will be devastated and is, perhaps, in no condition to endure the shock. He's not – or rather he wasn't – exactly in tune with his brother, but there was, nevertheless, a strong connection based in tradition and blood. I'm not sure telling Sweetie that her husband is dead will lead to any kind of sensible response. Then, there are Boris's other wives, each of whom has a claim on the knowledge.

She frowned.

A claim on his body, too, and on whatever material things he's left behind?

Zoe felt reluctant fully to climb out and disturb the carpet of white separating her from the terrace and what were, to her, the black mirrors of the dining-room windows. She sighed with exasperation.

And I didn't even pick up any of the hurricane lamps, which was my whole reason for coming here. Never mind. Though it's gloomy, the sun won't actually go down for five or six hours. Perhaps Monsieur Barge will have made it by then.

As if to give the lie to this misplaced optimism, the snow abruptly began falling more heavily, stinging her eyes and obscuring Château Palotte.

I'll tell Adélaïde. She can decide how to break it to her husband.

Forty

'Is She Deliberately Misunderstanding?'

Poised on the stairs of the reservoir, Zoe contemplated the snowy lawn.

I'm not going to take the direct route across the lawn to the terrace. I'll retrace my footsteps, like King Wenceslas's page, and go back in via the front door, the way I came.

Zoe checked her watch, trying to work out how much time had passed since she had embarked on her errands and, more importantly, when Didi Astor would arrive, carrying the two lasagne trays, piping hot and ready to eat.

I'd like to know if anyone's been out through the vegetable garden, from the lobby at the base of the eastern tower, under my room. Was it only yesterday that there was already a little drift of snow outside on the step, deep enough to deter Russell? It feels like a week ago.

She set off, leaving the reservoir door open.

Gaspard said forty minutes. I think I still have most of that, but I should hurry.

She followed her own footprints in reverse, diagonally across the lawn. The new snow was falling so heavily that they were already filling up, the indentations becoming blurred.

Boris didn't necessarily come out via the terrace. The front door wasn't locked overnight, remember. I'm sure I've read somewhere that new snow can be carefully brushed away, revealing hidden footprints left in the previous layer. I hope I'm not walking on them.

She climbed the steps between the lavenders and went inside, stamping her feet on the mat.

I suppose no one but Primo necessarily knew the house was unlocked?

Keeping her coat on because it was chilly indoors, she crept past the dining room – beyond whose closed door she could hear voices but no shouting or arguing – and went upstairs to her room. It had crossed her mind that the problem with the electrics might be connected to the loose wall socket beneath her bedside table.

I unplugged the boiler to prevent it from tripping the residual current device, but my lamp or even my phone charger could be another cause of the short circuit.

She removed both devices from the fragile double socket, redescended two flights to the basement kitchen, located the circuit breaker by touch and pushed it back up. To her great relief, the ceiling lights came back on. Her shoulders relaxed and she realised that she had been moving stealthily, as if under threat.

Why should that be? No one can possibly have a grudge against me. I'm just trying to help.

She plugged the boiler back in but, frustratingly, it remained inert.

I was right. It was failing, regardless of the short circuits. That's not good. In any case, it's imperative that I speak to Adélaïde.

She returned to the dining room, aware of the seconds and minutes chasing one another into oblivion. Opening the door, she found the whole family – except Boris, obviously, and Junior – assembled on upright chairs round the glorious mahogany table. Caroline sat apart, at the far end, on her phone. While Zoe had been away, Patrick had been downstairs to fetch some bottles of liquor from the cabinet in the kitchen, but no one had yet begun drinking.

She was welcomed as a saviour because everyone assumed that it was she who had 'fixed the lights'. Even Marie-France managed to express her gratitude, saying it was 'a mercy' that they wouldn't have to 'sit about with hurricane lamps, like unhappy boy scouts'.

Zoe accepted their praise and broke the bad news about the boiler to a chorus of dismay. Then she asked Adélaïde – she hoped, innocently – if she would like to see what she had done.

'In case it happens again?' Adélaïde asked.

'Yes,' said Zoe, looking meaningfully at her.

'Do you two have secrets you don't want to share?' asked Patrick, smiling.

Zoe laughed, hoping she wasn't overdoing it, and told him: 'No, but we did discover the problem together and Adélaïde was the one to speak to the engineer, Monsieur Barge.'

'If you say so,' said Patrick, apparently still in jest.

Is he actually suspicious for some reason?

'Don't be childish,' Minette told him.

Sweetie chimed in: 'I think it's a good idea that someone else knows what's happening. We can't expect Madame Pascal to do everything.'

'Go ahead, my dear,' Primo told Adélaïde. He had turned his chair to face the fire. 'Thank you for taking charge, Madame Pascal. I wish I could do so myself.' He sighed. 'But the slow shipwreck progresses.'

'We'll be as quick as we can,' said Adélaïde.

'Do what must be done,' he replied.

He only called her 'my dear' out of habit. The rift between them is still there, despite last night's comings and goings.

Zoe preceded Adélaïde downstairs, leading her into the boiler room with its cords and pulleys and drying rack, its washing machine, its now-meagre piles of logs and newspapers. She pulled the door closed behind them but, before she could begin her story, Adélaïde spoke.

'Primo had an awful turn. His face became congested and he was struggling to breathe. I've never seen him so bad.'

'How dreadful—' Zoe began.

'I feel so helpless every time it happens. I worry that it's something I've done to bring on the crisis and, of course, right now, perhaps it is. It's my fault the shadow of the past is lying so heavily upon us.'

'Yes, but—'

'Boris, of course,' Adélaïde continued in an angry, exasperated tone, 'has taken to his bed. I bet he's much less bad than poor Primo, sitting up in blissful solitude, eating biscuits from the breakfast tray. Meanwhile, Primo struggles on. In reality, the doctors are powerless to truly help. And the blood thinners – that are supposed to moderate his atrial fibrillation and ward off clots – mean that Primo gets cold very easily.'

'Was Boris prescribed blood thinners, too?'

'I believe so. Why?'

'I wondered about his eye? They might make a burst blood vessel more likely?'

'Yes, Primo had the same thing a couple of months ago.' Adélaïde gestured to the log pile. 'How long will we have to make these last? I will not have him uncomfortable or unhappy, if I can possibly help it.'

'All day, at least, I imagine.'

Adélaïde sighed. 'The boiler failing is the very worst thing that could have happened.'

'Not necessarily the worst,' said Zoe, gravely.

'What does that mean?'

'I have bad news.'

'You've lost my brooch,' said Adélaïde. 'I'm not surprised. I saw it was loose. Don't worry. It will turn up.'

'No,' replied Zoe, shaking her head. 'Or rather I did, but I found it again. That's not important right now. Listen, something truly terrible has occurred and I don't know what I ought to do – what we should do.'

'Go on,' said Adélaïde, warily.

Zoe left a small pause. She had abruptly realised that Adélaïde was the only person she had told of her intention to fetch the hurricane lamps from the reservoir.

And she didn't try to persuade me not to. That must mean that she didn't know what I would find there so I can assume that she has no guilty conscience—

'What is it, Zoe? You've gone blank.'

'I'm sorry. It's all a shock and a blur.'

Or she wanted it to be me who found him?

'What is?' demanded Adélaïde.

'Boris is down there.'

'Down where?'

'On the stage – the one that the musicians used.'

'What's he doing?'

'Nothing,' said Zoe, confused.

Is she deliberately misunderstanding?

'I don't understand,' complained Adélaïde. 'How can he be doing nothing?'

Zoe realised that she hadn't shared the most important detail of all.

'Because he's dead.'

V

MOTIVE AND OPPORTUNITY

Forty-One

'A MATTER OF LIFE AND DEATH'

Because Adélaïde was such a good actress, Zoe realised that she wasn't in a position to accurately judge the nature of her friend's response to the appalling news that her brother-in-law, Boris de Palotte, had died. Adélaïde appeared utterly composed, if a little withdrawn.

'I don't know what to do for the best,' Zoe told her, honestly. 'It crossed my mind that you should be the one to tell Primo? I suppose we should also call a doctor? Or the *pompiers*? They were very quick to turn up for Monsieur Alain.'

'That was before we became snowbound,' Adélaïde warned.

'Is there anyone in the village with authority to take charge, until somebody can come from Aix-en-Provence, for example? What about the policeman Patrick mentioned? The road from the west is more likely to be gritted and open than the one that has Monsieur Barge trapped on the far side of the Verdon Gorge.'

'Caroline says the road from Aix to Sainte-Catherine is shut,' Adélaïde reminded her. 'Look, Zoe, are you sure? There is no doubt in your mind?'

'About what?' Zoe asked.

'That he's gone.'

'No, none at all.'

Adélaïde put her head on one side. Zoe got the impression that she was being judged. Adélaïde said: 'Of course, this is not the first time that you have looked upon death.'

'I took my time. I checked.' Zoe felt herself blanch, remembering the awful sensation of touching Boris's lifeless flesh, like poor quality meat on a butcher's slab, moving slackly over the bones beneath. 'I will share the news myself, if you think it best. I could tell them now, before Didi Astor turns up with the lasagnes.'

'No.'

'What do you mean, "no"?'

'Not yet.'

'One of us has to.'

'We cannot tell Primo,' insisted Adélaïde. 'I cannot tell him. You mustn't, either.'

'You can't be serious.'

'It might be a matter of life or death,' said Adélaïde.

'It is already a matter of life or death.'

'Nothing can be done for Boris. I will not have Primo exposed to another shock. He can quite happily believe that his brother is resting upstairs.'

'When, all the while, he is lying cold and alone—'

'Not that cold, actually. Not as cold as we are going to get above ground if we run out of logs.'

This was not what Zoe had expected.

'Adélaïde, it seems wrong.'

'Of course it does,' she replied, with exasperation.

She's not cross with me. It's the awful circumstances.

'Tell me what you are thinking,' Zoe prompted.

'It's wrong in the same way that I was wrong to turn a blind eye to what I suspected was going on at Chichester Theare all those years ago. But I was young and stupid and heartless and, like I warned you, entirely self-centred.'

'So, you did have an idea about what was going to happen – a murder, live on stage.'

'Yes, and have regretted it ever since. That's why I try so hard with everyone, exhausting though it is. You can see it with Isabelle, for example, because I want forgiveness for what I did, for stealing the life she ought to have lived, the career and the marriage, though it wasn't my fault. It was just circumstances.'

'Yes, you are very kind to her, but we're getting off the point. Surely you see that the family has to be told.'

Adélaïde paid no attention. 'Murder is like an infection or a bad smell. Nothing and no one is left untainted.'

It was Zoe's turn not to answer. She was thinking once more about the undeniable fact that Adélaïde was a very good actress, but also about the utterly convincing frankness of her expression and tone. Then she gasped.

'I've just realised that he might have been down there, already dead, when I went looking for Russell.'

She gave Adélaïde the gist of what had happened, how she had missed the terrier and, finding him absent from his usual places indoors, had tried the reservoir and discovered him locked in and waiting for her, curled up on the chair that she herself had sat in.

'Russell might have gone and sniffed round the body and licked his hand,' Zoe said. 'Then, finding it cold, taken no more interest.'

'What a vivid imagination you have.'

'In order to understand the timeline of events, we would have to piece together everyone's movements. Do you know where you were between the end of the concert and when you finally went to bed?'

'Do you?'

'Well, yes,' said Zoe, surprised at her friend's combative tone. 'Doing chores, tidying, stacking the dishwasher, then in my room.'

'But afterwards, at some uncertain hour of the night, you went gadding about through the house and across the lawn to the reservoir.'

'Not that late, actually. And other people were up and about, including you, I assume. I heard footsteps on my way out and on my way in.'

'How long do you think that all took?'

'No more than ten minutes at the outside.'

'And what time was it?'

'That's the annoying thing. I took off my watch because it caught on the little lace fringe on the sleeve of the velvet coat.'

'But, when you went looking for Russell, you didn't see Boris?'

'Obviously not or I would have raised the alarm.'

'How could you have been down there without seeing him?'

'Because I was using my phone torch and the throw of the beam is very short and bright, meaning I could see what was close at hand but everything else was in shadow.'

'You were using your phone but you didn't check the time?'

'I may have seen it but it made no impression.'

'The hurricane lights had been extinguished?'

'Or perhaps simply run out of paraffin?' suggested Zoe. 'This morning was different because there was a shaft of light coming down through the sluice opening.' Zoe frowned, trying to get her ideas straight. 'That means that ten minutes earlier or later I wouldn't have seen him because the sunbeam wouldn't have been . . . Oh, no, that's not right. I was bound to notice him because I'd actually gone down there to fetch the hurricane lamps and they were grouped around the stage for the performance, close to where he lay.' Adélaïde said nothing. Her face was inscrutable. 'Where he still lies,' Zoe insisted.

The front doorbell rang.

'Lasagnes,' said Adélaïde, vaguely. Then her voice became insistent, commanding. 'Please, Zoe, don't tell anyone – not yet.'

Zoe was already on the move. From the staircase, feeling frustrated and compromised, she called back: 'All right, but we can't wait forever.'

She met Patrick in the hall.

'Wait for what? How's the conspiracy progressing?' he asked with annoying, jovial insistence.

'We've decided to write a screenplay,' Zoe told him. 'It's called *The French Bookshop Murder*, and we're going to sell it for a fortune to Hollywood.'

'Really?' he enthused. 'That's a brilliant idea. Maybe Isabelle can help?'

Zoe didn't know why he said that.

'No, of course not really,' Zoe replied, impatiently. 'We were discussing the electrics and the plumbing, nothing more, nothing less.'

Unsure why she had acceded to Adélaïde's urgent request to lie – or, at least, to withhold the truth for the time being – she opened the wide front door to find both Didi and Gaspard Astor on the rubber outdoor mat, the father preposterously underdressed in rolled-up shirtsleeves and a long white apron, his son wrapped up in what looked like a white, army-surplus duffel coat. The snow was swirling around their bare heads and flakes were settling on the steaming crusts of the pasta bakes, carried one each, their hands protected by bunched-up tea towels.

'*Nous voilà*,' said Gaspard. 'Here we are, as promised. We'll need to put them down sharpish.'

'Of course,' said Zoe. 'Patrick, would you spread some newspapers on the dining table?'

'It's already done.'

Zoe stepped aside then followed the three men. Gaspard and Didi hurried and were very pleased to relinquish their piping-hot burdens. Even with the full thickness of a copy of *Le Monde* beneath each, Zoe worried that the mahogany table would be marked. Then she pushed that thought aside.

That's not actually my business.

Adélaïde arrived from the kitchen with a pile of plates and cutlery, plus two large fish slices. She served Primo and then Marie-France before giving her utensil to Sweetie to help herself. Meanwhile, Patrick was expertly dishing up for his sister Minette, his mother Elizabeth, for Caroline and himself.

'I felt a chill as we came in,' said Gaspard. 'Is there a problem?'

'Yes,' said Adélaïde. 'You're a practical man, Monsieur Astor. Do you know anything about plumbing and electrics?'

'Enough to know I shouldn't fiddle with things I don't understand, begging your pardon.' He turned to his son. 'Run back and look after the shop, Didi.'

Without a word, but with a look of contempt for someone seated at the table – Zoe couldn't quite tell who – the young man left.

No one even acknowledged him.

In fact, the Palotte family hadn't troubled to thank either of the bakers for their kindness and were now busy eating.

Talking to one another as if Gaspard was somehow insignificant, transparent even, not really there at all.

Forty-Two

'Might I Have Met His Murderer?'

Zoe tried to feel more sympathy for the complicated Palotte family.

They are all famished. It's true, none of them was able to eat anything much last night, while they did their social duty.

Zoe led Gaspard out into the corridor and told him: 'We're in a bit of a jam with the boiler dead.'

'Have you called Laurent Barge?' he asked. Zoe explained why the regular maintenance man wasn't available. 'That's a shame,' he told her in a sympathetic tone. 'There's no one else in the village. I'm afraid anything I try will only make things worse.'

'Gaspard,' she asked, changing the subject, 'do you know about wood deliveries to the château? I assume Monsieur Alain always had it in hand?'

'Regular as clockwork, a nice load every week, all through the winter, from a cousin of mine. I believe you know him? His name's Gato Merino?'

'The handyman? Yes, he's done lots of jobs for me at the bookshop. He's wonderful.'

'The trouble is, it's been perishingly cold so he'll have had a lot of demand and I suppose you'll have been going through them? I wouldn't be surprised if you were running low?'

'We are.'

Gaspard pulled a sad face. 'There's no reason you should know, but tomorrow would normally be delivery day for Gato, but will he be able to get through?'

'Because of the snow and ice?'

'That's right. He's only got that little van of his, not much bigger than a postage stamp, so it can get up into the narrow lanes of the villages. He has to take care it doesn't get unstable and top-heavy loaded with logs. And, if he can't see where the side of the road ends and the ditches begin because of the drifts, well . . .'

He left the thought hanging.

'That is a worry,' said Zoe.

'You'll have to all cluster together till the day's end or until you run out, then go to bed – with the sun, perhaps.'

Zoe didn't share the fact that she had taken the precaution of bringing her own blower heater with her. She wondered if there might be similar appliances elsewhere in the château.

'Thank you for your advice,' she told him. 'And for helping to get some hot, nourishing food ready.'

'You're very welcome. Monsieur Primo has done – and I hope will continue to do – only good for the village.'

'I'm happy to hear it.'

She saw him out. He strolled away down the steps – not slipping this time – apparently impervious to the blizzard. With a sudden determination to get to the bottom of one of her many unanswered questions, she followed, catching up with him at the pedestrian gate.

'Monsieur Astor, Gaspard, I hope you don't mind me asking, but it seems to me that there's some kind of bad feeling between Didi and . . . Is it Elizabeth Lagrasse? Am I right? Can you tell me what it is?'

He turned slowly to face her, his face reflecting concern, but not deceit or trickery.

'You're thinking of what's happened?'

Zoe's heart lurched.

Does he know about Boris? How could he know? Unless Gaspard was the one to invite Boris to a clandestine meeting in the reservoir in order to do away with him? Or his son did?

'I'm not sure what I'm thinking,' she prevaricated.

Am I in danger?

'For you to ask that question,' he prompted, evenly, 'about my boy, you must have seen something?' He didn't sound angry or guilty.

'Yes, that's fair,' she said.

'Go on, then,' Gaspard told her with no tension in his eyes. 'Tell me what it was.'

Her pulse became steadier. 'I just noticed odd looks, at the drinks and nibbles last night and, perhaps, this morning – bad feeling between him and Madame Elizabeth.'

'Didi feels his mother's leaving very deeply,' he replied in a sombre voice.

'When he was a tiny baby?' she prompted.

'It was the affair that brought the marriage to an end.'

'You mean Elizabeth and Boris?'

'Yes, though they say she wasn't blameless, either, in having her wild oats to sow.'

'I'm sorry to appear dim,' said Zoe. 'You mean Boris de Palotte had an affair with your wife?'

He half-smiled, wiping the snowflakes from his face, the skin of his forearm tightened with goosebumps, but he wasn't feeling the chill like Zoe, who was shivering inside her ski jacket.

'I knew my Hélène wanted more from life,' said Gaspard, 'more than I was capable of offering. What could I provide? The same life, the same routine, every day and every week. I was lucky to keep her as long as I did.'

'She left soon after Didi was born?' Zoe asked.

'Yes, that's it. In his head, Didi's turned his mother into a wronged woman, a victim. In reality, she made her bed and was content to lie in it,' said Gaspard with a look that seemed to mean: *Pun intended.*

'The affair didn't last?'

'Oh, yes, it did. A few years, at least, with her in a Paris flat on Rue Jacob for Monsieur Boris's convenience. He's not been in the capital so much since money became tighter on the estate.'

Ah, that's interesting. It confirms what I had begun to suspect and ties in with the reason why Adélaïde has been contemplating doing the documentary, despite herself.

'Even though money is tight,' Zoe said, 'Monsieur Primo still makes his distribution of the profit on the rents that he invests – what people call their bonuses?'

'He does – and it was very welcome to me this year because I've got a leak in the roof at the back end of the mixing room and my van is on its last legs.'

'The tenants have come to depend on them?'

'When you tell people, outsiders, they say it sounds too good to be true – so it was no surprise when we all learned that this year might be the last.' He smiled, ruefully. 'Nothing good lasts for ever. Nothing bad, too, which is a mercy.'

'How many tenants are there in total?'

'A couple of dozen? No, maybe thirty, a few individuals but mostly families.'

In her head, Zoe was widening the range of potential grudge-bearers against Boris, the principal drain on the estate's finances. She asked: 'The place your wife moved to on Rue Jacob, is that the flat that Elizabeth Lagrasse now lives in?'

'I've never enquired nor been told but, if Didi got to hear about that, it would fire him up even more.' His half-smile became a frown. 'Rue Jacob was for Hélène's convenience, too, as well that of Monsieur Boris. She didn't bide there for his exclusive amusement. She had a life of her own, oth- erwise how would she have met someone else and taken it into her head to up sticks and go and live like a hippy in the old French colony of Pondicherry in India? Like I said, she always wanted more from life . . .'

There was a pause then Zoe said: 'You're very sanguine about it all.'

'It's a long time ago and my life is still a good one, so . . .'

He stopped again, without finishing his sentence, which Zoe recognised as characteristic of his conversational style. Her teeth beginning to chatter, she asked: 'Just one more thing, if you don't mind? After the concert, did you and Didi go straight to bed?'

'We're always up well before the sun. I was asleep within five minutes of entering our front door.'

'You wouldn't know if he'd gone back out?'

'He may have done. I did half hear the door, but I expect he was just putting out the bins. He's a good boy, despite appearances.' He frowned. 'You're shaking, Madame Pascal. You need to get off inside.'

'Yes, I do,' said Zoe, thankfully, but also with a sense that she had missed asking an important question. 'You've been very patient, Gaspard.'

'Oh, anything I can do to help, just ask.'

The burly baker turned away and disappeared through the gate into the snowy lanes of the village. Despite the cold, Zoe stayed where she was and watched him go, her eyes almost shut to protect them from the blizzard. She wasn't thinking about Gaspard, however. She was thinking about the fact that Didi might have been out and about in the small hours of the night.

I don't know exactly when or how Boris died. Should I assume that it was foul play? Not yet, perhaps? The idea I'm not enjoying is that he might have been there – alive or dead – when I went down looking for Russell.

At last, she roused her shivering limbs to hurry back up the steps and re-enter the house.

And, if he was, I didn't notice.

The hallway at the base of the western tower provided immediate shelter from the bitter wind, but it felt chilly and unwelcoming all the same.

Might Boris have still been alive on that first visit? And, if he was, might he have still been alive? Could I have saved him?

She rubbed her hands together, trying to return some circulation to her aching fingers.

Or might I have met his murderer?

Forty-Three

'WE UNDERSTAND ONE ANOTHER'

In the dining room, Zoe discovered two things that made her fume inside and obliged her to bite her tongue. The first was the fact that almost every single log she had brought upstairs from the boiler room had been piled in the hearth and they were all therefore being consumed at extravagant speed. The second was the fact that the two lasagne trays were completely empty, even of the tasty burnt bits round the edge.

Because I wasn't in the room while they were eating, I became irrelevant to them – out of sight, out of mind.

Looking very pleased with themselves, Patrick and Minette were taste-testing some tiny servings of Primo's finest whiskies. Primo himself was playing chess with Junior. Both looked pale for different reasons, the seventy-year-old because of his age and heart condition, the boy because he was naturally weedy and thin.

And he has no idea that his father is dead. Surely, I have to tell them—

Junior interrupted this thought by asking Zoe when the heating would be back on: 'It's very cold in my room – too cold for me to stay up there.'

'Zoe is not the new butler,' his mother told him, gently. 'It isn't up to her to sort it all out.'

'I didn't mean that,' complained Junior. 'It's just that she knows how to fix things and what's going on.'

'Madame Pascal is very clever,' said Sweetie. 'Did you know that she has a shop full of books? Some of them as long as the dictionary, I expect.'

'I must visit one day soon,' said Elizabeth who was turning the pages of a printed typescript with a blue biro in her hand.

Inevitably, in contrast to this sympathetic remark, Marie-France had something unkind to say about Sweetie's attempt at a few encouraging words, disparagingly using her given name, not her nickname: 'You say you "expect", Pauline. Is that because you've never been inside a bookshop?'

'Pauline was speaking for her son's attention,' said Primo. 'She is very well read in her field, I am sure.'

'You know she is,' said Elizabeth.

'What field might that be?' wondered Marie-France.

'You know Sweetie is well qualified as a personal assistant,' said Caroline who was watching this exchange with an expression of distaste.

'I thought Primo meant the field of gold-digging,' said Marie-France, brutally. 'But that would mean that her reading didn't prepare her to make a very good choice.'

Everyone looked at Sweetie who moved towards the door, as if she was going to stomp out and, in theatrical terms, 'make an exit'. Then, Zoe supposed, she remembered that she was in the only warm room in the house and changed her mind, going to stand at the French doors, looking out onto the dancing snowflakes. Elizabeth went and stood next to her, speaking very quietly.

'Where is Adélaïde?' Zoe asked.

The ones still round the table all looked at one another – Primo, Junior, Marie-France, Patrick, Minette and Caroline – and Zoe saw that none of them knew. From her position by the door, Sweetie said: 'She's outside, walking.'

Zoe caught a glimpse of Adélaïde through the glass, over Sweetie's shoulder, and felt a new surge of frustration.

She'll be obliterating any possible footprints in the snow. These people really are the limit.

Unable to trust herself not to tell the family off for their self-ishness, she fought the urge to clear the table of the two empty lasagne trays and left them to their bickering, retreating down-stairs to the kitchen. She ignited one of the gas burners on the stove and fetched the leftover pasta that she and Isabelle had prepared for their impromptu lunch. Because she was very hungry, she tossed in a few bits and pieces of preserved toma-toes and artichokes, adding to the sliced olives and tomatoes with which they had dressed the *penne*. She stirred through a large handful of grated Emmenthal and the whole mixture became gloopy and rich. She ate it at the kitchen table, grateful that no one came to interrupt her private feast.

No one, that is, until her final mouthful, when she became aware of Adélaïde lurking at the foot of the stairs.

'Thank you for keeping it to yourself.'

Zoe swallowed and retorted: 'How can you be sure I didn't ask Gaspard Astor to call the police?'

'Because you're my friend and because we understand one another.'

'Didn't you tell me earlier that . . . What was it? You said: "Perhaps you don't know me as well as you think." Well, whether I do or not, by keeping this secret, I can't help but feel I'm betraying myself in some way.'

'You sound very melodramatic.' Zoe didn't answer. Adélaïde went on. 'I'm worried about Primo and how his heart will react. Can't you see that there's a chance it will bring on a crisis?'

'But how long do you intend to oblige me to stay silent?'

'Don't fall out with me, please, Zoe,' said Adélaïde, desperately. 'You saw that Primo's a little better? Being with Junior, awful though he is, seems to calm him.'

'Is he letting you care for him? Have you talked about the—'

'The "flaw",' said Adélaïde, interrupting. 'No, I haven't.'

'I had an idea about that. Maisie should speak to him. She was there at the theatre all those years ago and she and Primo are more or less "of an age". She can reassure him that you did nothing to be ashamed of.'

'That would be very kind, if you could make that happen,' said Adélaïde, brightening. Then she sighed deeply. 'I've never carried my friendships with me. I don't know why. It's always seemed easier to leave the past behind. With you here in Château Palotte, you can see that I don't know how to be with you, even without all the drama and the worries: the boiler; how awful they are with Junior; money; what to do without Alain; Primo's "resuscitation", as he will insist on calling it; the awful thought of the hot wires of the ablation if the cardioversion doesn't work.'

'And Boris lying dead on the scaffolding planks of the stage in the reservoir?' asked Zoe quietly.

'I know,' said Adélaïde, desperately, 'but will you give me just until sunset? Or until someone decides that he's been too long in his room on his own and goes to look and finds it empty?'

'In order to do what?'

'To solve the mystery like you've done before.'

Forty-Four

'WE ARE TERRIBLE PEOPLE'

Zoe was about to argue that she was in no position to solve the mystery of Boris's death, but they were interrupted by footsteps in the corridor above and then descending the uneven stairs.

Elizabeth appeared carrying the empty metal cooking trays.

'I'm so sorry there was nothing left for you,' she said, her face convincingly apologetic. 'We are terrible people.'

'It doesn't matter,' said Zoe, untruthfully. 'I'm more concerned about running out of logs on this cold day.'

'Patrick and Minette have gone out wooding,' said Adélaïde.

'Good,' said Zoe, trying not to sound as though she thought it was about time someone in the family did something useful. 'Is everyone arguing still?'

'About the family church service,' said Elizabeth, making a sad face. 'Of all things.'

'How come?'

'It included an appeal for prosperity in the twelve months ahead,' said Elizabeth. 'I don't think anyone really believes in it, but you know how it is when things go well and you assume it's because of one small thing you did? The first "birthday blessing", as people call it, was back when Primo acceded to head of the estate.'

'Has the service brought good luck for all these years?'

'People say it has,' said Elizabeth.

'But things are no longer going well,' said Zoe. 'Prosperity is declining. Did the appeal strike too close to home?'

'Yes,' said Elizabeth, wearily. 'Things need to change.'

'They do,' said Adélaïde.

Zoe looked from Boris's second wife to Adélaïde and back. If there was one person who she thought she could trust with the knowledge that Boris was dead, it was Elizabeth.

She's clear-sighted. She works for a living. She is 'undeceived', as the poet says, by the various members of her family. And she's a practical person.

Inspired by the idea of another 'ally', Zoe decided to confront Elizabeth with what she had learned from Gaspard.

'I hope you don't mind me asking, but it seems to me that Didi Astor has . . . I'm not sure how to express it . . .'

'He hates me. He thinks that I'm the reason Boris took up with his mother, Hélène.'

'But why?'

'It's an internet thing, you know, those communities of sad boys and even sadder men who want to blame women for everything that's wrong in their lives when, in fact, it was a mutual attraction, with Boris offering the world – you know, wealth and opportunity and the bright lights of the capital – and Hélène bursting with unfulfilled desire.'

'You make it sound like a romance novel. Is that how you saw it, Adélaïde?'

'I wasn't there. It was before Primo and I met.'

'Oh, yes, of course it was.' Zoe turned back to Elizabeth. 'And everyone tells me you and Boris were living apart? Is that right?'

'No,' said Elizabeth, laughing. 'But perhaps they're using that as a euphemism for the fact that I was having my own affair with Patrick and Minette's father.'

'What was his name?'

'Patrick, also, but he called himself "Paddy" because he said it sounded chic. We were at school together and, when I discovered that Boris would never be what you might call an "attentive" husband, I found my own amusements.'

'So, your twins and Didier are of an age?'

'More or less.'

'What happened to Paddy? Is he still around?'

'No, he died.'

'Oh,' said Zoe. 'How awful. I'm sorry I asked.'

'That's all right. He was very dashing, a ski instructor, supremely overconfident. There was an avalanche at Courchevel. From eyewitness accounts, it seems he was flirting with it, convinced he could outrun it. He was wrong.' She sighed. 'I think that tragedy has shaped who Patrick and Minette have become – in their different ways.'

'How do you mean?'

'Patrick, like Paddy, happy-go-lucky, living for the moment; Minette careful and hard-working, worried about tomorrow.'

Zoe thought about what Caroline had said about Patrick spinning the car on a roundabout in the snow on the way back from Aix.

'Both are natural reactions,' said Adélaïde.

'My reaction,' said Elizabeth, 'was to drink too much. That was when Primo put a lock on the liquor cabinet.'

'Oh,' said Zoe again, then felt emboldened to ask: 'Is alcohol still a problem for you? I remember offering you some of that excellent white Burgundy last night. Was I pushy?'

'It isn't up to you to help me solve my flaws.'

There was a pause and Zoe was struck by the resemblance to her conversations about Primo discovering Adélaïde's 'flaw'.

Elizabeth turned away in order to fill the two lasagne trays with water in the big stainless-steel kitchen sink, adding a generous glug of washing-up liquid to each. Zoe addressed a quizzical look at Adélaïde who immediately understood her unspoken question – 'Should we tell Elizabeth?' Adélaïde firmly shook her head. Zoe sighed, looking down.

I am more and more uncomfortable with keeping this secret.

She had a horrible – disloyal – thought.

Is Adélaïde covering up for someone, like she did all those years ago in Chichester?

Then a new question and a new interpretation crystalised in her imagination, something she had believed resolved.

Could Adélaïde have had a motive for murdering Boris herself? I thought that was impossible because she didn't try to discourage me from going to get the hurricane lamps and, therefore, discovering what had happened, perhaps ahead of time, before she wanted it known. But that could have been a sort of double bluff, acting innocent, even encouraging me to go in there, because I would draw the obvious conclusion that she has nothing to hide.

Elizabeth turned back from the sink. Adélaïde's face expressed tension and worry.

But, if all that were true, what would be her reasoning for delaying the knowledge of Boris's death from becoming public?

To Zoe's surprise, Elizabeth went and briefly embraced Adélaïde, murmuring: 'Primo will come round.'

'Thank you,' said Adélaïde. 'What was the snow doing before you came down to the kitchen?'

'Heavier and heavier. Caroline had a look outside, you know, weighing things up, but she decided it was too dangerous for her to attempt the drive back to Aix. It would be so easy to get stuck somewhere and have to try and keep warm in your car until the fuel runs out.' Elizabeth turned to Zoe. 'You should have escaped when you had the chance.'

'I'm assuming the birthday events are over?' asked Zoe.

'Yes,' said Elizabeth.

'They are, finally,' said Adélaïde, with a tense half-smile. 'We could think of sunset as closure?'

Zoe understood what her friend meant.

She wants me to promise not to say anything until then. I suppose, at that point – maybe four o'clock? – it will have become impossible any longer to conceal Boris's absence.

'I suppose that's what it is,' said Zoe, agreeing. 'A sunset deadline.'

Forty-Five

'THE BOY ISN'T A PSYCHOPATH'

It was increasingly cold in the kitchen. Zoe wondered about keeping it habitable by bringing her blower heater down from her room.

I can always put it back when it's time for bed. Or should I offer it to Primo who is easily the frailest resident of the château?

'I just have to run upstairs,' she said. 'Why don't you go back to the dining room and keep warm?'

'Yes,' replied Elizabeth, heading for the boiler room. 'I'll take some of the last logs with me, though.'

'Yes, do.'

Adélaïde stayed where she was, immobile by the foot of the stairs. Zoe told her, very quietly: 'Try and find out who was where, when.'

Elizabeth re-emerged from the boiler room, her arms full, remarking with a grimace: 'It's all scraps and spiders. I hope Patrick and Minette have been successful in their scavenging.'

She embarked on the awkward stairs and Adélaïde followed. Zoe waited for the dining-room door to open and close, then ran up to the dingy first-floor corridor. In her room, she turned on the blower heater, using the solidly anchored plug socket near the door, rather than the problematic one under her bedside table. She angled it towards the end of the bed and sat down, hungry for its warmth.

It was interesting to discover that the liquor cabinet is locked because Elizabeth had a period of drinking too much. I imagine

Primo found that very hard to do. It would have offended his sense of self, his generosity and excellent manners.

Zoe held out her hands.

The Rue Jacob connection was interesting, too, and Didi Astor's silliness in believing that his mother's affair was the fault of the wronged wife rather than the philandering husband. I wonder who else has recognised his animosity? He made no attempt to hide it. Did he get the chance to talk directly to Elizabeth before the concert? Or was that what Minette drew Elizabeth outside to discuss? I can imagine Minette putting Didi straight – in no uncertain terms. If so, that conversation might easily have 'fired him up', as Gaspard said, against Boris instead.

She glanced at the window. The snow was still falling and the drift on the sill deepening. This reminded her of her emergency supplies, tucked behind the curtain. Because the modest pasta dish of leftovers hadn't satisfied her, she ate two slices of the – by now very firm – rye bread with both Emmenthal and *saucisson*. As she munched, contemplatively, she remembered, with exceptional clarity, her dialogue with Junior, when she had asked him why he had tried to drown Russell beneath the ice of the frozen lake.

He told me: 'I wanted to know what it would be like.' I asked him what he meant by that and he said something like: 'Not your dog. Just a thing. I wanted to know how it would make me feel.' And the reason must be that someone had asked him – commanded him? – to set the trap for Primo with the branch on the path. I'm sure that must be it. The boy isn't a psychopath, whatever some people have tried to convince me. And it would be entirely rational for him to want to know in advance how he might feel having done that terrible thing. It works with the timeline because the incident at the lake was before all these birthday shenanigans.

Zoe was beginning to feel more herself and realised that a combination of three things – cold, worry and hunger – had depressed her spirits more than she had allowed herself to recognise.

And made me more suspicious, perhaps? But this interpretation of Junior's behaviour does seem to me to be entirely convincing. Of course, it leads me back to the question of who would have the influence and authority to persuade him to do such a thing. His parents, obviously, are the prime candidates, but it could have been someone else. He's weak and, doubtless, easy to manipulate. Perhaps Patrick or Isabelle? I have no evidence of that. Primo is the only one who consistently tries to be nice to him, but that doesn't fit with the other details – the death of Monsieur Alain, who Primo seems to have been very close to. And the fact that, without Caroline's arrival, Primo himself would normally have been first down the steps.

She frowned.

Except, if Primo egged Junior on to do it, he could easily have contrived for Boris to precede him. Then, once Monsieur Alain had had his accident, it no longer mattered who went first. And the reason Primo has had such a bad crisis is because he was up in the depths of the night, killing his twin?

She pursed her lips.

But Primo was genuinely shocked to find Monsieur Alain on the steps. Was that shock brought on by guilt? Or could Monsieur Alain have been the intended victim – for something he knew, for example, that needed to be silenced?

She thought back to the moment when she had saved the branch from the fire and hidden it under some leaves, not far from the pedestrian gate into the village. She had glanced over her shoulder towards the western tower, wondering whose window it was on the first floor. From her clandestine exploration of Château Palotte, she now knew that it belonged to Marie-France.

There's someone with the harshness and the arrogance to commit a crime. Murder, though? Perhaps. She would certainly have the strength of mind to bend a ten-year-old boy to her will.

She heard footsteps overhead, coming from Junior's bedroom, and remembered hearing them – and the boy's sobs – on previous occasions, all of which were becoming a blur.

Someone told me that Junior ended up in Boris's dressing room last night, sharing the pull-out bed with his mother, Sweetie. I wish I knew what time that happened.

She thought again about the possibility of an interloper to Château Palotte, someone who snuck in with the tenants or the villagers for the concert.

Could it have been a stranger hiding up there? How about Patrick and Minette's father, Paddy? Oh, no. He died in an avalanche. I suppose that is an incontrovertible fact?

To make sure, using her phone, she made an internet search: *Paddy, ski instructor, avalanche, Courchevel, death.* The results took half a minute to load because the mobile data signal wasn't great, but what she found corresponded precisely to what Elizabeth had told her.

So that's a dead end. If I could question them all, one at a time, I feel I could get somewhere. I suppose I might be able to do so, before the sunset deadline that Adélaïde and I have agreed, but it will have to be a sly process, insinuated into general conversation. Which will be difficult if they all remain clustered round the dining table in the only warm room in the house.

She shook her head.

If it is still warm and they haven't burned up all the fuel.

Beginning to feel guilty about her prolonged absence, she wondered if Adélaïde had done as she had asked – in an urgent whisper – while Elizabeth was being useful and collecting up an armful of logs: 'Try and find out who was where when.'

I'm not sure she will even have tried. She's sort of checked out, just waiting for time to pass, hiding from the facts like an ostrich with her head in the sand. That's the impact of Primo's estrangement from her. Nothing else seems to matter.

Zoe leaned forward and turned off the blower heater. The air was becoming excessively dry, making her face feel tight.

I bet she knows about Elizabeth's large pot of caffeine pills. In fact, I bet everyone does. They all live together, on top of one another. It seems an extraordinary coincidence, given the fact that Primo and Boris both have a heart condition which – surely? – would respond terribly badly. Could that be the reason why Boris had that burst blood vessel – because someone dissolved caffeine tablets in his food or drink?

A shocking thought came into her mind.

Who made those lasagnes? They were just there, innocently, in the freezer compartment and I got them out without a thought. They might have been chock-full of ground-up pills, a fraction of the 'five hundred powerful doses of caffeine, soluble, fully vegan and without undesirable additives'.

She stood up, noticing that the quality of light in the room had changed. She went to the window and saw that the slot of clear sky in the east had expanded, the firmament clearing, with just a few wisps of ragged cloud against a dome of pure blue. Plus, the sun was more or less as high as it would get. The world looked bright and clean, albeit very cold.

I'll go down and speak to everyone and, maybe, persuade one or two of them to go for a walk – maybe do some wooding myself and a circuit with Russell. I'm sure the key is who was where when, from the argument at the end of the concert to sometime in the deep of the night. I need to establish their movements, preferably before the sun goes down, when I'll have to find a pretext for discovering Boris's body – in reality for a second time but no one must guess that – and finally reveal what only Adélaïde and I know.

She ate another corner of the wholesome but firm rye loaf.

And his murderer?

She put the emergency supplies away.

I wonder if Adélaïde has thought of a way of preparing Primo for the shock.

Then, all at once, she knew what her pretext for a second discovery could be.

I'll plug something back into the loose electrical socket under my bedside table and trip the electrics, including the lights, so we will need the hurricane lamps from the reservoir as evening comes on.

Forty-Six

'DON'T PRETEND TO BE OBTUSE'

Zoe turned off the blower heater and carried it out into the corridor, taking care to shut her door to keep in the warmth. She went all the way downstairs to plug it in and warm up the basement kitchen, then reascended to the dining room. She discovered that Patrick and Minette had been very successful, bringing in an impressive heap of fallen timber, some of it quite thick branches, torn from the estate's trees by the cold winter winds. The wood was burning more slowly than the well-seasoned logs because it was damp, but that meant it would last longer, draped out of the hearth into the space protected by the brass fender because, of course, none of it was cut to length. The room was a little smoky, even though the chimney was very hot and drawing well.

Zoe was about to congratulate the younger pair of twins when she noticed something that stopped her in her tracks. Perched on top of the fire was the branch she had saved from the flames, the one with the bare knuckle two-thirds of the way down that Junior had been trying to burn when he had blurted out: 'I didn't do anything.'

'We've done well, haven't we?' said Minette.

'Yes,' she told them, distracted. 'You have.'

'Junior helped,' said Patrick.

'That's good,' said Zoe. 'Where did you all look?' Junior's face was closed off. She insisted: 'By the gate into the village?'

He nodded, looking uncomfortable.

'He's a good boy,' said Primo. He and Junior were seated on the two dining chairs nearest to the blaze. 'Soon he'll be beating me at chess.'

'You must have searched under the leaves,' said Zoe.

'I did,' said Junior, quietly.

'That was very helpful,' said Primo. He moved one of his chess pieces. 'Your turn. When Boris comes down, perhaps we'll have a tournament.'

'No one's been up to check on him?' asked Zoe, as innocently as she was able.

'No one,' said Adélaïde. She was sitting on the far side of the table, leafing through Junior's magazine. Zoe supposed that was why she had heard footsteps above her room, because the boy had run up to fetch it. 'He needs to rest.'

'He's much better getting time to himself,' said Elizabeth with surprising sympathy, 'having been very poorly yesterday.'

'And very late to bed,' said Sweetie. She was next to Adélaïde, looking with interest at the Hollywood glamour photographs. 'I told him but he wouldn't listen.'

'Why was that?' asked Zoe, again with – she hoped – an air of inconsequence. She noticed Caroline observing her with a beady eye. 'Did someone tell me that indigestion is connected with atrial fibrillation? Was that it.'

'Sometimes he has to sit up until three or four in the morning,' said Sweetie, agreeing. 'He takes antacid medicine, but that's not good for his heart.'

Russell came nosing into the room and found Zoe near the door. He put his front paws on her leg, looking up at her with characteristic devotion – or, perhaps, manipulative appeal.

'Someone wants to go out,' said Marie-France, sitting very erect on the chair next to Caroline. Then she surprised Zoe by saying: 'I will come with you, if you don't mind, Zoe. The feeling of being trapped is increasingly oppressive.'

'Of course. Please do. Perhaps we should go out through the village, out of the wind?'

'Because?' demanded Marie-France.

'We will be more certain underfoot and we can bring back supplies from the general shop or the bakery?'

'If you wish.'

In reality, Zoe wanted to avoid anyone else traipsing out across the lawn because she was still nurturing the idea that footsteps in the snow – even those hidden beneath a layer of new snow – might be important. Then she realised that it was too late for that. Patrick and Minette and Junior had been out wooding.

And Junior found the incriminating branch under its pile of leaves and now it's being consumed by the flames.

Zoe noticed everyone looking at her.

'I'm sorry. I was thinking about something else.' She addressed Marie-France: 'Do you have better shoes?'

'I left my *après-ski* boots in the end cupboard.'

She and Zoe went to find them, with Russell at their heels. Marie-France took them into the lobby at the foot of the eastern tower and perched on a useful stool to put them on. Zoe opened the door to the vegetable garden, pulling it gently inwards, revealing an undisturbed drift of snow at the foot and a clean, unblemished carpet of white all the way to the gate that opened onto the lawn.

No one has been out this way, I'm sure.

They returned the length of the corridor, out through the front door onto the rubber mat. Marie-France stopped, indicating the place where Monsieur Alain had fallen with a narrow, liver-spotted hand.

'I see him still. I imagine I always will.'

'Yes,' said Zoe, thinking about how her imagination and memory were also haunted by the discovery of a corpse. 'It will never leave you. Do you want me to go first?'

'I will take my time.'

Marie-France descended the stone steps, feeling her way in the clumsy moonboots. Zoe followed, pulling down the top of the zip on her ski jacket a little because it was rubbing against her chin. Her gaze went to the pile of leaves by the gate, now scattered.

Is it possible that Junior saw me hiding the branch there? I don't think so. And I know whose room is above the front door. It's—

'This latch is stiff,' said Marie-France, struggling.

Zoe opened the gate. The timbers seemed to have swollen in the cold and damp – more evidence of the failing upkeep of the Château Palotte estate. They went out into the village, with Russell running ahead and back, sniffing at drainpipes and doorsteps. They passed the general store and the bakery and walked on into the market square with its open-sided post-and-beam hall. Marie-France said: 'Have you seen the church? Would you like to?'

'Yes, if you like.'

They had to climb a short distance along a lane that Zoe hadn't walked till now. It led to the south door of a Norman house of worship, protected by a porch. Marie-France took a seat on a bench on the left-hand side and invited Zoe to take her place opposite, adding: 'The lane leads on into the estate woods,' she said, 'but this is far enough. We will be comfortable here, warmed by the sun, sheltered from any breeze.'

Wondering what would come next, Zoe said: 'It's a lovely spot.'

Russell wandered away to take possession of some gravestones with his doggy scent.

'Yes.' Marie-France left a pause then her voice changed timbre, becoming more challenging: 'You have a keen eye. Nothing escapes your gaze. Will you share what has happened between Primo and Adélaïde?'

'What do you mean?'

'Please don't pretend to be obtuse. It is enough that Boris and Pauline both should, in reality, be obtuse.'

'I don't know what you are asking,' Zoe prevaricated.

'There is a new distance between them. It surprises me. Against all my expectations, Adélaïde has proved a devoted wife. I cannot imagine what it is that she could have done to alienate her husband, my brother-in-law. What have I missed?'

'I imagine you have missed nothing.'

'Yet there must be something?'

'I didn't say that.'

'An event I didn't witness, something I wasn't privy to or that happened elsewhere?' Zoe didn't answer, but Marie-France's beady eye must have read something in her face. 'Or at another time?' Zoe tried to remain impassive. 'I see that's it – a moment in Adélaïde's past.'

'I'm not comfortable discussing this,' said Zoe.

'You are not discussing it. I am discussing it and your pleasant features are too transparent to preserve your secret knowledge.'

'You wanted to come for a walk in order to question me on this?'

'I did.' Marie-France dropped her eyes, deep in thought, then raised them with a challenging expression. 'Is it to do with the mooted television programme, what Elizabeth calls "the true-crime doc", though why she has to abbreviate the inoffensive word "documentary" I cannot imagine.'

'What do you know about it?'

'Only what I have overheard in conversation.'

'How do you live?' Zoe asked, changing the subject, wanting to regain – if not the upper hand – at least some parity in their odd dialogue. 'What do you do with your time?'

'I exist. I socialise.'

'Do you read?'

'No.'

'Do you watch television?'

'I enjoy the daytime melodramas in the room on the top floor, above my own.'

'Anything else?'

'I knit. I embroider. I think about the past and what it can possibly have all meant.'

'What conclusions do you come to?'

'That only the present counts – the continuation of family and its traditions.'

'Your name was Montalbano before your marriage. That sounds very grand.'

'It does, I know. There are minor members of the Italian nobility among my antecedents, from before Garibaldi's republic.'

'How did you meet Boris?'

'Skiing – a foolish, expensive hobby but, because of its exclusivity, one favoured by people who like to flaunt their money. I invested a small inheritance in seeking a viable husband and believed, in Boris, that I had landed a wealthy fish, if you see what I mean? Because of my unwillingness to live a small, wifely life and the fact that he, once in possession of what he desired, found me no longer to his taste . . .' She sighed then resumed. 'I am speaking like a book. It is an unhappy habit, acquired many years ago in the formality of my Swiss finishing school. What I mean is this. Boris found me boring, once the threshold of physical intimacy was passed – once he had "possessed" me, as I believe the saying is. In my turn, I discovered that he was, himself, boring – not because the chase was ended, but because Primo had monopolised all the genes conferring intelligence and wit. By that time, though, I had become attached to my standing as a member of the Palotte family, invited to high-society events in Paris and in the south.'

'I understand that,' said Zoe, encouragingly.

'I don't think you do. I mean no offence when I say that you are far too practical and independent a person to have your values set and maintained by others.'

'Perhaps,' said Zoe carefully.

'I was young and desirous of seeing the world. The world, in those days, was mediated by men. So, I had an affair.' She paused. 'Or two or three.'

'Why are you telling me all this?'

'Because you don't seem to trust me. Perhaps that is because you trust no one? You believe Alain was murdered, isn't that so?'

'I don't know,' said Zoe, hiding her shock.

'And you and Adélaïde were plotting something this morning. Though she is an excellent actress, the pressure of Primo's coldness has made her more readable and your eyes, as I have remarked, are transparent – "windows to your soul", as it says in the *Bible*.'

Zoe didn't respond to this surprising speech straight away. She was, despite the odd conversation, enjoying the sunny, sheltered porch. There were even two or three brave fruit flies circling in the still air. Finally, coming out of her brief reverie, she asked: 'Your room is on the first floor in the western tower, over the front door?'

'Yes, it is.'

'Did you watch me hiding a branch under a pile of leaves by the gate from your bedroom window.'

'I did.'

'And?'

'What do you mean, "and"?'

'What did you deduce from that? Who have you told?'

'Why should I tell you? If you will not share the contretemps that has arisen between Adélaïde and Primo, you can't expect me to divulge—'

'You haven't told me why you want to know,' interrupted Zoe with impatience.

'Because I am as devoted to Château Palotte and to its traditions as Primo himself.'

'So devoted, in fact, that protecting them might make you compromise your own integrity?'

'You imagine I have integrity? You don't know me at all.' Marie-France stood up. 'This has been a frustrating conversation, for you as well as for me, I am sure. Perhaps, given time, you will unbend. Believe me, I am on Adélaïde's side, whatever she might have done.'

Zoe went to speak. The words 'she hasn't done anything' were almost out of her mouth, but she swallowed them and said instead: 'Will you be all right, walking back on your own?'

'I believe I will.'

'Did you stay up very late with all the others in the aftermath of the argument down in the reservoir?'

'I did.'

'Did you go from room to room, as Adélaïde did, trying to keep the peace?'

'I stayed where I was. People came to me.'

'Did anyone go out, do you know?'

'My curtains were drawn. I had no reason to look out.'

'But you did look out on me when I hid the branch.'

'Having watched you test how it might lodge between the lavenders, yes.'

After a moment to absorb this fact, Zoe asked: 'And your conclusion?'

'Madame Zoe Pascal, you will have to forgive me,' said Marie-France de Palotte, née Montalbano. 'You see, it seems to me unfair that, the more questions I answer, the more closed off you become.'

Forty-Seven

'No Comment'

Marie-France stalked away, leaving Zoe frustrated and pensive in the sunny church porch. After a minute or two, she went looking for Russell in the graveyard, finding him digging under a hedge, his front paws scraping at the cold dirt and snow. She called his name and he gave her the excited look that she had come to know as: *I think there are rabbits, here.*

Not wanting to dilly-dally, she picked him up and he scrabbled against her ski jacket.

Like he did against the velvet dress coat on the reservoir stairs.

She headed past the porch of the Norman church and down the lane towards the *boulangerie*. Seeing Gaspard behind his counter, with tall baskets of French bread behind him, she remembered Junior buttering a piece of warm toast for his father and placing it before him like an offering. She saw clearly, in memory, the expression on Junior's face as Boris drew him close with a wiry, liver-spotted hand.

It was a mixture of surprise and gratitude.

'Hello, Zoe,' came a poised, mellow voice from behind her. It was Isabelle. 'How is everyone? Were the arguments cathartic? Has the mood improved?'

'I'm not sure, but there are, in any case, new reasons for glumness.' Zoe told her about the electrics and the boiler. 'I was going to pick up some things to eat, but I'm in no hurry. I wonder if you might have a moment to talk?'

'Yes, if you wish.'

'Were you out shopping?'

'No, just walking, mulling something over.'

'Where might be convenient?'

'Come to my house. It isn't far.'

'You don't mind Russell?'

'Perhaps we'll wipe his feet first?' said Isabelle with her sudden and disconcertingly radiant smile.

The house turned out to be on the south side of the market square, facing north, therefore, with no sun to nurture window boxes or planters. Isabelle opened up without a key, reminding Zoe of the questions she had asked herself about security at the château. She followed inside and waited on the mat, Russell still in her arms so he didn't go dashing off, making a disgrace of himself. Isabelle returned with a tea towel that she said needed washing anyway and carefully wiped the dog's feet.

'Let's go upstairs.'

'You have an upside-down house?' asked Zoe.

'There is a roof terrace. In winter, it's the only place I like to sit. These old homes are designed for cool in the long summer months. They are so sad and dark on the ground floor.'

At the top of the staircase was a skylight which meant Zoe could tell that the treads were made of cherry wood – or another timber with an equally warm red tone. On the landing, she saw that the first floor had been divided in two, with the rear portion, facing the sun, converted into a conservatory, full of exotic plants.

'Are these memories of Martinique?' she asked.

'How clever of you,' said Isabelle. 'Yes, they are.'

'It's a lovely welcoming space.' In between the architectural leaves was a three-piece suite made of wicker, topped with colourful cushions. On each arm was a blanket, like in the television room in the château, suggesting that the conservatory became chilly at night, though it would still be a lovely place to sit. 'I'm tempted to say there's more oxygen in here than there is out of doors.'

'It really does feel like that,' Isabelle agreed.

The conservatory was warm from the sun through the glass and from an electric convector heater. On a bamboo side table, Zoe noticed a MacBook Air laptop and, next to it, a script. She asked Isabelle if she was auditioning or if she had been given a new part, adding: 'You gave the impression the other day, I suppose modestly, that you've not been working. I asked you how you had replaced the validation and acclaim of acting and you told me: "Nothing ever has." Or am I misremembering?'

'Your recollection is incomplete. I told you: "Nothing ever has, not fully." You see the nuance? I haven't been working as an actor but I do have a profession.'

'And what is that?'

'The worst of all the creative occupations,' she said soberly. She left a pause then, with mock gravitas, she added: 'I am a screenwriter.'

'How can that be the worst—?' Zoe began.

Isabelle anticipated her question.

'Because whatever you put down, however good, however clever, however intricate, there is always somebody more important than you in a position to change it for their own less considered purposes.'

'Yes,' said Zoe, sympathetically. 'I have heard that.'

Zoe remembered telling Patrick, in jest, that she and Adélaïde had decided to write a screenplay. He had replied: *'That's a brilliant idea. Maybe Isabelle can help?'* Now she knew why.

'When I saw you outside the *boulangerie*,' said Isabelle, composedly, 'I was mulling an idea as clever as anything that I fully expect to end up on the cutting room floor, even if it does survive to the final draft, which is less than doubtful.

You gave it to me when you were talking about the audience being overcome with bad air in the reservoir. Anyway, what did you want to talk about?'

Isabelle did her trick of sitting down without looking behind her, at one end of the two-person sofa. Zoe chose the left-hand armchair so she wouldn't be looking past Isabelle into the brightness of the sun. Russell curled up at her feet.

'I'd like to talk about what happened when you all left the reservoir and went back to the house. I understand you came in?'

'I did.'

'Of your own volition?'

'I was persuaded it might be a good idea to clear the air.'

'Was it?'

'I don't know. That's why I asked you, earlier on, if the mood had improved. A few home truths were spoken, but that isn't necessarily the same thing.'

'No, it isn't. Who was there?'

Isabelle looked confused. 'Everyone was there.'

'But not all in the same place?'

'We didn't assemble around that awful meeting table in the drawing room, if that's what you mean. It was sort of piecemeal, like I imagine negotiations at the United Nations must play out, with diplomats skulking in doorways and hush-hush bilateral conversations disappearing into bathrooms and cleaning closets.'

The vividness of this image made Zoe pause and gave her a sudden inspiration.

'If you're a writer, you didn't write Adélaïde's most recent success, did you? Are you the author of the one set in the Interpol offices?'

'Adélaïde told me how astute you are.'

'I watched it with Patrick and Minette yesterday afternoon. It was marvellous. How wonderful to have a shared success.'

'Oh, she's not supposed to know. My identity was concealed.'

'Why?'

'So that it couldn't be said – and, more importantly, so that I should never believe – that my services were chosen as part of Adélaïde's long and unending campaign to gain forgiveness for stealing my career breakthrough and my one true love.' Isabelle left a pause then smiled her dazzling smile. 'I'm joking, of course, but I do like the idea of being judged solely on my screenplay, not my connections or name.'

'Was that what you and Adélaïde were arguing about when everyone was cross round the dining-room table?'

'Not arguing, discussing,' said Isabelle, mildly. 'She asked me to come up early for a private chat, forgetting Monsieur Alain's death and thinking everyone else would be breakfasting in their rooms.'

'Who else knows you wrote it?'

'As an investor, Primo does. And I imagine his brother might, because Boris is a snoop.'

Momentarily forgetting herself, Zoe was on the point of saying: *'Boris is dead.'* Instead, she thought: *If Isabelle can mention Boris without qualms, does that mean she has nothing to do with his death, or does it just mean that she, like Adélaïde, is a very good actress?*

Isabelle went on, misinterpreting Zoe's expression: 'You look shocked. Does that surprise you?'

'It absolutely doesn't. Do you think it's possible that he's been snooping around the details of Adélaïde past?'

'I think it's inevitable.'

'Why?'

'Because he is concerned for his own welfare and, since Adélaïde arrived on the scene, he has been relegated to only second place in his brother's . . . I was going to say "affections", but that isn't the right word. In Primo's sense of his obligations.'

'Adélaïde is no more than an obligation?' asked Zoe with surprise.

'No, you misunderstand me. Primo, as you have noticed, has a very developed sense of duty.'

'Yes, that's true, but . . . Oh, I think I understand. With his marriage, Primo took on a new duty of love and care, above and beyond that owed to his twin.' Zoe paused, then asked: 'Coming back to yesterday evening, or early this morning, in fact, do you know what time it was when you left?'

'Soon after two.'

'Had the snow begun falling more heavily?'

'Yes. Everything was blurred with white.'

'Did you see anyone else outside?'

'I slipped away out of the front door and down through the gate into the village, with no reason to go searching for shadows on the lawn. Has there been an intruder? It happens sometimes, you know, the combination of the ancient pile and the celebrated actress whose early roles were so mouth-wateringly seductive.'

'I had to go out myself because Russell was lost and it turned out he was trapped down in the reservoir. Unfortunately, I have no real idea what time it was. As you were leaving, did you perhaps see if the horizontal door in the lawn was open or closed?'

'I'm afraid I didn't or, if I did, I don't remember.'

'No, why would you? Once everyone was back inside the château, Adélaïde says that she went from room to room, trying to keep the peace. What exactly were the arguments about?'

'For me, closest to home, there was a triangular conversation between Boris, Sweetie and myself. She put Junior to bed in the dressing room off their quarters because he was very fraught and wanted to be close by, then she impressed me, remaining surprisingly sanguine, no more histrionics or tears, accepting my explanation.'

'Even including the fact that you . . .' Zoe paused, not sure how to phrase what she was thinking. 'That you have carried a torch for Primo ever since you first met him and that your one-night stand with Boris was no more than a—'

'A vicarious drunken substitute for the real thing.'

'In a sense, then, she forgave you? Did she forgive her husband?'

'I don't think it applies. She hasn't – what's the word? – believed in him for quite some time.' Then Isabelle said something that echoed Zoe's conversation with Marie-France in the sunny porch of the Norman church in the centre of the village. 'I think Sweetie understands that her value for Boris was as a conquest. It is only his failing health that has made the marriage last so long.'

'You mean he hasn't been able to play the field, to act the philandering lothario. What else happened?'

'Marie-France would insist on discussing the possibility that Boris and Primo might each not be long for this world. She badgered them about their prognoses and insisted that Caroline should give her a legal opinion for what would happen in the event of two demises.'

'I imagine she felt compromised.'

'She didn't say so out loud but she was furious.'

'And then?'

'Primo appealed to her for an "off the record" comment, in order to set the record straight.'

Zoe creased her brow, remembering several different conversations, all of which impacted on the same question, and said: 'Succession is in the male line at Château Palotte. That would mean Junior?'

'Or Patrick,' said Isabelle.

'But he is not Boris's son.'

'That's the thing,' said Isabelle, composedly. 'It transpired that Marie-France has always believed that Patrick and Minette are, indeed, Boris's children, despite the fact that

302

Elizabeth had already taken up with Paddy, the dashing ski instructor.'

'Why does she think that?'

'There is a physical resemblance, don't you think? Plus, as everyone knows, Patrick has inherited Boris's goat-like desire for sexual conquest. And, of course, twins run in families. Boris and Primo are twins. Patrick and Minette are twins.'

'Has a paternity test been conducted?'

'It was mooted by Marie-France. She kept saying: "At my age, I must know where I stand." It's fair enough, I think.'

'And the outcome?'

'Patrick was happy to go ahead. Minette was indifferent – or she is a good liar. I think Elizabeth could see the possible advantage to her children.'

'That would suit my reading of her character. She is, above all, a practical person.' Zoe summed up: 'If Patrick is illegitimate, Junior would inherit and his mother and father would become sort of regents or guardians until he reaches eighteen?'

'Twenty-one. That was one of the details Caroline was prepared to commit to, as a question of notarial fact.'

'Meaning, if Primo died tomorrow, given Boris's infirmity, that Sweetie would effectively become the *châtelaine* for the next eleven years.'

'Eleven long years,' agreed Isabelle. 'Superseding Adélaïde, Elizabeth and Marie-France. Implausible, unimaginable – but yes.'

'Whereas,' Zoe continued, 'if legitimate, being the children of the second wife, Patrick and Minette would take precedence over Junior, the child of the third wife.'

'Patrick, only,' Isabelle reminded her. 'Male line only.'

Zoe acknowledged the point, wondering: *Would he be capable of 'the worst of crimes'? Or Minette, on his behalf, as it were? We know she wants more from life than what she called her 'kitchen-dungeon'.*

Isabelle waited, apparently sedately, then her eyes drifted to the script that she was working on, the pages on the bamboo table beside the sleek Apple laptop.

'I'm sorry,' said Zoe. 'I'm keeping you away from—'

'This feels important,' insisted Isabelle. 'You haven't shared why you are so interested in all this. I suppose you are about to tell me it's because you are Adélaïde's friend and you are concerned for her welfare?'

'That's right,' said Zoe, uncomfortable under the other woman's very direct gaze.

'But there is trouble in paradise,' said Isabelle, very quietly, with what Zoe heard as a sinister undertone. Isabelle added: 'Between Primo and his one true love. You can't deny it.'

'Does that please you?' Zoe asked.

For the first time, Isabelle lowered her eyes, as if to conceal a secret truth.

'No comment,' she said.

Forty-Eight

'The Stag in the Moonlight'

Once Zoe had left Isabelle's gloomy terraced village house with its delightful first-floor conservatory, she realised that there was a connection between what she had learned – about possible lines of succession – and something Marie-France had said. It had been towards the end of their conversation in the church porch. Frustrated, the older woman had stood up to complain about Zoe's reticence and discretion, adding: *'Believe me, I am on Adélaïde's side, whatever she might have done.'*

Caught on the hop, Zoe had, instinctively, wanted to defend her friend. Now, though, she could see that Marie-France was deeply concerned at the idea that Sweetie might inherit guardianship of the estate – with all kinds of potentially unhappy consequences for herself and for the other Palotte women.

Zoe let Russell back into the château grounds through the pedestrian gate, then returned to the *boulangerie*, finding it shut for a long lunch, reopening at three.

Of course. I should have thought of that.

She took out her mobile phone to ring Gato Merino, her handyman, and find out if, by any chance, he might be able to bring a load of logs. Because of the closed roads, the answer was negative but he repeated the hope that 'the weather might be about to break'.

She thought again of the deadline Adélaïde had set which she had – against her better judgement – agreed to. She looked up at the sky. The sun was quite low, of course, because it was early January, not far on from the shortest day. And it had moved a long way across the sky towards the west.

I still have some time. Almost by chance, I've managed to have two private conversations that have filled in some of the blanks. I wonder who I can find to continue my 'sly process' of talking to each of them in turn.

Down the side of the *boulangerie* was an alleyway whose timber gate was fragile with age. She pushed it aside, scraping a scar across the snow, the path otherwise unmarked. Above her head, bluish smoke rose from a metal vent into a sky that was just beginning to cover over with cloud once more. From somewhere close by came an insistent mechanical sound, like a pounding farm machine.

She followed the path to the corner of the building, by a green steel bowser in which, she supposed, Gaspard stored heating oil. Beyond was a small courtyard on whose far side was a posh-looking double-glazed shed inside which she could see gym equipment – a rowing machine, some free weights, and a running treadmill. Didi Astor was using it, his feet beating the insistent rhythm.

Zoe took a step forward, emerging from shadow. He saw her through the glass. His eyes widened and he lost his cadence, slipping backwards off the fast-moving belt. Zoe ran forward, worried she would find him flipped over by the dangerous machine. She opened the glass door and, to her relief, discovered that the treadmill was already still. The red safety string had been pulled from its magnetic socket, automatically stopping the motor, and dangled from the waistband of Didi's shorts, alongside his right thigh.

'You made me lose my balance,' he told her, his chest heaving in his off-white singlet. 'Are you looking for my father? He usually has a nap in the afternoon.'

'No, you, actually.'

Didi's eyes became suspicious. His breath still short, he asked: 'What's happened?'

'Nothing,' Zoe assured him.

'Shut the door,' he told her. 'You're letting the cold in.' She did as he asked, then he suggested: 'Actually, I'd nearly finished. We can go into the bakery. That will be more comfortable. There's no heating in here. Once the sun's gone off the glass, it gets freezing.' As he said this, he pulled a tracksuit on over his shorts and singlet – narrow blue trousers and a red jacket. Zoe recognised it as the colours of the Paris Saint-German football team. Once dressed, his breathing returning to normal, he asked: 'What do you want, though?'

'To have a word, that's all.'

'Because something's happened?' insisted Didi.

Recognising that both Marie-France and Isabelle had asked the same question, Zoe mentally cursed her inability to maintain a neutral expression and hide what she was thinking. She decided that her best gambit was what Maisie would have called 'the nuclear option'.

'I want to talk to you about your feud with Elizabeth Lagrasse.'

The air in the gym shed seemed to become very still. His eyes narrowed, but all he said was: 'Oh.' Then he dropped his gaze. Zoe grew aware of all the ambient smells: sweat, the rubber of the exercise mat on the floor, the oil on the moving parts of the treadmill and rowing machine. The combination was unpleasant and somehow desperate.

Like Didi himself. Didn't he tell me he was 'desperate' to get away from Saint-Paul-de-Palotte and that I shouldn't tell his father? I suppose he wants to go to Paris and watch his favourite football team every other week, marmalising the opposition because they have more money than everyone else.

She told him: 'The fact that Elizabeth's husband had an affair with your mother is not her fault. I'm not sure how you can imagine that it was.'

'It's always the woman's fault,' he told her, his eyes still down.

'That makes no sense. Boris is the one who—'

'You don't know. You weren't there.'

'I know enough to—'

'No,' he snapped. His face was pinched like a child on the verge of tears. 'She didn't do enough to keep him. She had affairs, so he did, too.'

'Where on earth have you found such ridiculous ideas? Boris has been a philanderer his whole life long. Elizabeth didn't push him into it. She didn't twist him from a faithful husband to—'

'It's the woman's role to satisfy her husband. If she doesn't, it's her fault that things break down.'

'No, it isn't,' said Zoe. 'Who have you been listening to? Is it people on the internet? You know they're taking advantage of you?'

'You have to understand power. Women have power and they need to be careful how they use it.'

Exasperated, Zoe didn't feel equipped to try and untangle Didi's indoctrination by internet misogynists.

'After the concert last night, what did you do?'

'We came home.'

Zoe decided to take a punt. 'And your father went to bed, I know. But you didn't. He heard you slip out.'

'So?'

'Where did you go?'

'Just for a walk.'

'A walk in the snow late at night?'

'It wasn't snowing at first.'

'Which path did you take?' Didi mumbled something that Zoe couldn't hear. 'What was that?'

'You wouldn't understand,' he told her.

'Try me.'

'You'll tell me I'm stupid.'

'I promise I won't.' Zoe waited. Her sense of Didi Astor was quickly evolving. She could see that he wanted her approval. The foolish ideas absorbed from the internet were no more than a veneer. His father, Gaspard, had brought him up better than that, despite the trauma of his wife's betrayal. 'It's important,' she told him. 'Or it could be, for reasons I can't share just now.'

'All right.' Didi sighed. 'You know the lane up to the church?'

'I do.'

'If you carry on that way out of the village, you emerge on the far side of the château and there's a public footpath through the woods and out into the fenced part of the estate.'

'Yes?'

'There was a good moon last night.'

'I know. I saw it. Why is that important?'

'Well, when the moon's bright, I like to . . .'

He stopped, dropping his gaze again.

'Please tell me. I'm imagining you walking through the trees, maybe as far as the open grassland.' Zoe had a sudden inspiration. 'Oh, is it the deer?'

'Yes,' he told her, quietly.

'You like to look at the stag in the moonlight.'

He sighed, apparently ashamed of his admission. Zoe could picture the scene – the young man with his confusion about the world and his place in it, watching the noble animal like a kind of avatar of triumphant masculinity.

'And then?' she asked.

'What, "and then"?'

'Where did you go after that?'

'I came back.'

Zoe thought she heard something not quite right in his tone.

'But you returned by another path?'

'Yes,' he admitted.

'Had it come on to snow at this point?'

'Yes, heavily. That's why I set off.'

'Which way did you go?'

'Down the far side of the lake and out of the main gates, then back up the road into the village.'

'Why didn't you go home the same way?'

'I don't know. I hadn't been out long enough. I was churned up with seeing that woman.'

'You mean Elizabeth.'

'I don't say her name.'

Zoe wanted to tell him: *Don't be so ridiculous*. She bit back the words.

'And what did you see?'

'One of them. I don't know which.'

'One of whom?'

'The twins.'

Zoe started with surprise as the door opened behind her. The dialogue had become so intense – and potentially important – that she hadn't been aware of Gaspard's approach.

'Good afternoon, Madame Pascal. How nice to see you again? Can I help you?'

'I'm sorry, I didn't realise you were shut for such a long time each afternoon and I came to see—'

'Yes, of course,' he said, comfortably. 'I hope Didi's not been trying to fill your head with any nonsense?'

'He was just telling me about going to see the stag and the other deer in the moonlight. It sounds wonderful.'

'Is he now?' Gaspard looked at his son. 'I hope he didn't try to tell you that the behaviour of that beast and his harem is a model for humans to emulate.'

'That's not what I think,' Didi whined.

'Could we just finish our train of thought?' Zoe asked, smiling at one then the other. 'Didi was just telling me about walking home through the snow.'

'Coming down heavy,' said Didi. 'I couldn't see well.'

'But it was one of the twins?' insisted Zoe.

'That's right.'

'Where was this?' asked Gaspard.

'Far side of the lawn. Where do you think?' snapped his son.

'When you say "twins", though,' insisted Zoe, 'do you mean Patrick and Minette?'

'No,' said Didi. 'Monsieur Boris or Monsieur Primo. But I couldn't tell which because of the snow and the moon gone behind the clouds.'

'Whoever it was, were they on their own, not followed by anyone else?'

'Not while I was looking, but I was soon gone out of sight.'

'Definitely a man?'

'I'd say so.'

'From his gait or size?'

'Just because that was the impression I got.'

Zoe had an idea and asked: 'What was the shape of the figure?'

'Like a person,' said Didi, confused.

'But his clothes. How was he dressed?'

A light came on in Didi's eyes and he said, as if talking to himself: 'Oh, yes. That must have been it.'

'Speak plainly, Didier,' said his father, with frustration.

'What have you remembered?' Zoe asked, on tenterhooks.

'He was sort of swamped in that coat of his, like a tent or a big lampshade.'

'Ah,' said Zoe, recognising an alternative description of the 'single European overcoat' and putting two and two together. 'Monsieur Boris.'

Forty-Nine

'THE DRAMAS OF THE FINAL ACT'

Gaspard wouldn't let Zoe leave without an armful of pastries – *croissants, pains au chocolat* and *pains aux raisins* – and two large pizzas, one with anchovies and one without: 'Because not everyone likes strong flavours. They'll be better if you heat them.'

Wandering back through the village, past the general store, Zoe felt that the weather and the air were changing at last, becoming less bitterly, crushingly cold. The zip of her jacket was still irritating her chin, made worse by the fact that there was a nasty dampness in the air, promising – she thought – rain.

Am I making too much of Didi's description? What he saw, albeit by bright moonlight, could have been somebody else, wearing Boris's coat.

She opened the gate, taking care not to drop her packages, and pushed through. Beyond the steps to the front door, lower down the drive beyond the carport, she could see three figures, maybe a hundred metres away, scavenging for wood beneath the mature trees – two grown-ups and one child.

That's Patrick, Minette and Junior. Even though they're not much more than silhouettes, they are recognisable.

She embarked up the steps.

I'd like to speak to Junior again, if I could just get him on his own. I do wonder if, perhaps, Marie-France saw him out of her window, placing the branch across the path, as well as seeing me hiding it later on. If she did and didn't warn anyone, she's partially responsible for Monsieur Alain's accident. And, if she kept schtum, is it because she, Marie-France, wanted either Primo or Boris to take a tumble?

The three mismatched figures were silhouettes because the sun had gone a long way down the sky in the west. The trees – whose fallen branches they were gathering – were casting them into profound shadow.

If the sun is going down, it's almost time.

Zoe felt a horrible nausea, like motion sickness, at the idea of returning to the reservoir.

And then having to act surprised, all because Adélaïde wanted time to prepare Primo for the shock.

Involuntarily, she shivered.

Unless Adélaïde had other reasons for wanting to delay – reasons that I haven't worked out but which . . .

She shook her head.

No, Adélaïde isn't a murderer. Maybe, when she was younger, she might have had the, well, the single-mindedness, the arrogance to act or to let someone else act, but not today, not having lived a full life, having experienced love and struggle and disappointment and triumph.

She checked the time of sunset on her phone.

Oh, that's a relief. I still have half an hour.

She climbed the slippery steps to the front door and hesitated on the rubber outdoor mat, watching the scavengers approaching, Junior carrying a thick bunch of twigs against the chest of his quilted anorak, Patrick and Minette laden with more substantial lengths of damp and mossy timber. Balancing her parcels awkwardly, she managed to turn the heavy iron lever to let them in ahead of her.

Minette told her: 'There's not much left out there. If we need more later – which I think we will – someone will have to go up into the fenced woods where the deer live.'

They trooped indoors. The others headed for the dining room while Zoe descended to the kitchen, now pleasantly warm because of her blower heater. She put her parcels on the plain boards of the table and set the oven to a low heat, getting ready to warm up the pizzas. Adélaïde came downstairs to find her, her face a picture of stress and frustration.

'You haven't managed to have a private word with Primo?' Zoe guessed.

'It's been impossible. There's always been people there and he hasn't moved because he feels the cold so terribly and there's nowhere else to go.'

'Even if there were,' said Zoe, 'creeping away for a private conversation would have been noticed.'

'I suppose.'

'Adélaïde,' Zoe warned, 'I won't delay any later than sunset.'

'I haven't asked you to.'

Zoe told Adélaïde about her plan deliberately to trip the electrics in order to give herself the excuse of going to fetch the hurricane lamps.

'Perhaps you could come with me and we can make our "discovery" together.'

'Yes, fine,' said Adélaïde on a weary exhalation. 'Of course. That would be only fair.'

'Do you mind if I put your velvet coat back on? The zip on this jacket keeps scratching my chin.'

'Whatever.'

Zoe ran upstairs to tell everyone in the dining room that Gaspard had provided two pizzas to share. Russell looked up at her enquiringly from a position in front of the fire.

'The oven's on,' she told them. 'Shall I put them in now?'

The consensus was yes. Primo thanked her courteously. Caroline, too. They were at the end of the table, looking at what seemed to be accounts ledgers. Close by, Elizabeth was working on one of her two typescripts – Zoe thought it was the true-crime book, *Baker's Dozen* – making notes by hand in the margins of the printed pages. She told Zoe: 'Gaspard likes anchovies. I love them too, but not everyone does and Junior needs something.'

Zoe assured her that there would be a choice.

Marie-France complained: 'Eating with one's hands isn't a meal.'

Elizabeth told her politely: 'You aren't obliged to have any if it's beneath you.'

To head off any further unpleasantness, Zoe told them about the pastries for dessert.

Marie-France exclaimed: 'Breakfast food? Then everything is upside down.'

No one – not even Elizabeth, the peacemaker, had the energy to engage.

At the opposite rounded end of the impressive mahogany table from Primo and Caroline, the *Star Wars* board game that Zoe had seen in Junior's bedroom had been released from its cellophane. Patrick, Minette, Sweetie and Junior were leaning in, apparently extremely engaged with the shiny cards, the plastic tokens and the grid of highly decorated spaces on the playing surface. Patrick and Minette both seemed flushed and were playing with noisy enthusiasm. Zoe assumed they had continued to enjoy Primo's exceptional liqueurs.

Sweetie asked her son: 'What do you say to Madame Pascal?'

'*Merci beaucoup.*'

'You're welcome, Junior,' said Zoe. 'I'll go and put them in. They'll only be five minutes.' Despite herself, unable to stifle her curiosity, she asked: 'Did anyone check on Monsieur Boris?'

'Junior kindly ran up,' said Primo. 'All is quiet – which is not unusual. My brother prefers his own company when unwell. You will remember how hard he found it when we had people in and he was poorly.'

'The door is locked,' said Junior. 'I turned the handle.' His mother looked on the point of offering a rebuke, but he forestalled her. 'I did it very quietly. So is the door from the dressing room.'

Poor boy. When he knows he was sent on a fool's errand, what will he think? He will lose the little trust he has in the adults who ought to be caring for him.

She returned to the kitchen to find that Adélaïde had already put the pizzas in and had found a large wooden board suitable for cutting them into triangular slices with a wide-bladed knife that Zoe recognised. Zoe told Adélaïde the story of the confrontation between Didi and Elizabeth over the quiche, the one in which somehow the sharp blade drew blood from Elizabeth's thumb.

'That sounds like a strange sort of accident,' said Adélaïde.

Zoe told her what she had learned about Didi's misogyny, the fact that he blamed Elizabeth for Boris's philandering with his mother, Hélène, Gaspard's wife. Then she told the story of Didi's moonlit walk.

'On his way home, from over on the far side of the lake, he saw Boris making his way to the reservoir. At least, he thinks it was Boris. From the way he described it and the fact that it coincided with the snow beginning to fall more heavily, I know it was after I went down to rescue Russell. I think the sequence is this. I left the reservoir and you all stayed, arguing, while I went back and forth tidying up. After a bit, you all returned to the château and had your various confabs in your different rooms. Meanwhile, I put on the dishwasher then read a book, lying on my bed. After half an hour, an hour at the most, I went out to search for Russell. Some if not all of you were still up, but not out of doors. I went back to bed. Sometime after that or maybe at the same time, Didi went past, seeing Boris on his way to what must have been a private rendezvous.'

'Why a rendezvous?'

'Do you really believe he went out in the dead of night in order to sit and think? Anyway, to continue, back in the château, everyone was finally going to bed. Isabelle left, she says, just before two. Marie-France and Elizabeth were, I think, each alone in their separate rooms, though they received visits. Patrick and Minette were together and, I suppose, can vouch for one another. You were alone in the dressing room beside your and Primo's palatial quarters. Likewise, Sweetie and Junior were on the *canapé-lit* alongside Boris's bedroom – but unaware that he wasn't there.'

'And the bedroom is locked,' said Adélaïde.

'I should have checked his pockets to find out if he has the key, but I didn't want to disturb his body. I'll have to do that when I go down shortly – when we go down shortly.' She frowned. 'Oh, and Caroline was, logically, in her room. I forgot about her. Did she take part in the late-night debates? Oh, yes, of course she did. She was called on to give her legal advice.'

'The pizzas smell ready,' said Adélaïde. She bent down and opened the oven. 'Yes, that will do.' Wearily, she took a tea towel from the worktop and slid the pizzas from their baking trays onto the large wooden board. They draped over the edges a little. 'Take them, will you?' Zoe picked them up. Adélaïde tucked a roll of kitchen paper under Zoe's arm saying, by way of explanation: 'Plates.'

'Are you not coming?'

'I can't face them. I have to have a couple more minutes to myself.' She sighed, deeply. 'All these years I've put up with them, for Primo's sake: Marie-France with her appalling entitlement; Boris spending Primo's money; poor Sweetie who is a victim in all this; Junior neglected and unhappy; even Patrick and Minette who don't see how dysfunctional it all is; and Caroline telling Primo what he can and can't do with his incomes and his trusts and . . .' She shook her head and tried to brighten her voice. 'I'm sorry. I know I asked you

317

to come. I shouldn't have. I think I was somehow aware that things were coming to a head, moving towards a crisis, and I would need a friend.'

'Did you enter the marriage blind?'

'In a way. Oh, I knew from the start that Primo came with burdens and responsibilities. I just didn't realise that they would weigh so heavily or for so long.' She forced herself to smile. 'Go, my friend, feed the hangers-on.'

'It will soon be over,' said Zoe, reassuringly.

'No, it won't,' Adélaïde told her, gloomily. 'I fear that the dramas of the final act are only just about to begin.'

Fifty

'NO, THAT DOESN'T MAKE SENSE'

Zoe went upstairs, put the board and the kitchen paper on some more newspapers on the mahogany table and used the wide-bladed knife – in the absence of a pizza wheel – to cut the two large pies into ten slices each. Everyone ate, Primo and Caroline without breaking off from their financial conversation, Marie-France punctiliously as if she was doing everyone else a favour, the *Star Wars* board-game team joyfully and with appetite. Elizabeth dripped some tomato sauce on her typescript and laughed, saying to no one in particular: 'Never mind. I can reprint that page.'

After five minutes, Adélaïde came in with the pastries, having warmed them through separately so they didn't take on the odour of anchovies. She had arranged them on a large platter with a gilt edge.

Primo said: 'Be careful with that antique dish, won't you?'

'I will, of course,' Adélaïde told him, quietly.

Zoe felt the brief moment was a microcosm of the current state of their relationship. Adélaïde wanted to do something to bring her and Primo closer together but was constrained, obviously, by the presence of what she had called the 'hangers-on'.

Beyond the French doors, the sky had almost completely darkened. She went to look and told everyone: 'I think it will soon come on to rain. I think I had better take Russell out before it does.' She turned to Adélaïde. 'Would you like to come, too?'

'I'm not sure . . .'

Zoe frowned.

Hang on. You promised to come with me.

Hoping Adélaïde would realise this if she gave her a couple of minutes, she said: 'I'll just run upstairs for something warm to wear.'

Zoe climbed to the first-floor corridor and walked along past the insipid watercolours. In her room, she pushed her arms into the sleeves of the velvet coat, then bent down, warily, to plug her beside lamp into the dodgy socket. There was a fizz and a spark. She snatched her hand away as the ceiling light went out.

I don't like doing this, but I do need a pretext for going back into the reservoir.

She did up the velvet coat, all the way down to her knees, and went back downstairs, meeting Adélaïde and Elizabeth in the gloomy ground-floor hallway, on their way back from the basement fuse box.

'The circuit breaker won't reset,' said Adélaïde.

'Oh dear,' said Zoe, hoping her eyes – the 'windows to the soul' – weren't giving away her subterfuge. 'What a disaster. I wish I'd fetched the hurricane lamps this morning.'

'Are we dressing up?' asked Elizabeth, noticing the velvet dress coat. 'Oh, I was going to ask, did you pick up Adélaïde's brooch? Primo loves that piece. I saw it on the reservoir stairs and meant to do so myself, but I became distracted by everyone complaining and bickering.'

'I did, yes,' Zoe reassured her, remembering the horrible arguments – and Junior crying – that she had been only too pleased to leave behind. 'Adélaïde, are you coming?'

'I can't, Zoe. I'm simply exhausted.'

Zoe swallowed her frustration.

'Are you sure? We do need those lamps. It might do you good.'

'I'm sorry. It's all become too much.'

There was mute appeal in Adélaïde's eyes. Zoe decided to let it go.

'Never mind. I'll be fine on my own.'

'I could come?' said Elizabeth. 'Eight lamps is quite a lot to carry.'

Zoe hesitated.

Is this a good idea? I suppose there's no harm in Elizabeth being a witness to my 'discovery'. And then, afterwards, she can help explain to everyone else.

'I suppose it would be useful to get all of them,' Zoe agreed.

They went into the dining room where everyone seemed to be talking over one another, with Minette and Patrick bickering about how best to build up the fire with the last of the outside timber in order to provide light as well as warmth. In the flickering flames, Zoe explained her plan.

'You are a blessing, Zoe,' said Primo.

Adélaïde went to sit next to him, pulling a chair close in. Zoe thought she was intending to prepare him for the news about his brother, but couldn't see either face clearly.

Russell yapped, briefly, in his decorous indoor voice. Zoe opened the French doors onto much milder air. She and Elizabeth stepped out onto the terrace. The snow underfoot was already becoming softer, almost slushy. Russell scampered off, leaving his own dancing paw-prints on the lawn.

'Primo is right. You've been so very helpful,' said Elizabeth. 'With each crisis, you've become more central to the smooth running of the household.'

'I hope you don't feel that I've trodden on your toes. That's your role, usually, isn't it? I mean, it has been, alongside poor Monsieur Alain.'

'Yes,' said Elizabeth. 'That's true.'

'You mean, yes, I've been intrusive?'

'No – at least not yet.' Elizabeth laughed but the sound was oddly grating.

Zoe said: 'I don't follow?'

Elizabeth smiled and told her: 'Forget I said it. I have two competing work deadlines, as you know, and each one distracts me from the other. I don't know what I'm thinking, let alone saying.'

By now, they were quite close to the horizontal door, held open on its chain, that gave access to the slippery stairs into the reservoir. Zoe felt she was obliged to forewarn her companion about what they were on their way to discover.

'I'm afraid you are about to experience a shock.'

'I am?'

'Yes, I don't quite know how to say it . . .' A few raindrops began falling out of the darkening sky, with just a hint of orange sun, low to the western horizon. 'I'm afraid—'

'Shall we get under cover before you do?' suggested Elizabeth.

'Good idea.'

Zoe called Russell who approached but, when she made for the entrance, refused to come in with them.

I totally understand, Russell. I don't want to go down there either.

Very gingerly, Zoe began her descent, her left hand on the damp wall. Doing so, her mind went back to the brooch that Russell had scrabbled from the front of her velvet coat and to the sequence of events that she had sketched out for Adélaïde in the basement kitchen.

Her steps faltered.

No, that doesn't make sense.

She turned. Elizabeth was standing on the top step, looming over her. The broad-bladed knife Zoe had used on the pizzas was in her right hand. Zoe could see dark splotches of tomato sauce adhering to the blade, like blood.

Fifty-One

'THIS NEEDN'T BE THE END'

'You've seen it, haven't you,' said Elizabeth, quietly. 'My mistake.'

Zoe's heart gave a lurch.

'I don't know what you mean.'

'Oh, but I think you do. I can see it on your face, in your very expressive eyes. You must have been a very attractive performer, as an actress.'

Zoe was four or five steps lower down the damp staircase into the reservoir. Elizabeth loomed over her.

'I think there's been a misunderstanding,' Zoe protested, descending backwards another step, her right hand against the subterranean brickwork, feeling very precarious. 'I was about to tell you—'

'There's nothing you need to tell me.' Elizabeth descended a step, the knife held threateningly out in front of her. 'But, if I could go back and edit my conversation, like I can with people's books, I would.' She sighed, theatrically. 'It happened later, didn't it?'

'This is very confusing—'

'No, it isn't,' Elizabeth suddenly shouted, loud and aggressive. 'Don't pretend. Don't play the fool. The brooch that fell from your borrowed coat – when did it fall?'

'Like you said—' Zoe began, reversing three more steps down, almost tripping on the skirts of her long coat.

'No, no, no,' shouted Elizabeth. 'It couldn't have been, not with everyone still here. Someone would have seen. And it's a treasured piece, glinting silver in the light of the hurricane lamps. Tell me the truth.'

Very frightened of the sharp blade with its evil point, Zoe retreated to the flat of the flagstones, relieved to be off the stone stairs, reaching behind her for the nearest pillar.

'All right. It was like this. Russell didn't come back indoors and I wondered where he'd got to. He must have got stuck when you all climbed out after the concert.'

'Ah, yes. I remember him sniffing about. So, you crept back down again later on and that's when you lost the brooch.' Elizabeth's voice became oddly dreamlike. 'So, when I told you I'd seen it on the floor, it was only a matter of time until you worked out that I must have come down here after that, after everyone else, and that I must have had a reason.'

'What was the reason?' asked Zoe. She had shuffled further away, semi-sheltered by a pillar, unsure what her next move should be. Elizabeth looked momentarily distracted. Zoe asked: 'How did you get Boris to agree to come down here in the middle of the night?'

'I worked out what he had done.'

'And what was that?'

'Marie-France told me she saw you on the front path, hiding the branch beneath some leaves. I expect you worked all that out, too.'

'I just wondered if Junior might have placed the branch between the lavenders as a kind of prank and—'

'Don't be absurd, Zoe. His father put him up to it. Boris has been jealous of Primo for seventy years. More than seventy years. It started in the womb, I'm sure.'

It was very gloomy in the reservoir. Zoe took out her phone again and reactivated the torch.

'Do you know this for certain, about Junior?'

Elizabeth sat down on the third from last step.

'I confronted Boris with it. He blustered and lied. Then the vessel burst in his eye and I thought: *That's a clue to how lying raises his blood pressure, isn't it, desperate to make up a plausible story?* He knew Junior would tell me, too, in the end. Junior likes me. I've been kind to him. When Junior went out wooding with Patrick and Minette, I told him to fetch the branch and burn it.'

Zoe hesitated, wondering if she could make a run for it and sort of jump past Elizabeth – like Bilbo Baggins escaping from Gollum in *The Hobbit* – and bounce away up the stairs.

In terms of physical abilities, we're more or less the same age. I think I'm fitter but she has the advantage of holding that enormous knife.

Then it was too late. Elizabeth was on her feet, pointing with the blade.

'I can't let you out of here.'

'That's ridiculous. What will you tell people?'

'That you tripped on the stairs and impaled yourself in an accident.'

'Why would I be carrying a knife? And that won't stand up to forensic scrutiny.'

'Then I'll cover you in paraffin and set light to you,' she said, sounding desperate. 'It will be an unfortunate accident with refilling the hurricane lamps.'

'But none of them are lit.'

'I could light them. People might expect you to have done the same to help you navigate back across the dark lawn.'

Zoe wanted to say that all this was completely deranged, but she didn't want to provoke her. Instead, she asked: 'How did you do it?'

'Do what?'

'Kill him.'

'I didn't. Go over there and you will see.'

'To Boris? You can't mean that.'

'I want you to know,' hissed Elizabeth, frighteningly.

Zoe retreated, half-stumbling against one of the many steel-framed chairs. She walked backwards to the edge of the stage, her eyes not leaving those of her unexpected enemy.

'What now?'

'Lift up his ludicrous coat.' Zoe did so, catching a glimpse of the flask she had seen on Elizabeth's desk. Elizabeth continued in a poised voice: 'I told him we would have to come and speak in private about his plot to kill his brother, using his son – his ten-year-old son, can you believe it? – as his weapon. He couldn't refuse. Then, when he got here, I thought I would give him my flask to drink from, thick with my soluble caffeine tablets. But he wouldn't take it.'

Zoe realised that there were now two more people hesitating at the top of the stairs, behind and above Elizabeth.

'Then what happened?'

'Have you ever seen,' Elizabeth asked, 'someone having a stroke? I mean in real life or, if it's done well, on television? I don't mean a minor one that makes their face droopy. I mean a deadly one.'

'No, I don't think I have.'

'It turns them off like a light.'

She prompted: 'What are you saying?'

'That's what happened. One moment he was there and the next—'

'In that case, you didn't kill him,' Zoe jumped in. 'You meant to, perhaps, but you didn't actually do it.' Out of the corner of her eye, Zoe recognised the shape of Patrick, silently descending the stairs. Minette was behind him. 'Was it you who wrote the threatening letter to Primo?'

'No, that was Boris, too. He even made Junior take it to the post box. He admitted that. He said he tried to make it sound like a child.'

'How did he know about Adélaïde's past?'

'He's a snoop,' said Elizabeth and Zoe recognised the word from her conversation with Marie-France. 'He goes through people's post, sneaks into their rooms to read their emails before they are logged out.'

'I thought someone had been in my room. This must have been very difficult for you.'

Elizabeth wailed: 'So what?' She dropped the knife and moved quickly away, across the damp flagstones. 'That doesn't justify what I meant to do.' She grasped the chain that controlled the sluice from the lake. 'I see that now. This has to end.'

'*Non, Maman*,' shouted Patrick.

'*Maman, arrête*,' called Minette.

Astonished, Elizabeth looked from one to the other, but she was insistent.

'I'm sorry. There's no other way. Primo will never forgive me. I'll be homeless. He'll cut me off without a cent.'

In a flash of understanding, Zoe saw that Primo's generosity had bred a sickly impotence throughout his family, an inability in each of his dependants to imagine standing alone.

'No, he won't,' said Minette, from the top of the stairs. 'You know that's not what he's like.'

Patrick came quickly further down: 'Stop it, *Maman*. Whatever has happened, don't make it worse.'

Zoe took a step towards Elizabeth, holding the woman's gaze.

'This needn't be the end,' she said quietly.

'Yes, it must.'

'Let there be a new start.'

'It's too late.'

Elizabeth hauled on the chain of the sluice. The mechanism failed to respond, but the rusted frame came loose from the opening. All of a sudden, it clattered to the floor, followed by the chain. Instantly, a cascade of freezing water

327

came surging down in an arc, striking Elizabeth from above and knocking her over onto the flagstones.

Zoe leapt forward, the weight of the sudden waterfall pummelling her shoulders, pushing her down. She groped through the flood for Elizabeth's hand, dragging her towards the steps.

Patrick hurried to join in. Together they heaved. Elizabeth was a dead weight, groggy from the sudden heavy impact. Several times they slipped, but she didn't fight them as they struggled to half carry and half drag her up the slippery stairs and out into the wet evening.

After the shock of the ice-cold lake water, the heavy rain felt warm on Zoe's face.

EPILOGUE

The final scene in the sequence of dramatic events that Zoe was already thinking of as 'the château murder' took place in the drawing room, with her blower heater on full blast in front of the empty fireplace. Because of the change of air outside, it would probably have been enough to make the room comfortable on its own, but – after a change of clothes for Elizabeth, Patrick and for her – Zoe had run over to Isabelle to borrow the space heater from her conservatory, too.

Of course, this meant that Zoe had to admit her subterfuge with tripping the electrics on purpose – but only to the small group now gathered not far from the baby-grand piano.

There were four armchairs. Primo was there, of course, looking small and shrunken, but more or less himself. Adélaïde at first perched on the arm of his chair, then he asked her quietly: 'Would you mind sitting separately, my dear?'

Zoe came next with Elizabeth fourth in line. Patrick and Minette stood behind their mother. With difficulty, Zoe had persuaded the others – Marie-France, Isabelle, Sweetie and Junior – to remain in the smoky dining room under Caroline's supervision.

Because she knew more than everyone else, Zoe took charge. She told them the story of her day, from the terrible discovery mid-morning, to Adélaïde's desire not to shock Primo into a crisis of atrial fibrillation, to her conversations with Gaspard, Marie-France, Isabelle and Didi. Once everyone understood how all that had played out, she narrated what she had learned in the reservoir, several times quoting Elizabeth directly but not allowing her to interrupt.

'Boris died,' she told them with determination, 'as a consequence of his disease, worsened by his own dissipation, gluttony and indigestion, and by his guilt at what he had tried to do – to murder his own brother, exploiting his ten-year-old son as his stooge in setting the trap, accidentally causing the death of a much-loved family servant as a consequence.'

There was a long silence. Zoe wasn't sure what would come next. She was still concerned for Adélaïde who seemed, understandably, immensely on edge.

She looks worse, in this moment, than her husband.

'Did you really mean to poison him, Elizabeth?' asked Primo, finally.

'I did,' said Elizabeth. 'And I was beginning to suspect that Zoe knew more than she was letting on when I brought the lasagne trays down to the kitchen. I tried to overhear what Zoe and Adélaïde were saying to one another.'

'But he didn't actually drink from your flask,' insisted Adélaïde.

'One moment, my dear,' said Primo and Zoe thought she heard a change in his tone – something much warmer. He went on: 'Yes, Elizabeth, you intended to make him drink, but you didn't do it.'

'No,' said Elizabeth, glancing back over each shoulder to her adult children. 'But that was just a chance event. I was lucky—'

'You didn't do it,' repeated Primo, as forcefully as his frailty would allow. 'And who's to say that you would have gone through with it – that you would have let him.'

'I think I would—'

'Or if it would have been successful in any case?'

'The dose would have been—'

'Atrial fibrillation,' Primo interrupted, 'is unpredictable. Sometimes the beta blockers I am prescribed have hardly any effect. None of us can be sure that your patent medicine would have proved fatal.'

'I meant for him to—' Elizabeth began.

'I am the guilty party,' said Primo with insistence. 'It is I, and only I, who permitted, indulged, encouraged and enabled my brother's appalling behaviour. To preserve the good name of my family, I paid his debts, explained away his philandering, excused his hypocrisy and tolerated his unkindness to that poor, poor boy.'

'We could all have done more,' said Adélaïde.

'And to cap it all,' said Primo, 'I've been sitting atop my ivory tower, judging you, my dear Adélaïde, for events of which I had no real knowledge from the dim and distant past. I should never have paid any attention to the poison-pen letter and, now that I know it was contrived by my own brother, I think . . .'

He stopped, his face drawn, and gasped. Adélaïde leaned over and took his hand.

'Are you all right? Do you need something?'

'Just to catch my breath,' he told her.

There was a pause. Zoe could hear the rain spattering against the dark windows.

The tension left Primo's eyes and he told Adélaïde: 'I just need to catch my breath and . . . you. I need you, my dear, if you'll forgive me.'

★

Two weeks later, Zoe was back at Château Palotte to celebrate the success of Primo's cardioversion – his 'resurrection', as he called it. Adélaïde had decided not to go ahead with the true-crime documentary and, without her collaboration, the project was dead in the water and no one cared any longer what had happened at Chichester Theatre so many years before.

Without the burden of Boris's expensive lifestyle, Primo was able to promise to help Elizabeth make some modest improvements to the apartment on Rue Jacob.

'I will be eternally grateful,' Elizabeth told him.

'There is no need,' he assured her.

Marie-France had several times declared: 'I have no need of things, just of security and time.'

Primo was able to reassure her that she now benefited from a life interest in her accommodation in the château.

Zoe learned that Sweetie – who now preferred to be known by her given name of Pauline – had taken her son's education and well-being much more closely in hand. Apparently, they were visiting a well-regarded family therapist in Aix-en-Provence and the boy was coming out of himself. Adélaïde told her that the irrational resentment felt by Didi Astor seemed to have been dissipated by bringing it out into the open, too, adding: 'Time will tell, however.'

Zoe also learned that Junior and his friend from the village had been trying their hand at fishing in the artificial lake, watched over by Pauline, who seemed to be taking a real pride in helping her son get over the loss of his father from stroke and heart failure – a simplified version of the facts, accepted by all.

Gato Merino and his son had been by to reinstate the sluice and pump out the flooded reservoir because, Primo said: 'The lake alone is a sufficient water reserve and I want to put on a series of summer concerts, giving back to the community.'

In further good news, it transpired that the European film studio responsible for the 'Interpol' movie was keen on a sequel, with Adélaïde in an enhanced role as 'number one on the call sheet' and Isabelle as screenwriter.

And the weather had definitely changed.

'Spring,' Zoe told everyone in English, 'has sprung.'

Then she had to explain the play on words in French, which proved quite difficult.

With the renewal of mild weather, Zoe helped Elizabeth to move the clay pots of herbs – rosemary, basil, thyme and oregano – out of doors to bask in the gentle sunshine. Then everyone waved goodbye as she pulled away in Renée the Renault.

All the way back to Sainte-Catherine, Russell sat with his front paws on the dashboard, enjoying the breeze from the vents, his nose pointing the way. Back at home, Zoe sketched a picture of him from memory, standing on the ice of the frozen lake, as a way of exorcising the terrible memory of when he almost drowned.

It helped but she wasn't entirely satisfied with her efforts.
I've made him look too wire-haired and whiskery.

*

Three weeks later still, Zoe invited Primo, Adélaïde and Caroline to join her for an *al fresco* lunch in Place Saint-Bertrand, prepared by Minette, served by Patrick, under the orange umbrellas at the Auberge Sainte-Catherine.

They were joined by some of Zoe's local friends – including Marcel Maurice, the winemaker, elderly Firmin Séchan, the vet, Elise Guillaume, the plant lady, and Julien Calmet, the local priest – which Zoe loved because it made her feel properly at home once more.

At the end of the meal, Patrick broke the news that he and Minette were to reopen the Auberge ahead of schedule, explaining: 'Maybe it's too late now for a paternity test, Boris Senior having been cremated. We thought about whether we could find out if we're related to Primo and Junior but the bottom line is – I don't want to take after him, whether he's my father or my stepfather. I think I've probably done enough sowing of wild oats.'

The delicious meal ended and the friendly party broke up. Caroline, who had helped Zoe through every step of the purchase of the wonderful 'bookshop of my dreams', *La Librairie de Mes Rêves*, walked her home through the beautiful cobbled square at the top of the town.

'It's time,' Zoe told her, 'for some well-deserved peace and quiet. Isn't that right?'

Caroline warned her: 'Don't speak too soon. These Provençal villages are full of mysteries.'

Zoe laughed.

'So it seems,' she agreed. 'So it very much seems.'

The End

ACKNOWLEDGEMENTS

Thanks to Luigi Bonomi whose idea it was that I should write cosy crime, and to the team at LBA; to my magnificent editor Audrey Linton, plus all her colleagues at Hodder & Stoughton; to the booksellers, festival co-ordinators, podcasters and all the others whose dedication and enthusiasm are so essential to a flourishing book industry; to all the generous writers whose support has been invaluable.

And, of course, to the person from whom I learned to write books – the best and only Kate Mosse.

Want to see more adventures from Zoe?
Go back to where it all began in
The French Bookshop Murder,
the first book in the
French Village Mystery Series

Love Greg Mosse?
Don't miss the Maisie Cooper Mystery series . . .

**. . . where crimes and murder
abound.**

RAISING READERS
Books Build Bright Futures

Dear Reader,

We'd love your attention for one more page to tell you about the crisis in children's reading, and what we can all do.

Studies have shown that reading for fun is the **single biggest predictor of a child's future life chances** – more than family circumstance, parents' educational background or income. It improves academic results, mental health, wealth, communication skills, ambition and happiness.[1]

The number of children reading for fun is in rapid decline. Young people have a lot of competition for their time. In 2024, 1 in 10 children and young people in the UK aged 5 to 18 did not own a single book at home.[2]

Hachette works extensively with schools, libraries and literacy charities, but here are some ways we can all raise more readers:

- Reading to children for just 10 minutes a day makes a difference
- Don't give up if children aren't regular readers – there will be books for them!
- Visit bookshops and libraries to get recommendations
- Encourage them to listen to audiobooks
- Support school libraries
- Give books as gifts

There's a lot more information about how to encourage children to read on our website: **www.RaisingReaders.co.uk**

Thank you for reading.

hachette
UK

[1] OECD, '21st-Century Readers: Developing Literacy Skills in a Digital World', 2021, https://www.oecd.org/en/publications/21st-century-readers_a83d84cb-en.html

[2] National Literacy Trust, 'Book Ownership in 2024', November 2024, https://literacytrust.org.uk/research-services/research-reports/book-ownership-in-2024